DEEP IN THE EARTH

a novel

Mary Bozeman Hodges

Sapling Grove Press
Jefferson City, Tennessee

DEEP IN THE EARTH
Mary Bozeman Hodges

A Sapling Grove Press Book

ISBN: 978-0-692-18276-5

Key search data: Mary Bozeman Hodges, author; novel; zinc mining;
early 20th century Appalachia; love story; family dynamics; small town
life; Tennessee; class struggles.

First Edition, year 2018.
Written by, and copyright © by Mary Bozeman Hodges.
Editing, design, and publication by Sapling Grove Press.
Cover photograph, anonymous, c. 1920's, East Tennessee.
Author photograph, © 2018, by Jimmy Hodges.
Printed in the United States of America.

www.saplinggrovepress.com

This book is dedicated to my father,
Paul L. Bozeman (1911–1998),
without whose storytelling and
love and knowledge of zinc mining,
farming and people of East Tennessee,
this book would not exist.

DEEP IN THE EARTH

Moss

My daddy left this world the night my brother was born. It was the worst night of my life.

My little sister Kathleen came tearing out to the barn, yelling, "Moss, come quick. The baby's coming."

I was throwing hay down from the loft to the cows, breathing hard, but my heart most stopped. Maw'd said the baby would come in March, and it'd just turned February. I stabbed my pitchfork into the hay and slid down the ladder, my feet hardly touching the rungs. Kathleen stood in the barn door, stiff as a board, her hands formed into tight fists.

"Hurry," she said, and I took off to the house with her running behind me, both of us ignoring the freezing air. I'd helped Paw deliver a few calves, but birthing a baby was a whole new row to plow. When I got to the house, Maw was lying on the bed, holding her belly.

"Lord God," I said to her. "What am I supposed to do?"

She patted my hand. "Nothing. Go get Aunt Lidy."

Suddenly she held her breath, arched her head back and clenched her teeth. I grabbed her hand, and she gripped mine so hard it hurt.

"I can't leave you. Tell me what to do."

After a moment she said in a quiet voice, "I'll be all right till you get back. Just hurry."

Paw wasn't home, which was nothing unusual. He'd been working at the mine for the last few months and came home only when he could get two days off together to help on the farm. He'd walk the eight miles or so both ways, except when he could catch a ride on a wagon, and work the whole time he was home. He'd said he was going to try to get some days off in March, but you never knew with Paw. He wasn't much a one to take time off, not even for births or deaths.

I had to leave my sisters alone with Maw while I went to get Aunt Lidy, and they were too little to know what to do if something happened before I got back. Not that I'd have known, either. I told Kathleen who was ten to do whatever Maw said. I figured it'd take at least a half an hour to get Aunt Lidy and back home. She wasn't really our aunt, but everybody called her that. She helped bring most everybody around these parts into the world. She was kin.

I didn't even take time to saddle Lady. The cold chilled me to the bone, and the wind was picking up, but me and Aunt Lidy made it back just before the snowstorm hit.

Aunt Lidy had hung on to me for dear life and hurried me along, saying, "Many babies as your maw's already had, that baby'll likely pop out like a corn kernel in a fire."

As she took off her coat and scarf, she set me to boiling water and Ellie and Kathleen to finding rags. By nighttime the snow was deep, and the wind was howling. But the baby had still not come. We heard Maw's muffled cries from behind the closed door to her and Paw's room. She rarely showed emotion or admitted pain, either in herself or in anyone else. Sometimes her cries merged with the howling of the wind, and you couldn't tell which was which.

I got the Bible from the table to try to get the girls' minds off Maw and the baby. Me and Kathleen pulled chairs up to the fireplace, and Ellie got her little chair that Paw had made for Kathleen when she was barely old enough to sit and which had become Ellie's. I turned to the story about Moses, Kathleen's favorite. She liked to read about Moses being found as a baby by the Egyptian princess and being raised as a prince, and then when he was grown up, returning to his people. When we got to the part about the baby being in danger and his mother putting him in a basket in the river, Ellie got up on my lap, and we had to balance the Bible on us both. When we'd hear Maw or the wind, she'd sink her little nails into my arm, but I didn't say nothing. It felt good, somehow. Kathleen pulled her chair up close to us and put her arm up on mine.

Just as we were getting to the part about the princess saving the baby, we heard a horse snorting outside. I went to the door, and as I opened it, a cold blast of air hit me. When I caught my breath, I saw our neighbor Raymond Lindsey getting down heavily off his big Appaloosa that pawed at the snow and created a cloud with his breath. Mr. Lindsey trudged through the snow, keeping his head down as he came up the three steps to the porch. He wore a leather hat, and his gloved hands covered his mouth and nose. Almost all the men around the area were gone, either to the war in Germany or to work in the mine at Outcropping. All except Mr. Lindsey and his boys. They raised so much food needed for the country and for troops they didn't have to go to the war, and they made enough money they didn't have to work in Outcropping, either. Mr. Lindsey wasn't one for social calls, even when it wasn't late or bad weather.

I said, "What's wrong, Mr. Lindsey?"

He looked up. "Evening, Moss. Could you get your maw for me?"

"She's, she's having the baby."

All he said was, "My god," and he just stood there. I told him to come in out of the cold and warm up. He pulled off his hat and gloves, hit them against his arm and stomped his feet to knock the snow off. Then he stepped far enough inside for me to shut the door. His eyes fell on the girls who huddled by the fire, watching me.

Ellie hugged the Bible to her and bent over it.

Kathleen said, "Evening, Mr. Lindsey. We're reading about Moses."

"Well, that's mighty fine, honey." Then he looked at me and said, "Cute little gals. Look like China dolls."

"I reckon," I said to be polite, but I didn't know as I'd ever seen a China doll, so I didn't rightly know. "They're scared," I added. So was I, but I didn't tell him.

"Sure," he said, still looking at them, "'course they are. Look like their paw, don't they?"

I nodded. "Yes, sir," though I really didn't see it except for their fair skin and light hair.

He looked back at me and paused, like he was trying to think of something else to say. I wished he'd just out with it. Finally he said, "You sure have growed up. Get taller by the day. Don't get around much to keep up with folks. You know how it is. Work all the time. How old're you now? Fifteen?"

"Be fourteen come summer." I motioned to my sisters. "The girls are ten and four."

He shook his head. "Time sure gets away from a body. You're a big one, tall like Bertha. Could pass for sixteen, easy. Dark like Bertha." His eyes peered into mine, and he added, "But you got Clyde's blue eyes. Dangedest thing I ever seen."

"That's what folks say," I said, and again asked him what was wrong.

He pulled his gloves back on, plopped his wet hat on his head and motioned towards the door. "What say, let's me and you go outside."

I grabbed my coat from the peg behind the door, pulled the collar up around my neck and told Ellie and Kathleen I'd be right back.

"Damn, it's cold," Mr. Lindsey said as the wind blew heavy flakes of snow around us, even on the porch. He crossed his big arms and squinted his bushy eyebrows as he stared at me.

"What brings you over on this bad night, Mr. Lindsey?" We weren't standing in the bitter cold for good news.

He shifted his eyes to his horse, then looked back at me. "Damn if I aint going to have that blame phone taken out. Wisht somebody else'd get one. Cost me a fortune to have the thing run out. Now I feel like the Grim Reaper with his sickle. Always the one to bring bad news."

I crammed my hands in my jacket pockets and hunched my shoulders up against the cold wind. I wanted to scream at him to tell me what he came for.

He took a moment to study his thick boots, and finally said, "Look, I got no way with words, boy, but we can't stand out here freezing all night, and I didn't want to say this in front of the little girls. They got enough to worry about tonight. But it's like this, some feller called from Outcropping, name of Johnson. It seems your paw and this here other man, I disremember his name, was blasting a wall of rock and some dynamite went off when they hit it with their drills. Man said that happens sometimes. Detonators don't work for some reason or 'nother, and the dynamite, well, it don't go off. Not till drillers hit it."

There was an explosion in my head. George Haskell's paw had been killed a few months earlier, and word was, there wasn't nothing left of him but a few pieces of flesh, all fitting into a small bag and weighing no more than a few pounds. Suddenly I was hot in the freezing cold. I wanted to sit down on the porch. I leaned against an icy post, seeing Paw's strong arms throwing hay up on the wagon, lifting me up on the horse for the first time, holding Ellie when she was a baby.

"He's dead, Moss," Mr. Lindsey said. "They both are, both men. I know it's about the worst news a body can hear, and I hate like hell to be the one come to tell you."

I pressed tight against the post and tried to keep standing. I stared into the blowing snow that was coming down so thick I could hardly see Mr. Lindsey's horse. But I could hear him pawing in the snow, wanting to go home. Mr. Lindsey asked what he could do, what we needed. I tried to think. I didn't have no idea what we needed, except to get Paw home to bury him, whatever of him there was to get. Paw always said he'd come home to the clean earth some day. Being buried wasn't exactly what he had in mind. Still, it had to be done. And there wasn't nobody else to do it. His'd be the second grave in our plot that he'd fixed up under a big oak on a hill behind the house when I was about eight years old and my baby sister had died at birth. As we fenced it in, he'd said he was making it big enough for our family and for some to come, and someday we'd all lie there, together in death as in life. Little Mattie died in the springtime. The ground had been soft from the spring rains, and we covered her grave with dogwood blossoms. I wondered how I'd be able to dig Paw's grave in the frozen ground, and what we'd put on it. There wouldn't be no spring flowers. Nothing but snow.

Mr. Lindsey was saying my name. I looked up and he asked again what he could do for us.

"All I know is, I got to bring him home. Maybe you could go to Outcropping with me."

"Lord only knows I'd be proud to help you get him and bury him if we could, but they said the blast caused a rock fall, and he's buried deep in the earth. Too dangerous to try to find remains. Said he'd have to stay there, him and the other man."

I felt as though my own chest was crushed. That my own limbs hung lifeless. Surely there was something to be found to bury, a hand at least.

"Sorry, Moss. Damn, I'm sorry."

Maw, oh my god, Maw. I didn't know how I could tell her, and especially that he couldn't even be buried with Mattie.

"They told me he had a few things in a room he rented at a place they called the dormitory," Mr. Lindsey said. "We can take my wagon to get them. May have to wait a couple days if this snow don't let up, and it don't look like it's going to any time soon. But we'll go soon as we can."

I thanked him for the offer, but said I'd go get his things myself in a few days. I didn't need a wagon for what little Paw'd took to Outcropping. And knowing Paw, I doubted he'd bought anything there he didn't have to have.

"If you change your mind and want some company, let me know," Mr. Lindsey said. "Want me to stay with you a while? Help you get the horse and cows put up?"

I shook my head, said I'd already taken care of them when it looked like a storm was brewing.

"Well, then, reckon I'll be getting back home. Tell Bertha when, uh, when the baby's born, my wife'll be over tomorrow with food, and she'll help with the little girls and the baby, do whatever you all need." He hit his gloved hands together and held them in a prayer position. Then he reached a big hand out, put it on my shoulder and said, "I know this aint the time, but if you need some work, hell, I can always use another hand on the farm. With the war going on, can't get no decent help no more, 'cept for my own boys. No men around worth shooting. Them as is, is in the mine. I'm, well, I'm awful sorry about this, Moss. But remember ... ." His voice trailed off, like he didn't seem to know what he wanted to tell me to remember, but he finally mumbled, "God's ways aren't man's ways."

I nodded, wondering how that was supposed to make me feel any better, and I wasn't sure that Mr. Lindsey knew either. I thanked him for riding over on such a bad night.

"Yeah, it's a bad night all right." He pulled his hat brim down, mumbled, "Shit," then left.

I watched him fade into the whiteness.

When I turned to go in, Aunt Lidy threw open the door. "Moss, it's a little boy. Aint that grand! Your paw'll be so proud."

———————————

When I told Aunt Lidy about Paw, she said, "Lord God, don't tell your maw yet. Wait till morning. I'll be staying a day or two to help you folks. Can't go home in this weather noway."

I thanked her, then went into Maw's room. She pulled the blankets aside to show me the baby. He was little and too still.

"Aint he beautiful?"

"Sure." He looked like a wrinkled red squirrel.

"Your paw'll be surprised to get home and see he's already born."

I fought back tears. "I'll see you in the morning. Aunt Lidy says you need to rest."

Aunt Lidy'd also said the baby might not live through the night, but he did, and the next morning I had to tell Maw what had happened. When I went in to her room, she lay on the bed with the baby sleeping in the crook of her arm. He was mostly blanket.

She pulled the blanket loose. "Think he looks like your paw?"

He still looked like a squirrel to me, but I didn't say so. "I need to talk to you about Paw."

She tucked the blanket tight around the baby.

"He's not coming home."

Her dark eyes shot up at me. "You mustn't talk like that. You know he don't plan to stay in Outcropping forever. It's not his fault he wasn't here when the baby was born. You can't hold that against him. He planned to take off."

"God help us, Maw, that aint what I'm talking about. He's gone."

"What do you mean, gone? Gone where?"

"He's dead, Maw. Mr. Lindsey came over last night. He'd got a phone call. A man from Outcropping told him Paw got buried in a rock fall yesterday with another man."

I figured there was no need to tell her he got blowed up, too.

She pulled the baby to her chest. "No. There must be a mistake."

The baby started to whine. His cry sounded like a helpless wail. Maw didn't say anything for a few minutes, just sat up straight as a poker and took deep breaths. Her dark face was as pale as ever I'd seen it.

Then she looked at me with her deep-set eyes, deep as wells. "You got to go get him so we can bury him with little Mattie."

"He's already buried. Can't nobody get to him."

She stared at the baby like she was boring a hole into him. "We got to name this one."

"We can do that later, when you're stronger."

"No. He needs a name. I'm going to call him Lazarus Clyde McCullen. Lazarus for the man in the Bible who died and come back to life. Clyde, cause Clyde's alive in this baby. We'll call him Clyde."

Thank God she wasn't going to call him Lazarus. But Clyde'd be a constant reminder of Paw. I couldn't call him Clyde, no matter what Maw named him, but he looked too weak to live long, anyway, so I didn't say nothing. I prayed he'd live, because Maw couldn't take losing them both. I told her I had to go get Paw's belongings in a few days, when the weather was better. I was afraid to tell her I was going to try to get work in the mine, pick up where Paw left off, hopefully someday see the place where he died, maybe even find something of his to bury. I decided I'd wait a few days till she felt better and till I saw if the baby was going to live.

A week later the baby was still alive. I knew she wouldn't like it, but putting it off wouldn't help. I told her I was leaving to get Paw's things and, while I was in Outcropping, I was going to see about a job. She sat at the table with her dark hair pulled back tight like always, drawing imaginary circles in the red and white checks of the tablecloth with one hand and holding the baby which didn't yet seem real to me with the other.

We sat in silence. Finally she said, "You can't leave."

"I'm just going for a while so we can stay together, so we can keep the land."

She laughed an unnatural laugh and said the land had already cost too much and it wasn't worth no more. "Clyde promised me you wouldn't never work in the mine. Told me that was why he was working there, so you wouldn't never have to." She said Mr. Lindsey could use me on his farm and she could get some laundry to do for folks. We'd keep selling eggs and butter, vegetables in the summer. "It's important to keep the family together," she said. "More important than anything. We'll get by."

"Paw wanted us to have a chance to do more than just scrape along. I can make decent money in the mine. Other boys do it. I got to go."

She stared at me hard. "No, no, you don't. You see what decent money's done for your paw, don't you? What it's done for all of us?"

Paw'd had such hopes when he went to work in the mine. He said a man had to do more than just eke out a living, barely able to feed his family. Said a man could move up in the ranks at the mine if he learned more and worked harder than anybody else. That's what he aimed to do, and I knew it was what I had to do for them, and for me, and for him. Paw'd said if he made foreman we could even go to college. That couldn't happen for me now, but I figured maybe the others could still go. He said if a man didn't raise himself in this world, what was it all worth.

Maw wouldn't understand. For her the work, the home, children, food on the table was enough. I guess because she never really had a home or family till she married Paw. She never said much about it except that her folks were dead, but Paw'd told me the story many times, how her mother had run off with a man who was an Indian or part Indian, nobody knew for sure, and how Maw's grandfather'd hunted them down and killed him and took his daughter back home. After Maw was born, her mother killed herself, and that left Maw alone, except for her grandparents. Her grandpaw wouldn't have nothing to do with her, but they kept her because of her grandmaw who said Maw was all she had left. It was Maw's grandmother I was named for. Her name was Mosheim. I reckon she was a good woman who lived with a bad man.

When she died, Maw was only thirteen, and her grandpaw run her off, said her maw's doings was what slow-killed his wife, and he didn't want to see my maw no more. "Go back to the Indians," he said. But she didn't know how to go back to the Indians. She didn't even know what her father's name was or who his family was or where he came from. She 'bout starved, sleeping in barns and whatever till a family took her in, in exchange for work—Paw's family, as it turned out. Then there must have been a big break-up, cause neither of them ever talked about Paw's family. They probably didn't want him marrying Maw. Lots of folks hate Indians. Paw told me he didn't ever want to worry about her not having a home again, that if anything ever happened to him, I must always take care of her and never leave her stranded without a home and family.

I didn't know what to say to Maw, so I just told her I was sorry, that I had to go. She nodded. We both sat quiet at the table, and I thought she wasn't going to say nothing more about my leaving. She never talks much, and when she says something, she don't waste words.

Finally she said, "Clyde worked so hard to get ahead. Had to prove he didn't need his folks. And they didn't even know. Work became a thing in itself for him. He drove hisself. He drove hisself to death. Don't do that to yourself, Moss. I don't hold no grudge against his folks or him. I'm telling you this because you have to know we can make it without you working in the mine. Man was made to till the earth, not work inside her, gutting her."

She'd never mentioned Paw's folks before, and I didn't want to argue with her. She wasn't much for arguing, anyway. I knew when I left, she wouldn't say no more. She'd said what she had to say, and it was a lot for her. Then she put the baby into his crib by the stove, the same crib we'd all slept in, and she sat back down and pounded the table with her fist over and over to a strange rhythm, keeping a tight line of her mouth. I asked her if we should try to contact Paw's folks, tell them he was dead. She said she knew I didn't understand, but she promised him she'd never contact them. That was all she said. I went on to bed and left her sitting at the table like that, her silence filling the room.

The next morning I got up early. Even though I knew how to get to Outcropping, I'd never actually been, and I wanted to get there at least by noon. Paw said the trip took him three or four hours. Maw was already up fixing breakfast, as always. The smell of coffee and the sizzling sound of bacon almost made it seem like any other morning. Maw served me, and I ate alone with neither of us saying a word. Then the girls got up, and while they picked at their food I finished packing a few things. When I started to leave, they begged Maw to let them walk to the edge of the farm with me. Maw nodded, and they ran to the loft to dress. While they got ready, Maw pulled some bills and change from her apron pocket.

"I got this money together last night. Ten dollars. Aint much but it's all I got."

I tried to say no, but she crammed it into my pocket. I took hold of her hand to stop her, but she grabbed my wrist.

"Take it. We got plenty to eat. Your paw always seen we had what we needed. They's meat in the smokehouse, flour in the bin and canned food in the cellar. You'll need cash more'n us. I couldn't bide you sleeping out in the cold till you find work."

At that moment I wanted her to take me in her strong arms and never let go, tell me again that everything would be all right, that I couldn't go. But the baby began to whine. She held my arm a moment longer and stared at me like she'd never see me again. Then she let me go, picked up the baby and clung to him as though he was going to be torn from her arms.

The girls and me walked down the lane, one on each side of me. Dawn was trying to break. It would've been lighter except for the brooding clouds. The fields and woods were dreary and bare. Some left-over dirty snow clung to the dead grass and stubble. I turned and looked back at the house. Light flickered in the front window, and I knew Maw was watching us, but she wasn't visible to me. At that moment I hated Paw for leaving us.

Ellie tugged on my hand. "Don't fall in that ol' hole."

I knew she was picturing the dark entrance to the mine Paw'd described. When he told a tale his words took on life, and you found yourself in another place, right there in his story. We'd all been at the edge of that opening and entered the dark hole.

"I won't fall in no hole." That was the least of my fears. Paw had told of the darkness of the mine, not a darkness like's on the surface of the earth even in the blackest night, but a darkness a man's eyes would never adjust to. He described miles of dark tunnels the men dug, like ground squirrels, he'd said, burrowing into the earth with only the flickering light on their hats. It was the darkness I dreaded.

"Don't get under no rock," Kathleen said, "and don't drill. She squeezed my hand tight. "Whatever you do, don't drill."

She listened to everything adults said. I'm sure she'd heard the story about Haskell's paw's drill hitting the misfired dynamite. I put down my bag to say good-bye and hugged her. "I'll be safe." I wanted to tell her to take care of Maw and the little ones, but when I looked down at her strained face and her wet eyes, all I could say was "Everything'll be okay, Kat. You take care of yourself and study hard."

"I will," she said.

Ellie reached her little arms to me, and I picked her up. "Take me with you. We'll come home when you're off, like Paw did."

"I can't take you, honey. Maw and Kat will need you too bad here on the farm. You'll help with the baby, won't you?"

She nodded. "But you'll be all by yourself. Who'll take care of you?"

She rubbed her eyes with the backs of her hands, not even trying to hide her tears. I held her tight and pressed her face into my shoulder so she could dry her eyes on my coat. I felt the warmth of her little body and the smoothness of her hair against my cheek.

Then I put her back down. "I'll be okay, and I'll buy you both something when I get my first paycheck. I got to go now. Y'all go back to the house, and I'll be home before you know it."

I walked on to the end of the lane without looking back, but when I got to the main road, I turned around. They were still there, waving and crying. Both girls' gold braids hung over their shoulders. Ellie's faded print dress made of flour sacks showed beneath her coat, and Kathleen's long coat hung to her ankles. I swore someday they'd have fine clothes like they deserved and I'd have a picture of them to keep. I tried to memorize everything about them. Then I waved them back toward the house.

As I turned and faced the wind, the cold burnt my eyes. I was glad they couldn't see my tears. I stuffed my hands into my pockets, rounded my shoulders and bent my head down. The only noise was the crunching of my own feet on the frozen road, rutted deep by wagon wheels. I passed Stiles' General Store, turned onto Stagecoach Highway, and then lost sight of anything familiar. But I knew the highway would lead me to Outcropping.

By late morning I saw a faded wooden sign that said, OUTCROPPING, TENNESSEE: ESTABLISHED 1880. PROPERTY OF THE INTERNATIONAL MINING COMPANY. Paw had said the company owned every house, every tree, every blade of grass, even the church. He'd said the land where the company had established itself was so rich in zinc, yellow gold, he called it, that it could be seen outcropping on the surface of the earth and that was how the town had gotten its name. He'd said the area was one of the richest sources of zinc anywhere in the world. But I didn't see any outcropping of the shiny ore, or anything yellow and bright. Nothing that reflected richness. Everything I saw was gray—gray dust, gray houses, gray buildings.

Shortly I saw the sign for the mine and the mill. They sat back off the road, and I couldn't tell much about them, but I could see the shaft rising high in the air like a giant gray beast. The road ran into a bridge and a smaller sign that said BLACKBERRY CREEK. Big gray walls were on either side of the creek. The mine and mill were on the west side of the creek, and a mountain of gray-white dust was on the east. It looked like a great storm cloud had settled itself on the whole town.

A little ways farther I came to a big gray building with a sign out front that said COMMISSARY. Paw had told us about the company store where the miners bought all their supplies. He said they had everything a person could dream of. That's the way Paw saw Outcropping, as a place that could fulfill a person's dreams. To him it offered work, money, and hope for his family. I stood straight, took in a deep breath of cold air and reached for the screen doors, each with a rectangle tin sign in the middle that said Merita Bread.

Bertha

I knew Moss'd go to Outcropping to work in that mine when Clyde got killed, even before he told me. Sometimes I hate Clyde for that. He was always talking about making it big and the mine being the only way to do that. Always talking about *being somebody*, like everybody aint somebody. But to him, a man had to have land, cows, horses, money. Reckon he grew up having them things and he never could get used to living without them. Always said he wanted things for me and the youngens, but it was him who wanted things, not us.

Course, he never thought nothing'd happen to him. I'll give him that. He convinced us that the mining accidents we were always hearing about came of men being foolhardy. When Hank Haskell got blowed up, Clyde said he probably cut fuses too short, got caught in the blast before he could get away, blowed hisself up—that's what Clyde said. When I said how bad it was Haskell's son George had to go to work in the mine at his young age, Clyde said lots of boys was there. George'd do all right if he'd work hard. Course nobody ever worked hard enough to suit Clyde. Except Moss. He had Moss doing a man's load of work on the farm when he wasn't no more than a kid. And Moss was always anxious to please him. He grew big and strong, and believed that whatever Clyde said was the gospel truth. That always scared me.

"My boy aint going to the mine," I told him.

"Hell, no, he aint," Clyde said. "Moss's going to be somebody. I'm going to see to it. He's special. Aint no end to what he can do, if he's given the chance. He needs him an education. And I aim to give it to him. I can't do it working on the farm."

Ever since we got married, all he ever talked about was getting ahead, as he called it. Now I aint no stranger to hard work. Can't never remember not working. But I believe in working to survive, not to kill yourself. I think Clyde's notion of having to prove hisself come of his folks turning him out, said they wouldn't have no Indian in the family. I worked for them on their big farm when I was just a girl. They took me in when I didn't have nowhere to go. I worshiped the ground they walked on, especially his mother. She made me a dress and bought me a pair of shoes.

Turned out, I was good enough to work for them, but they didn't intend for their son to fall in love with me. When they found out a baby was on the way, they tried to send me away. But Clyde wouldn't hear of it, said we was going to get married. When he wouldn't change his mind, they sent him off with enough money to buy a small place and get started on his own. Not much, but enough to get rid of us. Told us to move to another county, get far enough away they wouldn't never see us again or none of our brood. They didn't want people knowing their grandkids was half-breeds. I'm only half Cherokee myself or maybe not even that. I don't rightly know, but that didn't matter. Close enough, they said. They warned Clyde he'd live to regret marrying me, and they didn't want to be around to see it. They said we'd never make it. Said he better think twice about it, because he wasn't never to come back home crying to them once he left. That's the last thing Clyde'd ever a done, even if he had regretted it. So I guess I'll never know if he did or not. He never said nothing about it. He never so much as sent a message to them about one of the kids being born, or about little Mattie dying. And he made me promise never to contact them. So I aint. And I won't.

Clyde set out from the first to prove he didn't need them, that he could do fine without them. But he never made enough to suit hisself. The work became a thing in itself with him. His folks didn't know nor care. It was *him*, his own self that drove him so hard.

When he found out I was pregnant again, he did like so many others and went to the mine. I begged him not to go, but then, come to find out, if he hadn't gone, he'd probably a wound up in the war, a war that was all about some big-shot getting killed in some far off place. I never could make no sense of it, how any of that in Europe had anything to do with us in Tennessee. I didn't want him a way off in some foreign country where if he got killed we might never get his body back, couldn't put it to rest in the earth he loved. So, after knowing he'd be sent to the war if he didn't work in the mine, I couldn't say nothing about him working there, not that it'd a mattered if I had of. Clyde laughed at my worries, said he blasted rocks instead of men.

He was convinced he could move up to foreman in the mine and then he'd be able to send all the kids to school. We could've moved to Outcropping and Clyde wouldn't have had to walk back and forth every time he had a couple days off, trying to keep the farm going and work in the mine, too, but he wouldn't hear of it. Said he wasn't having his kids grow up in no mining town. Besides, he wasn't giving up his land. Said if we owned our own land, I'd never be without a home. So me and the kids kept the farm going with what help he could give when he came home. Moss could do about anything Clyde could, was always a boy going on a man. He grew up fast, saw hisself as the man of the house.

Now Moss has got the same itch as Clyde, trying to prove something to folks he's never seen, folks that don't care one way or the other. Thinks the mine's his only hope for a good life, just like Clyde. I see it as his death. Aint no point trying to talk him out of it, once he's made up his mind. He's like his paw that way. He's driven by something more powerful than me. And I don't think it's the good Lord.

Aunt Minnie

When Moss McCullen first came through them commissary doors, he was about the most pitifulest looking thing I ever seen. He was a big ol' boy, but he was all hunched over, looked plumb froze. He just stood there in the doorway with his dark hair glazed with ice, like he didn't know what to do next. Put me in the mind of a lost sheep like the Bible talks about.

I was helping Dicey Epps and couldn't see to him right that minute, so I said, "Be with you in a minute, sonny. I'm finishing up here. Pull you a chair there by the fire while you wait."

He nodded at me and said, "Thank you, ma'am." Then he went towards the way I pointed. When he passed the barrels of coffee, flour and meal, he slowed down and took in a deep breath. His eyes roamed over the jars of cookies and hard candy on the wooden counter. Reckon he was about as hungry as he was cold.

While I finished getting Dicey's order, she was in the dry good section looking at the overalls. She picked up a pair and tried to measure them up to her son Henry whose face was crammed into the folds of her skirt and whose little pants was way too short. He wouldn't budge, so she bent over him and held them up to his backside. Poor little boy hardly ever said a word, like his voice had been taken from him.

I walked over to them. "Need some help with them overalls, honey?"

She ran her rough hand over the material like it was velvet, folded them neatly and laid them back on the shelf. "Not this week. Groceries first."

"Know how that is. Folks got to eat. Now you take Henry over there to the counter and let him pick out a piece of candy to take with him while I ring up your groceries."

The tall lad at the stove was watching our every move. He seemed especially taken with Henry, who at the suggestion of candy peered out from Dicey's skirt. He pulled her toward the candy barrels with his scrawny hand. Dicey said she couldn't

25

afford the candy, and I told her it was my treat, that I wanted to give him a piece, that I liked to give the little ones a piece of candy from time to time.

"Get two pieces, honey," I said to Henry. "Give one to that young feller over there by the fire. He looks like he could use a piece."

When Henry and Dicey went toward the barrels, I tried to slip the overalls in with her supplies, but that boy kept watching me. He wasn't missing a thing. Never saw such blue eyes. Clear, like the sky. But his hair was dark as a raven, and his skin was too brown for that time of year. Indian maybe, I thought, but not full-blooded, not with them eyes.

I added up Dicey's groceries, but when I got the scrip book to tear out the amount of her purchases, I seen they was already drawn against Isaac's next pay. She reddened, so I reckon she could read the look on my face. The situation wasn't nothing new to her or to me.

"I don't need these here beans," she said, pulling them out of the sack. "I got some left at home. We got enough scrip to cover the rest?"

"Sure, honey. Go on and take them beans. I'll charge them against next time."

But she wouldn't hear of it. She thanked me for the candy and pushed Henry out from her skirts. "Go on now, give the boy his'n."

Henry inched over to the newcomer, hanging his head. When he stood near him, the boy looked down at the little feller holding out his hand to give him the candy and said, "You keep it. I got to eat my lunch."

Henry looked up and grinned, and his eyes suddenly became as bright as zinc. He ran back to Dicey and me and actually spoke, which was a rare thing. "Maw, he told me to keep it. He's got to eat his lunch." He looked back at the boy who nodded.

"That was mighty good of you," Dicey said. "Now, Henry, thank Aunt Minnie. We got to go."

Dicey's arms were full of groceries, and the child held a stick of candy in each hand. The young stranger went over to get the door for them, and I made a note of what I owed. It aint nothing for me to help folks out once in a while. I only got myself to feed. My paw always said if you don't help somebody else once in a while, you'll lose what you got, said helping somebody else was akin to helping Jesus. I been awful blessed, so I help out other folks when I can. But I have to be careful. Miners and their families is awful proud. When I finished, the boy came up to the counter. I looked up at him and squinted to get my glasses to slide farther up on my nose. The older I get, the shorter I get. It's got to where I look up to most everybody.

"What can I do for you, sonny? Where you headed?"

"Right here," he said. "Outcropping." He paused a moment and added, "My paw, he died. I need work."

"I'm sorry as I can be about that," I said, "but it looks like you need to eat first."

He stared at the cheese that sat on the counter under a glass cover, but he said, "Maw sent some lunch with me."

"Well, then, what're you waiting for? Eat. How about some hot coffee to go with your lunch?"

He put his hand in his pocket as though to pull out money, but then said, "No, thanks. I don't need any."

"I was just fixing to pour out what's left and wash the pot. It'll go to waste. Hate to pour out perfectly good coffee, don't you know. How about doing me a favor and finish it for me."

"Well, I guess, if you're sure it'd go to waste. "

"It will if you don't drink it. Now you go back over and sit by the fire, and I'll get it."

I doctored it up with some sugar and cream to where it was a pretty creamy color, and took it to him. He thanked me and put his hands around the mug's warmth.

"Name's Minerva Miller," I said. "Course nobody calls me Minerva. Nobody ever heard tell of Minerva around here, don't reckon. Minerva was the goddess of wisdom, don't you know? That's what my maw said. She read it somewhere. She read everything she could get her hands on. Folks thought she was a little strange that way. Anyway, everybody here calls me Minnie. Aunt Minnie it's come to be. You can call me that."

"Proud to meet you, Aunt Minnie. My name's Moss McCullen."

"Only knowed one other person named McCullen. You say your paw died? Didn't get killed in the mine, did he?"

He straightened. "Yes, ma'am."

"Then you must be Clyde McCullen's son."

He stared at the steaming liquid. "Yes, ma'am. That's right."

"I knowed him. Reckon I know everybody. Anybody that buys something buys it here. But I'd never a made the connection. You don't favor him none, do you? 'Cept for them eyes."

He looked uncomfortable. Sometimes I talk before I think, so I added, "Well, you're lucky. You must have a mighty handsome maw. You're better looking than yore paw."

He was, but I don't think that'd ever occurred to him, because he looked surprised, and he only said, "Folks think I have Maw's Cherokee looks. They always say that."

"What more could a man want?" I said.

He smiled a sort of half smile and again said he needed work and a place to stay, and did I know where he should go. I asked how old he was, and he said old enough to work. I figured from his answer he wasn't as old as he looked, but then I guess if a boy's paw gets killed, he's old enough. Besides with them rough hands and broad shoulders he looked like a body that was used to hard work. Figured he could load shelves just fine.

"You've walked into a job right here if'n you want it," I said. "Our stock boy Andrew Jones up and quit, just like that, only two days ago. Turned sixteen, lied about his age and joined the Army. I got no notion why these boys is so anxious to die. They're safe here, exempt from service, you know, cause of the mining. But some of them quit so's they can join up and get shot. Aint that the dickens?"

"Maybe they're safer overseas," he said, looking toward the mining equipment.

I saw his point. "Anyways, like I was saying, our boy Andrew quit, left us high and dry. How'd you like to work here? I can give you a place to sleep, too, at least for a while. They's a cot back in the storeroom if somebody gets sick or something. You can sleep there for now. If you're like your paw, we can sure use you. Word was, he worked like a son of a gun, and from the looks of you, you do, too. What'd you say?"

The boy looked like he didn't know what to do. Reckon he hadn't thought of doing nothing but working in the mine, like his paw, but I hate to see any boys go into the mine.

"Solve your immediate problem," I said. "You can think about the mine later."

He nodded his head slowly. "Thank you. I appreciate the offer. I need a job bad. But someday I will work in the mine. That's what I come here for. If you're okay with that, when do I start?"

"Right now," I said, before he had a chance to change his mind. "Come on, and I'll introduce you to Mr. Eslinger, the manager."

By the end of the day, I knew I wasn't wrong about Moss. He worked all afternoon, till dark. Mr. Eslinger had already gone home when I said, "It's about time to call it a day, sonny. You done real good. You aint eat yet, 'cept way back when you first got here, and you need to rest."

"I'm not hungry," he said, and I knowed he was lying. "But I am tired," he added, and I knowed he wasn't lying about that.

"Still you got to eat."

"Maybe I'll buy me some cheese."

"A little cheese aint no fitting meal for a growing boy. Tell you what, come on home with me, and I'll fix us both something hot."

"I don't want to put you out none. You been more'n good to me today. My maw wouldn't want me to take charity off nobody."

"Pshaw. Aint putting me out none. Got to cook me up something anyways. Eat by myself too much. Come on, I live just down the road here in Lowtown. Aint but a hop and a skip."

"That's mighty good of you, Aunt Minnie," he said, and that first night he walked me home and had supper with me.

Moss

I didn't know what to say when Aunt Minnie offered me a job at the commissary. I never heard of a man working for a woman, but I liked her, and I decided that for the moment I'd better take the bird in hand.

It didn't take me more'n that first day to see she ran the store, even though she had a boss. She might've been a little mite of a woman with a hump in her back, but she could work circles around most people, and she was sharp as a blade. When we were closing the store, she invited me to her house for supper, but before we got locked up, a man dressed in mining clothes covered with rock dust barged in. The screen door slammed behind him. Aunt Minnie was at the counter with her back to him. She jumped and turned around when the door slammed.

"Isaac Epps," she said, "what're you doing? It's done past closing time. Me and Moss here is just leaving."

"Well, you and Moss can stay long enough to help me." He looked at me and frowned. "Who the hell's Moss?"

"Our new stock boy. Took Andrew's place. Moss's paw died last week in that dynamite accident with Joe Lawson. You remember Clyde McCullen, don't you?"

"Yeah, yeah. Knew Joe better, though." He ran his dirty hand over his thick, dark whiskers. "Listen, I need me some scrip."

His gray eyes were hard, and his mouth turned downward on one side when he spoke. He smelled strongly of rock and dirt and tobacco, and he leaned over the counter, thrusting out one rough hand, but Aunt Minnie put her little knotted hands on the other side of the counter and said, "Now, Isaac, Dicey was in here today. She done bought your groceries. You don't need nothing. Go on home. I'm sure she's got supper waiting."

"Hell, she never gets everything, so afraid to spend money, like she's got anything to do with earning it. She'd starve me to death if I let her, but I don't want groceries. I want me a $10 book of scrip." He slammed his fist on the counter. "Now."

31

I began inching over to the hardware section for some kind of weapon, watching the man all the while. He wasn't paying me any attention, just scowling at Aunt Minnie.

She pushed her hands against the counter edge, leaned back straight as she could and said, "Can't get no scrip for you. Scrip is locked up for the day. Mr. Eslinger's got the key, and he aint here." She waved her hand at him like she was shooing away a dog. "Now, run along."

He jabbed his face forward, over the counter, one eyebrow higher than the other, and yelled, "I need that damn scrip or some money. Whichever. I don't care."

I picked up a sledge hammer and moved back towards them. Aunt Minnie came from behind the counter and stood squarely in front of the man, like a little female Napoleon. She only came to his chest, but she spread her feet, put her hands on her hips and stared at him with her head slanted backwards.

"Don't you come in here and yell at me, Isaac Epps, or I'll cut your water off for good. We both know what you want with that scrip, and you already owe more'n you got scrip to cover." She pointed a crooked finger toward the door and nodded in the same direction. "Now you just turn yourself right around and high-tail it out of here." She slapped the flat of her hand on the counter. "Store's closed."

I'd come up beside her, gripping the hammer behind my back. The man glared at her and at me, but to my surprise, he turned away grumbling. "Thought you people was supposed to be here to help a poor miner. Man can't have nothing. Works hisself to death for the company, and this here is the thanks he gets. Can't even have a little drink. I ort to leave this goddamn place and just tell the sons of bitches to go straight to hell." He staggered off and slammed the door even louder than when he had entered.

Aunt Minnie turned and looked at me as I stood there, still holding the hammer. She pointed to the counter, and I laid it down.

"Don't mind Isaac," she said. "He's just a harmless drunk. His loud mouth don't scare me none. Comes in here all the time like that, demanding scrip. You know what he wants it for, don't you? He'd take whatever I give him and sell it to anybody that'd buy it for whatever cash he can get so he can buy liquor, and when Dicey'd come in to buy groceries, she wouldn't have no scrip credited to them. You remember Dicey, that lady who was in here earlier today, the one with the little boy. Poor little feller. I don't think Isaac'd hurt nobody else, but it's painfully clear he takes his anger out on them. I'd like to skin Isaac alive when I see bruises on that poor little woman and boy. They aint neither one big as a flea. Reckon Isaac keeps hoping I'll give him scrip, but I won't. If I gave him all the scrip he'd built up, why, Dicey and that little youngen would starve to death."

"Why don't she take Henry and leave him?"

Aunt Minnie scrunched up her shoulders. "Where would she go? She only lives in the house she does because Isaac works for the company. Besides, she aint got no mind of her own no more. That's what happens to a woman who's treated like that. Becomes just a body walking around toting a shell with nothing inside."

"I think you should be careful of him," I said. "He don't look harmless to me."

She shook her head. "I aint scared of him. He's sorry, aint worth his weight in dirt, but some folks is just not strong as others. Don't know why." She stuck some loose gray-white hairs into the bun on her head. "I've turned away plenty drunk husbands. They aint too bright when they're needing liquor. I tell them Mr. Eslinger's got the key. He does." She patted her apron pocket, winked and added, "But so do I." She chuckled. "I aint never been hurt, and they's some a lot rougher'n Isaac." She gave one strong nod, and her glasses slipped to the tip of her nose again. "Besides, reckon if he'd a bothered me, you'd a been on him, you and that sledge hammer, like Jesus a running the money changers out of the temple."

I looked at the weapon and suddenly found myself leaning against the counter. A few minutes earlier I was ready to bash in a man's skull. I would've if he'd touched her, at least if I could've. I'd never before in my life thought of killing a man. I took a deep breath, and mumbled that I should put the hammer back on the shelf.

"Be a good idea," she said, as I went toward the hardware, thankful it wasn't covered in blood—neither mine or Isaac's. "Don't never fight, sonny," Aunt Minnie said, as though reading my mind, "least not if you can outsmart the other feller. Then, if you ever have to, you won't have to regret it later. And if you die in a fight, well, you'll know you died for a good reason, not for something stupid or that could have been avoided." She untied her apron, folded it and laid it behind the counter. "Lord a mercy, what do I know? I'm just a old woman. Come on. Let's me and you get on home and fix us a hot meal and forget about the likes of Isaac."

I followed Aunt Minnie to her house which stood in a row of others just like it—small, gray houses shaped like boxes. We entered the unlocked door, and she lit an oil lamp on a table near the door. I smelled the familiar kerosene as I looked around the room and saw an oak bed and a table with a worn Bible on it. A picture of Jesus surrounded by children of different races hung on the wall above the bed, though the colors were faded so that the children didn't look much different from each other. There wasn't a piece of glass over it, and the paper of the picture was wavy.

She saw me looking at the picture, and pointed to it. "The good Lord didn't see fit to bless me and Harold with no youngens of our own." Then she went over to a box beside a pot-bellied stove and got wood to start a fire. "Aint much," she said, stuffing wood into the stove, "but it's home. Be warm as toast in a few minutes." After she got the fire going, she pulled off her coat and gloves and scarf. "Here, let me have your coat." She hung it on a peg behind the door like we did at home. "We got to get you a scarf and gloves right away." She pointed to a chest and said, "Might be there's still some of Harold's in there. but first we got to get you something to eat. You like sausage and eggs?"

"Yes ma'am," I followed her to a small kitchen off the front room. My mouth watered as I watched her pull food from the icebox.

She pointed to a small white table and two chairs. "Sit down there and talk to me while I cook, sonny." She took some kindling from the woodbox and lit the fire in the cookstove.

I told her I'd like to help, and she said, "Well, thank you kindly. You can draw me some water." She pointed to a pail beside the back door. "Pump's right outside." When I returned with water, she said, "Now, you just sit down and rest. You've had quite a day. Tell me about yourself."

I sat at the table covered with a red-and-white checkered tablecloth, like ours at home. Aunt Minnie went over to a tall white kitchen cabinet and opened the upper side door behind which was the flour bin. Underneath the bin was a sifter and a bowl, just like Maw's. Aunt Minnie sifted flour like she didn't even have to think of what she was doing.

"You got brothers and sisters?" she asked as she began mixing the biscuit dough.

I told her I did and that my baby brother was born the past week, the day Paw was killed. "He's puny," I said, "born too soon."

She looked at me over her glasses. "You folks really has had your share of troubles lately, aint you?"

"We have, sure enough."

"How's your maw?"

"She's a strong woman, like you." At that moment I was thankful she'd never had to put up with anything like Isaac.

Aunt Minnie made a white streak across her wrinkled forehead as she pushed back a stray piece of hair. Then she began rolling out the dough. I watched her small shoulders move to the rhythm of her work. I figured Maw would be through with supper and would be putting the girls to bed, and the baby. It was hard to picture him. Ellie was still the baby to me.

35

"You buy them overalls for that little boy?" I said.

"You don't miss much."

"That was a fine thing to do for a man's family who treats you like Isaac does."

"What he does aint their fault. Dicey does the best she can by Henry, but her hands is tied with that no-count man."

"Don't he care about them?"

"Not as much as he cares about that moonshine. Gets a holt of a man." She punched the biscuit cutter into the dough with surprising force.

"Don't seem fair."

"Aint. But life here aint fair, sonny. These men never know if they're going to be alive from one day to the next. They all seen their buddies get crushed, blowed up, electrocuted, cough up their lungs. Now that aint no excuse, but I reckon it is a reason. Don't be too hard on them. You'll see plenty Isaacs around here. I 'spect they's plenty Isaacs everywhere."

"I'm glad Paw wasn't like that."

She popped the biscuits into the oven. "Glad my Harold wasn't neither. He was a good man, my Harold. Never knowed him to take a drop of liquor, 'cept when he was sick, of course. And he'd a cut his hand off afore he'd of raised it to me." She looked up and winked at me. "If he hadn't of, I would've."

"Where is. . . I mean, what happened to your man?"

"Passed on. Five year ago. Miners' TB. Spit up blood for years afore he died. But he worked almost till that day. God rest his soul." Her eyes moistened. "I'd been working in the commissary for some thirty year then, so I just kept on working. I was lucky. The company, they let me live on in this house. If I hadn't had me a job, I'd have had to move out. I got no idea where I'd have gone. Just goes to show, the good Lord'll take care of you, sure enough, if you let him, and if you help him out a little."

"You got any family around here?"

She shook her head. "Had a brother. Worked in a coal mine in Kentucky. Got killed in a cave-in. Lost touch with his family.

36

And, like I said, me and Harold, we never had no youngens. Aint complaining, mind you. Got lots of friends. You'll find folks here help each other out, 'cept maybe for the ones like Isaac who can't even take care of their own." She took down two plates and two forks from an open shelf and wiped off the gray dust with a piece of flour sackcloth. She filled a plate with sausage, eggs, biscuits and gravy and set it down in front of me. "Don't wait for me. Eat while it's hot. I'll pour you some milk."

"It looks mighty good." Between bites I said, "You cook good as my maw, and I didn't think nobody cooked as good as Maw."

As she filled her own plate she said, "Well, I've had plenty years of practice."

As we finished eating, she said it was too dark and cold for me to walk back to the commissary. "They's a bed in the front room. I sleep in this little room in the back here." She nodded toward a room that opened off the kitchen. I could see an old iron bed in it. "Harold built that room hisself. Just for me to do my sewing in. When he, well, when he passed on, I put me a little bed in there. Got it second-hand from a family that was moving on. They even come and set it up for me. Sorta feels nice to sleep in there, in the room Harold built. I spend most of my time at home there when I aint in the kitchen." She pulled in her breath hard and straightened as much as she could. "I like to sew. Point is, I got extra sleeping room, and you need a bed."

"You mean I can sleep here, in your house tonight?"

"Tell you what, you need you a place to stay. A storeroom in the commissary aint no fitting place for a boy. And you need hot meals. Why don't you move in here with me? Got plenty room, and we could help each other, me and you."

"How much you think that'd be worth?"

"Oh, cutting kindling, toting wash water and the like, on your part. I'll cook your meals, keep your clothes clean. Things like that. Sort of a give and take. What'd you think?"

While I was beholden to her I didn't want no charity. Didn't want her to feel sorry for me. I looked at her all hunched over her plate. "Don't seem fair to you, me living here just for doing chores."

"Why, it's a Lord's blessing, sonny. Been needing somebody to do chores for quite a spell. Shucks, I ought to pay you to stay here. Can't hardly tote that washtub no more. Told the good Lord just the other night, I said, Lord you going to have to help me find a way to stay in me and Harold's little house. And, here you are, sent by God hisself. It's fairly a miracle. The Lord works in mysterious ways, he surely does."

Paw'd said those same words when he'd laughed about going to work in Outcropping just in time not to have to go to war. But I couldn't see no way his death or my being in Outcropping could be the Lord's work.

I guess I sat silent too long, and Aunt Minnie said, "Now, if you don't want to move in here, I understand. That cot at the storeroom's yours if you want it, like I said, till you find something better. Maybe you don't want to live with a old woman. Couldn't blame you for that. Suit yourself."

"I'd be right proud to stay here. I can do lots of things to earn my keep."

"I'm sure you will, and they's plenty of chores to be done." She reached over and patted my hand. "Welcome home, Moss McCullen."

———————————

The second day after I started work at the commissary, I went over where Paw had lived to pick up his belongings. Everybody called where he stayed The House, or The Inn. It was a big rectangle-shaped building with an upstairs. Mostly single men or men working in Outcropping without their families like Paw, and even some boys who'd come to work in the mine, like me, lived at The House, which also provided meals for them. A lady led me up a flight of stairs to his room which was small and cold, with basically a cot, a small chest and a chair. She told me that the towels, bedding and furniture belonged to the company, but for me to take what I wanted of my father's things, and whatever I left she would see to it that somebody got it that could use it. Then she left me alone.

I stared around the room. Anybody could have lived in it. I went through the drawers, and there wasn't much of him in them: a change of work clothes, underwear, a shirt and pair of pants that I guess he wore when he wasn't working. An old pair of his shoes sat beside the bed. Nothing fit me. I decided to leave it for the lady to give away. In a corner of one of the drawers were a razor, a bar of soap and a comb. I also found a wooden cigar box that held some money which I guess he had been saving till the next time he went home. I put the razor and comb in the box and set it on the chest to take with me. Then I went through the drawers again to see if I'd missed something. I don't rightly know what I hoped to find—something, I reckon, that might be worth keeping, something that might remind me of him. Paw didn't waste anything, believed a man should work and save for what he saw as the important things like land, animals, and education, so I guess I shouldn't have expected nothing special in his room.

When I went back downstairs, carrying the box, the lady told me Paw ought to have some pay due him, that I should go over to the main office and ask. She said it'd probably stay right there if I didn't go get it. She showed me how to get there, and I thanked her. As I started to the office with the box tucked under my arm, I looked back at the old gray building. My stomach tightened, and I tried not to think of Paw living alone in that tiny room, putting his salary religiously into a cigar box.

He did have some money coming to him, which they gave me. I stuffed it in the box, too, and figured Maw would be glad to get it. On my way to the commissary, I thought of how little Paw had at the end of his life, very little to show he had ever lived and worked so hard. At least he left us his small farm and his dreams. I hoped we could make his dreams matter.

Bertha

First time Moss come home after setting out for Outcropping, my breath most left my body. The dogs were barking, and before I could put the baby down to see who was coming, Ellie and Kathleen were already tearing out of the house to meet him. One was on one side of him and one on the other as he come up the steps to the porch.

He looked good, not like somebody come from the grave, which was what I expected. The weather was still cold, and he had on a coat that fit him, wool gloves and scarf and a warm-looking hat with flaps that fell over his ears. He was toting a sack.

"Lord a' mercy," I said. "Get yourself in here out of the cold."

As he warmed by the fire, I told him he didn't look like no miner. I pictured him down in some deep hole like a grave, digging for zinc, and I didn't even know what zinc was.

"Not working in the mine," he said. "Working in the commissary, stocking shelves and anything else they need me to do."

I felt like a heavy rock rolled off my body. It was the best news I'd had in a long time. Before I could ask him about it, he pulled a package out of his sack and gave the girls both a red satin ribbon. Then he handed me a bolt of material. The lady he worked for said it'd make a pretty dress or two.

"They's enough here to make one for each of the girls," I said. "The red flowers in it will match their ribbons."

"Aunt Minnie was thinking you'd make yourself a dress."

"Aunt Minnie?"

"Everybody calls her Aunt Minnie," he said. "The first place I stopped at when I got to Outcropping was the commissary. She gave me a hot cup of coffee, and before I knew it she had give me a job."

"I'm beholden to her," I said, "but she didn't even know you."

40

"Said she knew Paw, and I reckon that was enough for her. She knows everybody."

"Well, it's a sight better than working in the mine."

"It's good for now," he said. "She gave me a place to live, too."

"Oh, where?"

"Her house. She has an extra room. Don't even cost me nothing. She's old, and she said we could help each other."

He handed me money wrapped in a rag. "This is for you and the girls."

I looked at it and said, "Why, son, there's a lot here. You need to keep some for yourself. Me and the girls is doing all right. The baby aint no trouble. We're selling eggs and taking in laundry from the Lindseys, and we're even baking pies and cakes for them. They got lots of mouths to feed over there, and Mrs. Lindsey can't begin to do all the work they is to do."

"It's not all mine," he said. "Some of it Paw had saved up, and some of it was due him from work. If you don't need it now, put it up for later for their school. I don't use much since I work for my room and board."

"But you've had to buy warm clothes," I said, pointing to the coat and scarf and gloves that he'd draped over the back of a chair.

"Oh, no. Those aint new. I've not bought nothing. All that was Aunt Minnie's husband's. He died a few years back, and she took them out of a chest and made me take them. Sometimes I deliver groceries, and she said I needed warm clothes."

"That's mighty fine," I said, knowing how hard it must have been for her to give them up. "You see you earn your keep. Now you must be hungry."

While I fixed food, he told me and the girls about Outcropping and the store where he worked. Their eyes lit up when he described all the things they sold. He told us about some of the customers that came to the store – and about Aunt Minnie. I can't hold no fault with her. I know I'll be forever indebted to her for taking in Moss.

I served the children and said, "Now, eat you some beans and cornbread."

I should have been thanking God that Moss had a place to live and good food and warm clothes, and I did, of course. But at the same time, I felt sad, like I was losing Moss to people and places I knew nothing about. The baby begun to fuss. He was hungry. He started out sort of poorly, but he was gaining weight and strength .

Moss didn't say much as I picked him up to feed him, just, "Looks like he's doing pretty good."

"Yes, he's a little fighter. Was sorta worried about him at first."

"He's got you," Moss said. "He'll be all right."

Moss had to go back to Outcropping the next afternoon. As he walked down the lane to the road with both girls beside him, I thought about our cow Bessie when Clyde sold off her baby. He said he'd gotten a good price and besides we needed another heifer, not a male. He laughed at my concerns over Bessie and said she was just a cow, didn't know the difference. But he was wrong. For days Bessie stood at the gate to the field where Clyde'd led out the little bull and bawled. It most broke my heart to see her grieve so.

When Moss got to the road, he hugged each of the girls and raised his hand in a final good bye toward the window where he knew I watched. I ran out the back door, leaned over the porch and threw up the meal of chicken and gravy I'd eaten with him and the girls. The baby cried a protest at the cold air that filled the house when I flung the door open.

Avery

One day when I went in the Commissary to buy a Moon Pie, a Co'cola and some thirty-aught shells a new boy was behind the counter. He looked to be about my age, so I told him who I was, and he told me he was Moss McCullen. He asked me what I was buying shells for, and I asked him if he'd ever been rat hunting.

He laughed and said, "Not by choice." Said he preferred squirrels and rabbits, said who'd eat a rat.

I come to learn he was always smart-alecky like that. I told him we didn't eat them. He said, then why did we hunt them.

"For fun," I said. "What else?"

I told him he ought to try it. He didn't have much time off between working at the commissary and going home to the farm where his family lived, but we set a day to hunt rats. I asked him if he had a gun, and he said only one he'd left with his maw. Me, I couldn't live without a gun. I told him he could use mine.

The day I come by to get him, he was waiting on the porch of the commissary like I told him to. He didn't know I was bringing Cleve, but Cleve goes with me most anywhere I go.

"This here's Cleve," I said. "He can't talk or hear."

"Why not?" he said.

"Just can't, but he knows what you're saying, leastways most of the time."

"Wow, that's pretty good."

I said I reckoned. Never particularly thought about it before. I don't think Moss'd ever met nobody like Cleve. Most people have to get used to him. They don't know what to think of him at first. They tend to talk loud, like maybe that'll somehow help him hear them. But Moss took right to him. Treated him just like he treated me. I was pretty impressed. I grew up next door to Cleve, and me and him learned to understand each other when we were both too young to use words, so I could purt near always figure out what he was thinking.

As we walked to the dump where we hunt rats, we had to go through Shantytown and Little Mexico, in that order. Them people live on top of each other, and the place stinks to high heaven.

"You don't deliver groceries out here, do you?" I said.

"Yeah, I go wherever they send me."

"You don't go in the houses, do you?"

He just shrugged and said, "Sure."

"Didn't they tell you not to do that?"

"Who?"

"Aunt Minnie or Mr. Eslinger—somebody for god's sake." I couldn't believe nobody warned him.

"No, nobody said nothing. Why shouldn't I take their groceries in?"

I told him them people aint clean.

"What'd you mean, not clean? Nothing's clean around here."

"They're nasty," I said.

I figured Moss probably hadn't seen a colored person before he came to Outcropping. Lots of folks aint. He said he didn't see as Shantytown was no worse than anywhere else, 'cept it was closer to the dump, and that wasn't the people's fault who lived there. I knew then Moss was some kind of do-gooder. I don't put much store by do-gooders.

"I have to deliver groceries."

"It's your life. But you won't catch me going in their houses."

"I don't see them asking you to come in."

I thought, buddy, you'll just have to learn the hard way, like everybody else, and I didn't say no more.

When we entered the dump, he wrinkled up his nose and said, "Damn."

"Well, what'd you expect? This aint Eden. But it's a rat's paradise."

Several rats were scurrying about, and Moss said, "I never saw such big ones, not even in the fields."

"We call them gopher rats. Get plenty to eat here at the dump. See why we kill them?"

Cleve began pulling on my shirtsleeve, wanting to shoot.

"Go ahead." I told Moss, "You just as well let him shoot and get it over with first thing, or he'll pester you to death."

Cleve yanked his gun up and fired—and missed, like always.

"Can't shoot, neither," I said to Moss. Then I shot, and of course made a kill. Always do. I handed Moss my gun. "Now you shoot."

He looked like he'd rather not, and I figured maybe he wasn't any good, but he took the gun and next thing I knowed he blowed one of them critters' heads clean off.

I whistled. "Good shooting."

"Luck," he said.

Cleve was all ready to have another turn and pulled his gun up, but he never took time to really aim. Moss put his hand on Cleve's gun and pushed it down. He looked at me. "You shoot good. Why don't you teach him how?"

"He's not my kid. Besides he can't learn how to shoot. But he has fun trying. Go ahead and let him shoot. Can't you see he's having a fit to?"

"Maybe he could do better if you taught him. Then he might have more fun."

"Maybe he could if *you* taught him. Be my guest."

Well, damned if he didn't. Took half the morning and a bunch of shells, but finally Cleve shot a rat.

"Shit fire," I said. "He aint never shot a rat before."

He was so excited, like a little kid. He was hugging me and hugging Moss, like we'd pulled him out of hell and given him new life. Moss just grinned and shrugged, said he bet Cleve could do it all along.

That's the way Moss is, always wanting to show everybody how to do everything. Then he pulls that humble act, but I can see through him. He's uppity and humble all at the same time. Irritating as hell. Like telling me I shoot real good, but saying I'm not taking time to teach Cleve to shoot. Like I aint been putting up with him all my life, when the other boys make fun of him. I've beat up many a boy over that. Course, Cleve thinks Moss walks on water now, and I'm still on the ground.

Aunt Minnie

I seen right away Moss was not your normal kid. He learned where everything in the store was in only a matter of days. I lived in dread of the time he'd tell me he was going underground. I knowed he wouldn't continue delivering groceries and stocking shelves for long. So I set out from the beginning trying to teach him everything I could, thinking someday he might take Mr. Eslinger's place, and that'd be a means to his ends, without working in the mine. I hoped against hope to keep him out of there.

I even got the butcher to teach him to cut meat. I couldn't cut meat too good, mainly because I didn't want to, but I could do about anything else around the store, except the heavy lifting. But anybody with a strong back can do that. I started teaching Moss to keep books and to know who you could help by giving credit to and who you couldn't and who you had to, anyway, because it's just what a body does. He was quick with math. He'd always gone to school before he came to Outcropping, so he had pretty much book learning.

I tried for a while to get him to quit work, ride the train to Knoxville and go to high school. Told him he could still live with me, do chores for his keep till he finished. Then he could work on getting ahead, be better prepared. He could go anywhere, wouldn't have to work in the mine. But I gave up on that pretty quick. He got real quiet whenever I brung up the subject. He said "Work, for the night is coming" was his father's words to live by, and I reckon Moss had made them his and there was no turning back. Work was everything, the way to get the young ones through school like his daddy wanted. He could go to school and help hisself, but he couldn't go to school and help his family. I don't think he ever had a chance to make a dream of his own. Don't think he even thought about the idea of hisself having a family one day. But there aint no way to really see that far ahead when you're young. Still, I encouraged him to work on his book learning much as I could.

In the evenings when we'd finish supper, I'd tell him my old eyes was too tired to read late at night and I'd like him to read from the Bible or sometimes the almanac or even from that copy of *Hamlet* he'd brought with him. Moss said his old schoolmaster had give it to him for helping him work with the younger kids his last couple of years in grade school. Them was the only three books we had.

He liked to read from the Bible, especially about the Old Testament heroes, about Abraham, Moses, David, Daniel. He said his little sisters always liked those stories, and I loved to hear him read in that clear, smooth voice of his. He never went through that period where his voice jumped up and down like lots of boys do. Or if he did, he went through it before I met him. Words always just seemed to roll off his tongue.

When he read, I'd always see something in the stories I'd never seen before. They'd fairly come to life. When he'd read about Abraham, I'd see the hurt in Sarah's face. Then I'd see the hurt in Hagar's eyes and I'd feel her pain in the desert when she didn't have no food for her little boy. I'd never thought much about Hagar before. Everybody I'd heard discuss the story had always focused on Sarah. To make matters worse, Moss always wanted to know why things happened. Now, I've never been much of a one to question anything in the Bible. Never even read it that close, I reckon. Took whatever the preacher said about the stories for the gospel truth. But not Moss. Instead of talking about how great Abraham was and how he was the father of many nations and God had worked through him and blessed him because he was faithful like the preacher always said, Moss'd want to know why it was okay for Abraham to sleep with his wife's handmaid and why he was willing to kill Isaac, and would he have really gone through with it if God hadn't told him any different. Why did he send Ishmael and Hagar away once he got a kid by his real wife? What if they'd died? He made my head hurt, and my heart, too. That's when I'd tell him I was getting too sleepy to think on all that. I'd go to bed, leaving him still poring over the book, worrying with questions that aint got no answers.

Sometimes when he'd start to read a story that depressed me too much, I'd just ask for him to read from the almanac. It was safer. I liked *Hamlet* cause I'd never heard that story before. But Moss took it awful serious, too. Hamlet was a dead king who comes back as a ghost. He tells his son, also named Hamlet, that his brother, young Hamlet's uncle, had killed him to take over the kingdom and to marry King Hamlet's wife. The ghost tells Hamlet to take revenge and kill his uncle who has made hisself king. The whole thing about drives young Hamlet crazy and finally he kills his uncle, but by then a whole bunch of other people has been killed or died. Moss said Hamlet's problem was that he couldn't bring hisself to do nothing, that he worried too much about his immortal soul and not enough about his father's murder and his father's wishes, and he quoted, "Conscience doth make cowards of us all." But I kinda liked the idea that Hamlet wasn't too anxious to kill his uncle, even if he was a snake in the grass. I couldn't believe old Hamlet would ask his son to seek vengeance and play God, for any reason, not even to get his own self out of Hell. Nobody can do God's job and not mess up. But Moss didn't like my thoughts on the subject, so I quit offering them, just let him read his favorite passages over and over. They was real beautiful speeches, like to be or not to be and who would bear the slings and arrows of outrageous fortune when they could take themselves out with a bodkin. It got to where he had so much of the play memorized, he'd look up and put such feeling in it that sometimes I'd forget it was Hamlet speaking and it'd seem like Moss.

I decided we needed some more books to read from, something a little more uplifting, and I got Mr. Lawson the schoolmaster to loan us some. When he met Moss, he kept trying to get him to go back to school until Moss got to avoiding him. I told Mr. Lawson if he really wanted to help Moss, to let up on the school thing and to give me some books for him to read. He did, and gradually Moss warmed to him again. I knew Moss hadn't give up on the idea of someday going to work in the mine, but he fairly drunk up all them books Mr. Lawson shared with him. Every other Saturday, Mr. Lawson'd pick up the books from the last time and leave some more, except for a few he let Moss keep. Sometimes on Sunday afternoons he'd try to spend a little time with Moss, talking about whatever subject Moss wanted to talk about.

Sometimes they'd get to talking about history and stuff. I never knew there was so much out there in the world. It was interesting, but after a while I'd tune them out because I had too much to worry about in Outcropping. Couldn't be worrying about the rest of the world.

Avery

That Moss can be a real ass, but most everybody likes him, and it's good to have a friend like that. You never know when it'll come in handy, but sometimes it aint easy putting up with him. He always wants to talk about some book or about the government or about making money, boring stuff like that. He even bores Cleve with all that shit, but poor Cleve'll let him go on and on and act like he's interested, even though he can't study none of that stuff and I don't reckon he can understand a word of it, and of course he can't get a job. I feel sorry for him when Moss gets to going, and I cut him off quick as I can. There was one time he told us the history books call America the melting pot of peoples, but he said Outcropping seemed like a bottle of milk to him where only a few was on the top and most settled to the bottom.

"Aint nothing wrong with being on the bottom," I said. "I like the milk in the bottom a lot better'n I like the cream on top."

He shut up then, just looked at me and shook his head. Guess he couldn't argue that point. When he knows you're right, he shuts up. But he'll never admit you've made your point.

About the middle of the first summer Moss spent in Outcropping, past planting time, I finally got him to relax a little when he had a day off and do something besides go see his family. Me and Cleve introduced him to the swimming hole. Turned out, he's a good swimmer, said he'd always swam in the Holston that ran near their place. I should a knowed he could swim. You can't teach Moss nothing, cause he already knows everything. He said his paw taught him to swim in the river by throwing him in and he had to swim out. I reckon that'd be one way to learn all right, or die trying.

Folks on Nobb Hill have their own pool to swim in, but it's only for the big shots. I call it the Snob Hill Pool. But the company dammed up Blackberry Creek for the rest of us. They got big concrete walls on both banks, and you have to walk down steep steps to the creek. First time Moss went to the edge of the wall to go down the steps, he stood there a moment and stared. I have to admit, they don't look so high from the road, and there's not really no other way down to the swimming hole 'cept to go way past the limefield on the east side or past the mill on the west side and work your way back down the creek.

"What's a matter?" I said. "Scared of heights?"

He said no, but you never knew with Moss, because he'd never admit it if he was.

When we climbed down to the ledge below and looked back up at the walls on either side, I said, "Nice view, huh? Just for our benefit. Big, gray concrete walls."

"Kind of makes you feel trapped, don't it?" he said.

Before I could answer, Jim Johnson, who was sitting on the ledge, said, "Them walls keep limestone out of the water."

Like any fool wouldn't know that. Jim Johnson is the mine manager, head foreman, big shot, and he's another one who thinks he knows more than anybody. Folks say he reads everything coming and going. He aint hardly ever at the swimming hole, cause he's another one that works all the time. I don't talk to him. My daddy warned me not to get him going, but I didn't get no chance to warn Moss, and Johnson just kept talking, sharing his vast knowledge and sitting there straight as a poker to impress everybody, and he is about as tall as House Mountain. He looked up at us with his hands shielding his eyes from the sun. He's got the hairiest arms and the biggest hands I ever seen.

"We get our drinking water from the creek," he said, like nobody else had a brain. I guess since he had a new audience with Moss he decided to really lay it on thick. He pointed to the west bank. "See that big gray building over there? That's the mill where the zinc is separated from the limestone rock that's sent up from the mine. Once they break up the rock and get out the zinc, they grind the waste to where it aint nothing more'n powder, mix it with water to pump it to the side of the creek you climbed down from." He pointed and said, "That's what the milky-looking stuff belched out of that big pipe is—water and lime. When it dries up, only lime's left, not good for nothing. Started out as a little pile of lime. Then it became a hill, now it's a goddamn mountain." He shook his head like lime was the worst thing in the world. "Reckon we'll all suffocate in it one of these days, or drown in it, but that don't seem to worry folks much. State finally made the company put up these walls to keep it from seeping into the creek and on into the Holston. Don't completely stop it. Better'n nothing, I reckon."

Hadn't hurt me none nor nobody else, best as I could tell, but Johnson said, "You see what it does to the lungs. All these old timers 'round here spitting up blood from breathing them rock slivers."

Some folks has to gripe about everything. My mama says that white stuff puts food on the table. If it weren't for that rock dust, Johnson wouldn't have a job. For that matter, neither would Moss. Reckon they don't neither one think about that. And them men with miner's TB that Johnson was talking about are old. Old folks always die of something. My paw says you're going to die one way or another, and if it comes your time to go, won't make no difference if you're in the mine or in the middle of a cornfield. I was getting anxious to swim. I tried to motion to Moss to get in the pool, but he didn't pay me no mind.

He made the mistake of asking about the overhead cars that carry the rock from the mine to the mill, and Johnson started again. "Them cars look little from down here," he said, "but they each carry about two ton of rock. Run all the time. That's a hell of a lot of rock to come out of the earth all day long. Hell of a lot of rock to be running over our heads all the time, too. But we aint never had a cable break yet." He pointed to the limefield, which I'll have to agree did look more like a mountain than a field. "Takes a lot of rock to be crushed into that much lime."

I finally said, "Come on, Moss. We aint going to have no time to swim before you got to go to work."

Johnson frowned at me and said to Moss, "Go ahead. Have fun with your friends."

53

Moss said, "He'll wait."

Right, I thought, don't worry about Avery. Sometimes I think I work my life around Moss's schedule.

"Aint you the new kid in the commissary?" Johnson said to him.

"Been there a few months. Seen you come in a time or two."

"I thought I recognized you. Name's Moss, right? I drop in every now and then, mostly on Saturdays. You're usually closed by the time I get off work during the week."

Course Johnson had to let everybody know he works longer than anybody else. I'd about had it with both of them. "I aint waiting no longer, Moss."

"Go on, kid," Johnson said to Moss. "Your friend there has ants in his pants. I'll see you around."

I'd like to put ants in his pants. Moss told him he'd enjoyed talking to him and such stuff as that, like he always does. I swear he knows more people in Outcropping than I do, and I've lived here all my life. Course I don't bother to know everybody. Some folks just aint worth knowing. Moss acts like he's best buddies with the world, even the Mexicans and coloreds. He sure can be stupid.

When Moss dove into the creek, he practically came up on the other side. He's about as tall as Johnson. Well, not quite, but he don't miss it far. Then he hollered, "Come on, Avery. What're you waiting for? I thought you were in a hurry."

Sometimes I'd like to beat the hell out of him. Some day I just might.

When I swam out to him, he said, "So, that's the man."

"Yeah, that's the man. Thinks he's God. I can't stand him. Don't care who he is. Started out toting water, like anybody else. Now he's made foreman, he thinks he's so smart. He'd a talked your head off if I hadn't a saved you. Lord, everybody knows them overhead cars carry rock. What else around here is there to carry? Rock and more rock."

54

"But who'd believe they carry such a load?"

"I really don't give a good damn. Come on, let's swim on over to the side."

"I bet he knew my father," Moss said. "In fact, a man named Johnson called my neighbor the night Paw was killed."

Moss has a way sometimes of making you feel like shit. I guess he would've liked to have asked Johnson about his paw, but, hell, I aint no mind reader. He hadn't ever told me that before. I said I was sure Johnson'd talk to him about his paw if he wanted him to. Course there aint no telling what he'd say. Johnson's got a way of calling a spade a spade. If he has a gripe with you, he'll tell you right out. He sure chewed my paw up and spit him out for laying out of work one day. Paw aint never laid out again, not without good reason. But I didn't tell Moss that. I figured he could find out for hisself. Do him good to be took down a peg or two, and Johnson'd be the man to do it.

Thelma

First time I seen Moss McCullen he come bringing groceries to the fellowship hall in Shantytown, brung them right through the big screened-in porch, past all the picnic tables we use for dinners and socials, and he come right on into the kitchen, calling my name, *Thelma Strong, groceries for Thelma Strong. It's Moss McCullen from the commissary.*

Me and my husband Lightning runs the hall for the coloreds. Everybody in Outcropping like to dance and eat, and the company provides us a place like they do the whites. Ours is supposed to be for everybody that aint white, but the Mexicans don't come around. They know they aint welcome. Sad, but I can't change folks' thinking. I pretty much run the center, cause Lightning, he works at the mine. Tote a little moonshine, too. Lightning got a way of making money and getting most anything he want, including me. He say he can't run the center with all he got to do, so I run it for him cause he wants the money the company pays him for the job.

Anyway, I's surprised Moss brung my groceries inside for me. Aint no other delivery boy ever brung them in to the kitchen. Leave them at the door for me to tote in. I thank Mr. Moss over and over.

I say, "You must be a new boy."

He say he is, and I tell him the commissary help is getting better and that he got to have a piece of my sweet potato pie. I make the best sweet potato pie in the world—in Outcropping anyways. To be honest, I aint been nowhere else in the world. Moss say I don't owe him nothing, he just doing his job. I tell him to sit down and not argue. Then I say he can take it with him if he rather. But he sat right down and say maybe the others would've brought in my groceries if I'd offered them a piece of my pie. I look at his eyes, and he give me a big wink.

"They wouldn't bring in my groceries if I offered them the whole damn pie." We both laugh.

He say my pie about the best he ever put in his mouth, but not to tell Aunt Minnie he say so. He tell me he's living with Aunt Minnie and that she cook real good, but she don't make pie like mine.

"Why, boy," I say, "how you manage that?"

"I don't rightly know," he say. "I reckon somebody up there's watching out for me. First day I come to Outcropping, she gave me the job at the commissary and offered me a place to live, too."

We talk about Aunt Minnie and what a fine woman she is. Most folks don't know what all Aunt Minnie do for folks on our side of town. She's like the man Jesus told about who prays in the closet 'stead of on the street corner. I say they aint no better person. She never put herself above nobody, not even the Mexicans. I tell him I feel bad for them, and that Aunt Minnie do, too.

"Here they are, far from home," I say, "trying to make a little money, do the worst jobs in the mine, make the least pay, try to give their kids a chance, like the rest of us, and don't nobody like them."

Moss say he can relate to that, which I think is odd for a white boy to say.

He look up at me with them deep eyes of his and say, "Why do folks always got to put somebody down, Miss Thelma?"

"Don't know. Seems folks got to have a pecking order. A body'd think them that's been through hard times would feel sorry for others that's suffering. But it don't seem to work that way."

—————————————————

Some months later, after the war ended and the company wasn't selling so much zinc, lots of men was laid off and most of the Mexicans was gone. Got laid off first. Don't know where they went. Just left. Maybe back to Mexico. Mr. Moss come delivering groceries, come on the porch like always, heading for the kitchen. Big Jim Nash sitting in there, leaning on a table, wasting his time, like always when he laid off, him and some other men that used to bust rocks at the mine. The rest of them stay where they at, not paying Moss no mind, but not Jim.

He get right up in that boy's face, him big as a bulkhead, and he say, "Hey, boy, what you doing?"

Moss say delivering groceries, and he try to go around Big Jim. But Jim move with him, blocking Moss, saying, "Now, you don't wants to come in here with us po' ole darkies, does you, white boy?"

Moss stop trying to get around him, look like he studying in his mind what to do.

Jim say, "You scared, boy? If you is, you can just leave them pokes right there. I take them on in."

Moss a big boy, but Jim as big as Boss Johnson, probably outweigh him. Nobody in their right mind would want to tackle either one of them. But Moss stood face to face with Jim, like he trying to decide whether to take a licking or eat dirt. So I decide it be time I do something. I grab a fry pan and butt in between them.

I look up at Jim and say, "You get out of this boy's way." I push one hand against his broad chest and aim the fry pan at him with the other. "Get out of the way, and let this boy through or you be seeing stars."

I held that heavy fry pan above my head, and if he hadn't back down, I'd a busted him up the side of the head, for sure.

He took a step back, and I say to Moss, "Now, come on in here with them pokes, honey."

Jim take a few steps, swaying like me, mocking, saying, "Come on in, honey," but he don't do no threatening no more.

Moss follow me in, close on my tail. Big Jim, he glare at us both, like a angry bull, but he don't do nothing, just come up to the door looking at us. He don't want to mess with Lightning, and messing with me's messing with Lightning. Lightning was at the mine. He ain't never out of work. Mules too important, and nobody can handle them like Lightning. They got to be taken care of whether they's mining work to be done or not. Big Jim's not afraid of Lightning. He aint scared of the devil hisself, but he don't want his supply of moonshine cut off, and Lightning'd do it. And you can think what you like about Lightning toting 'shine, but folks got to have their liquor, and it aint just the coloreds. The white folk like to brag about how they aint no liquor in Outcropping, meaning on their side of town. But I know the truth about that, cause Lightning making money off them.

I say to Moss, "You got to forgive that big ox. He frustrated cause he aint got no work right now with the war over and all. Aint no cause to take it out on you, but he too much a fool to see that." I stare over at Jim and add, "Or maybe he just too drunk. How 'bout some nice hot cornbread before you go? Just got it fried up."

Big Jim's mouth fell open. "You didn't offer me no cornbread, Thelma."

"Well," I said, "if you come in with Moss and act like somebody, I fix you a piece, too, and a big glass of cold milk. Now aint you something, acting like a big ole bully to the only boy that'll bring my groceries in this kitchen. I never see you ever get off your sorry ass to carry them in."

Then I say to Moss, "It's the old white lightning in him, honey." I point to the other men sitting on the porch. "They here a drinking, wasting hard-earned money, acting like big shots, trying to forget they aint. You 'member that, Mr. Moss. Too much liquor don't make you look big, it make you look stupid. Why, Big Jim here, he usually gentle as a lamb. I know he out of work, but that aint no excuse to be mean. Now, my Lightning, he may peddle liquor, but he don't drink it, 'cept when he sick, of course."

He shook his head and said, "Folks are fools, aint they, Thelma?"

"For the most part, reckon they is."

Jim, he just hang his head and eat his cornbread dripping with butter. After that Jim nor none of the rest of the men ever bothered Moss again. Sometime they even offer him a drink, but he never take it. Don't know whether because he don't want it or whether he want to impress me. I don't care what keep him away from it, just so he stay away. He joke with the men and tell them when he was a little boy, his pappy's hogs'd root on House Mountain during the day. They'd come back at night, drunk as skunks. He say, after that he can't never drink the stuff for picturing pigs wallowing in the vats where it was made.

The men roar with laughter and say, 'You kidding, right?"

He say, "Would I lie to you?" But he gives a big wink, and you can't be sure.

Madeline

Mama died last year when I was fourteen. Excuse me, *Mother* died. Father always says *Mama* is common. Correct language is a big issue with Father. He doesn't think anyone in Outcropping speaks correctly, especially coloreds. He tried to change Annie for a while, said her way of talking was a bad influence on me. Mama said Annie had raised her and it didn't hurt *her* language any, that she'd done just fine and that I would, too. Father didn't understand.

Annie had come with Mama from The Willows where she'd grown up, her beautiful brick home with white columns overlooking the Holston River, where all the McMahans had lived for generations. Annie's people date back as far at The Willows as Mama's. They were bought fresh from Africa, way before the Civil War. Mama said some of the bricks in The Willows have fingerprints of Annie's ancestors. She'd run her hands over a brick to show me, put her prints right in the slave prints, and she'd tell me I must always take care of Annie, because her blood was as much in that house as mine was. Annie'd always been with Mama, ever since Mama was born in 1880. Annie delivered her, and Annie nursed her. Annie's husband had just been killed cutting a tree when he and some other men were clearing a field for Grandfather, and her little baby died of pneumonia about the same time. She nursed Mama instead so Grandmother wouldn't lose her figure. But she lost it anyway, and she lost my mama, too, because I think Mama loved Annie better than anyone in the world, except maybe me. When she married my father and moved to Outcropping, she begged her parents to let Annie go with her. And when I was born, she made Annie promise she'd always take care of me. But nobody controls Father.

He finally gave up on Annie and proper speech, said you couldn't teach coloreds to talk correctly. Still he had Annie correcting me. She could talk the way she wanted, he said, since she didn't know any better, but she had to see to it that I didn't talk like her. I love the musical flow of her words and the richness of her expressions. I can imitate her to a T, but if I'd say, "Where my mama?" like she might say it, she'd shake her long finger at me and say, "Now, Missy, you knows for you, that's *Where* is my *mother*?" Then she'd wink and say, "And if you really wants to know, your mama at the doctor's."

It got so Mama spent a lot of time at the doctor's, and then when she got worse Dr. Timer came to our home to see her. She began to spit up blood and was short of breath. Silicosis, Dr. Timer said. Father smirked and said *we* didn't get silicosis, only miners got silicosis. He said "miners" in the same tone as he said "silicosis." Even though Daddy was the chief engineer for the mining company, he never considered himself a miner.

When Daddy told Dr. Timer only men who mine get silicosis, Dr. Timer shook his head and said, "Tell that to all the women and children I've buried."

"But not *us*, not up here on the Hill," Father said. We live on Nobb Hill where only the highest level of management lives, and he believes that makes us special.

Dr. Timer said, "You think that white dust doesn't travel up here? With all due respect, sir, you do live in Outcropping. Granted, you're safer up here than the miners are, but don't think you're immune. Your wife does have silicosis, and it is caused from breathing zinc dust. Some folks seem more susceptible to it than others. Don't know why. Perhaps you might consider moving her out of town. Why don't you move to her folks' farm? Fresh air might give her a little more time."

I begged Father to move Mama and me and Annie to The Willows, even if he didn't want to go himself. The Willows was much more than just a beautiful house. It was an Eden with hundreds of acres and many animals. Grandmother had come from a large adjoining farm, and when she married my grandfather, the two farms were merged, and The Willows became even bigger and finer. The air there was clean and fresh, and Mama could've sat on the big porches and watched the peaceful river and the animals grazing in the fields. I think heaven must be like The Willows. Surely Mama would've gotten better there. Grandfather wanted us to come, too, but Father wouldn't hear of it, and we just watched Mama quite literally cough up her lungs. By the time Mama died, she was white as lime dust. Pale as an angel, Annie said.

I still miss her so. I'll never forgive Father for letting her die like that. She was all I had except for Grandfather and Annie. Grandmother had already passed when Mama died, and one day shortly after she died Grandfather just fell over and he was gone. Dr. Timer said probably of a broken heart.

Father never does anything but work. And all he wants me to do is play the piano and read and look pretty when I'm not in school. He won't hear of letting me associate with the young people of Outcropping, and there aren't that many here on Nobb Hill. He says if I become refined, I will marry a rich man and never have to work. He has no idea what's in my mind, in my heart. I don't know, either. There's only a rock there since Mama died.

I hate it here, especially summers when I don't go to school in Knoxville. Even the pool the company had built on the hill for the staff is boring. Only a few little children come, and a fourteen-year-old boy who looks like a walrus with glasses and stares at me all the time. The mothers at the pool perch on the deck, trying to look like models in *Vogue*. Mama was afraid of the water, so she wouldn't get in and play with me, and Father was too busy to swim. He saw it as a waste of time. And, of course, he wouldn't hear of my playing with the miners' children in Blackberry Creek where the company dammed it up for the hourly paid workers. He thinks they're all nasty and uncultured.

I guess that sort of thinking is why those of us on the hill have a concrete pool, which seems unnatural for a body of water. It's been here longer than I can remember. I suppose some of the folks on Nobb Hill that came from elsewhere, like Father, couldn't fathom being in water with local people, or being in water that might have something alive in it besides people, for that matter.

Sometimes when Father's not home, I walk down to the bridge over Blackberry Creek where I can watch the people of Outcropping play in the swimming hole. Watching people in the creek from the bridge is like looking down into a fairyland. Mothers are often there and in the water, too, sometimes even fathers. And if they're not, the children go in alone. They jump in, splash and yell and race each other across. Father says folks don't watch out for them, that's it's a wonder they don't drown, but it looks to me as though everyone watches out for everyone else. They all look like they're having such a good time. I would love to be there with them. They don't have any cares in the world.

Father says I'll go to college in two years when I finish high school. Thank goodness. Then I can do whatever I want, except I'll miss Annie. He says she can't go with me. I've never been without her. I love her dearly, and she'll always be in my heart, like Mama. But I can't wait to leave Father. When I get to college, I'm going to find the most objectionable person at Vanderbilt to date, if there is anyone objectionable at Vanderbilt. I'm sure Father doesn't think there is, but there must be someone, perhaps a tall, dark poet like Lord Byron. I'm sure Father'd hate a poet. He'd prefer a doctor.

I'll miss sneaking off to The Willows, too. My grandfather wasn't dead a month before Father sold off all the animals and equipment. I still walk out there sometimes. Annie doesn't like me to go because she's afraid something might happen to me. But she'd never tell on me. Mama and I always wanted to move there, even before she got sick. But Father said the closest he ever wanted to get to a cow was seeing it on his plate in the form of a steak.

Father was college-educated, but I guess he wasn't what Mama's folks considered old money. Education wasn't enough for them. His people didn't have *land*. And Father's people didn't like the idea of Father marrying Mama, either, because they thought Mama's people were too stuck up, since land was all the thing with them. *Glorified farmers*, they called Mama's people. So we never saw much of them. They came to Outcropping once, and were appalled. They said they couldn't believe Father was actually bringing me up in such a "dingy, poverty-stricken little town." Grandmother carried around a lace handkerchief which she kept scented with perfume, and she was forever wiping her forehead and saying, "Mercy, I've not been clean since I've been here. I'm always covered in that nasty zinc dust." She said Father simply must get his family out of Outcropping and go back with them to Winston-Salem, that they'd find something fitting for him to do. I don't think they ever liked Father's being an engineer. They wanted him to be a lawyer and settle in North Carolina near them and raise them some grandchildren, specifically a grandson. They only had my father. So I guess their need to reproduce fell on him, and he wasn't much up to it either. He only had me.

Avery

Me and Cleve spend a lot of time at the swimming hole when the weather gets warm, at least we used to. Moss came when he could—course he always thinks he's got to work in the commissary or go home and work on the farm. But sometimes, if he only had a day off, which wasn't enough time to go home, he'd mosey down to the creek.

There's always lots of kids swimming in the creek. Sometimes a few adults—men off from work or mamas that can spare a little time from their chores. But kids come with or without their folks. Everybody watches out for the little ones. Sometimes it's a pain in the ass and I'd like to let them sink or swim, but I can't let no kid drown.

The second summer Moss was in Outcropping and we'd all turned fifteen was when everything changed. Thanks to Moss—and Cleve, too. But Moss is mostly to blame.

Cleve could always dive better than anybody I ever seen. Boss Johnson says Cleve's so good he could get paid money for diving. Maybe some other place, but aint nobody in Outcropping going to pay nobody to dive, and that's a fact.

One day when me and Cleve and Moss was all at the hole, diving off the ledge and racing across the creek like always, Cleve got a wild hair about jumping off the big pipe that runs over the creek from the mill side to the limefield. He kept pointing up at the pipe and making bird dives with his hands, and we didn't have no notion what in heaven's name he was trying to say. We tried to get his mind off it, tried to get him to dive in with us and swim to the far side, but he never let up with the arm motions.

Finally Moss and me raced across. Course Moss won. It's cause he's taller'n me so he don't have as far to go. Aint fair. When we got back to the side where we'd started, everybody was all in a dither and pointing up to the overhead pipe. We looked up and blame if that crazy Cleve wasn't climbing up one of them A-frames that support the pipe on either side of the creek.

66

Everybody was yelling Cleve's name, but of course he never heard them.

"What the hell's he doing?" people shouted.

"He's going to fall off that thing."

"Somebody better go get him."

But nobody offered to go up on the A-frame.

Moss looked at me and said, "He's going to dive off that pipe."

"Oh, hell, no," I said. "He aint that stupid."

Moss didn't even answer, just swam to the far side of the creek again where Cleve was. Then he ran up to the A-frame and started climbing after him.

"Shit," I said and swam across, too. I was getting sick and tired of taking care of Cleve. When I got to the foot of the frame, I yelled to Moss, "You two are going to kill yourselves. Get back down here."

But Moss kept climbing. I told him he was crazy as Cleve, who'd started walking out on the pipe. By the time Moss made it to the pipe, Cleve had walked out to the center. He stood there, looking down. Then he looked back to the side and saw Moss walking out to him. I was half-way up the frame, wondering why I was risking my life for two fools.

Next thing I knew Cleve had dove off the pipe head-first. Folks in the water had all got away from the middle and Cleve hit the water before I could take it all in. I most lost my breath and held onto the frame for dear life, fighting the need to vomit.

I figured Cleve was dead as Adam, and I didn't want to look. But when I opened my eyes, expecting to see the water red with blood, like in the story of Moses, I saw Cleve's head pop out of the water. Everyone started yelling and clapping. Suddenly they all got quiet again, as they looked back up and seen Moss balancing on the pipe about where Cleve had dived from.

I yelled again at Moss to come back, but he hollered, "I think it'd be safer to just dive in the creek." And he did, just like that.

67

When they both got to the side and climbed back on the ledge, they laid down in the warm sun, breathing hard. I climbed back down and swam over to them. I was worn out myself, so I laid down beside them.

"Y'all are plumb crazy," I said.

Moss was panting as he said, "I guess. But it was fun as hell."

"Fun my ass," I said, "It's a wonder either of you's alive. You could've busted your damn brains out. What little you got."

But they started laughing like hyenas. Both of them, laying on the ledge, laughing their fool heads off.

I got to get me some more friends, I thought. These two'll get me killed sure as sin.

———————————

Once that crazy Moss and Cleve discovered they could dive off that damned pipe, they started jumping off it for fun. Now it don't take no genius to see the stupidity of that. You aint going to catch me up there. They can splat themselves out like pancakes if they want to. It's got to be at least thirty feet high up there if it's an inch, and the creek's only about five feet deep, and that's assuming you hit the center—at least according to Jim Johnson, the *World Book Encyclopedia* of Outcropping. And when they dive, nothing simple like jumping feet first. Oh, no. It aint enough to risk busting up their feet. They got to chance busting their heads open. But they're not the only fools around. A few other idiots join them. Everybody else watches them. That's why they do it, to show off. They've become the town entertainment, the town clowns. If there was anything else in the world to do in this durn town, I'd quit going down there.

When they'd been diving off there for about three summers, there was talk the mine was going to make the pipe off limits. Didn't do it soon enough. But, shit, you shouldn't need somebody else tell you jumping off a thirty foot high pipe's a fool thing to do, even if the creek was deep, which it aint.

68

One Saturday morning when I got to the hole, Moss and Cleve was there already. Cleve was scrambling up the frame to the pipe. Moss sat on the ledge, and I joined him. When Cleve got on the pipe, he started waving at us. Moss waved back, and I just sat there. Cleve waved so hard I thought he'd fall off the blame thing.

"Wave at him, Avery," Moss said. "He wants to know you're watching him."

"Hell," I said, "I'm not his daddy or brother. And you aint the boss of me, neither." But I finally gave Cleve a weak wave because I was afraid he was going to fall, flailing around up there, if I didn't.

"He's good," Moss said.

"Yeah, good and crazy. Now he can do something, he thinks he has to show out for the world. And what'll he get out of it? Nothing, except maybe a cracked skull. You can't make no money diving."

"He's having fun. It really is great fun."

That's Moss's way of reminding me that he can do it, too. I still think if Moss hadn't done it, Cleve wouldn't have kept doing it. I didn't say nothing, and Moss got in the water and swam across the creek to climb up to the pipe. The rest of the fools started doing it, too, and the show got underway for the day. The pipe got so wet it was glistening in the sun. They didn't even give it time to dry between dives. When Moss went up for at least the fifth time, he was about out to the usual diving spot, and it looked like he almost fell, but then I thought he'd regained his balance. Next thing I knew, he slipped right off, falling headfirst, but he hadn't formed his dive. I turned away from looking. I thought, hell, what'd you expect. I told them it was stupid from the first. I figured that'd put an end to their showing off.

Moss

Diving off the big overhead pipe at the swimming hole was about the most fun thing I ever did in my life. The most stupid, too. Well the second most stupid, but the most stupid up to that point. I knew it was crazy from the start, but it didn't seem that dangerous once we discovered we could do it if we hit just right. But when I slipped off that thing when I was eighteen, I knew the fun hadn't been worth it. I fell head-first and tried to get turned around so I'd enter the water with my feet first, but it was too late. The last thought I had was of Mom and the girls. It would've been one thing to die in the mine working, but this was another, to die playing, risking my life for fun. At that moment I knew I didn't have no right to be mad at Paw for dying in the mine. At least he died working for a living.

Then it was as if Paw said—or maybe it was God, or maybe it was me—*take it with your arms, boy*. All I know is, I tried to lock my arms. Breaking them would be better than breaking my skull. That's the last thing I remember before I woke up in the water. I don't know how long I was in the creek. Not long I reckon, or I'd have drowned. I just remember trying to figure out which way the surface was. My arms wouldn't pull me up, and my legs wouldn't let me stand. Everything was fuzzy and red and distorted. I saw arms, many big, long arms that lifted me up. I wondered if that was what it was like to die, and then I couldn't think at all.

When I woke up the next time I was on the ledge. I heard voices, but I couldn't place them, saying things like *Is he dead? He's coming around. Oh, my god....*

My eyes were clouded with blood, and the faces above me swayed. I tried to grab hold of one to keep it still, but my arms wouldn't work. Then somebody was holding my hand. It was Cleve, and he squeezed hard.

"Am I alive?" I said.

I could see his head nodding, real fast. It made me dizzy.

"Only by the grace of God," said Gadget, the head mechanic at the mine. Everybody called him Gadget, because he could do anything with a tool. His real name was George Taylor, but I don't expect many people even remembered that. Only way I knew his real name was because of his account at the commissary.

"Where's Avery?" I said.

"Right here. Come on over here, Avery."

In a moment, Avery was kneeling beside me saying, "I'm here, buddy. You gonna be all right. I tried to tell you, you all was crazy. I guess you'll stay off that pipe now."

"I think … I must've busted my head …. I feel like I pushed my arms into my feet."

"Your arms is still in your shoulders," Gadget said. "It's your head you best be worried about. We got to get you to Doc's. We'll make a pack saddle to get you up the steps."

Doc's office was only down the hill from the swimming hole, right near the commissary.

"I can walk," I said, and struggled to get up.

I wiped my eyes, and Gadget said, "You're smearing blood all over your face. He yanked up a towel and wiped me off as best he could. Then he said, "Here, hold this on your head. And don't be a fool. You can't get up them steps."

"Maybe, if you help me up."

"Well, damn it," he said, but he lifted me to my feet. I felt like a big, long rag doll holding onto him. We made our way over to the steps, with Gadget practically carrying me. He said, "I'll come behind you. Cleve can walk up front. You can hold onto him. If you feel yourself falling, don't worry, I'll get you."

He called his boys over, gave them some change for Co'colas and told them to run on to the commissary, he'd pick them up later. I remember thinking he was a good father.

Gadget had a huge barrel chest and powerful arms. I knew he wouldn't let me fall. I really felt safer in front of him than if they'd tried to carry me up the steps. I made it a few steps, then said, "I feel funny, Gadget."

"I got you," he said, and I felt his strong arms holding me up from the back.

It seemed like a long time before we got up the steps. Avery had followed Gadget, and Gadget told him and Cleve to get me in his car. I said I couldn't get in the car.

"Why not?" he said. "We can get you in. We got up the steps."

"All this blood. It'll ruin your new car."

Gadget cussed and said I was crazy. My head hurt like hell, but I thought I was perfectly fine, as far as my thinking. Not many folks had cars in Outcropping. I couldn't mess up Gadget's new one. I tried to explain that, but no one seemed to understand. I had trouble thinking of the right words to say.

"You're going to bleed to death while we stand here pow-wowing about blood in the damn automobile," Gadget said. "We all got blood on us, anyway. Now get in."

My head was pounding, but I said, "It aint far. I can stand on the running board."

"Damn it to hell," he said. "Ride on the running board if you want to. I'm surprised that fall busted your head, it's so hard. I think you'll live. You're too stubborn not to." He put a hand on Cleve's shoulder and motioned. "Get up there with him." He looked at Avery and said, "You, too. See he don't fall off."

We rolled down the hill to Dr. Timer's office with me sandwiched on the running board between Cleve and Avery. By the time we arrived, my head felt like crushed rock. Blood was all over the running board, but it could be washed off. I don't remember going into Doctor Timer's office.

But I do remember Miss Sadie, the nurse, looking at my head and asking what happened. She was real pretty with light brown hair under her starched white cap and eyes the color of the first leaves in the springtime. All the men were about half in love with her.

When she found out what I'd done, she said, "Well, that's really smart. I thought the company'd made that pipe off limits."

"Not yet," Gadget said, "but they will now."

As she guided us to an examining table, Miss Sadie said, "I knew somebody would get hurt there sooner or later. Aren't there enough ways for people to get hurt around here without doing something that stupid?"

"Well, Sadie, you know how boys are."

She cocked her head and said, "No, Gadget, how are boys? These boys are old enough to know better."

He hung his head and cleared his throat. I felt bad he was taking the scolding I should be getting, so I said, "Pretty stupid, wasn't it?"

"Very stupid. Lie down so you won't lose so much blood."

I decided against telling her my arms felt like they'd been wrenched from their sockets. She was mad enough about my head. Amazingly they didn't seem to be broken.

She poked a spoonful of a yellow-brown liquid down me and said, "This paregoric'll help dull the pain. It's all I can do till Dr. Timer gets back, except clean the wound and bandage you up. He's gone to deliver a baby. Could be a good while. First baby." She pressed a hand against my chest. "Didn't I tell you to lie down?"

I guess I forgot. I wasn't thinking too good. When she went to wash her hands and get supplies, I looked at Gadget and pointed to the bottle. 'Good stuff," I whispered, "Get me some more."

"I can't do that."

"I'll do it," Avery said, handing it to me. He probably hoped I'd get in trouble. I took a quick gulp and handed it back, and he returned it to the shelf.

When Miss Sadie finished washing her hands, she said to Gadget, "You all may as well go on home. Moss can't leave until he sees the doctor. I'm sure he'll send him on to Knoxville. You can check back later in the day to see what's going on."

Gadget nodded to Avery, nudged Cleve and said, "Let's go, boys. I got to pick up my youngens. We can't do nothing more here."

I thanked Gadget for taking care of me.

He smiled and said, "We got to take care of each other. Sorry I was rough on you, but damn if you didn't scare the blessed hell out of me."

"Drop by the commissary and tell Aunt Minnie that Moss won't be coming to work," Sadie told him. I noticed she never asked or said please when she told somebody to do something.

"Going there anyway to pick up my boys."

"They're expecting me at work by noon," I said to Sadie.

"They'll survive without you. We're all expendable. You've been around here long enough to know that. Your head's got to be sewn up. I'm going to clean you up and try to stop the bleeding. You need to be still till Dr. Timer returns. You won't be going to work today. You have a concussion." I guess she could tell by the look on my face that I had no idea what she was talking about because she added, "Bleeding inside your head. You need to stay down for a few days. You could get very sick, maybe pass out. Or worse."

If I hadn't been so light-headed all that might have scared me, like it should've. Nothing much was bothering me, except that I might be late to work. I told her she could sew up my head. Said I'd seen my paw sew up a cow before. She said she wasn't my paw and I wasn't a cow, a mule maybe. Her nostrils flared. I asked her how old she was.

She raised her eyebrows and said, "Too old for you! I can't believe you're flirting. I must have given you too much paregoric. You ought to feel like Humpty Dumpty. "

I didn't know I was flirting. "Sorry," I said, "but I have to think about something other than my head, something good. That's the way folks take pain, you know. My maw taught me."

"Is that some old Indian notion?"

I said I didn't know, but it worked.

74

"Well, then, why don't you think about the fun you had diving off the pipe. That ought to get your mind off the pain."

"That might've worked yesterday," I said.

"The bleeding's slowing up. Relax while you wait for the doctor and think of something good like your mama taught you."

I shut my eyes and thought of something Maw didn't have in mind.

The next thing I knew, Sadie roused me and said, "Don't go to sleep."

"You told me to relax."

"Relax, not go to sleep. I have to watch your eyes."

"Good," I tried to wink so she'd know I was teasing, but I couldn't make my eye close.

"You're as drunk as a miner on Friday night,' she said.

I laughed and started to sit up, but my head started pounding again, and I grabbed it in both hands.

She put a hand on my shoulder and said in a softer tone, "Be still. Moving around is going to make your head hurt worse and bleed more. I told you, you could be bleeding inside. Dr. Timer will send you to Knoxville when he gets here. Now quit acting like a child."

She was right. Diving off the pipe when I should have been at work was acting like a child. Everybody always said I acted like an adult, but this sure had taught me a lesson. I wasn't as grown up as I thought. I could've died and that wouldn't have helped anyone. Or, worse, it could have been Cleve that had fallen and maybe died. I'd have never gotten over that. But I wasn't going to any hospital. The only people I knew that had been to a hospital never came back.

I laid back down and said, "I can't go to Knoxville. And I really got to get to work."

"I swear, you're like the miners who come in here needing pieces of rock removed from eyes, gashes sewn up, limbs set, and a thousand other things, and most of the time, unless they've lost an arm or leg or unless they die, the crazy things leave here saying

75

they have to get back to work. I don't want to scare you, but this head injury could be very serious."

"I bet you've put in stitches before."

"Only on my mother's cat." She cocked one eyebrow and said, "He's hardheaded, like some people."

"He lived, didn't he?"

"Sure, but cats have nine lives. Seriously, sewing it up will hurt with nothing stronger than I can give you, and besides the gash runs onto your forehead and it'll leave a scar. You don't want that, do you?"

"I reckon it'll make a scar, anyway, won't it?"

"Yes, but it won't be as bad if it's done right."

"Maw says scars are trophies, reminding us of what we can get through in this life. If you don't want to sew it, just pull it together and bandage it up. I've seen Maw fix some pretty bad cuts before. One time she set my arm and the bone was sticking clean through the skin. She did it all by herself." I held up my arm and said, "See? Good as new. There's the scar."

"God have mercy on your mother." She took in a deep breath, closed her eyes for a minute and said, "If Dr. Timer finds out I sewed you up, God have mercy on me and you both." I smiled, and she said, "You needn't smile. It'll hurt."

"Trust me. It can't hurt no more than it does already."

"Don't bank on it," she said, as she took scissors and cut my hair around the wound. Then she shaved it even closer. "Once we start, we'll have to go through with it. You can't get sick on me."

"I'm ready," I said.

She bit her lip as she stuck the needle into my head, and I realized she was right about a couple of things. She wasn't used to doing it and it could hurt worse than it already did. She stuck the needle in slow, like a miner tamping a stick of dynamite into a hole in a rock. I told her to hurry, but she told me to shut up. I tried to concentrate on her scent instead of the strong smell of alcohol and blood, which smelled stronger than before. As I gripped the edges of the table, my arms hurt, but that pain took a back seat to the pain in my head. The scene of falling and locking my arms to break the blow to my head came flooding back.

I was trying to get out of the water when Sadie finally said, "All done. I need to sit down for a few minutes. Just lie there."

She sat down in a chair and leaned her head against the wall behind it. She was pale and not so confident-looking as before. I wasn't feeling so well myself. I must've fallen asleep. When I woke up, she was still sitting there, watching me. I grinned, and she smiled back.

"You got a couple of Co'colas here?" I said.

"In the icebox back there in the storeroom."

"Is it all right if I get us one?"

"No, it isn't. But I'll get us one."

I could already taste the Co'cola when I put my hands around the frosty green bottle and tried to guide it to my mouth. She sat back down, and we drank without saying a word. I watched her neck as she swallowed and thought how white it was, like that of a swan. As my gaze travelled down to her dress, I saw all the blood.

"I'm sorry I put you through that," I said, "and I'm sorry I got your dress bloody.

"You should be. Now go home, get an old quilt, find you a nice shade-tree and rest. Take a couple days off work. If you die, we're both in trouble. We'll have to take out those stitches in a few days without Dr. Timer knowing. Then we'll see about you going back to work."

"Maybe we could take the stitches out on a picnic," I said. "You have a boyfriend?"

"I have a friend, and he's as stubborn as you." She stared at me and said, "Don't let your devotion to some ideal of hard work and company loyalty keep you from having a life before it's too late."

I didn't quite understand what she was saying. I figured it was because of my sore head. Then she called for the company chauffeur to come take me home. I couldn't believe it, me riding in the car for the big shots.

When the chauffeur came in the office, he looked at me and said to Sadie, "You want me to take this boy home?"

"That's why I called you. He can't walk that far now. Help him in the house when you get there. He lives with Aunt Minnie."

He tipped his hat at her. "Yes, ma'am. Whatever you say."

Monday morning Sadie came to the commissary bright and early with a list of supplies for the clinic and she was carrying a little poke. When she saw me stocking shelves, she took in a deep breath. She stood up straight and placed her hands on her hips. Everybody looked at her. You couldn't have kept from looking at her if you wanted to.

"I thought I told you not to come to work today," she said, "but I figured you'd be here unless you died."

I mumbled I felt okay and asked if I could help her with something.

Mr. Eslinger stopped working and eased over to listen. Aunt Minnie was behind the counter, and she looked up over her glasses and frowned at me.

"You need to grow up, Moss McCullen," Sadie said, "and realize that this commissary will keep going with or without you, as will the rest of the world. You're a fool, you know that? Just like all men. You're a fool for diving off that pipe in the first place. You were a fool to let me sew up your head, and you're even more of a fool for working with a concussion. And I'm the biggest fool of all for helping you." She threw her hand in the air, set the little bag on the counter and said, "Get Aunt Minnie to take the stitches out in a few days. She may hurt you a little more than I would, but what's a little pain? Right?" She jerked her head in Aunt Minnie's direction, pointed to the supplies and said to her, "Here's fresh bandages. His wound needs to be changed every day. Use some iodine and scissors when you take the stitches out in a couple of days."

With that she whipped around and left. Mr. Eslinger raised his eyebrows and watched her strut out. He grinned at me and said, "Mighty handsome woman when she's mad. Never knew she could take such a personal interest in a patient."

Aunt Minnie wasn't smiling. All she said was, "Guess she told you what for. I told you, you shouldn't a come to work today. That Sadie's the kind of woman you need. Maybe you ought to run after her and tell her you'll go home for the day."

But I didn't. For one thing, I was afraid of what she'd say, and for another, I wasn't sure I was ready for a woman like Sadie, or if I ever would be. Reckon it's a good thing I did leave her alone. She wound up being Captain Johnson's woman.

Hope

Big as my belly is, you'd think this baby'd fill up the hole that's been inside me ever since Paw died. The baby has filled up a lot of it, but they's still tunnels running here and there. I reckon our bodies are like the earth. We can lose a lot of ourselves and keep on going. Folks take pieces of us, but we don't cave in, unless too much is taken out. That's what Stub says about mining. He says that the tunnels and holes underneath Outcropping don't cause the earth to crash in if they leave enough pillars to hold it up.

I called him Uncle Stub when I was little. He's actually my third or fourth cousin, something like that. He was my Daddy's second cousin, so whatever that makes us. Except for him, it was always just me and Paw. I can't hardly remember my mother. But sometimes I have visions of her. I can't see her features in my mind no more, but I see long, curly hair the color of a new penny and blue eyes and pale, pale skin. I hear coughing and retching. And I see lots of black and red. She died of black lung in a coal camp in Kentucky. At least we won't die of black lung, Paw said, when he moved us to Outcropping. But he didn't know about miners' TB. Paw didn't live long enough to worry about that, though. Got his head cut off when a cable broke over a year ago when I was only sixteen. They wouldn't even let me see him. Guess it didn't matter. It wouldn't have been Paw.

They sent Stub over to tell me. When I opened the door, he had tears in his eyes, and I knew something was bad. He wiped his eyes with his sleeve, and he told me Paw'd been killed. I couldn't talk or cry or nothing. Stub had to remind me to breathe when I almost passed out. I didn't know what to do without Paw. I felt like I was dead myself. Don't remember much of those first few days. Stub saw to getting him buried.

When I began to realize I was always going to be in a world without Paw, I wondered where that would be. Paw and me lived in a company house, but houses were only for miners and I had no idea where I would go. To the company I wasn't nobody without

80

Paw. I felt like nobody, too, like part of me was in the earth with him, and my body was still here somehow, walking around like an empty shell.

Stub said to not worry. I could stay in the house 'cause he'd get it put in his name, since he qualified for a house if he wanted it. Stub's wife and baby had died of typhoid back in Kentucky in the coal camp, and he never got remarried. When Paw decided to pack up and move to Tennessee, Stub came along, said he also needed to leave Kentucky and too many memories. Since him and Daddy'd both worked in the coal mine, they got jobs right away. Then the war broke out, and they did pretty good. Paw said zinc gets valuable in a war. They use it to keep things like guns from rusting and they put it in tires and I don't know what all. Paw said we done right, moving to Tennessee. Then he got killed anyway.

I couldn't have got through those first few weeks without Stub. He was so much like Paw, even smelt like him, like rock and cigarettes. He'd hold me when I cried at night, and that was the only time I felt safe.

After about a year of us living in the house, he told me to sit down, that he needed to talk to me. Said he couldn't keep on living with me like he was. We were going to have to make other arrangements. I started shaking, because I didn't know where I'd go, and he put his arms around me and said he didn't mean for me to move out. He said he didn't see no other way than for us to get married. I said I reckoned we might as well. He said he guessed it was time I quit wearing pigtails down my back and put my braids on top of my head. I laughed and cried at the same time, and he did, too. I still didn't care much what happened to me at that point, not having Paw no more.

But now I got a baby coming, and I got something to live for. Things have a way of working out, like Paw always said. You just got to keep the faith and find a way to keep living till you can see some good in the world again. That's the hard part.

Kathleen

I know it's wrong for me to say so, but Moss's leaving home was harder for me than Paw's dying. Both of them going at once was too much. Moss was like a father to me and Ellie. I know Ellie's always been his favorite, but I loved him more than anything. When he left, I thought my heart would break. Maw said he left to make a living for us all. I didn't want money. I wanted Moss. The first time he came home after he got his first paycheck he brought me and Ellie each a hair ribbon. Ellie wears hers, but I won't wear mine. If I ever have a little girl, I'll pass it on to her.

I took on chores that Moss used to do and helped Maw with some of the laundry she started taking in for folks. I thought if we made enough money, Moss'd come home. Then he wouldn't see the need to work in the mine. He'd come to work on the farm sometimes, like Paw used to. But it seemed no matter how much we made, he wasn't coming to stay. The only way I ever got to talk with him was to work alongside of him, so I did.

I didn't want to go on to high school when my elementary school days were over. I thought I'd just work, and maybe Moss could come home, but he wouldn't hear of me not going. I started high school three years after he left, and I knew then he'd never come home to live, 'cause after I finished there'd be Ellie, then LC. Moss doesn't pay him much attention, but Moss is the one who dubbed him LC. Once he started calling him that, of course Ellie and I did. Finally Maw gave up on calling him Clyde, too. By the time we all get through school, Moss'll have a whole other life without us—or he'll be dead.

I had to walk down to the main road to catch the bus to go to school in Knoxville, and Maw worked it out that I could walk with Joe, the youngest Lindsey boy who started high school the same year I did. We sat together on the bus coming and going, and that's when I learned Joe's maw was sick. They didn't say nothing to nobody for a long time about it, but finally she got so bad she couldn't keep up with all the work on their place—four boys to feed, plus farmhands, as well as all the washing and everything else. His maw had something wrong with her heart. Myself, I think it had something to do with the fact that her oldest son Caleb got killed in the war. He didn't even have to go, and he didn't go until the war was almost over because his paw was so dead set against his going. Still, he went down and volunteered and wound up in Europe faster'n you could shake a stick, and he got shot about that quick too.

That's when Mrs. Lindsey started failing. Mr. Lindsey had got Maw to do a lot of their laundry, dropping it off at our place and picking it up when it was done, even before we knew why. We also started cooking and canning for them. They always had so much to do on their place that they needed help.

All that made me worry, not only about being without Moss, but about what we'd do if something happened to him. I decided I wasn't going to mourn myself to death if everybody around me dropped dead. I was going to be able to take care of myself. So I asked Joe what he thought about me working after school for them, maybe helping with supper and whatever was needed since his maw was sick. He said they sure needed some help, that Mrs. Rice who used to help his maw clean and do laundry had got too old and sick to work anymore, and why didn't I stop in on the way home and talk to his paw.

That's when I started working for them. And it was work, feeding that mob of people. Even Max Hendrix, the new schoolmaster, had a room in their house in exchange for helping on the farm, and he ate with them, too. For the first year Mrs. Lindsey worked with me a little when she was able, but then during my sophomore year she took to her bed, and it was just me in the evenings to fix supper. Max or Joe'd help me clean up afterwards, and one of them would walk me home in the winters or we'd ride horses 'cause it'd be dark by the time I left.

Moss didn't know I was working at first. I knew he'd have a fit, and I didn't want to hear it. But with school going to be out for the summer, Mr. Lindsey wanted me to work during the days and I said I would. I had to tell Moss before he found out on his own. I figured Maw could tell him herself that she was going to be working over at the Lindseys', too. I'm glad, because it's getting to be more than I can do to keep up with all the laundry and cooking and cleaning and seeing to Mrs. Lindsey as well. Maw can bring Ellie and LC with her when she works so they won't be alone. Ellie can actually be a help, and she can play with LC to keep him entertained. Moss won't like it, but we can't depend on him for everything.

One Sunday when he came home, I joined him on the porch while Maw and Ellie washed the dishes and LC played with the new kittens on the steps. I took off my apron, folded it over the back of a rocker and sat down in the swing beside him. Big trees shaded the front porch, and for a while we just swung back and forth, watching the maple leaves shine like silver in the breeze. We could hear LC's laughter and Ellie singing "Amazing Grace" from the kitchen. She was our singer. I don't know where that voice came from. None of the rest of us can sing a lick, but I thank God for her voice. On days that I'd get so down, I'd hear her singing. She sang all the time as she played and worked, and it'd lift my heart. That evening on the porch, I breathed in deeply and tried to savor every minute of the peaceful scene. Once I talked to Moss, the tone would change. It was the first time Moss and I'd actually sat down together since he'd left, except when we ate. It was the first time I ever stood up to him, too. But it wasn't the last.

"I got to tell you something," I finally said.

"What's wrong, Kat?"

"Nothing's wrong." I took in a deep breath. Then I said, "I been working for the Lindseys in the afternoons after school, and I'm working this summer, too."

He stopped the swing instantly, and I caught my breath. We hung there suspended with his long legs holding the swing. At first he didn't say anything. Just looked at me. Then he said, "I want you to do well in school. I want you to keep up with your studies, not work."

"I do keep up," I said, "but Mrs. Lindsey is real poorly and can't manage like she used to. During school, I only worked in the afternoons when I got home until after supper. Helped her get everyone fed." I didn't tell him how late that sometimes got to be.

"You shouldn't walk home at night by yourself."

"Mr. Lindsey always sends Joe or Max with me when it's dark."

"Who's Max?"

"You know, the new schoolmaster. Ellie's teacher. He has a room with the Lindseys. He works for Mr. Lindsey, too, after school and on Saturdays, in exchange for his room and board. With Albert off to college, Mr. Lindsey needs all the farm help he can get. You know they lost Caleb in the war."

"You call him Max?"

"He's not my teacher," I said.

"I don't like it. You don't have to work for anybody, especially a bunch of men. Tell them they'll have to get someone else."

"I can't do that, Moss. It's not just a bunch of men. It's our neighbors. Don't you understand? I'm helping them, and I'm helping us, too. I make enough to pay to ride the bus to school and even have some left, and Mrs. Lindsey gives me material to make dresses for me and Ellie, too. She showed me how to make them real pretty before she got so bad off. With me working for them, you can keep more of your paycheck for yourself. You deserve to have a life, too."

"I got a life."

"Well, I'm not going to quit working for them," I said, "and that's all there is to it."

"I can't believe Maw lets you do this." He tried telling me I was too young, but I reminded him I was older than he was when he left for Outcropping.

"Maw lets me so we're able to help support ourselves," I said. "Just because you're a man doesn't mean you're the only person in the house who can work."

85

I looked at the nasty scar on his forehead that he had avoided answering questions about during supper. He'd just said something about falling, gave the impression he'd fallen at the store. But I thought, if he fell at the store, he must've fallen all the way down the basement steps. And if he did, I didn't see why he didn't just come out and say so. Moss'd never tell an outright lie, but he was good at avoiding what he didn't want you to know.

"What if something happens to you?" I said.

He tried to pull some hair down over the scar, but his hair'd been cut all around it and it still hadn't grown out much. He turned away from me and stared out across the fields. "Nothing's going to happen to me."

"That scar says different," I said, "and the Lindseys need me this summer. They're really up against it. They've lost Caleb, and now Mrs. Lindsey's dying. That's enough to deal with without worrying about how they're going to have meals and clean clothes."

"They're not the only folks who've lost family members."

"I know that," I said. "And we all have to go on the best way we can. Mrs. Lindsey don't need to be worrying about how her family is going to go on. She's been real good to me. They've all been real good to me, to all of us. Mr. Lindsey even sends one of the boys over to do the plowing for our garden when you can't get enough time off to do it. Last week he sent two of them over to fix our leaking roof. He always sends what's left over from a meal home with me."

"You don't have to take leftovers."

"I work hard for that food," I said, "but Mr. Lindsey still don't have to give it to me. No, I'm not going to abandon them, and you can't make me."

I felt terrible talking to him like that when he'd spent his whole life taking care of us, even before Paw died. One thing working has done for me is help me appreciate what Moss has done for us, and it keeps me so busy I don't have so much time to fret about his being gone. And, even if he don't know it, he needs

86

to have some of his burden lifted. Besides, Moss can't leave us and still tell us what to do. We have to live when he's not here.

Annie

I knew we was in big trouble the summer when Miss Madeline run into Mr. Moss. And when I say run into, I mean *run into*. She hop in that little yellow car of hers she aint got no business having in the first place and tear out that driveway backwards so fast, she never see Mr. Moss in the company truck come to deliver groceries. Thank goodness he not still driving that old hack they used to have when he started working there. That poor old mare would've been deader'n a doorknob. Only reason Madeline didn't bang up both vehicles is Mr. Moss see her coming and take to the ditch. Blooded his mouth all up.

I see trouble coming when she lead him into the kitchen, telling me to get some towels and warm water. He embarrassed about the whole thing. He keep saying he be okay, and she keep saying she going to make sure. I don't 'spect he used to nobody making over him so much. She tell me, go next door and get Dr. Timer.

"Lord, child," I say, "the boy don't need no doctor. He just got a busted lip. Now get out of my way and I fix him up."

But she insisted on cleaning his face. That didn't make no sense. She aint so much as cleaned up a dog or cat. I tell her to let me do it, she mess up her fancy dress. She say it don't make no difference. She fussing around about how sorry she is and how bad she feel. I don't reckon she feel bad as Mr. Moss. But he sat there all wide-eyed, staring at everything, especially Miss Madeline, and breathing hard. I don't reckon he ever see a house like the one he sitting in. And I know he never see a girl like Miss Madeline, cause nobody has. She the prettiest thing on earth, with her long blond hair and soft, white skin and eyes as blue as a summer sky.

I raised her since the day she was born and I still amazed at how beautiful she is. Just like her mama, God rest her soul. Raised her, too. When she was born, her pappy, Mr. Payne sent out word to the workers who lived in houses at The Willows, which he owned, was there anybody could nurse a baby. I could. My

88

husband had got killed a few months earlier when him and some other men was clearing pasture land at The Willows. Tree fell on him. Our baby was born shortly before the Paynes' baby, but she only live a few days. Poor little thing. Maybe she want to be with her pappy. I wanted to go with them both, but God didn't see fit to take me. I say I never want another man or another baby long as I live. My mama tell me, why don't I go nurse Mrs. Payne's baby in the big house. I did. Don't know what I expected, but when I held that tiny thing in my arms and she nurse from my breast, I didn't care if she white or black or blue or purple. I grew to love that little girl like my own, and I love her baby the same way. If I hadn't love them so much, maybe in time I would have had another family, in spite of how I felt when I first lost them. But I think there some reason I be sent to take care of Mrs. Payne's baby.

I look at Miss Madeline's delicate hands, ringing out the rag in the bowl of water, and it turn pink.

I tell her again, "I take care of Mr. Moss."

But she just say bring some bandages.

"How you going to bandage a lip?" I say.

She look at me with her eyebrows raised and say she don't know. I say, you aint. She tell me to fix him something to eat before he go back to work, but he say he don't think he can eat nothing and besides he got to get back to work right away, that he still got groceries to deliver. She say he can't go back to work, he injured. Again he say he got to. She say she'll call the store, say he can't go back to work for a while. He laugh as best he can with his lip still bleeding and starting to swell. Miss Madeline, she don't know nothing about working. She aint never had to. I tell her Mr. Moss be okay. He tell her he be okay, too, but he don't leave before she got him coming back for dinner the next night. I know that'll be big trouble. He do, too, but he can't resist her. Can't nobody.

Moss

I was driving the new 1924 Dodge delivery truck the afternoon I
met Madeline. Well, actually I met her when I ran off the road to
keep her from hitting me. It was a good thing I was driving slow. If
I'd wrecked the truck, there'd a been hell to pay.

I always went slow around Nobb Hill. I liked to look at the
big homes with beautiful porches and imagine what it must be like
to live there. I studied the colorful flowers until I had them all
memorized. I knew every walk, tree, shrub, and flower in every
yard. I hadn't been doing deliveries much since I'd become the
assistant manager of the store, but the new boy was out walking
some orders near the commissary, and Aunt Minnie said, "Why
don't you take the truck, get outside for a little while, and take
three orders that's been called in from the Hill?" She knew I'd be
glad for a chance to get outdoors.

We'd had a wet spring, so by early summer the trees and
bushes and flowers were all lush. The yards were splashed with
red, white, pink and purple. Even the lime dust couldn't hide the
brilliant colors. I thought of Maw as I looked at the flower gardens,
which she would've seen as wasteful. She always said anything
time and money were spent on ought to be edible. About that time
of the day she'd be working in her vegetable garden. One of the
girls would be with her. The other would be seeing to the baby.
Well, he wasn't a baby any more. He was old enough to help out a
little. Maybe he'd actually be tending the garden with them. Or
maybe he'd be gathering eggs. I rarely thought about LC, and
when I was home, he spent most of his time playing with the
animals. Maw would always say he was "tending" to them.

I was roused from my thoughts when a shiny yellow
Maxwell came flying backwards down the driveway at Mr. Rogers'
home. I swerved sharply to the right and slammed on the brakes to
miss it. I pitched forward and smashed into the steering wheel. As
I tasted blood, I thought how rich people have no problems and no

concern for anybody or anything. I figured the Maxwell would already have disappeared, leaving me in the ditch.

Had to be Mr. Rogers' daughter. Everybody knew she drove the only Maxwell in town. I'd never met her before, but I knew about her. Working in the commissary, I knew everybody, or at least I knew about them. I knew the girl's mother had died and that she'd been sent away to college and recently had finished. She never went to school with the children in Outcropping, never came to the commissary. Once when I was at the swimming hole with Avery and Cleve, I saw a young girl standing up on the bridge above the creek, looking like a princess with her long blond hair, like Rapunzel high in her tower. I asked Avery who she was and he said Mr. Rogers' daughter. Said she never went anywhere in town except Nobb Hill. "Too good for us, I reckon," he added.

As I was pulling my handkerchief out to wipe my face, I heard her say, "I'm so sorry. Are you all right?"

I looked up and saw a beautiful face framed in gold. Thought I must've died and gone to heaven. Her moist blue eyes looked straight at my face.

"My god, you're hurt," she said. "I knew it."

Her blond hair fell over her shoulders as her hand reached inside the truck and actually touched my chin and raised my face.

"Look at me," she said.

I couldn't have looked anywhere else if my life had depended on it. All I could think of was that she looked like an angel and smelt of roses.

"Oh, lord, you're bleeding. I've never made anyone bleed."

My mouth was cut inside as well as out, and I probably looked worse than I was.

"Getting in a rush wasn't worth it," she said.

I decided if she'd keep holding my chin in her hand, it was worth it to me. I didn't know if any damage had been done to the truck or not, but at that moment I thought, to hell with the truck. I was struck dumb as Paul on the road to Damascus and could not move.

She opened the door and said, "Can you stand up?"

Of course I could stand up, but she reached for my arm to help me. The pressure of her hand on my arm sent shivers up my spine. I came back to the real world as my mouth began to throb and I tasted blood. I turned away from her and spat.

"I'm fine," I said. "Really. You don't need to worry."

I started to get back in the truck, but she held my arm tighter and said, "You're not driving before you rest and get cleaned up. I'll send for the doctor right away."

"I don't need a doctor. It's just a busted mouth. It's not the first one I've ever had."

She tightened her hold on my arm and said, "Well, I'll clean you up and make sure you're okay."

I couldn't believe anyone so beautiful and so sweet could be holding my arm. I wouldn't have believed anyone on the Hill would've cared if I'd knocked out all my teeth.

"Come on," she said, pulling me toward the house.

She was fairly tall for a girl, coming up to my nose, but she was slender and if I'd really needed help, I didn't think she could've supported me. She wasn't like the girls I knew who had to work hard. Her arms and hands were soft, and she wore a light pink sundress and pink slippers with high heels. I thought of Ellie and Kathleen's rough little hands, their faded dresses, and their bare feet. The girl's flowing hair was soft and shiny, not bound up tight in pigtails, and the wind blew wisps of it onto my neck. I was afraid it'd blow onto the blood. I suddenly felt hot and sweaty and dirty. I knew I'd made a mistake to go with her as we entered through the front door. I'd never gone in that way. Groceries were delivered through the back doors on the Hill.

"Your father is at work, isn't he?" I said.

"He's always at work."

She led me down a hall into a large, airy kitchen with a big fan humming overhead. A tall colored lady in a black dress and a white apron was busily cleaning god-knows-what. It was the shiniest, cleanest kitchen I'd ever seen.

"Oh my lord, Miss Madeline," the woman said, "what done happened? This boy's bleeding."

"I almost ran into him backing out the driveway. He swerved his truck off the road to avoid me."

"What I tell you, Miss Madeline? You got to slow that thing down."

"I know, I know. Right now I've got to wash him off. Get me a pan of water."

"I clean him. You get your dress dirty."

"I caused this," Madeline said, "and I'll take care of him. Just fix me a pan with some warm water." As she talked, she took me over to a white kitchen chair and pointed for me to sit down.

The maid frowned, shook her head and muttered that Madeline'd made a lot of messes she hadn't cleaned up and it'd never bothered her before, but she brought a basin of water and a cloth to the table where I sat. Madeline wet the cloth and began washing blood from my face and neck. I was embarrassed to see the white cloth turn red. Madeline pressed too hard on my mouth, and I didn't know if I felt more pain or pleasure. I'd have sat there for her to cut my head off.

When she put the cloth to my mouth, it bled more, and she jumped back and said, "Oh, Lord. Annie, I've hurt him. Come help. Oh, oh, I'm so sorry."

"It's okay," I said. "Maw says bleeding cleans the wound." But I tasted hot blood afresh, and since I wasn't outside, I couldn't spit it out. I had to do something with it, so I swallowed it.

Annie was watching us with eagle eyes. She handed me a glass and said, "Salt water. Come over to the sink and wash your mouth out. Blood'll make you sick as a dog."

I looked over at the shiny white sink, and Annie said, "It'll clean. Now rinse and spit out the blood."

I watched the blood and water swirl down the drain. I looked for something to clean the sink with, but Annie shooed me away. "My sink. I take care of it. You go sit back down."

Then Madeline dampened another clean cloth, this time with cool water, and again wiped my face. The coolness felt good. I shut my eyes, and I could've been in paradise. But when I looked up, she was studying my forehead. I thought of the gray dust that was always in my hair, which was too long, but at least it covered my scar. Then she pushed my hair off my brow and stared at the scar. I figured she was wondering how I got it. Probably thought all the townspeople were rough, maybe dangerous. She had been protected from the rest of us. She'd been sent to school in Knoxville, driven by a chauffeur along with other clean and starched children from the Hill.

"I got to go," I said, getting up. "Got deliveries to make. Your groceries are in the truck. I'll get them. I've bothered you folks enough. Thank you for taking care of me."

"Surely someone can come to finish making your deliveries. You can stay and have dinner with us. Oh, I am so rude. I haven't even properly introduced myself. I'm Madeline, Madeline Rogers, and this is Annie." Annie nodded, and Madeline said, "You might even know my father, Carl Rogers. And what's your name?"

"Moss McCullen."

"Moss? What a funny name. Oh, I mean it's unusual. I like it."

"It's not so unusual where I come from," I said, "but Madeline is."

She smiled. "Do you know my father?"

Everybody knew Carl Rogers, the chief mining engineer. "Heard of him," I said. "I've really got to go or I might get fired." Especially if your father catches me here, I thought.

"How dreadful," she said. "I don't want to cause you any more trouble, but I don't really think anything bad will happen. You're angry with me, aren't you?"

If she hadn't been so beautiful and so sweet, I could've hated her for not knowing how easily trouble can come to a person. But how could she know about life not being fair, living in a beautiful home with a maid who cleaned invisible dirt and a

94

shiny new car and the chance to go to school. Even though she'd grown up in Outcropping, she couldn't have been raised farther from me if she'd been raised on another planet. She was a year or two older than me and many worlds away. Her father wouldn't want me in his home and he'd have been very angry if he found out I'd entered through the front door. I'd be in trouble at the store, too, if people called in and said they hadn't gotten their groceries. I didn't want to hurt Madeline's feelings, but I had to get out of there.

"I'm not mad," I said. "You've been very good to me, but I shouldn't be here, and I don't want you to get in trouble."

"I'm glad you're not angry with me," she said. "And you can't possibly get me in trouble. I can take care of myself." She crossed her arms and added, "You must let me make this up to you. I'll be at the store tomorrow to check on you and to make arrangements for you to have dinner with us tomorrow evening."

"Miss Madeline, you aint never set foot in the commissary," Annie said, "and this aint no good time to start."

"Well, there's nothing that says I can't go. It will be all right with you, won't it, Moss?"

I didn't know what to say. A run-in with her father could cause me to lose my job and keep me out of the mine, too. "You're very kind to worry about me," I said, "but it's not necessary."

"Well, I'll be there anyway. And you can come here tomorrow night when you get off from work. Annie'll fix things you can eat like mashed potatoes, maybe some soup. Won't you, Annie?"

Annie stood with her eyebrows knitted and her arms crossed over her apron, saying nothing.

Madeline ignored her. "Do you like chocolate mousse? You should be able to eat that well. And Annie makes the best you've ever eaten."

All I could do was picture a large antlered animal, even though I knew she must've meant something else, something other

95

than meat. I wondered what the Rogers did eat. I figured not beans and cornbread.

"Thank you again for taking care of me," I said, heading for the back door and thinking that Madeline wouldn't really come to the store and that she'd forget all about dinner the next evening.

As I hurried down the driveway, anxious to get their groceries from the truck and leave, Annie called out my name. I looked around, and she was running to catch up with me as fast as she could, carrying a glass of tea.

She handed me the tea and said, "You take this, Mr. Moss. I'll take the groceries in."

I set the glass on the running board and opened the truck door. "The box is kind of heavy," I said, getting it out.

"I've toted many a load heavier than this," she said, taking it from my hands. "Now you go on."

"But what about the glass?"

"Don't worry none 'bout the glass, Mr. Moss. One more or less won't make no difference. They got more glasses in that house than you and me'll ever have in our lifetimes put together. But what I really wants to say is about you and Miss Madeline. I seen the way you look at her." I started to object, but she pointed her index finger at me. "Don't be shaking your head at me, Mr. Moss. I wasn't borned yesterday. I know what you'se thinking. Worse, I know what *she* thinking. She sweet a child as God ever put on earth, but she don't know nothing about life. Aint never had to want for nothing, and she likes you. Won't see no reason why she can't see you. Oh, she knows about a person's place and all that, but she just don't think she got to pay no heed to it. Rules are for other folks. You got to be the one with the level head, 'cause you the one knows 'bout these things." She looked me straight in the eye. "You knows what I means, Mr. Moss?"

I nodded. "Yes, ma'am, I do. My head's reasonable enough, but it aint my head that's a going crazy."

"Lord, Mr. Moss," she said with a wave of her hand, "you better be careful. Her pappy not so sweet as she is, as I'm sure you've heard."

"I don't think you got anything to worry about," I said. "She couldn't care about the likes of me."

"I hope you right."

I looked back at her when I got in the cab, waved, and said, "You're worrying about nothing."

I pulled away hopelessly in love with Madeline Rogers.

The day after I almost wrecked the commissary truck was a Saturday, and Jim Johnson dropped by that morning to buy a plug of tobacco as I came up the basement steps carrying a 100-pound bag of beans to put in the bin. I put the sack at the top of the stairs and started back to get more when I saw Mr. Johnson leaning on the counter, watching me.

"Morning," I said, and tried to smile, even though my mouth hurt.

"Lord, boy," he said, "what the hell happened to you?" He grinned. "You get too fresh with your girlfriend?"

"Had to stop the truck too fast and smashed into the steering wheel. It's all right."

"Don't look all right. How's the truck?"

"It's all right, too."

Then he pointed towards the bean sacks and said, "Why didn't you bring up another bag?"

I laughed in spite of my sore mouth. "Aunt Minnie says I shouldn't strain myself."

"You saying you could bring up two?" he said, crossing his arms and looking at me without cracking a grin.

His comment took me by surprise. Finally I said, "I don't see no point in that."

He slapped a bill on the counter and said, "There's a reason. That ten says you can't. You come up them steps with two,

97

it's yours. All you got to do is get to the top step. If you don't, well, I keep my ten and you don't owe me nothing."

I planned to try to get a job in the mine soon, and ten dollars was a lot of money for anyone to lose. But the situation was already there, and I didn't see any way it could turn out good. Either I looked like a show-off or a scaredy-cat.

"Carrying up sacks is part of my job," I said.

"Well, let's find out if you can do it." He lit cigarette, then added, "Unless you don't want to try."

I went down the stairs and picked up one sack in each hand. Made me feel sorry for pack mules. One more bag made a big difference, but I'd done it before. When I got back up, I put down the sacks and leaned over and stretched.

Then I stood up, looked at Mr. Johnson and said, "You don't have to pay me."

He dropped his cigarette, put it out with his boot and said, "Shit, you're crazy. But you're strong as a damn ox." Then he slammed out the screen door, leaving the money.

I stuffed it in my pocket, feeling pretty grim, and bent over to pick up one of the bags to empty into the bins. As I got up, holding the sack, I saw Madeline. Again I had the sensation that I'd somehow stumbled into heaven. I wondered how long she'd been there as I stared at her, unable to speak. I hoped she hadn't seen me make a fool out of myself.

"I didn't know you were a gambling man," she said.

"What?"

She looked at the bean bags.

"I didn't mean for that to happen," I said. "I'm not usually that stupid."

She nodded.

"And I'm not a gambler. It wasn't a real bet 'cause I didn't put any money down. And I didn't intend to keep his money."

"I know," she said. "I saw. You're very strong." Her face lit up as she smiled. "I didn't mean to embarrass you. But I couldn't resist." She looked like summer with her hair pulled back in a yellow ribbon and her crisp white dress.

I tried to smile back. "What can I help you with?"

"Nothing. Annie does all our shopping, orders most of it. But you already know that. I wanted to see that you were all right after the unfortunate incident yesterday."

"I don't see it as unfortunate," I said. I couldn't believe I was brave enough to say that.

She smiled again and said, "I told you I'd be here today. You didn't think I'd come, did you?"

"No, I guess I didn't."

"I have to say Annie tried to talk me out of it, but here I am. And I'm glad I got to see such a show. Ah, your mouth still looks pretty bad." She put a delicate finger up to her own mouth.

I swallowed hard. I felt like she'd slammed into me again with the power of her presence, her body, the smell of roses. I leaned against the counter and tried to make my mouth work, to say something, but all I could think of was putting my mouth on hers. I touched my own lip and remembered that it did indeed hurt.

"Been hurt worse," I stammered. I followed her eyes as they moved from my mouth to my forehead. I ran my fingers through my hair and pulled it down thicker over the scar.

"I don't mean to stare," she said, "but I feel terrible about the accident. It was my fault, and you're being so generous. You must come have dinner with us today and let me make amends."

"You don't owe me nothing, Miss Rogers," I said, hoping no one could hear us. I didn't see anyone close, but Aunt Minnie had great hearing for someone her age.

"Then come anyway, just because I'd like you to. There are so few young people on the Hill. I hate summers since . . . since . . . well, anyway, please say yes. And, remember, the name is Madeline."

When I said I couldn't, she looked disappointed. I wanted to tell her the truth, that her father would not want me to eat at his house, but I didn't want to hurt her feelings. I said, "I work late."

"We eat late," she said. "I won't take no for an answer."

The "we" scared me. I assumed she meant her father and her. She surely knew her father would resent my being at his home, especially to see her. Delivering groceries was okay, courting was quite another matter.

"I can't eat much these days." I pointed to my mouth and smiled. "I got this cut in my mouth."

"Oh, please, don't tease. It pains me just to look at that nasty bruise. And especially to know I caused it. You're not afraid your girlfriend will object, are you?"

"I don't have a girlfriend."

"Then it's settled. I mean, since there's no one to object."

No one but your father, I thought. All that time she'd been talking to me I'd seen only her, as though she was in a picture frame. Suddenly I heard Aunt Minnie clear her throat. She'd come up to the counter and was standing there, frowning. Her entire body registered disapproval from the glasses dropping on her nose to her hands on her hips. I winked at her, but she still frowned.

"Come about 7:00," Madeline said as she turned to go.

"Wait."

"What is it now?" She cocked her head to the side, and her hair fell across her shoulder. "Don't tell me you're going to make another excuse. I declare, I almost think you don't like me."

"No. I mean, it's just that, well, what about your father? He won't want me there. He'll—maybe he'll think I want to court you."

"My father lets me make my own decisions," she said.

I doubted she'd ever made decisions he had any reason to object to.

"Do you?" she said.

"What?" My head was spinning.

"Want to court me, silly?"

Aunt Minnie coughed.

I said, "Well, have you ever been out with anyone who works in the mine?"

"No, but you don't work in the mine. Of course, I haven't dated anyone who works at the commissary, either."

"Someday I will work in the mine."

It was past time I got on underground. The commissary'd been a good thing for me, but it was a dead end. I could only go one step higher and could never make much more money. At thirteen I hadn't really been ready for the mine. But after six years, I'd begun to feel the need to do what Paw meant to do. And I had also come to believe that mining could be made safer, that too many needless accidents happened, like what happened to Paw. Besides, I wanted to go down under to see where he was buried. Suddenly that was more important than ever to me.

"You haven't answered my question," she said. "Do you want to see me?"

I knew I was playing with dynamite. A relationship with Madeline was doomed before it began, for no matter what she said, her father wouldn't let me see her, and if I tried, I'd probably wreck any future I had in Outcropping at the commissary or the mine. I also knew she couldn't ever be serious about someone like me and she'd waltz right out of my life when she tired of me. Still I said, "Yes, I sure would like that."

"Good," she said, swinging around toward the door, "See you tonight."

I watched her go, then walked to the front of the store and watched her drive away until I could no longer see her.

Aunt Minnie followed me. "What in the world do you think you're doing, Moss?" she said, pointing a crooked finger at me. "I'll tell you what you're a-doing. You're not courting a girl, you're a courting disaster. And you're a going to be hurt. You're going to be hurt real bad."

"I know," I said, looking out the door in the direction of Nobb Hill, "but I'm going to feel real good first."

———————————

When I walked up to the Rogers' door, I knew it was a big mistake. I figured I'd be turned away. But Annie answered the bell, and she said, "Evening, Mr. Moss. Come on in," and she leaned near me and whispered, "Lord have mercy on you."

I entered a large hall, and Annie pointed to a room off to the right. Mr. Rogers stood in the room, smoking a pipe and staring into an empty fireplace. He had on dark dress pants and a neatly pressed white shirt. Madeline was sitting in a straight chair with velvet upholstery. She jumped up to greet me even before Annie announced me. She looked beautiful in a white dress with lilacs on it and a lilac ribbon at her slender waist. I had come from work, so still had on my khaki pants and shirt. I cleared my throat and tucked my shirt in a little better.

Madeline came right up to me, took my hand and led me into the room where Mr. Rogers was and said, "This is the young man I told you about, Father. This is Moss McCullen."

He turned around and looked at me but didn't say anything. I stepped forward, extended my hand and said, "How do you do, sir?"

"I've been better," he said, without acknowledging my hand. "What kind of a name is Moss?"

Madeline put her arm through mine and said, "Dinner's ready. Come on."

We walked into the dining room, and her father came in after us. A large dark wooden table was set with a lace tablecloth and lots of fancy dishes and silverware. There was a huge cabinet with glass doors, full of more fine dishes and crystal than I'd ever seen. They could've served an army. Madeline looked perfectly comfortable, and it was clear to me she belonged in the setting, and I did not.

When we began eating, she was at home with the delicate china and crystal and silver. There were too many dishes and too much silverware and a lace tablecloth that would stain if anything got on it. I had no idea what I was supposed to do with all the forks and spoons. All I could do was follow her lead. I didn't pick up anything until she did. Then I used it for whatever she used it for. Annie didn't sit down. She served us, and ran back and forth from the kitchen to the dining room, taking dishes back and forth.

Madeline's father said, "So, young man, Mr. McCullen, you look familiar. I understand you work at the commissary." He looked as if he had just eaten a green persimmon.

"Yes, sir."

"And what do you intend to do this fall?"

"This fall, sir?"

"This fall. Will you be going off to college?"

I didn't know if he was trying to torment me, or if he actually thought normal young people in Outcropping contemplated going off to college in the fall. I said, "No, sir. I'm the assistant manager at the commissary. I've worked there for a long time." I thought better of saying six years.

"I see," he said slowly, looking at Madeline with one bushy brown eyebrow lowered. He wasn't going to tolerate any friendship between Madeline and me. Mr. Rogers wasn't exactly known for his generous disposition. Madeline was probably the only person who seldom felt his wrath. I figured he'd make an exception with her tonight, though, after I left. Madeline's eyes dropped under his stare, and his steel gray eyes turned back to me.

"Just what do you plan to do with your life, young man?"

I squirmed in my chair. "Do with my life, sir?"

"Yes, your life. What are your goals?"

I figured my plans wouldn't amount to "goals" in his book. I was suddenly hot, even though a cool breeze blew through the large open window behind my back.

"Daddy, really," Madeline said, "Moss is very young. He probably doesn't know what he wants to do yet."

"Madeline, by nineteen or twenty a man must know where he is going and how he is going to get there. Isn't that right, Mr. McCullen?"

"I suppose so, sir. I imagine most men in Outcropping know what they're going to do. They're going to work in the mine. They don't exactly have choices."

"Well, I'm sure an enterprising young man could find a way to get away from here and do something more lucrative. Surely you don't plan to work in the commissary all your life."

His eyes were two hot coals, burning holes in me. Suddenly I was also angry, too angry to be defensive. "You're right," I said. "I don't plan to work in the commissary all my life."

He raised his eyebrows and said, "No?"

"No. I plan to work in the mine as soon as I can get on."

I loved the look on his face, even though I knew I'd dug myself into a hole I couldn't get out of. He drew in his breath and rearranged himself in his chair. Madeline visibly sank into hers.

No one said anything for a moment.

"Why would you want to do a thing like that? If you're going to continue to work in this town, you would certainly be better off in the commissary than in the mine."

"Not in the long run. I can advance in the mine. The most I can do in the commissary is become manager, and I wouldn't earn much more than I do now. Besides, Mr. Eslinger is only forty years old . . ."

Mr. Rogers was staring at me, and I knew it didn't make any difference what I said then, so I didn't see any point in continuing.

Fortunately Annie came in with dessert, chocolate pudding, or at least it looked like chocolate pudding, but it was in fancy little dishes that stood on stems. Coffee was served, too, and I discovered what the last two spoons were for, but it certainly seemed like a lot of trouble to keep switching from one spoon to another, not to speak of the extra work for Annie. Everything about the evening was a chore, except watching Madeline.

I poured more cream than usual in my coffee to cool it down so as not to burn my sore mouth, and I tried not to clang the silver spoon against the delicate china. My hand shook as I lifted the fragile cup to my lips. I winced as I drank the hot liquid, some of which spilt onto my chin. My mouth hurt, my head hurt, my shoulders were stiff, and I felt sick. I could feel Mr. Rogers' eyes on me. It was hopeless to gain his approval to see Madeline, and I figured she couldn't possibly care much, anyway. I gulped down the small bowl of mousse, left the rest of the coffee, and asked to be excused, saying I had to go to work early the next day.

"But it's not late," Madeline said. "Please stay and visit with us for a while. It's a lovely evening. We could sit out on the porch." She stared at her father and said, "I've never had a young man sit in the swing here with me."

Mr. Rogers clenched his teeth. He rose from his chair and said, "Madeline, I am sure Mr. McCullen has to get his rest. He works for a living. Isn't that right, Mr. McCullen?"

"Yes, sir, it is," I said, getting up. "I work for a living, just like you do."

I'd taken enough off him for one evening. If his eyes could have shot real nails, I'd have been pinned to the wall.

He said, "I'm sorry for any inconvenience you have been caused by the unfortunate accident, young man. If I owe you any compensation, let me know."

"Sir, you don't owe me anything. I'll be going now." I looked toward the kitchen where Annie stood watching us and wringing her apron. I nodded to her. "It was real good, ma'am."

In spite of Mr. Roger's glare, Annie replied, "Thank you, Mr. Moss. Hope it didn't hurt your sore mouth."

"It was well worth a little pain," I said, "as anything good is."

Then I headed for the front door, determined not to go out the back, and Madeline ran behind me saying, "Moss, wait."

I kept going. I didn't want to get her in trouble, and I didn't see any point in making her father more angry than he already was. I should've had better sense than to go in the first place. I only had myself to blame. Madeline must have been very lonely on

Nobb Hill and desperate to be with someone her own age, and I'd taken advantage of that.

As I hurried down the front steps, she followed me. She grabbed my arm and said, "Please don't go yet. It's early."

"I don't have any choice, Ma'am."

"Don't call me ma'am," she said, not letting go of my arm. "You can stay for a few minutes."

"You don't really think your father is going let us sit out here on the porch, do you?"

"Then meet me somewhere else."

"This isn't some kind of a game, Madeline. You surely know we can't hide in this small town."

"Just for a little while. I can talk to him and change his mind in time. Maybe you could go to college, and he'd be okay with that."

"Even if I could, which I can't, that'd not be good enough for him. I'm not from money or education, and I'm sure that's what he expects for you. And I don't blame him. You don't need to be wasting your time with me."

"I don't think I'd be wasting my time."

"Where do you think this is going?"

"I don't know. But I have to see you again."

"My god, this is going to come at a big price."

"Am I worth it?"

"If it could work, but it can't."

"Why don't you let me worry about that."

Her father called her name, and he didn't sound happy.

"I'll get word to you through Annie," she said, and before I could answer she ran back inside. As I left, I felt as though I was falling into a hole as deep as the mine, but I was helpless to stop the fall.

———————————

When I got off work the next day, Madeline was waiting for me in her car in front of the commissary.

I went to the driver's side, leaned over and said, "Hey, lady, is it safe to get near this car?"

She looked up at me with wet eyes, and I had the uneasy feeling that this was only the beginning of tears I would see from her. I thought, what the hell are you doing? But I had no answers.

"Get in, please," she said.

My brain said run, but my body got in. She started the car and headed in the direction of the river. Shortly we turned off the main road and later turned onto what was actually no more than a driveway. I had no idea where we were going, but said nothing as we drove along the river at least a quarter of a mile. The lane, bordered by trees, led to a stately old house that sat on a hill above the river. Though somewhat neglected, the two-story brick house was a beautiful place, with chimneys that seemed to rise from everywhere, and with white pillars on the front porch.

She pulled up in front and stopped the car.

"Where are we?" I said.

"This was my grandparents' home."

'It's like something in a book."

"Beautiful, isn't it?" she said, staring at the house. "It was mother's parents'. They're dead now. We still own this land but haven't done anything with it since my grandfather died. He farmed all nine hundred acres."

She spread her graceful arm out and moved it slowly from left to right. I didn't see the land, only her arm.

"They're dead now. My grandfather, my grandmother, my mother, all gone. I come here when I want to be alone." She looked up at me. "This is where I was heading when I almost killed you." I smiled at the exaggeration, but she didn't. "When Mother died, I would sometimes walk all the way out here, just to feel her and my grandmother's presence. Now I can drive to my escape." She managed a smile and said, "I must be more careful."

"Coming out here with me is not being careful," I said. "Why did you bring me here?"

"I had to talk to you, and I couldn't do it in town." Tears welled up in her eyes again. "You were right. Father won't even talk to me about you. He absolutely forbade me to see you and told me I was never to mention your name again." She dropped her head and added, "He said you couldn't trust a person that didn't . . . stay . . . in his place. I'm sorry, but that's what he said. I knew he wouldn't like my seeing you, but I didn't think he'd actually tell me I couldn't. I've never seen him so stubborn. I can almost always get him to do what I want. He was so mean, so unfair."

"It's okay," I said. "I understand."

"No, it's not okay, and I don't understand. I've been so lonely here since Mother died. There's only Annie. Father goes to work early and comes home late. He doesn't want me to work at home, or anywhere, for that matter. He fusses at me if he catches me doing what he thinks is Annie's work. I'll be going to graduate school this fall. I want to do so many things. I want to go to Annie's. He won't even entertain that idea. I want to know about the people of Outcropping. When I went to the commissary yesterday, that was the first time I'd ever been in it. Everyone else seems to know each other, and there's something so special in that, you know? And when I find someone so nice and interesting as you, I don't see what that's got to do with anybody not 'staying in his place.' I want to know about you. I want to know all about your life, what you do, what you think. Is that so wrong?"

Her hands gripped the steering wheel so hard her knuckles were white. I don't know what possessed me, but I reached over and took one hand from the wheel and lifted it to my sore mouth and kissed it and smelled its sweetness, felt the smoothness of her thin fingers. I felt her fingers tighten around mine.

"Your hands are so . . . hard," she said.

"I don't want to cause you problems. Nothing would work between us, you know."

Her fingers tightened more, and she said, "If people like each other, where they work or live shouldn't be a problem."

"It is to a lot of folks," I said.

"Sad, isn't it?"

I nodded. "Thank you for explaining to me what happened, though, and I do understand. If you were my daughter, I wouldn't want you to end up in one of the little matchbox houses in Outcropping. I would want you to have a fine house and a maid and anything else you want. I could never give you all that."

"I already have all that," she said.

"Your father'd want you to have someone who could give you more."

A tear ran down her cheek. I started to wipe it, but she reached up and ran her finger along my bruised lip. The next thing I knew she was in my arms, and I was kissing her and touching her soft hair, her ears, her eyes. I tasted the saltiness of her wet cheeks and the sweetness of her lips. She clung to me and her body trembled. I'm sure mine did, too.

She pushed back enough to look at me and said, "When I told him I would see you anyway, he said he'd make life hard for you if I did."

I knew he could. I could never really have her, not for more than the summer, then she'd be gone, and it could cost me everything I'd worked so hard for. Life would still go on, but everything would be different for me, and not for the better.

Still, I said, "What can he do?"

Inside I was yelling, *What else can I do?* I got no education, no influence except maybe in the store, and I might be losing that this very minute if Mr. Rogers knows I'm with Madeline. I had nowhere else to work, and I had to take care of Maw and the kids. I looked back, down the lonely dusty lane. Then I looked to the side at the flowing river which went on and on, oblivious to our pain or pleasure.

"I'd feel awful if you lost your job," she said.

Not as much as I would, I thought. But I said, "I'll get something else." I couldn't leave Maw and the girls to go somewhere else to find work, but looking down into Madeline's sad eyes, I couldn't think of things of this world. My blood was racing faster than the river.

"We'll be together out here," she said. "No one else ever comes here. He won't find out," and the next thing I knew we were kissing again, and kissing, and kissing, and the pain in my mouth mingled with the sweetness of hers, and soon I was aware of nothing but a pleasure I'd never known.

Madeline

Moss was the most exciting person I ever met. I think I was in love with him from the time I almost hit his truck in front of our house. I ran up to his window, and when he looked up at me with his deep blue eyes, my legs went weak. I'd never seen anyone so handsome. I knew right away he was my Lord Byron.

Father forbade me to see him, but I was determined to do so. Still, I worried about what he would do if he found out I was seeing Moss. On the rare times he had a day off—that is, when he didn't go to his mother's—we went to The Willows to get away from all other eyes but ours. The river became our own separate world where no one and nothing could hurt us.

Annie reluctantly carried messages for us. When we met, I would pick him up outside the city limits of Outcropping, down a deserted side road. My heart would be pounding even before I saw him. I could feel him before I touched him. I'd hold my breath, worrying that there wouldn't be a next time.

At the river, we'd lie on an old quilt, and I'd bring something to eat and drink. We were in a world of our own, untouched by what anyone else thought. He was always excited to see what kind of treats Annie had prepared for us. He said it was like manna from heaven, mysterious, delicious and fed to him by an angel.

To him the river and land were a paradise, and he couldn't understand why anybody wouldn't tend the rich and fertile earth. It was a shame for it not to be used. I told him my grandfather raised cattle and corn and hay, and everything was beautiful.

"Why doesn't your father move out here and hire people to farm it?" he said. "He's got a car. He could drive back and forth to Outcropping."

"Mother and I could never get him to come out here to live," I said. "He said he would be too far from his work. I think he wanted to be where he always felt in control, and he didn't know anything about farming. He would hardly even come to visit. He never liked to ride the horses, and he didn't appreciate the fields of corn and wheat. And, to be truthful, I think he was afraid of the cows."

I looked at Moss and thought he'd not be afraid of anything. Then I said, "Father was never very close to the earth. Strange, when he makes his living in mining. Grandfather said that my father takes from the earth, but he doesn't know how to give back, to keep it producing."

He said, "I can't imagine a man who had the opportunity to live and work on such a place not wanting to do so."

"He's a stuffy snob," I said and laughed.

He laughed, too. It was fun to be able to be honest about Father. I never talked to anyone else about him.

"Come on," Moss said, "let's go swimming."

"We can't," I said. "We don't have suits."

He grinned, and I knew what he was thinking. I smiled and said, "Next time let's wear our suits under our clothes." And that's what we did, or at least I did. He swam in his pants and brought another pair to wear back home.

Moss loved the water. He'd dive in and glide like a fish. I loved to watch him. He looked as comfortable in the river as on land. He seemed at home anywhere, except in our dining room. He always tried to get me to swim. I put him off, saying I just wanted to bask in the sun and watch him. One day he walked up to the blanket, leaned over me and shook the water out of his hair onto me. I jumped up, squealing, but he pulled me back and lay down beside me laughing.

"Come on in," he said. 'Don't you like to swim?'

"I'm not too brave in the water. I'm not like you. I can't swim."

He was amazed. He thought everyone from Outcropping knew how to swim. He told me I could learn, and he picked me up and started for the river. I held onto his neck tightly and begged him not to throw me in.

He put me down and said, "I'm sorry. I didn't mean to scare you. I wasn't going to throw you in. I'd never do that. Don't you trust me?"

"Of course I do," I said, "or I wouldn't be here."

He walked back to the blanket, leading me by the hand. He sat down, resting his arms on his knees, and I lay down beside him. "What do you want to do?" he said.

"I just want to watch you. You're so tan and strong, not pale and soft like the college boys who live with their noses stuck in books."

He rested on one arm, and leaned towards me, fingering the strands of hair around my face. I reached up and brushed his hair off his forehead.

"What caused this scar?" I said, running my finger along it.

"Well, I wasn't so natural in the water the day I got that. You know where the swimming hole is?"

"Yes. When I was a little girl, I would sneak out to the bridge and watch all the people having such a good time there. I used to beg Father to take me there. He told me I should swim at our pool where it was safe and where unruly children wouldn't bother me or hurt me. That'd be unruly children like yourself." I pressed my finger into his forehead and laughed. "Is that how you hurt your head, jumping off the ledges?"

"I was up on the pipe that crosses the creek. It's pretty high, you know, and we, us unruly children, dove off it."

"Are you brave or just crazy?" I said.

"Sometimes it's hard to know the difference. I could ask you the same thing."

"Oh, I'd never do something like that."

"You're here with me."

I nestled into his body. "I can't explain that."

"We are on dangerous ground," he said. "You know that."

"I know, but I don't feel in danger when I'm with you."

"See, you're braver than me," he said.

Moss

One day when Madeline and I went to the river, it was raining. We sat for a few moments in the car, but it was hot and muggy, and every time we tried to put the windows down, we got wet.

She looked over at me and said, "Would you like to see inside the house?"

"Your grandmother's homeplace?"

"Yes. Why not? Let me show you where I spent the best days of my life—well, up to now. Besides, it's too hot to sit out here in the car."

"But it's all locked up."

She put her hand on my upper arm, ran it down slowly, and said, "Can't you take care of that? It's not like breaking in. After all, it belongs to my family."

If I got caught breaking in, what she said wouldn't make much difference. I pulled off my shirt so we could use it as a sort of make-shift umbrella, and we ran up the brick walk through the rain, huddling under the shirt. When we got to the door, we looked at each other, and she said, "Well, open it.'

I wound my shirt around my hand and broke the glass, then reached in and unlocked it.

We entered the formal hall, much bigger than the one in Madeline's house in Outcropping. Dark woodwork lined the floor and doors. The winding staircase was beautiful, but everything was covered with dust and smelled musty. We slipped our shoes off. I was soaking wet and was afraid to move. But she took my hand and we began our journey through the house.

In the parlor we stood in front of an old piano with the word Steinway on it, and Madeline ran her fingers over the keys, easily fingering out a familiar tune without even sitting down. We went from one large room with high ceilings to another, with Madeline touching every item of furniture, leaving her fingerprints in the dust. For the first time since I'd met her, she was unaware of me. She was in a time and place that belonged to her and her

114

family. I was afraid to touch her or even speak. I followed her as she looked into gold framed mirrors and sat on chairs with fancy carving.

Every now and then she would say, "My grandfather brought this over from England," or "This is from Germany."

After seeing the entire first floor, we climbed the staircase. Madeline walked down the wide hall to the last bedroom on the right, with me following like a soaked dog. She stood in the doorway, looking all around, and then went in.

She sat on the brass bed. Then she looked up and patted the quilt beside her. I looked down at my wet pants. She said, "Sit down."

Next to the bed was a brass doll bed, made like the one we sat on, with a pink spread with ruffles. Madeline leaned over and pulled out a doll with a lacy dress. She hugged it to her, then turned to me with dreamy eyes. I felt as if I were being pulled into her world by a powerful magnet. I took her upturned face in my hands and kissed her. She dropped the doll to the floor, put her arms around me and pulled me into the soft bed.

When I went home that summer, I didn't want to. I felt so guilty, but all I wanted to do was spend time with Madeline. Anything else I had to do was in the way of my being with her. My family and the farm were still important to me. My life with Madeline was like a dream, and that dream was stronger than anything else.

Once when I was home, Ellie was tagging along with me as I hoed corn, and she wasn't singing or dancing around me, just poking along with her head down, dragging a tow sack to collect the ripe ears. Maw'd said we'd eat them for supper. I asked Ellie what was wrong. At first she said, "Nothing," but I told her nothing didn't make her so down in the mouth. Then she asked if I had a girlfriend. I lied and said no. Maybe I didn't lie. Madeline wasn't really my girlfriend, at least not what I thought of a girl that you went places with and took home for your family to meet. I didn't really know what she was to me, except the most important thing in the world.

"Kathleen says you got to have a girlfriend or you'd come home more," Ellie said.

"Well," I stammered, "I'm very busy, you know."

"You sure you don't have a girl?"

"If I did, I'd still love you as much as ever."

"But you don't want to be with me."

I promised her I'd come home more, knowing I wouldn't. As we walked back to the house, Ellie dragged her sack of corn, and I was drowning in a wave of guilt about not seeing my family more, about not helping on the farm more, about risking my job for a girl I could never have.

Avery

The day I got on at the mine I stopped by the commissary to tell
Moss. My paw'd told me it was high time I got a job, and I reckon
it was. Summers were getting boring. Since Moss'd busted his
head open the past summer, he'd all but quit coming to the
swimming hole. And since the company'd put the pipe off limits,
most of the boys that used to swim at the creek finally went to
work, too. Cleve still swims, but he aint got nothing else to do,
'cept when somebody hires him for some kind of odd job, and
most folks aint got no money to hire him. Them on the Hill won't
hire him, probably think he's crazy or something.

I got me some stick candy out of the jar and waited for
Moss to finish filling an order. When he come over to the counter,
I gave him a piece and told him about my job.

"That's great," he said. "What'll you be doing?"

That was a dumb question. Most everybody starts as a
roustabout unless they got some kind of experience. I told him I
was going to try to get on as a mechanic after I put in my time as a
roustabout. I said, "Figure that's one of the safest jobs I could do."

"Gadget'll help you get the job," he said. "Talk to him about
it."

"Yeah, I will. Where you been? Aint seen you much this
summer."

"Too much to do between the store and the farm, and after
last summer I can't get too excited about going to the creek."

"Aint got you a girlfriend, have you?" I said.

"When have I got time for a girlfriend?"

He looked down when he said it, like he was looking for
something. Moss'd never exactly lie to you, but he had a way of
getting around telling you anything he didn't want you to know.

About that time the door opened, and I looked to see who'd
come in. It was Hope Goddard. She always took my breath away,
with her curly hair the color of a new penny and her eyes as deep
and blue as the river, but she never acted like she saw me. She was

so shy. I'd always liked her, but far as I knew she never went out with nobody. Then, the next thing I knew she was married.

"Look at that," I whispered to Moss, jabbing my thumb toward her. "Aint she about the prettiest sight you've ever seen?"

He looked at her, leaned over the counter toward me and said, "You know who she is, don't you?"

"I know she's married, if that's what you mean. You know her husband?"

"Not really. Never comes in. Don't come to church with her. But all the miners like him. Got a lot of experience."

"Well, I know one thing," I said. "He's a old man,"

"He's not that old."

"Old enough to be her paw," I said. "Say you see her at church?"

"When I go. Like I said, he's never there, but folks say he's a good man."

I grinned. "Can't be that good. What she needs is some young blood, don't you think?"

I kept looking at her while we talked, but she hung around the door, looking away from us.

"I think you better back off," Moss said.

"You aint my boss."

"I got work to do," he said.

Then he asked if he could help her.

She came up to us, looking away the whole time, and handed him a list. He went to fill her order, and she walked back to the front door and looked out while she waited.

"Nice day, aint it?" I said, walking over to her. "Could use some rain, though. Break the heat."

She nodded.

Figured she was afraid if she talked to me, she might like me.

Moss came back to the counter, set down a small box and said, "Groceries are ready, ma'am. Anything else I can help you with?"

She shook her head and reached for the box. As she went to leave, I reached out for it and said, "Let me help you with that."

She pulled it away from me and said, "No, thanks. It's not heavy."

I reached for it again and said, "Too heavy for a pretty little thing like you."

"Excuse me," she said, and went back to the counter and asked Moss where the material was. Even I knew where the material was. Anyway he pointed towards it, and she said, "Could you help me, please?"

"Sure," he said,"but I don't know much about picking material. You want me to go get Aunt Minnie?"

"No. You can help," she said. As they walked over to the dry goods, she said something else I couldn't hear. I went over and got me a Co'cola, but I kept an eye to them. They were talking soft. No telling what he told her. After a few minutes, she went back to pick up her box of groceries without buying any material.

He walked with her to the door and said, "You have a nice day, now."

She didn't say nothing. Just walked off.

I started to leave and said, "Think I'll go help her carry that box home."

"Quit pestering her," Moss said.

"What's it to you?"

"Nothing, just leave her alone."

"You want her for yourself?"

"She's married."

"Aint you heard, forbidden fruit's the sweetest."

"Haven't you heard, eating it's a good way to die?"

"I aint scared," I said, "and it's none of your goddamn business."

"She's not interested."

"How do you know?"

"Well, if she were, she had plenty of time to let you know."

"I was just having a little fun," I said, and slammed out the door. One of these days he's going to push me too far.

Moss

The last time I went to meet Madeline that summer, I waited for over an hour. I'd never waited that long. I thought maybe she'd had a wreck. She always drove too fast. Then again, maybe someone came as she was leaving the house and she couldn't get away. Or worse, her father might've found out about us and wouldn't let her come. I decided I'd stay another thirty minutes and if she hadn't come by then I'd leave.

I sat down beside the road. The warm sun felt good on my face, and I began to think of Madeline's room. I thought of her slender body that smelt so good and of the way it fit so perfectly against mine. The time we spent at The Willows was like being in another world, and I never wanted it to end. But I always knew it would. Her father planned to send her off to graduate school when the college term started. She insisted she wouldn't go, but I was sure she wouldn't stand up to him. And, I didn't know what I'd do with her if she did. I wasn't in any position to marry her. I pictured her fancy dresses and shoes, her fine furniture, her little car, and I knew she would never be happy in a gray shack in Lowtown with me and Aunt Minnie where most of the miners lived. If I went to work in the mine and someday make foreman, I could live on Engineers' Row. The houses there were nicer, though nothing like those on The Hill. Her little car and her fancy clothes would still be out of place. My chance of making foreman was slim anyway, and I was possibly blowing it completely by being with Madeline. Definitely if Mr. Rogers found out.

I didn't know what we were supposed to do. We couldn't live together, and we couldn't be apart. Or at least I couldn't live without any hope of her. I told myself that our lives were connected in a way that was bigger than Outcropping and its divisions.

I was getting a headache. The sun's warmth that had felt good earlier began to get hot. Too much time had passed. I started walking towards her house. Then I began to run. When I got there,

I took the front steps all in one leap. I didn't even knock. Nobody ever locked their doors in Outcropping, and Mr. Rogers would be at work.

No one was downstairs. I yelled for Annie. Finally I heard Annie call my name from upstairs. Said to wait, she'd be right down. I hit the stairs two at a time.

When I got to the second floor, Annie came out of a room and said, "Mr. Moss, you shouldn't be ...."

Before she could finish her sentence I pushed past her. Madeline was in the bed. I leaned over her. She was pale with black circles under her eyes. She looked up weakly at me and began to vomit. I grabbed a bowl that was on a table beside the bed. After she finished, I wiped her face with a towel that lay on the bed near her.

All she said was, "I'm so sorry."

"No, no, it's okay," I said and pushed her damp hair away from her face.

"Move aside, Mr. Moss." I looked up and saw Annie with a pitcher in her hand, and when I moved she wet the towel and wiped Madeline's forehead.

"What's the matter with her?"

"She sick, and we needs to let her rest." She pointed toward the door. "Go on downstairs. Aint proper for you to be up here, not that I reckon it makes no difference. I be right down."

I didn't want to leave Madeline, but I thought maybe Annie wanted to talk to me about what was wrong. I leaned over and kissed her white forehead and said, "I'll be right back. Everything's all right. Go to sleep and you'll feel better."

She looked up at me like a sick child. Then she closed her eyes. For the first time in a long while, I thought of little Mattie.

Annie joined me in the hallway, and I asked her again what was wrong.

"I told you, she's sick."

"But what does she have? How long's she going to be sick?"

"Well, I'd say about another month."

122

"My god, has the doctor seen her?"

Annie stood with one hand on the banister and one hand wiping her eyes. "You really don't know, do you, Mr. Moss?"

"What?"

"Lord above, what you should a seen all along. You knowed it was all wrong. Why couldn't you have let her alone?"

I leaned against the wall and said, "What are you telling me?"

"Oh, I think you know now. And Mr. Rogers, he going to kill us all dead."

I felt as though I'd been hit in the stomach with a shovel. I said, "Are you sure?"

"I aint dreaming up this mess you all done made," she said, as she turned away from me and walked down the stairs. When she got to the bottom, she waited for me and said, "Sure wish I was wrong. But I aint."

I sank down on the bottom step and said, "Has Dr. Timer seen her? Maybe she's got some disease."

"We get the doctor in here and we all dead ducks. She'll get over this being sick in a few weeks. And my suggestion is that, when she does, you take her away from here as fast as you can get."

"How? I've not got much money. I don't have a car. And I can't leave my mother and sisters and brother."

She frowned at me. "Fine time to be a thinking of all that, Mr. Moss. Your mama and sisters and brother'll live, I reckon. I be the one to die. I got a little money put back. They don't let me want for nothing. Miss Madeline, she got some of her own, too. And she got a car, which you knows, which we all know. If she hadn't had that fancy car, we wouldn't be in this mess. Lordy, Mr. Rogers'll skin me clean as a chicken. But I aint got long no way. And don't reckon it matters much what happens to me if I aint going to have Madeline."

"I sure made a mess of things for everybody."

"Yes, sir, you sure did. You both did. But they aint no point crying over spilt milk. You want this baby, don't you?"

In spite of my fears, happiness was trying to rise like water in a well at the thought of Madeline carrying my baby. "I love her, Annie," I said.

"If I didn't know you do, I hit you up the side of the head. Now, listen to me. Take her away from here, soon as she feel better. You'll find a way to take care of her. The good Lord provides. Don't worry none about nobody else. You be all right. And so will everybody else. Lots of folks is worse off."

"You really think she'll come with me?"

"I do, but you got to be patient with her. She always been took care of."

"Come with us, Annie," I said. "She won't know how to raise a baby."

Her face lit up, and she said, "You got that right, Mr. Moss. But for right now, you get out of here and don't be coming back. I get news to you when she able to leave. You best be thinking about which direction you want to go in and how you going to get there."

I didn't want to leave Madeline, but Annie was right. If Mr. Rogers found me there, we'd never get away together. So, I left, feeling as though I were leaving a part of myself.

Annie

I finally went to the store to see Mr. Moss. I know he sick with worry. So was I. He see me on the porch, motioning him to come outside. When he come, he hit me with a heap of questions, which I didn't have no answers to. Finally he noticed my swollen eye and ask me if Mr. Rogers do that.

"It don't matter," I say. "Mr. Rogers so mad, he got to have someone to blame. When he come home and find her sick, he call Dr. Timer. When he find out what's wrong, he grab me by the arm and pull me out of the room. When we in the hall, he hit me so hard I fall back into the wall. He never done nothing like that before. He say if I done what I ought a done, this wouldn't have happened. And I reckon he right. The doctor come out of the room, his eyebrows all knitted up, and he say to Mr. Rogers, we aint going to have no more of that. Mr. Rogers, he say he sorry, but when the Dr. Timer leave, he tell me to get out of his house and not come back. I aint heard nothing since. Don't know what he done with her. What we going to do, Mr. Moss?"

"I'm going to go over there."

"I wouldn't do that," I say. "She not there no way. Mr. Rogers, he get my niece Maggie to work for him after he send me away. She say Madeline done gone. Not hide nor hair of her in that house. Mr. Rogers tell her Madeline in school again. I think he done sent her away, probably to some of his people over in North Caroliny till she have that baby. She don't hardly know them folks. How we going to talk to her? Poor child. She got to be so scared."

Mr. Moss say Madeline get word to us. She know where we are, and we don't know where she is. He say she'll write soon. But I don't think so. I think she so scared of her pappy she won't never come back. Mr. Moss ask me where I living, and I say with that no count brother of mine. He drink too much, but I got nowhere else to go. He happy to have me, as he got somebody to cook and clean for him. Can't keep a woman. He works just enough for the company that they aint fired him yet. Mr. Moss promise me he let me know soon as he hear from Madeline. I aint holding my breath. Poor baby, poor baby, she aint got no more control of her life than I got of mine.

Annie warned me not to go to see Mr. Rogers, but after a few more weeks we'd still not heard a word. It was driving me crazy wondering where Madeline was, who was taking care of her, whether or not she was really going to have our baby. I was determined to find answers and to go get her wherever she was, though I had no idea how I'd do that with no car.

One day after work I walked over to her house. I stood on the porch for several minutes getting up my nerve to ring the bell. I was even more scared than the first time I went there.

Mr. Rogers came to the door. His face looked like it was chiseled in rock. "It's late to be delivering groceries," he said. "Go to the back door."

I took a deep breath. "I didn't come here to deliver groceries."

"Then you're in the wrong part of town."

"Where is Madeline?" I said.

"That's none of your affair."

"Oh, yes, it is."

He acted like he didn't know what I was talking about and said she'd gone back to school, and he added, "Her life has nothing to do with you."

If she'd left to go back to school, she'd have told me. At least she'd have told Annie. I said, "I have to know where she is, Mr. Rogers."

He narrowed his eyes. "You were a diversion for her in a boring summer. Beyond that, she has no interest in you. Now go back to the commissary where you belong."

He tried to shut the door, but I pushed it open, knocking him backwards. "Tell me where she is."

He regained his footing, straightened his clothing, then put his hand on my chest and said, "Get out of this house. You have overstepped your bounds, and I'll see to it that you never work another day in this town."

127

I lifted his hand off my chest and said, "I don't think you'll do that."

"You'll find out when you show up for work tomorrow."

"You mess with my job," I said, "or any job I ever try to get in this town, and I'll tell everyone why."

He turned pale as lime. I wouldn't have told anyone about Madeline, but he didn't know me well enough to know that. "What do you think folks would think if they knew I was the father of your grandchild?" I said. "Whose story do you think they'd rather believe, and whose story will pan out to be true?"

"You wouldn't," he said.

"Oh, but I will, and you'll topple right off your high and mighty pedestal, just like rock down a tipple."

Then I backed out of the house, not taking my eyes off him till the door shut. If I stayed another minute, I'd have knocked his teeth down his throat. I didn't sleep at all that night. Nobody said anything about Madeline or my job when I went to work the next day, or the next or the next.

———————————

The last thing I wanted to do was to tell Maw about Madeline, let her know what a fool I'd been. She was proud of me, always thought I was so grown up. Kathleen and Ellie thought of me as more than a brother. I was almost like a father to them, and I never wanted to let them know I'd failed them. I was sick with dread as to what they'd think about me. But I had to prepare them in case something happened and I had to leave Outcropping fast to bring Madeline home or to settle somewhere else with her and the baby, maybe on the farm, at least till I could figure out what else to do. I took half of what money I'd saved to give to Maw and kept the rest back in case I needed it.

They weren't surprised when I told them about Madeline, except when I told them who she was. Still, Maw told me I should follow my heart. She didn't elaborate, and I wondered if she was thinking about her and Paw and about how his parents wouldn't help him. She refused to take my money, said she and the girls were doing fine. She told me I should save all I could to be prepared for whatever happened with Madeline, that they didn't need part of my paycheck. She said not to worry, that I must do what I had to do, and if it was meant to be that me and Madeline would be together, we would be. But if it wasn't, I must not live in the past.

That was the deepest talk me and Maw had ever had, probably the deepest we'll ever have. But it was good to know she didn't think any less of me. Kathleen and Ellie both told me I should come back home and that Madeline was crazy not to have stayed with me. LC said he didn't like girls anyway, except for Kathleen and Ellie. It was all so much easier than I thought it would be. I told them I'd make it up to them someday, and they said there was nothing to make up.

After Madeline had been gone for several more weeks and I hadn't heard anything, I had to accept she wouldn't be coming back for a long time, maybe never. It was time for a change, time to go underground. I'd been putting that off long enough.

Even if it hadn't been for my father and the fact that I really believed mining could be made less dangerous, I still couldn't have worked in the store on and on. It was safe work, and I loved working with Aunt Minnie and getting to meet the people of Outcropping, but it wasn't work I could feel in my bones. The only kind of work I loved like that was working on the farm, but that wasn't no way to make a living unless a person had lots of acres like the Lindseys. It was the store or the mine for me, and it had to be the mine, and I needed to get on with it. It would take years, if ever, before I could work up to a position where I'd be able to make much money or have any influence on the way mining was done.

And now I had another reason for going to the mine. If I could move up and if Madeline returned, life with me would be easier for her, and more fitting. So, on one of my days off, I went to Jim Johnson's office early in the morning before daylight to catch him before he went underground. I started to knock just as he came to the door on his way out.

"Well, if it aint the bean man," he said. "Little out of your way, aint you?"

"Well, no, sir," I stammered. "I wanted to see you, if you got a minute."

He backed into his office and said, "Come on in." He sat down behind a large wooden desk and pointed to a chair beside it. "Sit down, boy. What's on your mind?"

"I came to see if maybe you could use me in the mine."

He raised his eyebrows and leaned his chair back. "You telling me you want a job underground?"

I nodded. "I do."

"What for? You got a good job. Jobs on the surface aint easy to come by. Most men go underground 'cause they aint got a job."

"I've wanted to work in the mine since I came to Outcropping."

He crossed his arms behind his head and said, "This got something to do with your Paw getting killed?"

"Maybe, but that aint the only reason. I need a better job."

"You know you won't make any more'n you do now."

"Not at first, but if I work hard, real hard, of course, and learn everything I can, maybe someday I could move up to foreman . . . someday . . . maybe."

I felt stupid stammering around, but he nodded, and we sat there staring at each other, me wondering what he'd be like to work for if he'd hire me, which I wasn't sure of. I hoped he wasn't still angry over his ten dollars.

Finally he said, "Not many do."

"You did, sir," I said.

He leaned forward in his chair and said, "So that's it. If I can do it, you can, too."

"Well, yes, something like that. Men like you that work their way up can do a lot for the miner. I'd like to do that, have ever since Paw . . ."

"You can't undo the past," he said.

"No, but maybe something can be done now."

"Don't get your hopes up, boy. Changing the company or mining, even the men, is like busting hard rock. If you're on a mission, I suggest you join the church and go to Africa." He stared at me, and I thought it was all over. Then he slowly smiled, which I was to discover he rarely did, and he said, "I like your gumption. I knowed your paw. He was a good man, and that's a credit to you. He was a real miner, too. Could do any job I put him on. Learned quick." He snapped his fingers in the air and added, "Just like that. He would a made foreman some day. No doubt about it. Damn shame what happened to him."

"Will I be able to see where he died?"

"You can see a mountain of rock. No way to ever find anything of him, if that's what you're thinking."

I looked down and nodded.

"That make you scared of the mine, boy?"

"It's dangerous, yes, sir."

"Think you could drill? Blast rock?"

"Yes, sir."

"You scared of dynamite?"

When I said yes, I figured he'd tell me to go back to the store, but he looked me straight in the eye and said, "Any son of a bitch that aint scared of dynamite's crazy as hell and I don't want him in my mine. The question is, can you work with it?"

"If I have to," I said. "I've done a lot of things I didn't think I could."

"You've done some things I didn't think you could do, too."

I mustered up a grin, knowing he was still thinking of the beans and not sure if that was good or bad.

But he said, "You can start as a roustabout, like everybody else. I know you got work experience, but let's face it, upping the counters at the store aint got much to do with mining. Roustabouting aint fun and the pay aint good, but it'll give you a chance to learn something about everything. Start at thirty cents an hour. Be ten hours a day, six days a week, most of the time. How much notice you aim to give the commissary?"

"Four, maybe six weeks, if they need it. They been mighty good to me. I wouldn't want to leave them in a bind."

"I can appreciate that," he said. "How 'bout you come tell me a day or so before you're ready to start. I'll put you to work. And, who knows, maybe by then you'll change your mind."

"Thank you, sir. I appreciate it. I won't change my mind. And you won't be sorry."

He reached out his hand to me and said, "I bet I won't. You got grit, and that's what it takes to be a good miner. I lost one bet on you. Don't aim to lose this one. If I do, I'll lose more'n ten dollars."

Aunt Minnie

Lord, I felt like my heart turned over when Moss told me he was going to work at the mine. I'd done everything I could to keep him at the commissary. I think what caused him to go to the mine when he did had something to do with that Madeline who'd disappeared, gone back to school, according to her paw. That was a subject me and Moss didn't discuss 'cause I wasn't supposed to know. But when she come into the store for the first time in her life and started talking to him, I watched her, and the looks between them said it all. I may be old, but not so old I don't know fire when I see it.

I begged him not to go to the mine, told him someday he'd be the manager of the store, that he had a good, safe future. I said, "Biggest danger you'll ever meet there is drunks like Isaac, and I don't see you reaching for hammers no more." He smiled a little, but I couldn't move him.

He said, "I know it's safer at the commissary, but I got to do it. It aint that I don't appreciate my job at the store. I'll always be indebted to you. When I came here as a kid, you don't know how scared and alone I felt. Then you were so good to me that first day. Suddenly I was warm and safe, and I had a job and a home. But, well, I come to Outcropping to work in the mine, and that's what I got to do."

I could feel my heart beat in my chest, and my hand began to shake. I held it with the other hand. I didn't want him to do nothing—or not do nothing—on account of me. I said, "I reckon I always knew that. You got to do what you got to do. You're a good boy, Moss, a good man." I had a real hard time asking the next question. "You, uh, you think you'll be moving?"

I was never so relieved when he said, "Why, no. I mean I hadn't thought about it," and I really don't think he had. He said, "I left one home. I'm not anxious to leave another, that is, unless you'd like to have your house to yourself again."

When he said that, it was like a ton of rock was lifted off me. I smiled and said, "Lord, no, I don't want to be alone. Why I aint heisted a wash tub or nothing heavy in years. I done let my old muscles get soft. And, you, why you'll need hot meals more than ever now."

"I will, for sure," he said.

Then he actually came over and hugged me. I said, "We'll go right on like before. We'll stay together, you and me."

Moss

On my last day of work at the commissary, Aunt Minnie helped me gather supplies I needed for the mine. She'd insisted on buying my lamp, because she said it would be my light to see by in the dark of the mine. I didn't expect it to be so hard to leave the store, but when we left that last evening, the screen door seemed to slam louder than usual.

I walked to the mine on my first morning underground, carrying my black lunch pail like all the miners. I also had a sack full of boots, socks, overalls and a hat with a mounting bracket for the carbide lamp. The sky was clear, and there were some lights around the town. The colors of fall were never quite as rich in Outcropping as at home because of the rock dust. The leaves were falling, going back to the earth.

That was where I was going, deep in the earth, in the hole Ellie had warned me not to fall in. I couldn't imagine men, mules and machines underground. There was a whole other world down there. People were drilling and blasting into the rock. I shivered. If my hands hadn't been so full, I'd have stuffed them into my pockets. I was scared. It was one reason I'd put off going to the mine sooner. But I was determined no one else would know. I pulled myself up as tall as I could, slung my head to the side to get my hair off my forehead, and picked up my pace as I approached the walk which led up to the mining operations.

I went to Jim Johnson's office. Captain to me now. That was what all the miners called him. He told me to come with him and he'd show me the ropes. He took me to the change house and told me to get on my mining clothes and to be quick about it.

The house looked like a giant meat locker with hooks on which the men hung their digging clothes and boots. The hooks were attached to chains so that the clothes and boots could be raised up about eight feet off the floor to allow them to air dry. Showers were to the back. Like everything else, the room was painted gray, and it smelled strongly of rock from where the men

135

left their clothes overnight, every night. Sort of like rust and dirt mixed together. It smelled like the men never carried their clothes home to be washed.

Scrambling into my work clothes, I remembered coming to Outcropping before the government required changing areas for the men. The miners never looked clean. The dirt from mining wasn't like dirt from farming. It seemed to become a part of the men, settling in the lines of their faces and hands, dark stains that never washed out. I used to cringe watching the gray figures walk home like ghosts at the end of their shifts. Maw had always said that cleanliness was next to godliness, and I'd decided Outcropping must be a long way from godly. When I was younger I used to wonder how far down in the earth a person had to go to get to hell. Figured I'd get as close to it in the mine as I ever wanted to.

Captain stuck his head in the change house and said, "Come on, boy. Hurry up. You aint going to church, you know."

"Ready, Mr. Johnson," I said, joining him. "Let's go."

"Call me Captain, Moss, so you won't sound too much like the new boy in the mine. You're going to take enough ribbing as it is. No point asking for it."

"I'll remember that, Captain."

"Good. Now, before we go below, we're going to make a quick stop at the General Office Building so I can introduce you to Mr. Frazier."

I couldn't imagine why the mining supervisor would want to meet me. My expression must have registered my surprise, and he said, "Mr. Frazier meets all the new men. Knows ever man that works here by name, day and night shifts. He puts in his time. Usually the first one here in the morning and the last one to leave at the end of the day shift." He grinned and added, "'Cept for me, of course."

As we passed the changing room for blacks and Mexicans, I prayed we wouldn't run into Mr. Rogers when we got to the Office Building. We walked down the hall on the way to Mr. Frazier's office, and I saw a sign on a door which read, "Carl Rogers, Chief

Engineer." I swallowed hard, and Captain said, "That's Mr. Rogers's office. Know him?"

I nodded and said, "When I see him."

"Well," he said, "that's about all you'll ever know him. He aint much of one for socializing. Not that nobody cares. Don't never go underground unless he absolutely has to, afraid he might pick up a little dirt, I reckon. Don't much like us mountain folk, especially ones like me that moves up through the ranks. Great believer in a man staying in his place. Immovable as rock."

I coughed and was thankful it was too early for most of the staff to be at work. After the last time I saw Mr. Rogers, I didn't think he'd do anything to keep me from working in the mine, but just the same I wasn't anxious to run into him.

"Don't worry," Captain said. "It don't matter what Rogers thinks. If Mr. Frazier likes you, that's all that matters. He judges a man on what he can do, and if you can mine as well as you can carry beans, he won't care what the chief engineer thinks."

When we arrived at Mr. Frazier's office, Captain knocked lightly, even though the door was opened. A sign above it said "Frederick Frazier, General Mining Superintendent." Mr. Frazier looked up from his desk, saw us and came to the door. He reached out a hand to me, and before Captain could make the introduction, he said, "You must be the new man, Moss McCullen."

"Yes, sir." I extended my hand and said, "Proud to meet you."

"Glad to have you, son. Knew your father. He was a fine miner. One of the best I ever saw."

"Thank you, sir."

"Jim here tells me you'll make a good miner, too."

"I intend to, sir."

"Good." He nodded to Captain and said, "Looks like a good choice."

"He is, sir. Strongest kid I ever seen. We're headed for the cage, but I knew you'd want to meet him."

"Glad you brought him by." He looked at me and said, "Don't get scared off the first day. Give us a chance."

"Pleased to meet you, Mr. Frazier," I said.

"You, too, Moss. Good luck on your first day."

As we walked to the cage, Captain said, "You know Harvey Miller, the hoistman?"

Like many of the miners, Harvey had often dropped by the store for a Co'cola or a plug of tobacco. When he saw me, he said, "Moss, what you doing here? Commissary shut down?"

"We're gonna make a miner out of him," Captain said.

"Well, he'll make a good'un," Harvey said.

"That's what I'm betting on. Let us down." Captain winked at Harvey and pointed his thumb downward.

Harvey grinned and made a salute. "Anything you say, Captain."

When the cage door clanged shut, I flinched. A door had been shut in my life, and I could not go back through it. Suddenly I grabbed for the sides of the cage as I felt myself free-falling. I dropped my hat and lunch pail. My stomach felt the way it did when I dove off the pipe, only then I knew I was going to hit water, not rock.

Then I saw Captain grinning, and remembered hearing tales about the hoistman's initiation for each new man. As the roustabout took his first ride into the mine, the hoistman would drop the cage quickly, catching it at the bottom, just before it crashed into the rock floor. It wasn't any great comfort to remember that, but I told myself to stay calm. It was just a game, they weren't going to kill me. But I didn't like it. Sure enough, just at the right moment, the cage jerked to a halt, and I slammed into the door. Even Captain lost his footing as he grabbed at the walls of the cage, and we both found ourselves sprawled on the cage floor.

Captain laughed, and I stared out into the mine. Then I picked up my lunch pail and my hat and thought, what a crazy game. No wonder miners get killed.

Captain straightened himself, then reached over, slapped me on the back, and said, "Welcome to the pit, boy." He pointed into the mine as we stepped out of the cage. "This here's hard rock mining. They say zinc was formed from volcanoes. It was once a hot liquid, hotter'n hell. Then it set into rock. Hard rock mining aint like mining for coal in that old soft shale, like they do in West Virginia and Kentucky. No, sir, this here's solid rock—hard, bloody rock. Them yellow streaks of zinc is the life blood of the rock, only thing that makes it worth anything. How far down you reckon you are?"

"Deep. Over 600 feet I been told."

"You been told right, son. Scares some folks. Lots of men come down one time, and we never see them again after that first day. We're down where the sun don't shine. That yellow zinc is our sun."

As we walked across the big open space in front of the cage, he said, "This area's called the yard." It was pretty well lit with wires and bare bulbs running overhead, and I was surprised that it was so big. Probably about fifteen feet high, two hundred or so feet long and thirty feet or more wide. It was alive with activity. Several tracks ran through the yard, and while I watched, some cars loaded with rock and pulled by a mule came in from a drift. The mule trudged toward an area in the yard called a tipple where the ore was dumped into a hole called a skip pocket. Eventually the rock would be crushed into the fine powder that was dumped onto the lime field.

As we walked farther into the yard, Captain pointed to a small building, and he said, "Yonder's my underground office. Aint high enough yet to stay on top all day. Probably won't ever be. I'm still a underground man." He laughed and said, "So don't get your hopes up too high."

At the far end of the yard was a blacksmith's shop and stables where the mules were kept. Looked pretty much like those I'd always seen, except they were nestled in areas where the rock had been blasted out.

Captain said, "Something to see such fine stables way down here, aint it? Company takes better care of them damn mules than they do the men. Costs a lot of money to replace a mule. Have to take them ornery beasts up topside once a week to keep them from going blind. Thank God that's not my job."

"They don't look like they'd fit into the cage."

"Don't," he said. "So durn big they can't stand up. Aint easy getting them in there. Have to back them in and force them to sit down. Look like big old dogs, sitting there, waiting to be taken out. As you might guess, they don't like being backed up, especially into a small place."

After we passed the stables, the opening began to narrow into a tunnel cut into the rock. Captain pointed to it. "This here is the main drift. We cut us a tunnel into the rock till we get to the ore body." He sliced the air with his hand and added, "We open out a stope there, then we continue to cut out the drift or we cut us a cross-cut towards ore somewheres else."

The drift was darker, and I couldn't see how far it went. Captain reached up to light his carbide lamp on his hat that looked something like a baseball cap, except its bill had a leather holder for a brass lamp containing small pebbles of carbide. He opened a small valve which controlled the amount of water that was added to it through a straw-like stem to make acetylene gas, and with the skill of an expert miner, he hit the lamp with the palm of his hand, causing a piece of flint to spark and ignite the gas.

"Get your light going, boy. Dark in here. Always remember, your light's your life."

While I was trying to figure out how he'd done that trick with his hand, he lifted his lamp from his hat, reached over and lit mine with its flame. I thought of Aunt Minnie as the lamp lit the passageway in front of me.

"I'll teach you how to jar a flame up like I did sometime when we have time. It's the sign of a good miner, so you'll have to do it. But first thing you got to learn is, never let it burn out."

We walked along the track down the main drift. Soon we came to another large open area that was cut into the rock off the drift, but it wasn't as big as the yard. Captain said I was looking at a stope. Even though I thought I had a pretty good idea of what a mine was like from Paw's stories, as well as from stories I'd heard at the commissary, nothing could have prepared me for what I saw and heard as I stood at the edge of the stope. Men working on ledges—twenty feet, forty feet, even eighty feet up on the walls of rock as they followed the ore body at different levels.

"See them men," Captain said, pointing up high. "They're cutting a bench so we can mine up there. They cut into the rock till they uncover big bodies of zinc ore."

A whistle blew, and he put a hand across my chest and said, "Whoa." We watched as two men jumped over a ledge they were working on, hardly touching the rope ladder as they scuttled down it. When they hit the bottom, they ran a few feet and hunkered down just as I felt a rumble and heard the blast. Smoke and rock dust poured over the ledge where the men had been. After the blast, the men climbed back up into the gray-white cloud, even before it completely settled, and began to drill like nothing unusual had happened. Sweat dropped off my forehead in the cool mine as I wondered how I would stand all the rock and dust and noise for ten or more hours a day. Not to mention sliding down rope ladders from such a height after my fall at the creek. What those men were doing was what Paw was doing when he got blown up. They said he was in the main stope, too, so he must have been somewhere near where we stood.

Captain put his hand on my shoulder and said, "Whatever happens down here, boy, you can't panic. Got to always think, sometimes fast as lightning."

We walked on down the drift, and I wondered if Paw had known he was going to die, or if he had died so quickly he didn't have time to think about it. Soon we came to a cross-cut formation where the men were blasting out a new tunnel.

"This here's Sparky," Captain said as we walked up to a tall, lanky young man. "He's hanging wire to light up this drift. You help him today, and he can learn you all you'll ever need to know about electric power."

Sparky flashed a toothless grin at me. I nodded, thinking that someday I might answer to a name other than Moss. From the miners coming in the commissary, I already knew about the nicknames the miners gave one another. Sometimes their names were fitting to their specialty, as in the case of Sparky and Gadget, and sometimes names had to do with the way they acted or the way they looked. Romeo loved women, and Mouth talked all the time. Then there was Big Red and Fats. Some names were given as jokes. Curly didn't have a hair on his head, and Tiny was huge. Accidents were the trigger for some names. Patch had an eye blown out from misfired dynamite, and Shaky had been hit in the head by a falling rock. I hoped if I were given a nickname, it wouldn't be as a result of an accident.

After my first day in the mine working with Sparky, I learned of a danger I'd not thought much of before—live wires running overhead above the car tracks. The only safety measures were not to touch them. I discovered that the biggest protection from most dangers in the mine was using your common sense and staying alert.

Lightning

Mr. Moss worked with me and the mules once in a while when he was roustabouting. Thelma tell me about him bringing in her groceries. When she find out he working at the mine, she tell me to help him out. Miners can be pretty hard on a new man, and besides I don't cross Thelma. That's how we get along so good. So I take the boy under my wing.

Most of the men hate working with the mules. See it as a job only for coloreds, like busting rock. I's lucky to get to work with the mules. They got more sense than people, and it aint near as hard as using a sledge hammer. Them poor men breathe that old dust all day long, and break their backs doing it.

Mr. Moss, he good with the mules, say working with the them remind him of working on his family's farm. Mules aint easy to deal with if you don't know how to treat them. Most folks think mules only good for doing heavy work and don't worry about no plan to get them to do it, 'cept to beat them. That aint good for no animal. Mr. Moss, he know that. Learn it from his pappy. Still, he tell me I learn him more about animals in one day than he learn in all his days on the farm.

"Bet you been brung up to believe mules is dumb, aint you?" I say.

He grin. "Never thought about them being smart."

"That's what everybody say, but these critters smart a animal as God ever made. Take old Joe here." I pat his back. "He got a headful of sense. Aint you, old boy? You give him a load too heavy to tote, he aint going to pull it till he fall over dead. No, suh, not Joe. He just sit down on these tracks. Got more sense than to break his back for zinc that's no use to him. Now, Captain tell one of these poor miners to do something they can't do, they'll do it anyway, or die trying. So afraid somebody going to take away they job. What good a job if it kill you? Lord, rather work with mules any day."

Mr. Moss, he laugh, and I laugh with him.

143

"It's the truth," I say. "Folks say mules stubborn. Hell, stubbornness save their lives. Company'd work them to death, like they do men, if they let them. Oh, I know they takes them out once a week so they don't go blind and can't work no more. But they can kill them working them too hard. Joe, he get too tired, he know if he turn away from the track just a certain way, his harness'll come loose and he can just mosey on back into a old used-up stope and hide till suppertime. Reckon I wouldn't never find him, if his eyes didn't light up red when I shine my lamp in his face. That's one thing he aint learn yet. I 'spect any day now he'll learn to shut his eyes. And if I don't find him, it don't make no difference. He got to eat, and come meal time, he'll come back out of the stope. Yes, suh, Joe know when to rest and when to eat. Now, you take a man. He aint got sense enough to know his harness'll come loose. Men work in the same traps till they fall over deader'n four o'clock. Not mules."

"You like your mules," Mr. Moss say. "I can see that."

"I do, and I aint ashamed of it, neither. Let me tell you something else, Mr. Moss. Mules know how to have fun. Ever now and then they decide to take them a joy ride. If I don't brake the car fast enough, that old car behind them get to going too fast and a bumping their heels. They don't stand for it. They just plops right back into that car and ride it down the hill, all four hooves sticking straight up in the air." I held both my arms out front, and that boy laughed so hard he bout bent double. "Damnedest thing you ever see," I say, "Big animal like that, a riding a car down the hill, having a good old time. You tell me a man that's got that much sense. Aint no man smart like a mule. You 'member that, and you and me and the mules'll get along just fine."

Avery

I didn't no more get on at the mine than Moss decided he would, too, and him already with a good job. Didn't need to come to the mine. Reckon he did it because I did. Next thing, he'll be after my job. When he got on, I was helping Gadget as a mechanic assistant.

Moss started out as a roustabout like everybody. Bet that hurt his soul. Probably thought he'd start out as president of the company. One day he was sent to work with us, and Gadget put him to repairing a motor with me. I figured pretty soon he'd be the one repairing the motor instead of me.

I said, "You still going to be president of the company someday?"

"Yeah, that's why they've got me training under you, so I can be president of the company."

He laughed, but I didn't think it was funny. I said, "Maybe you'll just take my job."

Said he didn't want my job. He's so damn uppity. "Aint good enough for you?" I said. "I forgot, you're going for bossman, foreman, like Johnson. Been watching you kiss everybody's ass, trying to learn everybody's job. Guess if you're going to be boss, you got to, aint that right?"

"Isn't that the way to become a good miner?"

"I don't like you a using your friends to move up."

Naturally about that time Gadget came up. Reckon he heard us, and he said, "What's the matter with a feller trying to better hisself? If a feller's friends don't help him, who will?"

I should've known Gadget'd take Moss's side. I said, "Well, he's just trying to be better'n everybody else."

"Aw, get off your high horse," he said. "Boy's just trying to do the best he can. Aint no law again that. Wisht I'd a tried to learn everything I could've when I was young. Maybe you ort to do the same."

"And maybe you ort to just mind your own damn business."

145

"If I'd a minded my own damn business, you wouldn't be no mechanic today. And if it hadn't a been for Moss here telling me I should give you a chance to work into a mechanic's job, I'd never a fooled with you noway. He aint interested in your job. If he was, I'd give it to him." He stood up straight and gripped his wrench with his big hand and added, "Better watch your mouth afore you get yourself into trouble with the wrong person. I made you a mechanic's helper, and I can put you back roustabouting."

How does Moss somehow always wind up making me look like a fool? I had to apologize to Gadget because I didn't want to lose my job, but I didn't apologize to Moss.

After that, when Moss had to work with the mechanics, Gadget had him work with him or Greasy, who was too stupid to care who he worked with, and that suited me just fine.

Moss

From the moment I saw Stub I knew how he'd gotten his nickname. Before I met him I'd heard his name, and I didn't know if he was missing a finger or what. As it turned out, he was a small man, but he had a large torso. Looked like the top of him had outgrown the bottom.

He looked up at me and said, "My god, they're growing them big these days. You're the new man."

I nodded. "Captain sent me. Said he wanted me to learn from the best."

"Been working in the mine since I was ten year old, and that's longer ago than I care to remember," he said. "Reckon I can learn you just about anything they is to know about dynamite. What's your name, boy?" He grinned at me and extended his hand.

"Moss, Moss McCullen."

"Oh, yeah. Heard tell of you. Clyde McCullen's son. Good man, Clyde was. Right proud to meet his son."

I nodded, and he said, "Name's Stub. Actually it's Steve Goddard, but nobody calls me that. I 'bout forget what it is myself. Call me Stub. Well, enough gab. We don't make no money standing around chewing the fat. Job ahead of us is to open a new stope. We got it started. See that ledge up there?" He pointed up toward a high ledge that I figured to be over fifty feet. "You and me's gotta cut into that stope bench. We gonna go up that rope ladder and blow the hell out of it. Now, I'm going up first and take this here rope. You stay down and tie the dynamite on the rope so's I can pull it up. Got that? Once I get the dynamite, you come on up."

He went up the rope ladder so fast, if I hadn't seen it, I wouldn't have believed it. He pulled the dynamite up, then threw down the ladder and yelled, "Well, come on. Get a move on. Aint got all day."

I put my feet into the foot loops and began to climb. Stub leaned over the edge and said, "You're going to work out all right, boy. You climb up this ladder easy as a squirrel running up a tree."

It didn't feel that easy to me. When I was on the ledge, Stub nodded toward the wall of rock in front of us.

"See these here holes? I done had them drilled." He pointed up above his head. "I got some drilled up there, too. Now, your job is to load them with dynamite." He picked up a wooden pole lying on the ledge. "Tamp real careful-like." He took a stick of dynamite and wedged it into a hole and gently tapped it in with the pole. "You don't want to cut the fuses as you tamp. When the dynamite's in real good, then you cut the fuses to about five feet on the first stick of dynamite and make each one about four inches shorter'n the one before as you go down the row so's they'll blow one after another when I light them."

"Wait a minute," I said. "How're we going to light all those fuses and get down the ladder before they start blowing?"

"Hell, you got forty-five seconds a foot from the time you light a fuse. How long's that take you before the first one blows?"

"About three and a half minutes," I said.

"Well, by god. They finally sent me a man that can figger as well as climb ropes. Always sending me boys that can't work with numbers. Now, mind you, I don't hold no fault with a man that can't figger, but he sure as hell don't need to be dynamiting. It's the idiots topside that's stupid, sending a man down to do a job where he could get hisself killed—or somebody else, like me. They's the ones supposed to run this here show." He shook his head and muttered, "Can't have no dynamite man that can't figger. And ciphering on the job aint like figgering on paper. Anyways, like you said, we got to get back down that ladder in three and a half minutes from the time I light the first set of dynamite. We stay up here longer'n that, we'll be blowed to kingdom come."

"That cutting it a little tight?" I said. "Three extra feet would give us over two extra minutes to get all the fuses lit. You got a lot of sticks here."

148

"Hell, we don't need all that time. Trust me, been doing this longer'n you been borned. Shit, boy, time's money. Aint got none to waste. Them fuses is a lot longer than they ought to be, and we aint got all day. Get busy trimming. Piddling around don't help a man relax around dynamite. Once you live through a blast, you'll see you got all the time you need—if you don't mess up. Mess up one time, it's your last."

As he started up the ladder to the next ledge I said, "I don't intend to get killed."

He looked down at me and said, "Me neither."

As I cut the fuses, sweat poured off my forehead. When I finished trimming the last one, Stub lit the fuse on the first stick of dynamite, then another and he was going down the line before I realized he'd lit them. He never said a word. I lunged for the rope ladder and slid down without touching my feet to the foot holes. Stub was right behind me.

As he landed, he said, "Run."

We got to safety just as the dynamite went off. After we hit the ground and the dust cleared and my heart stopped pounding, I grabbed his collar and pulled him clean off his feet.

"What were you trying to do?" I said. "You didn't even tell me you were setting off the fuses. You could have blowed us both to bits. Or I could have broke my goddamn neck coming down the goddamn ladder. If you weren't so old, I'd smash your teeth down your throat."

He started coughing, as best he could with me holding him up by his collar. I put him down, and he bent double hacking into his handkerchief. When he stopped, he folded the bloody handkerchief and gripped it in his shaking fist.

"I'm sorry," I said, "but you could have killed us both."

Still bent over, he put his hands on his knees and tried to get his breath. When he could talk, he said, "You think I want to get my helper killed and break my perfect record? Shit, I knowed you'd be okay. A man can always go down a ladder faster'n he can go up it. Besides, a man's got to be ready for anything when handling dynamite. Might as well learn right off not to wait for nobody to tell you nothing. Best lesson I can give you is to always be alert."

"You think I'm a fool?" I said. "You expect me to believe that was the usual way of dynamiting up that high."

He grinned and straightened his clothes. "Well, I guess I was trying to get your goat a little. You know we always got to break in the new fellers. Don't hurt nobody, just have a little fun."

"You call that fun? Hell, I can take a joke as well as the next man, but that was a damn fool thing to do."

He looked down at his boots. Everything about him was gray, even his skin—I hoped not from choking. How much of his hair was naturally gray and how much was due to rock dust I couldn't tell. Once I cooled down I knew he wasn't lying about not aiming to get me hurt. Captain had told me Stub had a perfect safety record, but he'd added I best be careful, as there'd been a couple of close calls since Stub'd gotten older. I wasn't so sure I hadn't just witnessed another close call.

He wiped his mouth and forehead and looked up at me. He wasn't grinning any more. "You got to loosen up, boy," he said. "You get too serious down here, you mess up. I promise I won't never let you nor nobody else get hurt. You can count on that. From now on, I'll warn you ahead of time what I'm doing. And I won't never have you do nothing I don't do right along with you. Anybody'll tell you that. You still want to work with me?"

"I reckon," I said, "but I'd appreciate it if you wouldn't joke around dynamite."

He crossed his heart and said, "No more joking."

I figured I could learn a lot from Stub, if I lived long enough.

Stub

I'm the one who give Moss his nickname Chief. Met him when he came to work as my helper. After a while, I asked Captain if I couldn't keep him as a permanent helper. I needed a man like him. I liked all the boys Captain sent me well enough, but some of them weren't worth a pile of lime dust as dynamite men. Either they was too scared to make good workers or they couldn't do nothing other than what I told them to do. Got to be able to think on your feet when you work with dynamite. I told Captain, Moss was a real good miner, had what it took to be a contractor hisself in time. Captain said it was okay with him if it was okay with Moss.

Moss said he'd stay as my helper, but he'd not cut fuses short any more. If I didn't want him, that was all right.

"Look, kid," I said, "you're really trying my patience, you know that? Them regulations is meant to be broke. It takes them blame fuses forever to go off when you leave them eight feet long. Hell, I got time to read a book while we wait, and I don't read so well. I keep telling you, time is money. When am I ever going to learn you that you got plenty a time to get away from the blasting when you cut them fuses a few inches shorter than you're supposed to?"

"Never. You're only saving a few seconds. And risking our lives is not worth a few seconds."

"Nothing ever happens, nothing aint never happened, and nothing aint going to. Who's the expert here? I been cutting fuses short since before you was thought of, and I'm still around."

"By the grace of God," he said, and he told me I wasn't going to get him blowed up because he wasn't going to let me.

"Damn," I said, "if you aint about more trouble than you're worth. You ought to be a pulling them cars instead of dynamiting. You the mule-headedest helper I've ever had, but you're the damn best one, too. Here I am trying to give you a break, and you're telling me what you're going to do. Reckon the other men think

I'm the helper and you're the contractor. You're the chief, and I'm the Indian. Hey, that's it."

"What?"

"That's the name we've been hunting for you—Chief. You look the part, and you act the part."

It wasn't long before all the miners were calling him Chief, and it stuck.

Time passed fast working underground. Mostly I went to work in the dark and came home in the dark. Every day I learned something new. But not a day passed that I didn't think about Madeline and wonder if I had a child somewhere.

Three years after she left, I still hadn't heard a word from her. Mr. Rogers said little to anyone about Madeline, or about anything, for that matter. I guess he knew anything he said would spread all over Outcropping. Gossip traveled through the air like rock dust. Reckon he wanted to protect his image more than he wanted to hurt me. The only thing I heard was she'd married a doctor somewhere in North Carolina, she never came home, and Mr. Rogers seldom went there.

Annie hadn't heard anything either. I knew it was killing her inside, but she never complained. I didn't understand. It would be like if I left and never contacted Maw. Sometimes on a weekend if I didn't go home I'd go see Annie and take her a package of meat from the commissary or a bolt of cloth that Aunt Minnie'd pick out. Her brother drunk up most of what he made, and she didn't have what she needed. I hated seeing what I'd caused, even though she never reminded me. She always acted like she was happy to see me.

On a beautiful June day, about the time of year I'd met Madeline, I decided to walk out to the farm to do a little work and see everybody. I needed to get away from the dirt and heat of Outcropping and breathe clean air.

As I walked home, I thought of Madeline. When I came to the road that went toward the river, I found myself turning down it and walking to the riverbank near the old house. I sat at the place where we used to sit on that old quilt. I looked up at the house for some evidence that she'd been there, knowing there'd be nothing. I gazed into the river, and my thoughts flowed with it. I didn't believe any man had ever loved a woman as I'd loved Madeline. The time with her had been the happiest of my life, and I was afraid to let it drift away, but that life was beginning to seem more and more unreal. Even though I'd long since resigned myself to the fact that she'd been unable to accept a life with me, I never wanted to stop remembering. At twenty-three, I believed the best part of my life would always be in the past.

"What do you think our children will be like?" she would ask, leaning on one arm and looking at me seriously.

"Like you, I hope," I'd say, imagining a little girl with blond curls. In my mind I pictured Ellie as she'd been before I left home.

"Oh, no, not if he's a boy," she'd say. "He should be tall and broad-shouldered with dark hair."

"Never can tell. I don't look nothing like my father."

"Who do you favor?"

"My maw. She's tall and dark." I wondered what Madeline thought about my being as dark as I was. She'd never said anything.

"Your mother must be a handsome woman," she said.

"I guess she is, but she never had no time or money to show her beauty off."

A frown clouded her face. "How sad."

"Maybe he'll look like your father," I said. For all my dislike for the man, I had to admit he was impressive with his tall, thin aristocratic build and his thick brown hair and neatly trimmed mustache.

I was surprised when she said, "I don't really care what he looks like, just so he acts like you."

I turned to kiss her and felt the empty air. I was brought back to the lonely riverbank and the river that flowed on and on as though nothing had happened. Sometimes I wanted to go with it, pull up stakes and go anywhere. Not to our farm. Somewhere I'd never been.

I'd always known Madeline had some unreal notion of me. Maybe that was why she left and never came back. For the first two years, I really believed she would return, for Annie if for no other reason. I trusted that one day she and our baby would appear.

Even as I realized that wasn't going to happen, I still went to the river, just to remember. In my mind I'd make love to her. I could see and feel and smell every inch of her body. I didn't think the pain would ever go away. And I didn't want it to, because if it did, the memories would have to disappear.

Kathleen

I dreaded telling Moss about me and Max getting married. I knew he'd never understand. All he ever talked about was me and Ellie and LC going to college. I lacked two years finishing at the university, but we were still going to get married. Mr. Lindsey begged Max to stay at his farm and keep helping after school. Said he didn't know what he'd do without him, or me. Mrs. Lindsey had died, and Maw and I and even Ellie still worked for him and the boys. He told Max if we'd stay, he and his boys'd build us a little house on the edge of the farm, and we could live there free as long as Max wanted to work on the farm. I could work as much or as little as I wanted while I finished school. He was thankful for any help. There was no end to what needed to be done on that farm and in that big house. But Moss had his own dreams for us, and they didn't have anything to do with helping Mr. Lindsey.

He said, "You can't give up college just to get married."

"I'm not giving it up," I said. "You don't understand. You never take time to be in love. All you love is work." I told him how Max and I'd planned it all out, that I'd still catch the bus in to Knoxville every day, and with living free we could afford my tuition. I told him Max had been saving for three years for us to do this.

He took a step back. "You mean you all've been planning on marrying since you were in high school?"

"Well, he has been," I said.

Then he asked what if I got pregnant, and I said if I did before I finished, well, it'd take a little longer, but I still would get through. Maw'd help out with a baby. When he saw he wasn't going to change my mind, he said he'd keep helping with my tuition, but I said, no, Max wouldn't hear of it.

"You don't know what you're doing, Kat," he said. "You'll be so sorry. Life won't be easy."

"Life's never easy, Moss. Nobody wanted you to leave, either, but you did."

He looked so sad, it was almost enough to change my mind, but not quite. I told him it wouldn't be long before Ellie and LC would be going, and he needed to be saving for them.

He just said, "You've got to finish, Kat. You're so smart. Promise me, if you need help, you'll let me know."

"Promise." I lied.

Stub helped me in the mine more than anyone else. Sometimes he'd bring an extra piece of cake in his lunch pail. I didn't need it, 'cause Aunt Minnie packed my lunch, always with cake or pie or a piece of fruit. But it made me feel good that he thought of me. He started asking me to drop by after work sometimes for some stew or meatloaf. It took my mind off Madeline and Kathleen.

His son William took right to me. Always wanted to show me something like a shovel or mule or rail car that Stub had carved out of wood. We'd get down on the floor and play with them. Sometimes when I'd look at his blond hair as he was bent over the toys, I'd think of LC. I never played with my brother. I hardly listened when he tried to tell me something he had learned at school or at the Lindseys' farm. I just kept working at whatever I was doing. I knew more about William than I did him.

Once I said something to Stub about William making me think of LC. After that he'd push me to take his old truck to drive out to see my family so I could see them more often. I didn't want to take his truck, worried about something happening to it, but he insisted. Once in a while when I was just going out for a Sunday afternoon, William would tag along. He'd press his little face against the truck window to see the cows and horses we'd pass in the fields along the way. When we'd get to the farm, he and LC would spend the whole time with the animals.

After I'd worked for Stub a while, I became a contractor, too. I knew he'd gone to bat for me. At twenty-four I was the youngest contractor in the mine. Since I was paid on a percentage basis instead of by the hour, I made a hell of a lot more money. I was pretty much my own man, too, except Captain would tell us where he wanted us to open up new drifts or stopes. But he didn't hover over us. Didn't have to. Money was the driver, since we earned according to the zinc we mined.

I always had one helper with a little experience assigned to me, and the two of us would dynamite the rock. Roustabouts with sledgehammers crushed the big chunks of rock left from the dynamiting into pieces small enough to be transported. Other workers shoveled these into cars pulled on tracks by Lightning's mules to the main drift and switched out for the motorman to move it to the tipple.

The contracting system worked well for the company. The contractors'd push the men, so the company didn't have to. Sometimes we could make more than the foremen if we put in a lot of hours, but our poor helpers got paid by the hour, and they didn't get no more money no matter how hard they worked or how much ore they uncovered. But they still worked hard with the hope of making contractor some day. I knew if a union ever came, which there was talk about, the contractors like me would be a thing of the past.

The last year I was a contractor, we had an especially wet spring. Blackberry Creek overflowed its banks, and river-bottom land along the Holston was all under water. Pools, even lakes, of water stood in low-lying areas that were usually dry. Farmers worried about spring planting. We worried about the mine flooding.

By the middle of April 1928, Captain had us running pumps around the clock, and still more water was coming in than was being pumped out. He came up to the north end of the mine where me and my men were working deep under the river, trying to follow a rich vein even deeper into the earth, but we were about to get flooded out.

He said, "Damn, it's bad down here."

"Yeah," I said, "It's coming in faster'n it's being pumped out. I think we're going to have to pull out."

"Not yet. We might try building a bulkhead. See if that works. I'm going to get Mr. Frazier down here."

Mr. Frazier came, and the three of us stood looking at the water. "It's bad, all right. In all my years in the mine, I've never seen so much water," he said. "Hate to give up this vein if we don't have to. We probably will, but let's try a bulkhead first."

159

"I'm not sure it'll stop the water," Captain said. "It's real bad."

"I know, but if we can cut off the worst of where it's pouring in, we can maybe handle the rest of it with pumps. If we shut down altogether, the mine will flood out. Company won't make any money, and the men'll be out of work a mighty long time."

"They're getting worried. Some of them remember the last time the mine closed down because of flooding and a lot of people went hungry."

"We pulled out that time before it got as bad as this," Mr. Frizier said. "Course, we didn't have the number of pumps we got now. If we can manage to only shut off this new end and keep the rest of the mine going, we won't have to lay but off a few men."

Captain looked at Mr. Frazier and said, "It's a tough call. I hate to see men out of work, but I hate to put them in this kind of danger, too. If you say the word, I'll get some workers on a bulkhead right away."

"Do it. Get some good white oak logs, and shut off this drift. But keep a close eye on it. If the water don't let up soon, it won't hold."

The bulkhead covered the eight-by-eight foot opening of the new drift tunnel. When the workers finished with it, Captain pounded his fist against the heavy timbers and said, "Good job, men. Solid as the rock of Gibraltar. That'll hold her for a while at least. Now we can get back to the business of mining."

He told me to keep my best men working and to go work with Stub where he and his men were driving the main drift farther south.

A while later he pulled Stub and me aside. "We got to keep a real close eye on that bulkhead," he said. "Water's building up behind the timbers, and I don't have to tell you, if it builds up too much behind it, it could break."

"I aint never seen that happen," Stub said.

"Me neither, but I've heard tell of it. Happened in a mine out in the west once and every damn person in the mine drowned. Just between us, we should already have shut down the mine. I want one of you to go down to that area every couple of hours or so and check on it. You see water seeping out around the logs above five feet or so, or if you hear rumbling, and especially if you see the timbers shaking or water oozing out, come get me."

"What if we aint sure if it's bad enough?" Stub said.

"If you aint sure, it's bad enough."

The bulkhead held for a while, but the rains kept coming and the creeks and the river kept rising, and when it was bad above ground, it was bad below. A couple of days after the bulkhead was built, Stub and me were sitting on a ledge eating lunch, and I said I was going back down to check on it.

"I's down there about an hour or so ago," Stub said. "Didn't hear no rumbling."

But he couldn't hear thunder, so I said, "Well, I think I'll go check before I get busy again."

"Suit yourself. You usually do."

As I went down the long drift toward the crosscut, I passed Lightning in the opening of a stope, struggling with his mule.

"Whoa, Joe, whoa," he said as he held the reins and the mule kicked and pulled back. "Take it easy, old boy."

A short Irishman the men called Leprechaun was loading rock onto the cars the mule was pulling. "What is it that's wrong with your mule?" he said to Lightning.

"Don't know, Lep. Started acting crazy-like. Blame rats gone crazy, too. Listen at them."

Rats were squealing and scurrying everywhere. They were as good as the chicken the inspector brought with him to warn of dangers like gas or balk ground. They sensed moving ground before men had any signs of it. Lightning, Lep and I all stood listening, smelling, staring down the drift into the big rock opening. We saw no water, but the animals knew trouble was coming. I told Lightning to get his load up to the yard and then for him and Lep to get out of the mine.

"On my way," he said, "soon as I can get Joe to cooperate."

Lep stopped loading to help Lightning with the mule. I went on down the drift toward the bulkhead. As I approached it, I heard rumblings, and when I got close enough, I could see the timbers shaking and water pouring from between the logs, even up toward the top, higher than me. I ran back to the drift and saw Lep and Lightning and Joe heading toward the yard.

"You seen Captain?" I yelled.

"Yes, sir," Lightning said. "Passed us a few minutes ago. He's up ahead."

"That bulkhead's about to go. We got to get the men out of this mine. Go to all the stopes in this area and send everybody to the yard. I'm going to run on and tell Captain."

"What about Joe?" Lightning said.

"I'm sorry," I said. "If we can get everybody out in time, we'll come back for Joe and the other mules. I'll help you. Right now, get the men out."

I ran past them to find Captain. When I saw him, I hollered for him to wait up.

"What's wrong, son?" Then without waiting for an answer, he said, "Shit, it's the bulkhead, aint it?"

I nodded. "It's going to go."

"Let's take a look."

"No. We won't make it. I've already started getting the men out."

"Couldn't we wait till this shift is over?"

"Water's leaking out," I said, breathing hard, "even at the top."

"Damnation," he said, thrusting a fist into his other hand.

"I already sent Lightning and Lep to tell everybody up at the cross-cut to head for the yard. It'll take a while to get them all out of the mine."

"You better be right about this, Moss."

"Let's hope I'm not."

Leprechaun came running up and said he'd told everybody he'd passed and that Lightning was checking all the stopes for men.

"Good," Captain said, "Get to the cage, Lep."

"I'm going on to the south end to warn Stub," I said. "He and our men are the farthest away from the cage. I'll warn Preacher and Steel. They're down that way. If the bulkhead goes, it'll pour through here, past the cage and beyond, and won't none of them be able to get out."

"Okay. I'm going to the cage. Hopefully most of the men are on their way there." He put his hand on my shoulder and said, "If you get trapped, son, there's an old air shaft back up there, beyond where your men are working. Stub'll know where it is. You all can get out through it if you have to. Now run like fire on a fuse."

I ran so hard I felt my lungs would burst, hollering at everyone I passed to hightail it to the yard. Then Lightning yelled my name.

"How the hell did you get here so fast?" I said.

"They don't call me Lightning just because of moonshine, you know."

"Why aren't you at the yard?'

"Why aint you?"

"I'm heading to the south end to warn Stub."

"You aint going down there alone."

"Get out while you still can. We could get trapped up at the south end."

"Well, then, I reckon we all be trapped."

We tore on down the drift. When we got to Steel and Preacher, I told them the new bulkhead was giving way and for them to get to the cage.

Preacher dropped his drill and said to Steel, "Come on."

"We aint going to let a muler and a stock boy tell us what to do, are we?"

"I sure am. Throw your drill down and let's get out of here."

"You aint my boss. We got us a good load here."

"Don't be a fool," Preacher said. "I'll pray for you." Then he took off.

"Look," I said to Steel, "Aint got time to argue with you. I'm going to warn Stub. Go with Preacher, come with us, or stay the hell here and drown."

"Aint never seen a damn bulkhead break yet," Steel said, but he threw his drill down and took off toward the cage. Me and Lightning ran on. After we'd gone only a hundred yards of so, it sounded like somebody had blasted the whole mine out. We stopped dead in our tracks.

"That aint dynamite blasting," said Lightning.

'I know," I said, as water poured up the drift toward us.

"Lord God A'mighty," said Lightning, "The rest of the mine must be flooded, and the whole Holston River must be pouring in."

"Hurry," I said, as water swirled around out feet. By the time we got to Stub, water was rising up there, too.

"What in tarnation?" Stub said when he saw us. Then he looked down at his wet feet. "The bulkhead" was all he said.

I nodded.

"Poor old Steel and Preacher," said Lightning. "Aint no way they could've got to the cage."

"Did the men get out?" Stub said.

"When we came up here, everyone was heading for the yard." I said. "Hopefully they got out. But I don't see no way Preacher and Steel could've made it."

Lightning hung his head. "Old Joe's gone, for sure." He looked at the rising water. "We's trapped up here, aint we?"

The lights went out, and all we could see with our carbide lamps was water. We shivered in cold and fear.

164

"The air shaft," I said. "Captain said if we got trapped, to get to the air shaft."

"It's beyond us a ways," said Stub. "The water'll rise slow enough back here for us to get to it. We can climb up the steps through the manhole to the outside. It aint the usual way of getting out, but we can do it. Follow me." We waded through the cold water for the air shaft, and hopefully for life.

Stub

I coughed up more blood than usual after the flood and finally had to take off work for a while, though it like to a killed my soul. Sometimes I couldn't get my breath. It's a awful feeling when you can't get air.

Doc Timer said he was afraid it was pneumony. Told me he knew I wouldn't want to stay down, but with the silicosis, it could get real bad if I didn't. He told Hope to give me plenty of chicken soup and keep me in bed. He looked at us both. "I know that's asking a lot." He pointed his finger at me and said, "But if you want to live, you'll do it." He shook his head, closed his bag and left, saying he'd be by the next day.

Moss and me'd become good friends, and once in a while he'd come by the house, even eat supper with us. Sometimes he used my old truck and took our little boy William with him to the country. When William'd come home, all he could talk about was chickens, cows, and horses. Moss was a good man, one you could trust. He was who he was, and nothing more. When he came by after the flood, Hope told him what the doctor'd said. It was as hard for me to talk as it was to breathe because I kept coughing. She handed me a fresh handkerchief and put a can beside the bed for me to spit into. Moss looked like he'd lost his best friend.

Between coughs, I said, "I aint dead yet."

"If I'd made you go with me to check on the bulkhead," he said, "you could've stopped at the cage and not wound up in that cold water."

"Hell, you couldn't have made me go with you. I'd just come from up there, and I wasn't going to go all that way back. Besides, I aint going to let a little pneumony get me. No, sir, when I go, I'm going out in a blast, going to be blown right up to heaven. Got to make sure they hear me coming."

"Well, don't rush it," he said. "You better stay off and enjoy this pretty woman waiting on you while you can."

"I'll stay off a few days."

"Make it a few weeks," he said.

"Hell, no. You trying to kill me?"

"I'm trying to keep you alive in spite of yourself. Now, I got to go and let you rest. You need anything?"

"Nothing except to get out of here," I said, "and I know you aint going to help me there."

Death was in my lungs, and I knew it. I'd coughed up blood for years, but this was worse. I couldn't eat or sleep or hardly breathe for coughing. I'd skirted death every day in the mine, and I didn't want to die in my bed. I stayed down for a while, but I had things to take care of before I left this earth.

Moss

Stub often asked me to supper after we got off from work. I went some, but recently I'd been making excuses, told him I had to get home, Aunt Minnie'd be expecting me. To tell the truth, Hope made me uncomfortable. Not that she tried to. But there was something between us we both tried to ignore. She was pretty with her coppery hair and her big blue eyes. But it was more than that. Her eyes were so deep I felt I could drown in them. They reflected such a good soul, and I would love to have known her better. But I'd learned a hard lesson about taking what wasn't mine. Still, after Stub got sick, I felt I needed to go by more often.

Stub knew how I felt about Hope. He'd catch me staring at her while we ate or when we'd sit around the stove in the evening. But he didn't seem upset about it. In fact, we never mentioned it. Not until one day after he got sick. After supper we sat on the porch in two rockers Hope'd put out there for us. The two of us were about all the little porch would hold. Out of nowhere he asked me how I felt about Hope.

I nearly fell out of my chair. When I could get my breath, I said, "She's a great person. You're a lucky man."

"Quit beating around the bush. You know what I'm talking about. I aint got forever." He squinted his eyes at me. "You in love with her?"

I gripped the arm of the chair to keep my hand from shaking. "She's not my wife."

"That aint what I asked. It's okay. I got to know."

"I try not to think about it."

"That answers my question."

"This aint no regular conversation," I said.

"This aint no regular situation," he said.

"Why're you talking to me like this?"

He coughed hard, then said, "I'm not going to be around much longer. We all know that."

"Shoot, you'll bury me."

"We both know that aint true. I got to know her and William will be okay when I'm gone. I want you to take care of them, but only if you want to. Got a little money put back. They aint going to be desperate. I'd like for her to be happy, to be with someone that can do more than take care of her, someone that can make her happy. You know, she aint never had what you can give her. I gave that to Maritsa."

"Maritsa?"

"My first wife. When we got married, we was crazy in love. Her face'd light up when I come in a room. That's what I want for Hope. I want to look down and see her face light up like that."

"I'll take care of them. I promise. But I don't know if she'll want me, well, that way."

"She'll want you. And I'm glad. She aint had much pleasure in her life. And she deserves some. She is a good woman."

"Yes, she is," I said. "And you're a good husband."

"Hell, I'm a sick, old man."

"You've been good to her. You're better'n most husbands around here."

"Well," he said. "I don't know about that. She married me 'cause there wasn't nothing else for her to do. Don't want her to have to marry for that reason again, not even to you. Don't forget this talk when the time comes."

When I walked home that evening, I didn't know what to think about what Stub had said. I'd never heard of such a thing. I'd heard of men fighting over women, even killing each other. But this was different. I'd never known anybody who loved like Stub, enough to give up his wife to someone else for her to be happy. I'd thought no one could ever love someone like I'd loved Madeline, but I was just beginning to learn what love was.

Ellie

I've always been around a farm and loved the smells of plowing, planting and harvesting. Knew I wanted to spend my whole life in the country and raise my children on a farm. There's nothing as appealing as a man who's worked all day on the land, coming in at night smelling of dirt, hay, sweat and tobacco. Me and Joe Lindsey'd known each other all our lives, and I'd been in love with him since I was at least ten, but he didn't pay me no mind until I was about fifteen. After that, he started finding more and more reasons to be around me. Getting married seemed the natural thing to do. We decided to tie the knot the summer after I graduated from high school.

I knew Moss'd be disappointed. He had plans for me to go on to college to study voice. 'Course he'd have wanted me to go to college if I'd sung like a bullfrog. I love to sing, but I don't care nothing about school, and I couldn't imagine going for another four years. Kathleen wasn't any help. She said I had too good a voice to throw it away, which was a silly thing to say. How can you throw away your voice?

She didn't have any room to talk. She got married when she was only two years older than me, though I have to admit she went on to college and finished after she and Max were married and after Maxine was born. But Kathleen loved reading and studying. When she wasn't working she had her nose in a book. And, that's okay, but it wasn't for me. Maw don't care if I marry Joe. Actually I think she's glad, because she knows I'll always live right next door to her. In fact, we plan to move in with her and LC until we can build a house on Joe's land. Joe has worked on his paw's farm all his life, and he plans to always do that.

His paw is tickled to death because he wants Joe to keep the farm, him and his brother Fred. He's going to divide it up between the two of them. None of the rest of the boys is interested in it. James made a doctor, married a girl from Cincinnati and moved up there to go into practice with her paw. Gifford teaches agriculture and lives near the university. Ezra always said he was going to get away from the farm as soon as he was old enough and never come back. He did, too. He was studying to be a lawyer at the university and got in a fight over a girl and killed a man. He's in Brushy Mountain Prison, but I'm not supposed to know that. Caleb, God rest his soul, got killed in the war.

I aint going into this marriage with my eyes shut. Farming's a hard life. I've seen it firsthand, because Maw and Kat and I've been working for the Lindseys ever since Mrs. Lindsey took sick. We cook for the men, wash dishes, do laundry, clean the house, mend clothes, feed chickens, pick corn and vegetables from the garden, and do countless other chores. But just 'cause you got to work for something don't mean you don't love it.

Moss came home one Sunday when I was about to graduate from high school, and I decided to tell him. Had to face him sometime. Kathleen helped Maw with the dishes after supper so I could go out on the porch to talk to him.

He was so upset he couldn't even talk at first. Finally he said, "But you've never even courted anyone else."

"That's right," I said. "Don't never intend to."

"But you're still a girl. You don't know how you'll change."

"I may change in a lot of ways," I said, "but I'll never change in the way I feel about Joe."

"You don't know that."

"Yes, I do."

"What about school? You have a voice that makes folks forget their troubles. Don't seem right not to use it. You've always planned to study voice at the university."

I said, no, he'd always planned for me to study voice at the university, and that I did use my voice, and I always would. I said, "I sing at weddings and funerals and parties. If everybody that has a talent gets educated and moves off, who's going to do that around here? Folks here need someone to sing for them."

"But what if you ever want to move?"

"I won't. I'll always stay here with Joe. Some folks don't want to move away. All I heard from Maw when I was little was that you were working so we could stay on the land forever. Now you're saying you don't want me to live here. I'm probably the only one who's really interested in actually keeping the farm. Mr. Lindsey's giving Joe the half of his farm that joins ours. We'll always farm it. Unless you want it, of course."

"That's not the point," he said. "I want you to be able to leave if you should ever want to, or ever have to. What if something should happen to Joe and you have to support you and your children? I don't want you to have no control over your life. Please, don't do this, Ellie. Not yet. Go to the university for at least two years, like Kathleen did. Then you'll know if it's worth finishing. I won't say nothing if you decide to get married then."

"I won't take the chance of losing Joe," I said. "He's six years older than me, and he's ready to get married."

"If he loves you he'll wait."

"And if I love him, I won't make him wait."

Moss

The day after the flood Mr. Frazier sent for me. I knew I should have waited for Captain to give the order to pull the men out of the mine, but there wasn't time. No telling what Mr. Frazier thought about it. When I got to his office I leaned against the door a moment, took a deep breath, then knocked lightly.

Mr. Frazier didn't sound upset as he said, "Come in, come in."

When I stepped inside he stood up, shook my hand and said, "Good to see you, Moss."

I breathed a little easier. He lit a Lucky Strike and offered me one.

"No, thank you, sir. Captain said you wanted to see me."

He threw the pack of cigarettes on his desk and said, "I do, indeed, son. Have a seat." He sat down in his gray leather swivel chair behind his desk and pointed to a straight chair on the other side. "How are you after yesterday's heroics?"

"I didn't see heroics," I said. "It was mostly chaos with everybody trying to get out of the mine before they drowned."

"Well, Johnson tells me you saved a lot of lives."

"Lost two men and some mules. I didn't mean to act out of turn, sir, and I'm sorry about that, but there wasn't time. . ."

"Damn straight, there wasn't time. You got nothing to be sorry for. Jim says if you'd waited for his orders, you'd have died and other men with you."

"I didn't think I had a choice, sir."

"Nobody's questioning your judgment, Moss. We're lucky as hell you started getting the men out when you did. Going over authority when you know you have to is a sign of a leader. Lots of men won't do it, even if they know they're right. And you were."

"What if the bulkhead hadn't broke?"

"It did, and more men would've died if you hadn't followed your instincts."

"Hell, I didn't want to die. And everybody helped. Stub led us out through the air shaft."

"Enough modesty. You set it in motion, knowing you could get yourself in a lot of trouble if you were wrong."

"I'd have been wrong not to."

"Exactly my point." He took a long draw on his cigarette, coughed deeply and looked at a large map that covered the better part of one of the walls in his office. He pointed toward the wall. "Map of the whole operations. Go on. Take a look."

He followed me over to it. I found the drift under the river where the bulkhead had given way. *Fault Line* was written around the area. The drift that Steel and Preacher had been driving under the river was marked with a broken line.

Mr. Frazier pointed to it with his finger. "We still got us a mess down there."

"Yes, sir, we sure do. We got a pump going on the cage."

"Good. Get as many pumps going as you can, soon as it's safe to go into the yard area. We can still get the zinc under the river by going around the flooded area, driving a drift right here." He traced his finger along a line on the map. "It's a rich load. We don't want to lose it. I want my best men on it. Stub and his men, if he's able."

"Sir, it's not my place to say so, but none of that area is stable, and Stub don't hear the rumbling of balk ground no more. If it goes to popping, he won't know it. And the men are bad to ignore it so they can keep working. Let me and my men work with him. Stub and I are a good team, and an extra crew won't hurt."

He squinted his eyes and squashed out his cigarette. "That'd be two contractors in the same area at the same time. You and your men could do the job without Stub's crew."

"I figure the company'll come out good if it means doing the work in half the time, especially with the danger back there. When the floods let up, we can pull one crew off."

Mr. Frazier leaned against his desk, crossed his arms over his chest and stared at the map for a while without saying a word. Finally he said, "Sit back down a minute, son."

I figured I'd get a lecture about overstepping my bounds. While my stomach did somersaults, he went back to his chair, coughed and reached again for his pack of Luckies. He held it in his fist and ran his index finger over the top of it without taking a cigarette out. "My night shift foreman Ed Morgan got his eyes blown out showing Whitey where to drill the other day. I'm sure you know about that."

Whitey had been killed in that incident—the same kind of accident that killed my father and so many others, hitting a stick of dynamite that'd failed to go off in the initial blast. I wiped my forehead with my handkerchief and said, "Yes, I know." I tried to relax the set of my mouth and the veins throbbing in my neck.

He frowned and pulled out a cigarette. "I know your father died hitting misfired dynamite. Damn shame."

"Didn't have to happen. I've read that some of those kinds of accidents with dynamite can be prevented by having the men wash out the sockets of the drill holes."

"Where'd you read that?"

"In a mining journal."

He lit his cigarette, then said, "Where did you get a mining journal?"

"From Captain's office. We were talking about wet drilling, and he'd read an article about it so he loaned the journal to me."

Mr. Frazier pointed his cigarette at me and said, "I assume there's a point to this."

I cleared my throat. Washing out holes was a touchy subject. I was on balk ground. "I've got my men washing out the holes before they fire," I said. "If that'd been done when my paw was drilling, he might be alive today. Whitey, too. And Ed Morgan might still be able to see."

Mr. Frazier smoothed his graying moustache with his thumb and his index finger and looked at me through a cloud of smoke. "Well, son, we've all known about wetting holes for some time, but nobody wants to do it, especially the men. Gums up the drills. Foremen ignore it because the men put up such a fuss. Company ignores it because it slows up the mining process."

"It may slow up the drilling time a little, but time's cheaper than the lives of men."

"Nobody likes changes. How do you get your men to do it?"

"They're my men. I tell them to do it."

"That leadership quality in you is why I wanted to talk to you. You make it sound easy to get men to do what you say, but it's not. Takes a special kind of man. Like Jim Johnson. You remind me of him when he was younger. I need a new night shift foreman, and Johnson says you know more about mining than any contractor he's seen—except himself before he made foreman."

I smiled. "Captain's a fair man," I said. "Some managers would've been mad if I went over their head about shutting down the mine and would've fired me instead of recommending me for a promotion."

"Let's be honest. Most would've taken the credit themselves," Mr. Frazier said. "Jim's a good man. Picked him myself. He knows how to mine better than any man I've ever known. I swear, I think he can smell zinc. But he also knows how to work with the men—like you. It's been hard on him, moving through the ranks, giving orders to men that taught him to mine. He's dealt with resentment, anger, jealousy. It's been a fight all the way, but the men have come to respect him."

"I don't know anyone who doesn't," I said. "I've never known a more honest man."

"I'm sorry the position came open the way it did, but we've known for a long time you'd be the next foreman whenever we needed one. And I have to tell you, you'll be facing problems Jim didn't have. There's all this union talk now, as I'm sure you know. Men probably expect you to be a leader in that. They'll see you as a traitor."

From night shift foreman I'd move to day shift foreman, if I didn't mess up—or get killed. Of course I was worried about what would happen if a union came, but the chance for a staff position was what I'd worked so hard for. It was what Paw'd wanted.

Mr. Frazier was watching me, leaning back in his chair and blowing rings of smoke. Finally he said, "Want to think about it?"

"No, sir. I'll take the job. I'll do the best I can."

"I know you will, son."

"Thank you, sir," I stammered.

"Good to have you on staff, Moss."

"When do I start?"

"Right now. While the mine's still flooded, you'll work with Jim. You'll supervise at night, he'll take over in the day. You boys do whatever needs to be done with the pumps to get the mine in working order again. Work as many of your best men on your shift as you can rationalize to headquarters. Don't want to lose good miners while we're shut down." He paused and inhaled deeply. "I need to talk to you about something else. This may not be the right time. I was going to wait, but what the hell." He looked down at the cigarette in his hand for a moment, then squashed it out in a tin ashtray. "What I'm about to tell you is not to be spread around yet. Just between me and you, understand?"

"Yes, sir."

"News'll get out soon enough. But there's a lot going on with the flood and men getting laid off and union rumblings. Don't want to scare everybody with too many fast changes. But this is the deal—Jim Johnson's being promoted to superintendent."

"You're retiring?"

"Oh, no, not yet. What I mean is, Jim's going to take Mr. Walker's place at our mine in New Mexico."

"New Mexico? Captain's going to New Mexico?" Jim Johnson was a legend in Outcropping. I couldn't believe he'd ever leave, even for a promotion.

"That's right," he said. "Hate to see him go, especially right now, but I can't hold him back just because I'm caught between a rock and a hard place. He's given too much of his life to this mine as it is. When he leaves, you'll take his place, that is, if you want the job, and we'll bring in a man to take your place for the night shift. Jim says you know this operation as well as he does. I'm counting on it. So, that's the long-range plan. You'll work with him on the night shift till he leaves. What'd you say?"

"It's all so fast. You think I'm ready?"

"I wouldn't be offering you the job if I didn't think you were ready. And no matter how you cut it, I've got to get two new foremen quick. It's rare to lose both so near the same time. I could have the company send in a man to take Jim's place, but the men'll resent an outsider even more than they'll resent you. Things are tense enough as it is. God only knows what's going to happen. So, I'm laying it on the line. Bringing you on at this time serves a two-fold purpose. Jim says you want changes and you'll work through the company or the union to get them, whoever gives you the chance first, and he also says whoever has you on their side's got the advantage." He ran his hand through his thinning hair and took out another cigarette.

"Since you're shooting straight with me," I said, "I'm going to do the same. If I'd stayed in the ranks, I probably would have joined the union. For years I've seen men get hurt and killed for no good reason. Heaven knows, there's enough dangers that can't get fixed. But some things can be done to help. If the company'd done some of those things, union might not've gotten a foothold."

Mr. Frazier sat staring at me, his unlit cigarette dangling from his fingers. It was hard to tell what he was thinking.

"Way I see it," I said, "it's in the company's best interest to make some changes, or this union thing can get real nasty." I took a deep breath and added, "I know the men's got to work with the company, too. There're some real hotheads you can't please no matter what you do, but there's also lots of good men who'll listen to reason. Maybe I can help, if you still want me—and if I don't get killed." I worked at a laugh, but Mr. Frazier never cracked a smile.

178

He ran his fingers down his cigarette and tapped it against his desk, then lit it slowly, watching me all the while. "I'm glad you understand the men's grievances," he said. "We have been dragging our feet about making changes. But both sides will have to give some. If things get too bad, the company'll pull out. They'd lose a good load of zinc here, and the men'd lose their jobs. Wouldn't be good for nobody. But with the economy like it is, it's a possibility. I'd like to keep it from happening, and I think you can help us. But you have to decide where your allegiance lies. It's going to be hell for you either way. If you decide to stay with the men and join the union, I can respect that, and at least we'd be dealing with a union leader that's open to reason."

"If you still want me," I said, "I'll stay with the company."

"It's a big promotion, especially moving to day shift, but you'll pay dearly for it." He coughed hard, then said, "This union thing's like a tidal wave that's building up, and you're going to be right in the goddamn middle. But I'm glad you're with us. Now, go out there and earn that foreman's salary."

We shook hands, and I hoped I was doing the right thing. The promotion was the fulfillment of a dream for me and maybe a way to help the men, so why did I feel like Benedict Arnold?

Stub

Moss came by the house the day he made head foreman. Asked me if I felt well enough to sit on the porch, said he wanted to talk to me. I took a blanket out as it was getting late in the day. We propped our feet up on a post, and he said, "Turning fall."

"Yeah, getting grayer'n usual," I said. "I hate to see cold weather come. Gets in my bones."

He cleared his throat and said, "I need to tell you something."

"Shoot."

"You might not like it, "he said.

Then he told me about his promotion. I was surprised, but reckon I shouldn't have been.

"It's what I've always worked for, you know that," he said. "But it's come at a rough time with all this union talk."

"You know that's why they want you."

"Yeah. They're probably hoping I can do something to change the men's minds."

"Don't think you can," I said.

"Me neither, and the company won't like that, and the men'll resent me for becoming staff."

"They gave Johnson a hell of a time when he went staff," I said, "and he didn't have to deal with all this union stuff. Might be, you ought to give it some more thought."

"But what if we don't get the union established? There's still a lot of changes that needs to be made." He grinned and said, "Like enforcing the rule about not cutting fuses short."

"Even the union'll have a hard time enforcing that one." I laughed, which caused me to cough. "But, mark my word, the union will happen. And I don't want you to get caught in the crossfire."

"Between you and me," Moss said, "I hope the union does come. Don't think any serious changes will happen if it don't. The men did probably think I'd be a part of it. Guess I would've been if

I hadn't already made foreman. But there's going to be foremen whether there's a union or not. Maybe we can all work together to make life a little better for the men and their families—and even for the company. Without the company none of us has a job."

"Maybe," I said.

"Well, it's got to be better if someone on staff cares about the men and understands what their lives are like. You'll still be my friend, won't you?"

"What kind of fool question is that?"

"I'm sure I'll lose some friends over this."

"You will," I said, "but not me. And, you might make some friends, too. You're right, union or not, they'll always be foremen. And it'll be better if one of them is you. I just hope you don't get hurt. But you got to do what you think is right. That's all any of us can do."

We sat and rocked for a few minutes, neither of us saying nothing. Moss just stared out at the evening sky. Reminded me of the picture we got of a Indian sitting on a horse, no saddle or nothing to hold on to, just looking up at the sky, with his arms out to his side, like he's lost between two worlds.

When I moved into Captain's office, one of the first things I did was to get a job for Cleve. I'd sworn to myself I'd get him a job if I ever could.

Cleve's father had died the previous year in a dynamite accident, and Cleve and his mother had to move out of their home. The miners' houses were so small that neither his brother or sister and their families had room for them both, so his mother moved in with Cleve's brother, and Cleve moved in with his sister Maude and her family. Cleve still worked at odd jobs when he could get them, but he had no security of a home if Maude's husband died. If Cleve worked for the company, he could qualify for a house or he could live in the dormitory.

I knew the company wouldn't consider him for an underground job, but one day I was in Mr. Frazier's office shortly after Captain had left and we were working on plans for a new cross-cut, and that was when I knew how to get Cleve on. Dust was everywhere, even more than usual. I wiped it off the table and even the map with the back of my hand. Finally I hunted for a rag. Then Mr. Frazier wanted some coffee. There was an old pot on a stove in a corner of his office, but he said he didn't know how to make it, and I said I'd do it. The coffee left in the pot looked like it'd been there for days.

"It'll take me a few minutes," I said. "Got to clean the pot first."

He said he was sorry, that old Zeke who had cleaned the offices for years had been off more than he'd been on over the past months, and he didn't really think he'd come back to work this time. Said Zeke's lungs were about to get him, and he was moving in with his daughter and her husband.

"Don't you think it's time for us to get a new man?" I said while I scrubbed the pot. "This whole building is a mess."

He said he'd been putting it off in case Zeke did come back. He didn't want to hurt his feelings.

"We still need someone who can work hard and get this building cleaned up," I said. "If Zeke comes back, he's not going to be able to work like he did. There's enough for two to do, anyway."

As the coffee began to perk and the smell made us anxious for a cup, Mr. Frazier asked if I had someone in mind. I said, yes. He said, get him, and I did. He didn't even ask me who it was, and he was shocked when Cleve came to work with me the next day. I told him to give Cleve a chance, that he could do anything. We went through the whole thing about him not being able to hear or speak, but I finally convinced him to give him a two weeks' trial period. I told him Cleve could understand most anything anyone said to him.

The day before, when I'd gone to tell Cleve about the job, his sister Maude answered the door. "Come on in this house, Moss McCullen," she said. "It's been a spell since you been here."

"Too long," I said. "Been mighty busy at work."

"I know you have. We're so proud of you, making foreman and all. My husband, he's so glad you're the boss."

"He is?"

"He sure is."

"Well, he's probably one of the few."

"Now that aint true, Moss," she said. "You got lots of friends, spite of this union talk."

"Well, thanks for saying that," I said.

"Lord a mercy, it don't seem no time, you and Cleve and that Avery Hought used to go down to that smelly old trash dump and shoot rats. Don't seem possible. All you was just boys. Time moves on, don't it?" She sighed and said, "I'm forgetting my manners. How about a cup of coffee?"

"That sounds mighty good. Cleve around?"

"Why yes, he is. He's out back chopping wood. He'll be ready for a break. You two can have coffee and I'll let you boys visit."

"I'll go get him," I said. "I need to talk to him, anyway."

183

"You're the only person in the world that ever really talks to Cleve," she said, "except me and Mama. We've always loved you for that."

I looked toward the back door and said, "He's my friend, Maude. He was since I first came here as a kid. He never quits being my friend. He don't care if I'm a stock boy or a roustabout or foreman."

About that time, Cleve came in. He held out a long, skinny hand to me after wiping it on his overalls.

"Hey, Cleve," I said, "how're you doing?"

He smiled and nodded his head. I never knew how Cleve could understand most of what anyone said if he was looking at them and if you did a little gesturing for effect.

"I came over to see if I could interest you in a job. Work."

Maude was starting to pour coffee, and she stood there, with the pot slightly tilted. Cleve put his hand on his chest.

"Yes, you," I said. "Want a job? We need us a man to clean the General Office Building." I pointed in the direction of the mine and moved around as though I was sweeping and dusting.

Cleve grinned and nodded.

I looked at Maude and said, "Poor old Zeke's not well and won't be with us much longer, if at all. We need somebody we can count on."

She sat the pot down and leaned against the back of the nearest chair.

"Be sure he's ready by 6:00 in the morning. I'll come by and walk with him on my way to work. Take him to the office."

I held up six fingers to Cleve. He grabbed my hand again and pumped it up and down.

Maude took my other hand and said, "How can we ever thank you, Moss?"

I said they might be cussing me after a few days. I told her there was a lot to do, that Zeke hadn't done much for a long time and the place was a mess. "We'll show him what we need done, Maude. I know once he gets used to it, he'll do fine."

184

She wiped the corners of her eyes with her apron. "They'd never of hired him if it wasn't for you."

I tried to tell her that wasn't true, but she said, "Yes, it is. I know that. But you'll be proud. I promise you that. He can do anything. Why, he makes enough money just doing odd jobs to support hisself. We don't never have to give him a dime, except to feed him. We won't be forgetting you for this, Moss."

"Money's not great, but they'll pay him like they would anybody else. I'll see to that. I've wanted to do this for a long time. Sorry I couldn't do it before now." I looked at Cleve, pointed to Maude's coffee pot, acted like I was drinking from a cup, and told him to be sure Mr. Frazier had a fresh pot of coffee every day. If he did, he'd keep him on forever. Cleve did, and he set into cleaning the office from top to bottom. He was so thankful to have a job that Mr. Frazier said he had to make him take a lunch break. Said he wished he'd had Cleve working for years.

Moss sure made the most out of the fact that we had to run the pumps around the clock to keep the water down. Lots of them were so old we had to work on them all the time. Company was too cheap to get new ones. But it gave Moss a great chance to push his weight around, always ordering us to work on this pump or that pump.

One day he come up to where I was working on a motor and said, "Where's the pump Gadget said he told you to fix?" Didn't even say, Hey, Avery, how're you doing, kiss my foot, or nothing, just "Where's the pump?" Like I knew which pump he was talking about. I was always fixing a damn pump.

I kept working on the motor and said, "Hell, they's always a pump needing to be fixed. Right now I'm working on this motor. Sometimes something breaks down besides a pump."

"If we don't keep the pumps going," he said, "it won't matter what else breaks because we'll have to close the mine."

I got that. I didn't want the mine closed any more than nobody else, but he had to add, like a bigshot, "Don't act like you don't know what I'm talking about. I just spoke to Gadget and he said he told you to fix it and to get it to us."

"Keep your shirt on," I said, trying my best not to throw my wrench at him. "I'll get to it. You'll get your pump."

"Get to it now," he ordered, his words slow and heavy.

I slammed my wrench against the motor and said, "Aint we the high and mighty one these days?"

"What's that supposed to mean?" he said, like he couldn't understand English.

I spat and said, "You're always throwing your weight around, giving orders anytime you get the chance, even when you know something's going to get done anyway."

"It doesn't look to me like the pump's getting fixed. It was supposed to have already been working again. I'm just doing my job, Avery. What's wrong with you? Why're you always mad? Always wanting a confrontation."

I stood up and stepped away from the motor, still gripping my wrench. "Aint nothing wrong with me. Aint me that's become a company man and left my friends."

"I didn't leave nobody," he said. "We all work for the company."

I pointed the wrench at him and said, "Where you gonna be when the union comes in, huh? Tell me that, boss man. We all thought you'd help us. Now you're gonna be our enemy."

He took a step back and said, "Just 'cause I can't join the union don't make me anybody's enemy."

"Well, you sure as hell aint gonna be on our side," I yelled. "Company's agin the union."

"They're not against the men. They're scared of the union. They're not sure where this is all going. In time, though, the company and the union'll have to work together to help the miners."

I shook the wrench and said, "Company's not gonna do one shitting thing for us unless it has to. That's why we need the union."

He was too stupid or too cocky to know how close I was to smashing his head in. All he said was, "With or without the union, the company'll do more if there're men in it that cares."

"Oh, yeah, men like you, huh? Shit, you don't care about nothing but your own hide. You just think your're better'n us and always have to have a good job. That's all you've ever cared about. Company's got you locked in tighter'n a bulkhead. Don't you know, you gonna be the hard wall the company'll use to try to stop the flow? They only want you 'cause you're big and stupid and strong." I pointed the wrench at his face again and said, "But you can't stop it, no more'n you can stop the Holston from flowing. Can't nobody."

He spread his feet and took in a deep breath, like he thought I was going to lunge at him. I knew him well enough to know if I took a step towards him, he'd take me on, even with the wrench in my hand. Then, win or lose, he'd fire me. That was the only thing that kept me from attacking him. But for a moment I thought he was going to come at me.

Instead he straightened and said, "Well, heaven knows I can't control everything, but I can see that the pump gets fixed so the men can use it. You're slowing them up. Now lower that wrench and go fix it. Or use it for what you want to, and we'll get this thing settled once and for all."

I cursed and threw the wrench down. "Yes, sir, bossman. I'll fix your precious pump, but remember, they's them in this mine that don't like staff. If I was you, I'd be looking over my shoulder."

"You threatening me, Avery?"

I stared hard at him and said, "Hell, no, man. That aint no threat. That's a warning. In case you don't know, you aint exactly the most loved person in this here mine. I can fix the damn pump, but I can't fix hard feelings. You best be careful."

I got Moss to help me get on at the mine just about the time all the union fires were heating up. I knew he wouldn't want me in the mine, or Maw either. All I'd heard my whole life was how I was going to college. I did want to go to college, had to, because I wanted to be a doctor for animals or people. Wasn't sure which, but I wanted to go to medical school, and didn't want Moss to put me through. I'd heard enough of how he'd given up his childhood for all of us. I wanted everybody to see I could do something for myself. I'd started school when I was four. Maw let me go so she could work, and I begged to go with Ellie. I'd graduated from high school early and was young to start college, so I figured I could work in the mine two or three years and make some money. I don't think Moss or Maw had any idea how many years or how much money my education would take.

Moss and I'd never really talked, so I didn't know how to begin to ask him to help me get on. One day when we were in the barn after a day's work, I finally just blurted out that I wanted him to get me a job at the mine to make some money for college. He was unhitching the mule, and he stopped right in the middle of it. He stared at me like he'd never seen me. To him I was always the little brother he had to take care of.

"You aint going to the mine," he said.

"Got a better idea?"

"Keep working here at the farm and over at Mr. Lindsey's for a year or so more. You're too young to go to the mine."

"I can't hang around here all that time. I need to be making real money. It's my education we're talking about. Lots of boys my age work at the mine. You did."

"You don't know what it's like," he said, "and besides Maw would never agree to it. She'd kill us both."

"It'll take years for me to study to be a doctor, Moss," I said, "It'll cost a lot. I'm still young for college. I can work till I'm twenty or so, save my money."

"I can put you through."

"Maybe, but that aint the point," I said. "I want to do it. You don't have to do everything for everybody. If you don't help me get on, I'll find another job. But you know I can't make as much money anywhere else around here."

"I want you to live to spend it."

"I will. I'll do whatever job that's open."

"Aint as many jobs as there used to be. I wouldn't mind so bad if I could get you something on the surface, but I know you'd have to start as roustabout, like everybody else. Underground, doing a little bit of everything."

"Let me try. If I don't suit you after a few weeks, I'll come back home, get another job."

He took me back with him when he left, but he wasn't happy. Maw was so upset she hardly spoke to either of us the day we headed to Outcropping. I moved in with Moss and Aunt Minnie. He told her he didn't expect her to take care of me, that it was too much for her to do my laundry and cook for me and that he was going to get someone to help her. She said from the looks of me I didn't need taking care of. I just needed a home. But he insisted, saying she needed someone to help her anyway.

Aunt Minnie was real good to me. And so was Maggie who Moss got to work for us. I missed Maw and my sisters, but it wasn't long before I began to feel at home.

Things went okay until the miners got really serious about establishing a union. They all knew I was Moss's brother, and since he was a part of the staff, they didn't trust either one of us, except some of Moss's real good friends like Stub and Gadget and George Haskell that Moss'd gone to school with when they were both young. Moss really wanted me to quit, but I wasn't ready to. Working in the mine was hard work, but I'd have died before I admitted it. Some nights I could hardly move. The worst part was feeling closed in by the earth and the darkness. No matter how much the mine was lit up, it was still dark. I got used to it, but I never liked it, not like Moss.

Moss

As union talk got more heated, whenever I'd come up on men talking, they'd shut up. One day I went up to a table where some of them, including Avery, were eating their lunches to get two men to work on the opening of a new drift. Anger hung like a black cloud, so I decided against sitting down for a few minutes, as I normally would have done.

Instead, I just told Abe Black and Isaac when they got through to come on up to the north drift to drill the new heading and I'd meet them there in a few minutes. Abe never liked to take orders, always had a way of making it look as though he were doing you a favor when he did as he was told. It wasn't a good idea to give him the job, especially as he had an audience to show out in front of, but he and Isaac needed a new assignment, and I wanted somebody experienced to open the new heading.

He stuck his hands under his overall straps, stretched his heavy legs out like two big logs and said, "What you want to open a new drift out thataway for, Chief? Company tell you that's where the ore's at? How's a old country boy like you that don't know nothing 'bout nothing but upping the counters know what's behind that hard rock?"

The men laughed. I was used to them making jokes about my days at the commissary, especially when they didn't agree with me. This time Abe's face was red and distorted. It would've been easier to open the wall of rock than to change Abe's hard head.

"There's ore there," I said. "Bring twenty-five detonators and dynamite and let's shoot the heading."

"Maybe I will." He looked around the table at the other men who began to sneer, and he added, "Maybe I won't. What'd you think, Isaac?"

Isaac grinned and spat.

Abe pointed in the opposite direction and said, "Think maybe we'll just drive us a drift over yonderways,"

192

I looked at them, then at the other men. I wished I'd asked any other miner to drill the heading even if Abe'd sat around idle all afternoon, but it was too late to change the order. "Drill where you're told," I said. "You, too, Isaac."

Isaac started to get up, but Abe rubbed his whiskers and said, "I know as much about where they's ore as you do. And I'm a gonna blow over there."

The men yelled encouragement, anxious to see what he'd do—or more importantly what I'd do. If I ignored the situation, I'd never have any respect from them. I'd not had a real run-in with Abe before, but I'd heard about the famous fight between him and Jim Johnson many years before. The men said it was like two bulls going at it. Abe'd wound up with a broken nose and some days off work without pay, and Jim had gotten a black eye. Jim could've fired Abe, and at that moment I sure wished he had.

I stared at Abe and said, "Ore body's ahead of you there in the drift, and that's where we're going. You and Isaac get the dynamite and detonators like I said and come on. The rest of you men finish your lunch and get back to work."

Abe glared at me. He got up and stepped away from the table. He was a bulky man with a crooked nose and a scar across his left cheek that ran from his jaw line to the corner of his eye. I'd heard it was a result of a drunken fight which'd left the other man dead. But that'd happened years before I came to Outcropping. Apparently self-defense had been the excuse, and no action was taken.

"What if'n I say I aint going to do it?" Abe said, tightening his fists.

"Either do it or get your things and leave," I said, trying to watch both him and Isaac, who'd also gotten up and moved around to the left of me.

Abe spat a brown stream of tobacco juice and said, "You firing me, Chief? I don't think so. I aint going nowheres. And you aint gonna make me, neither."

"It's one or the other, Abe."

"Then I reckon you going to have to try to make me. You as good as Johnson, boy?"

I glanced back at the table. I couldn't take all the men on, and wasn't sure if I had any backers among them. I wasn't even sure about Avery, who gave no indication as to whether he would be with me or against me. He wasn't jeering, but he wasn't trying to stop it.

I knew it'd be the fight of my life. Abe outweighed me by a good fifty pounds, but he was a few years older than when he'd fought Jim. I hoped none of the other men would jump in. Abe moved toward me while Isaac circled around to my backside. I glanced from one to the other.

Abe lunged at me and threw a powerful blow at my face. It'd have knocked me down for sure, but I ducked and drove my fist hard into his over-sized belly. He slumped, but Isaac kicked me across my lower legs from the back and my feet flew out from under me. My instincts told me to roll. As I did, Isaac dropped a big rock where my face would've been. A rough edge of it caught my right shoulder. I jumped up and swung a punch at his face with my left hand so fast that he didn't dodge, and his jaw popped like a broken cable. Blood spurted over his face as his jaw flopped loose, and he fell to the ground.

I looked back towards Abe who was now coming at me with a shovel, looking like a big cave man carrying his club into battle. Out of the corner of my eye I saw the men from the table moving in on me from my left.

Abe saw, too, and grinned. "What now, company man? You gonna beat us all up? I got this here shovel I'm gonna kill you with and bury you with, too. Say yore prayers. Only God aint down here."

He took a step forward, holding the shovel in front of him with both hands. His eyes bore into me like drill bits. I knew there was no stopping this flow, but I decided to take care of Abe before the others got to us. I had to act quickly, but suddenly Abe stood still. The other men stopped moving, too. They were looking to my right, and I glanced around quickly and saw a group of black workers led by Lightning—including Big Jim—carrying their shovels and sledgehammers. LC was with them. He moved towards me, but Lightning held him back. About that time Stub, Gadget, Cleve's brother-in-law Winston, George Haskell and a few other miners came running toward us.

Gadget stepped out from the group. He thrust out his chest and said, "This here aint right. You fellers know it. Aint fair, one man again two, let alone again all you'ens." He gripped a hammer and jerked it forward. "Now stay back, I say, and let Chief and Abe fight it out or, by God, you'll be taking us all on." He looked at Avery and said, "Get your ass over here."

No one moved, except Avery. I watched Abe. His face had turned an ugly shade of red, except for his white scar. Suddenly he roared like a wild beast, raised his shovel above his right shoulder and ran at me. He swung the shovel toward my head, but I ducked as it whipped above me. As he missed, he was off balance, and I jerked the shovel from him, threw it to the side and lunged at him, taking him to the ground in a thud. Abe gasped for breath. I got off him, grabbed the shovel and stood over him with one foot on his chest and both my hands holding the shovel above his neck. I was ready to push it all the way to his backbone.

Stub ran up and said, "Don't do it, Chief."

"Back off, Stub," I said, breathing hard.

Abe raised one hand in a pleading motion. I raised the shovel and brought it down with all my might beside his face. He arched his body and yelled, then lay limp when he saw he wasn't hit.

I threw the shovel aside and said, "Get up. Get your things and get out." I looked at Isaac who was holding his jaw with bloody hands. I pointed at him and said, "You're lucky I'm not firing you, too. You're off for a week without pay." I looked at Avery who started to say something, but I interrupted him and said, "You and George take Isaac topside. Use the company truck and get him to Doc's."

I pitched the keys to him and he said, "Moss, you know I wouldn't have. . ."

"I don't know nothing," I said. "Just get Isaac to Doc's, and the name's Chief." I turned to the men who had been ready to attack me and said, "Anybody else got anything to prove?" No one moved or said a word. "Then get back to work," I said.

They all went back to their jobs. I should've fired all their sorry asses. I rubbed my sore shoulder and looked toward the group of men who had come to my defense and said, "Thanks." They nodded and started back to work, too. I said, "Stub, you and your men leave what you're working on and start on the north drift for now. Gadget, you and Winston see to it that Abe gets his gear and leaves the mine. Go along with them, Lightning, and if he gives them any trouble, come get me."

———————————

The next day, Aunt Minnie stayed off work. She'd been staying home more and more often. I'd never known her to miss work in the past. All she'd say was that she was tired and that her back was bothering her. We'd moved from Lowtown to Engineer's Row when I made head foreman, and we had an inside bath and a tub she could soak in. I'd fixed her a swing on the front porch and made the garden along the edge of the porch so she could see the flowers when she sat outside. I'd always wanted some flowers, ever since I'd seen them decorate the houses on the Hill.

Aunt Minnie came to the table after me and LC had already eaten. She looked as though it hurt to put one foot in front of the other. I poured her a cup of coffee and sat down.

"You want me to fix you some eggs?"

"No, no, you don't have time. Maggie'll be along soon. She'll take care of me. What a mess I've come to, having folks wait on me. And they's so much to do at the store. I feel awful not going in."

"You don't owe them nothing."

"I know you're thinking they don't pay me enough for me to fret about it. But at least I got me a job. What do you think I'd have done when Hubert died, God rest his soul, if I hadn't had my work? Company kept me on, and I didn't have to move out of our house. I worked hard and made them need me so bad they wouldn't trade me in on no man. Reckon they took advantage of the fact that I had to be needed, but that aint so bad. Feels good to be needed." Her eyes disappeared into a smile. "And they want me all right, I seen to that."

"I guess they'll close the doors when you quit," I said.

She smiled and said, "Life goes on, don't it? The world can move on without any of us. Reckon I'll have to put in my notice. What would you think about that?"

"You know what I think." I squeezed her knotted hand. I'd been trying to get her to quit for a long time. She kept saying folks were supposed to work as long as they were alive. I was so worried about her, I finally talked to Doc. He'd said she might risk getting hurt by continuing to work but, on the other hand, maybe working helped her forget about her pain. At any rate, he'd said, let her be the one to make the decision. It's not just the money, he said. She knows she's got a home with you, but she'd feel useless. He said there were worse things than dying on your feet.

I told Aunt Minnie I had to get going or they'd fire me and we'd both be without a job. "You get Maggie to fix you a salts bath to soak in after you eat breakfast."

I packed LC's and my lunches. He gave Aunt Minnie a peck on the cheek as he picked up his pail and went out on the porch to wait for me. I said I'd be on out in a minute.

"He likes to spend a few minutes with his pets before he goes to work, don't he?" Aunt Minnie said. "Lord, we're going to have us a regular Noah's ark here if he picks up any more strays."

"I'll say something to him about that."

"Oh, no, I didn't mean that. Leave him alone. Gives him something useful to do when he's off. Everybody's got to have something or someone that needs him."

I went over and put a hand on her shoulder. "I'm real glad you've decided to quit. It's time."

"Knowing it and liking it's two different things." She tried to look up at me, but put her hand on her neck and rubbed it.

"Don't strain," I said, and knelt beside her.

She reached for my hand. When she squeezed it, I was surprised at the strength she still had.

"You be careful today, and watch out for LC," she said. "I know they's problems at the mine. Me and Maggie'll have you all a good supper when you come home tonight, something special."

I'd tried to make excuses for my torn shirt and sore shoulder when I'd come home the day before, but I was sure she'd heard comments before she'd left that day. The commissary was better than a party line for the spreading of news.

"Don't worry," I said. "We'll be all right."

Maggie

The day of the blast I went to work like always. Aunt Annie got me the job working for Mr. Moss when his little brother come to Outcropping and moved in with him and Aunt Minnie. He asked Annie about working for them. She say she appreciate his offer, but she can't do him a good job no more. She too old and she can't take his money. When he asked her if she know anyone he could get, she tell him me, and I been working ever since.

After I left Mr. Rogers when I was going to have my baby, I swear I never work for no white folks again. I learn right quick that they use you for whatever they want. When it comes down to it, that's what you are to them—something to be used, and that's all. When they finish, you out the door. But Annie tell me I be happy working for Mr. Moss and Aunt Minnie, to give it a try, and I aint regretted it one day. Mostly aint nobody home while I work at Mr. Moss's, but that day when I go in, Aunt Minnie sitting at the kitchen table, sipping on a cup of coffee. That's been happening more and more often.

"Why, Aunt Minnie," I say, "you feeling poorly again?"

"Just a little tired," she say, but her face was pinched and gray. I ask her if she had any breakfast, and she say no. I fix her some eggs and biscuits. She got to where she eat like a bird, but I tell her Thelma sent her some of her blackberry jam, and she try to eat a little.

"Why don't you let me fix you in there on the couch," I say, "and you can prop your feet up and rest."

She stare at the table. "I'm going to get plenty of rest soon enough."

I refilling her coffee cup and shake so I spill it over into the saucer.

She must've read my mind, and she say, "I aint gonna die, at least not yet. I mean I'm quitting work, soon as I give notice." I breathe a sigh of relief, and she add, "Sinful, aint it? And me with you to wait on me hand and foot. Never thought I'd live to see the day I'd quit work, let alone have somebody cooking my breakfast."

I tell her she done earned her rest. She don't need to go feeling bad 'bout it.

She sit up straight as her back would let her, and she say, "Folks don't earn no rest, Maggie. Long as the good Lord gives a body breath, why, a person ought to pull their weight. A body's got to have a purpose, you know."

"You think you aint got a purpose?" I say. "Your job is to let us all enjoy having you around."

She patted my hand. "You're a good person." Then she just sat silent and run her finger along the rim of her plate. Finally she say, "Never thought I'd have nobody to take care of me when I got old. Just figured I'd die on my feet. Hoped I would, still hope I will, but we never know what the good Lord has in store for us, do we?"

"We surely don't," I said.

"I never had no kids, I mean, none of my own, you know," she said, "and I didn't have nobody to fall back on. But my maw always used to say that there wasn't no kindness done that weren't paid back twofold, and I reckon it's the truth. There I was all them years ago, a taking some poor hungry kid home, a meaning to do him a kindness, and here he is helping me more'n I ever helped him. Nothing would do him when he moved in this fine house but for me to move with him. Now here he's got me to see to."

"That aint the way folks around here see it," I say, "and that aint the way Mr. Moss see it. You been good to him as his own mama, and he loves you. He wouldn't know what to do without you."

She sniffed, raised her head as high as she could and sighed. "I aint gonna complain no more. Onliest thing worse'n a body that don't work is a body that gripes." She press both of her hands flat against the top of the table and say, "That's enough talk about a old woman. How's your little boy, Maggie?"

200

"Oh, David, he doing real good," I say. "So healthy and smart. I sure is lucky. Yes, ma'am, aint no complaining here. I aim to bring him over and let you see him one of these days."

"I wish you would," she say. Then she ask me, don't I miss being with him.

"Yes'um, I do. But Annie, she take care of him when I work. She been a real help to me. When everybody else fussing at me for a having him and seeing him like he just another mouth to feed— and worse, me not married at the time and all—Annie, she take care of us and she say to everbody, 'Looky here, world, look at my grandbaby.' She call him her grandbaby. Aint nobody in Shantytown going to say nothing to Annie, so they accept him, too. And he so good for her. She lost her 'baby' as she call that white girl she raised. She left town and don't even send Annie so much as a card or letter. Anyway, she pining for her until she have my boy to take care of. And it all come around, see, Aunt Minnie, because some day she be need'n us, me and my boy, and we be there for her, like Mr. Moss here for you. Aint no shame in that. They's honor."

Aunt Minnie rub her hand across her eyes. "Thank you for that, Maggie. You're wise for your years." Then she start to get up, but grab onto the table for support.

I run up and say, "Where is it you wants to go? You wants to take a nice salts bath? I fix it for you."

She say, "No, not yet. Maybe later. I thought I might go sit in my swing and enjoy the morning sun and my fall flowers. Did you notice my asters that Moss planted, all red and yellow and purple?

"Why, I seen them bright colors first thing as I walk up to the house, and I think to myself, my, aint them pretty flowers. Made me feel better, just looking at them."

"You pick you some to take home with you," she say. "Take Annie some."

"I'll do that, but it's a bit chilly to be out there this morning. You sure you want to sit outside?"

"I am. I won't get to enjoy my flowers much longer." I raise my eyebrows and she say, "Now, don't get the wrong idea again. All I mean is it'll be getting too cold soon, and the frost'll get them. I best be enjoying them while I can."

I laugh a little and say, "Well, if that's what you wants, we get you a pillow and a couple of quilts and I wrap you up all snug as a caterpillar in a cocoon if you done set on going out."

"Thank you. I'd like that."

I put a quilt under Aunt Minnie and one over her and propped her up with a couple of pillows. "You sure you be all right? They's a chill in the air. Want another hot cup of coffee to help keep you warm?"

"No, no," she say. "I'm fine." LC's cat Hopper jump up with her, and she pull him close to her. She say, "He's warm."

"Then keep him with you," I say, and go back to the kitchen, leaving the door open so I can keep an eye on her and hear her if she ask for anything.

After cleaning the kitchen, I go to the living room. I look out and she just laying in the swing, rubbing the cat and mumbling to him about the pretty flowers, like he was human. I dusting around in the living room when I hear a loud truck, speeding down the street.

Aunt Minnie say, "Well, lawsy me. What a way to bring something by a body's house."

I look out the window and she pushing aside the quilt, trying to get up to see what'd been thrown into the flowers. I head for the door to tell her not to try to get it when I hear the truck screech to a halt. I come to the door in time to see a big man get out and yell, "No! No! Get back."

The next thing I hear a big blast and find myself laying under a heap of planks and busted furniture. I can't see nothing. The front of the house all blown in. I yell, "Aunt Minnie! Aunt Minnie! Oh, Lord, don't let this be happening, please, Jesus, don't let this be happening."

Then I hear Miss Marie, the next door lady, hollering our names. I yell back and say I'm in the house. Then I don't remember nothing till I hear my name being called again. I open my eyes and some neighbor ladies moving stuff off me.

They say, "You all right? What on earth happened?"

I say I don't know, maybe the world coming to an end, but please get Aunt Minnie.

They say where is she, that the porch is all fallen in, that they hope none of LC's cats there.

"*She* on the porch. She out there."

Miss Marie say, "Oh, God, no. What was she doing on the porch?"

"Resting on the swing, looking at her flowers. Find her, please."

They get me out from under all the rubble, then they plow through the glass and boards and try to get to her, but they can't lift enough stuff. Shortly some men come running, and they uncover what was left of that poor old soul. They tell us women to go to the kitchen. Miss Marie wash my cuts and check me out for broken bones, but I fine 'cept scared to death and sick at heart. I say, "I got to clean up the house."

Miss Marie say, "We'll clean up. Mr. McCullen will be here soon. You come with me to my house till someone can take you home. I'll fix some coffee for you."

I grab her arm and say again, "*She* on the porch! Oh, God, *she* on the porch!"

"We know, honey, we know, but we can't do nothing now. And you need to rest. Come with me." She led me over to her house and put me on her couch, propped my feet up and fixed coffee for me.

About 8:30 the morning of the blast, Mr. Frazier sent word for me to come topside and report to his office. He rarely called me up. If he needed something, he saw me before I went under or when I came up at the end of the day.

The door to his office was ajar, and I knocked softly. He told me to come in. He was leaning against the edge of his desk, and he pointed to a chair. "Sit down, please."

I sat, but he remained standing.

"What is it?" I said. "What's wrong?"

"I have some bad news, son. Real bad news."

I had the same feeling of dread I'd felt on that bitter February morning fifteen years ago.

"It's Aunt Minnie."

I gripped the sides of the chair. "I've been afraid she'd fall. She's so frail these days."

Mr. Frazier lit a cigarette. He offered me one. I shook my head. "She didn't fall," he said. "She's. . . she's dead."

My heart stopped. I felt as though I'd fallen off a ledge in the mine. I knocked away tears with the back of my hand and finally muttered, "No, no. She can't be dead. There must be a mistake. She was fine when I left. I mean, she was tired and stayed at home, but it was the usual thing with her back. Maggie was with her."

"I'm so sorry," he said, "but there's no mistake."

I slumped back into the chair and tried to breathe deeply. "How?" I finally said. "What happened?"

He held his Lucky Strike out at arm length, stared at it and frowned. "It was dynamite."

I jumped up and said, "Dynamite?'

"Somebody threw it at your house. I'm sure no one meant to hurt anybody. Just scare you. Whatever sorry son of a bitch that threw the dynamite probably figured no one would be home in the morning." He shook his head and said, "Wouldn't have hurt her even then if she hadn't been on the porch."

"The porch? She was on the porch?"

He nodded. "Seems she was in the swing, enjoying her flowers, and somebody threw dynamite into the flower bed." He squashed out his cigarette into the ashtray on the desk and said, "Damn union bunch, no doubt."

I reeled around to the map and smashed my hand into the site of the fight. "It was him."

"Nobody saw it happen. Maggie said when she was going to the porch to check on her, she saw a heavy-set man running from the area of your yard across the street to a black truck, but she didn't know who it was. Some of the neighbor ladies said they heard an old truck speeding down the road, but no one paid it any mind until they heard the explosion. At that point they all ran to your house. I'm afraid whoever did it got away."

Still staring at the area of the fight, I said, "I know it was Abe. You know it, too. I should have killed the son of a bitch when I had the chance. I wanted to. I really wanted to." I turned back around, looked at Mr. Frazier and said through clinched teeth, "If I ever see him this side of the grave, I will. I swear to God I will."

"I'm sure he knows that, and I'm sure he'll never show his face in Outcropping again."

————————————

"Dust to dust" the preacher kept saying. I'd thought I'd finally gotten Aunt Minnie away from the worst of the dust when we moved to Engineers Row. Gray flecks hung in the air as the bright autumn light filtered through the church windows in the late afternoon. You can't get away from the dust in this town, not even in church.

The building was filled, as though the entire town had gathered for the service. Even the coloreds and what few Mexicans that'd stayed after the war stood outside on the church lawn in the best clothes they owned, and when LC and I went in, the men took off their hats and put them over their hearts, and those with no hats put their hands on their chests. Thelma and Lightning nodded to me, and I raised my hand to them. Even Annie was there, and she hadn't been getting out much. I'd not been going to see her as much as I should've. It was hard because she always asked about Madeline, and she knew as much as I did—nothing. But I needed to go see her once in a while. God knew she'd given up enough for me. Seemed kind of stupid, some of the people who'd done the most for me and Aunt Minnie were outside standing, even old women, while assholes like Isaac were inside.

Abe's family wasn't there. When he ran off, they moved out of the company house to a scrub piece of property they still owned nearby from before they'd come to Outcropping. I had to admit he was better to his kids than Isaac was to his. In spite of what Mr. Frazier said, I knew Abe'd be back someday to see his children. Mr. Frazier didn't understand the people of Outcropping. To him they were just worker bees.

I rearranged myself on the wooden pew and looked at the picture of the last supper at the front of the church, hanging above Aunt Minnie's casket, faded and wrinkled in its old wooden frame. Judas stood behind Jesus, looking suspicious. That was Abe, the son of a bitch. I hoped he hung himself, except that I wouldn't have the pleasure of taking him out of his misery.

Preacher Smith stood, cleared his throat and started talking about how good Aunt Minnie was. Apparently folks had told him stories about her, and he was sharing them with everybody, things Aunt Minnie never talked about. He said her life was a better sermon than any he could ever preach, but then he went on to preach one. He worked it around Jesus teaching about "Whatsoever ye have done unto one of the least of these. . .," but Aunt Minnie would've turned over in her coffin if she could've heard him. She never did anything for show. I blocked his words out.

I looked around the crowded church. I saw Dicey, pitifully thin and shabbily dressed, only a ghost of the pretty young woman

206

I'd first seen in the commissary fifteen years earlier. Lines of pain and age were engraved on her face. Henry sat beside her, now a pale, thin young man. I couldn't bear to look at Isaac and others who had been ready to beat me up or kill me only a few days earlier. Damn hypocrites. Everybody knew Abe'd thrown the dynamite, but others probably helped come up with the idea. Abe was too stupid. Everybody said they were sure no one meant to hurt anybody. I didn't care whether anybody meant to hurt her or not. She was dead because of mean, lowdown, stupid people. But who besides Abe and probably Isaac? My eyes fell on Avery. I hoped not Avery. I'd probably never know who all else might've had something to do with her death. I took a deep breath and tried to pray, but I was pretty rusty. It was a thought more than a prayer. I hoped to get over the hate I was feeling because Aunt Minnie wouldn't want me to hate anybody, not even Abe.

LC squirmed next to me. He was looking down at his slender hands which were folded together in his lap. I felt a sudden, unfamiliar surge of pity for him. He'd never known Paw, and I'd certainly never done anything to fill that role, like I'd done for Ellie and Kat. He was living away from Maw, and Aunt Minnie was like a grandmother to him. She'd taken him in like she took in me when I came to Outcropping, when I'd felt so alone in the world. And now she was gone. My head throbbed and my throat tightened.

The words of a hymn floated through the church, *Rock of ages. . . let me hide myself in thee.* I hadn't even noticed the preacher had shut up. I'd never really paid much attention to the words of the hymn before, but I'd heard the melody since I was a little boy and the song had always made me feel safe. For once I would liked to have been deep in the earth and to have hidden myself in the rock, the hard rock I'd fought with for so many years, the rock under which my father was buried. I'd never found him in the rock. The area where he was buried kept falling in. His grave was covered with tons of rock, like a gigantic tombstone that made no sense.

While the people sang, we left the church and carried our burden to the graveyard on the hill behind the church—me, LC, Stub, Gadget, Cleve and Mr. Eslinger. Stub was really too weak to carry the casket, but we put him between me and Gadget. Aunt Minnie's grave was covered with flowers, mostly asters and mums that were still blooming around Outcropping, but they were dwarfed by the large spread of roses that had been sent by the company to cover the coffin. They would all die quickly.

When the service was over, people came up to me and LC to express their sympathy, even Isaac with his mouth wired shut. Once again I heard the words of the hymn *save from wrath. . . ,* and that kept me from smashing his already broken jaw, but the words wouldn't keep me from killing Abe if I ever found him, even though Aunt Minnie would say, "He didn't mean to hurt nobody, Moss."

Then Cleve was beside me. His eyes and his silent comfort offered what little peace I found that day. Why was it that Cleve with all his goodness could not speak while those with so much anger could be heard so loudly?

As people filtered away, Hope came up quietly as I stood alone beside the mound of dirt hidden by flowers. She slid her arm through mine, and in spite of my dark feelings, I was strongly aware of her presence. She said, "You and LC come on home with us. We'll fix you some supper. People's brought all kinds of food over. They brought it to our house since. . . You need to eat."

I grasped her arm tightly and said, "She took care of me ever since I been a kid. You don't never get too old to need that, you know."

"I know."

"You all go on home," I said. "I'd appreciate it if you'd take LC. Fix him something to eat. I'll be on over in a while. Don't worry about me. I just need a little time with her."

"Take as long as you want," she said. "We'll see you when you get there."

"Thanks. It'd be—It'd be bad, real bad, without you all."

Stub stood at the edge of the cemetery, and LC was with him, his face full of uncertainty, as though he were not sure if I wanted his comfort or if I'd give him any. I'd been so used to taking care of myself it hadn't occurred to me that LC might need to be needed. I pictured his pale face in the mine the day of the fight with the men that had come to help me. He was right out front with Lightning, even though he didn't know the first thing about fighting. I motioned to him and Stub, and LC walked quickly to me and I opened my arms to him. I was surprised at the strength in his arms as we hugged.

When we separated, I put my hand on his shoulder and said, "I'm glad you're here."

"Me, too," he said. "What'll we do now without her?"

"I don't know, but we'll be all right. We still got each other."

He nodded and looked at the mound of earth.

"Come on," Hope said. "Moss'll be along in a while."

"Go on home with them and have some supper. I'll be over later."

As they walked away, Stub came up to me, and we shook hands. He said, "Look, kid, what can I say? It's a damn shame. She was the best soul that ever lived."

All I could say was, "Why did I plant them asters?"

"You planted them flowers 'cause you loved her. You didn't do this. What happened wasn't your fault."

"I'm just so damn mad."

"It's all right to be mad, but don't go blaming this kind of meanness on something that was good. It aint fitting."

I nodded. "I'm just not myself right now. I need to be alone."

"Come on to the house when you're ready," he said and walked away.

When they'd all left, I dropped to my knees beside the grave. I reached over and picked up a blood red rose. I looked at the flower, then squashed it. I'd always thought flowers covered the ugliness on this old earth, but they were only covers. I got back up, dropped the rose and stepped on it.

"It seems like I hurt everything I touch, Aunt Minnie," I said. "I want to fix everything, everybody, and instead I'm pretty good at making things worse. I guess you know how I feel about Hope. You don't miss much. Stub don't, either. He knows. And it don't matter to him. I've never seen a man love his friends and family like that man. And in case you're worried, I'm not going to hurt him. I'm surprised you didn't ask me about her. Guess you knew it was hopeless, just like you knew I could never have Madeline. You didn't say much then, either. It wouldn't have mattered. I've always had to learn the hard way. At least this time I got enough sense to know that wanting don't make it right. What would I ever have done without you? What will I do now? You brought peace everywhere you went."

In a few days I had to go back to the house to see what was worth saving. I'd have rather they'd just burned it down and everything in it. But they insisted I get out what I wanted to keep.

The first thing I did was go to Aunt Minnie's pie safe in the kitchen. She'd always told me that when something happened to her, I was to look for her will there between two pie pans. Sure enough I found it and read it, along with some money, and an apple pie she'd obviously made shortly before she was killed, maybe the day before. There was over five hundred dollars in an envelope. She said it was to go to me, and I could do with it whatever I wanted. I was surprised she had so much. She wasn't big on saving, always giving things to other people, and she never made much money. But she had told me a person ought to keep a little back, so as not to ever be a burden to anybody.

She also wrote about a locket and told me where I could find it. It was in the almanac we used to read, hidden where she'd cut out pages for it to fit into, right in a chapter that told about when it was best to plant. In the will she'd said I could give the locket to my mother, or I could save it for my wife, if and when I ever got married. When I found the locket, I opened it, and inside was a picture of a young woman and a young man—Aunt Minnie when she was young and her husband, younger than me. I shut the locket and squeezed it, thinking of her with so much life ahead.

Someday I'd be gone, too, and somebody'd be looking at what little of myself I'd left behind. I wondered what a person could leave that would matter, when all was said and done. A little money, some furniture, *things*. Nothing no one else would really have to have to live. The only thing that mattered of Aunt Minnie was what she'd put in my heart. Everything else would go away in time. All that stuff folks worked for, what did it matter?

––––––––––––––––––

A week after Aunt Minnie's funeral, the men went on strike and were off work for six weeks. An uneasy peace existed. Both the men and the staff refrained from any real violence, and both seemed anxious to end the strike. We settled without either side being completely satisfied. But at least it was over, and the union was recognized.

Nobody had seen or heard from Abe, and that wasn't satisfying either. The one constable, the only law enforcement officer in Outcropping, wasn't doing anything. We didn't have much use for the law. Folks never called in the feds in Outcropping. Handled everything themselves, one way or another. For one thing, nothing much happened. If there was theft in the store or something like that, the person was fired and told to move on and that settled that. A killing was unheard of unless it was in a fight, and that was usually considered self-defense.

In Aunt Minnie's case, Abe had left, and that seemed enough. No one wanted the government involved. Abe had left his family high and dry, and folks actually made up money to help them, but nobody asked me to contribute. Maybe I would've. Don't know. It wasn't his family's fault. But I wanted Abe bad. When I talked to our constable, Bill Bates, he said Abe was like Cain, fated to roam without family or friends and to live with his own conscience. He said, leave it to God. I said that wasn't good enough, but Bates said he was sure Abe didn't aim to hurt Aunt Minnie. I said he tried to kill me. And I was sure others were in on what happened. There'd been reports of a couple of men around Outcropping that no one knew, probably union men, but they'd also disappeared since the blast. No way to trace them. Bates kept saying they all had to live with what they did, and they'd carry the guilt of killing an old woman to their grave. That wasn't punishment enough to suit me.

Once the strike was officially over, I went into the mine with a skeleton crew to inspect the condition of the machinery and equipment, to check the stables, and in general to see that the mine would be in operating condition by the beginning of the week. I sent the men in twos to check on different areas.

I took LC with me to check out the stables. As we neared the area, we heard squealing, high-pitched sounds and caught whiffs of a sickening smell, which worsened the closer we got to the area.

When we entered the stope, we stared in disbelief, trying not to breathe. It stank of blood and shit and death. Dead rats lay all around, some partially eaten. Big ones like the gopher rats me and Avery and Cleve used to shoot at the dump. The frantic screeching had to be coming from other rats, but we saw no live ones. LC said he'd always seen rats in the barn and the fields, but he'd never really heard them make sounds, certainly nothing like what we were hearing.

"Well, it's rats making the racket," I said. "But where are they? Damn, if this don't look like hell."

"What's been eating on them?" LC asked.

"Must have been other rats," I said, as I looked all around. "Nothing else down here. Keep your eyes open. If they'll eat on each other, I reckon they'll eat on anything they can find."

"They're usually so harmless. Sit like dogs and wait for leftovers when we eat our lunches. What's happened to them?"

"They're starving. Looks like they've eaten all the leftovers they could find since the strike. Think about it, nobody's been bringing down oats or hay for the mules since the strike, and there's been no miners to throw them food. Reckon there're like people, they get hungry enough, they'll eat anything, even each other."

"Let's get out of here, Moss."

"We will, but I got to find out where they are and get rid of them. We can't open up the stables with a bunch of crazed rats down here."

The wailing was coming from the feed barrels where oats had been kept for the mules. They sat at the back of the stope against a wall of rock. I pointed to them, and said, "That's where they are."

"But how could they get in?"

"See that ledge in the rock behind the barrels? They've run up there and jumped in. Now they can't get out. At least they can't get to us. Let's take a look."

"Let's go get some of the other men. We can't watch every direction at the same time. There might be other rats still around, not in the barrels. We need help."

"I don't want to get bit any more'n you do, and I don't intend to." I picked up a piece of steel that was always laying around the mine, and handed LC one. "Keep a look out."

I started toward the rats, and LC grabbed me by the shirtsleeve and said, "No, Moss. Don't go near them. Maybe we could blow them up."

I removed his hand. "I'm thinking of something easier and less dangerous. Why not drown them with the watering hose?" It lay near a trough for the mules.

"What if you run them over the top and they've not yet drowned?"

"I won't," I said, and went for the hose. I ignored the fact that LC wasn't going with me. I didn't need him, anyway. I went over to the pipeline to cut the water on and carried the hose to the barrels. The shrieking grew louder as I got near them, like they sensed me. Some of the rats were dead, and those that were alive fought savagely to get on top of each other as I let the water pour in. The noise became so loud I wanted to put my hands over my ears. I yanked the hose out before the water got high enough that the ones still alive could jump out. Bloody teeth and claws reached up toward me. I turned away. Finally there was silence. I glanced back toward LC who stood frozen where I'd left him. I was glad none of the other men were there to see his fear.

I went to turn off the water. Neither of us saw the rat that crept from somewhere in the stope toward where LC stood. When he screamed, I looked up, and his pale face glistened under the light of his hat. The rat had latched onto his leg.

"Don't run," I yelled. "Get him with your carbide."

As I tore across the stope, LC dropped his piece of steel and grabbed his light off his hat, shook it to make the flame shoot out farther and just as I got to him he touched the rat with the flame. It let go of his leg, and LC jerked his hand back as the rat's sharp teeth snapped into the air toward it. I jabbed my knife into its back, and it rolled its wild head around in slow motion, mouth spread wide hunting anything to bite, but before it could latch onto either of us, it died, eyes staring and mouth opened.

"My god," LC said. He sat down on the rock floor, staring alternately at the bleeding rat and his bleeding leg.

I yanked my knife out of the rat and looked all around for other living ones. I wiped the blood off the knife on my pants leg, folded it back up and stuffed it into my pocket. I looked at LC holding his leg. He'd been right. I should've gone for help before doing anything. But instead, like always, I thought I could take of things. It was my job.

"You did good, LC," I said, "real good. Now we got to get out of here, in case there's more where that one came from."

214

As I helped him get up on his bleeding leg, I knew he had no business being there. No business being in the mine. He was just a kid. No wonder he was scared. If I'd had a lick of sense I'd have been scared myself. I had to get him out of the mine—permanently. I decided he'd not spend another day under ground, no matter what I had to do. He reached out to me for support, and I started to carry him on my back.

"I can walk, damn it," he said.

As we headed to the cage, Avery and Gadget were checking out machinery, and when they saw us, they came running to meet us.

"You won't believe what happened," I said.

"Got bit by a damn rat," LC said.

"But the rat got the worse end of the deal. LC burned him with his light."

"Yeah, then Moss stabbed him."

"A rat?" Gadget said.

"Yeah. They went crazy with no food. There's a mess to clean up back there at the stables. We need to get Avery and George to go rat hunting. Right now we got to get LC to Doc's as fast as we can."

In minutes we were in the cage, waiting for the hoistman to take us up to light and safety.

When Moss and I came to the stable area after the strike, I was scared of those crazy rats with their sharp and bloody teeth that were eating on each other like some sort of demons. We'd come upon a level of hell right out of Dante's *Inferno.*

Moss wasn't afraid of the devil himself. All he could think about was taking care of the rats, and all I could think of was getting out of there. But when I got bit, I realized Moss was scared of something bad happening to someone he loved. And I learned that day what kind of person he was. He'd always been my big brother, of course, and he took care of us. I'd always seen him as someone who thought he knew everything there was to know. Never saw that as something good. But that day in the darkness of the mine he was the man who knew how to get rid of the rats. He knew what to do when I got bit and when the rat almost bit me again. Who kills a rat with a pocket knife? By the time he was my age, he was completely on his own. He'd had to learn quickly how to survive. Never had the choice of giving up or not accepting a challenge. I wanted to be that kind of man.

At the clinic, Dr. Timer took one look at me and said to Moss, "Get him on a table. I take it this is your brother I've been hearing about?"

He nodded and said, "LC."

"Sorry we couldn't meet in better circumstances, LC," Doc said as he cut my pants leg up the center, but this is the way I meet most people." He inspected the wound, then looked up at Moss over his glasses that slid down on his nose. "This is not a dog bite."

"No, it ain't," Moss said. "Got bit by a rat."

Doc stood up straight and his eyes opened wide. "It must have been a whale of a rat."

"Big as a cat. Like the ones at the dump. And sick, too."

"O Lord, not rabid?"

"No, it wasn't mad," Moss said. "Just crazy with hunger."

"Thank God," Doc said. "If it'd been rabies, we would've been in big trouble. Where'd this happen?"

"In the mine," I said, "in the stables. A whole bunch of them were trying to get food from the barrels. Moss drowned them."

"You got bit by a rat in the mine?"

"There's always rats in the mine," Moss said. "Never bother us, but since the strike they've gone crazy because they don't have food. When LC and me came upon them in the stables, they'd been eating each other."

Doc shook his head. "Well, why not rats? If it's not rats, it's rock falls. If it's not rock falls, it's dynamite. If it's not dynamite, it's gas. . ."

He cleaned my leg, still muttering to himself. After a few moments, he looked up at me and said, "Punctures are dangerous. How do you feel, boy?"

"Not so good. My leg hurts bad."

"I'm sure it does. I have to open up the skin around the wound to get some air to it. You understand?"

I nodded. "Tell me everything you're going to do."

"You don't have to watch. I can give you some paregoric for the pain."

"Take it," Moss said. "It'll help."

"No. I want to watch what he's doing."

Moss started to say something else, but just shrugged.

"What's this boy doing in the mine, Moss?" Doc said. "He's too young."

I sat up straight. "I'm stronger'n I look. My paw, he wasn't big, either, and he was a good miner. Everybody says so. Tell him, Moss."

Moss ran his hand through his hair. "He's doing the same thing as the rest of them's doing in the mine—eating. Putting food on the table. They're all too young. If fact, you don't get old enough."

"Sorry, Moss. You're right. But this boy don't look like a miner." Doc pointed the scalpel at me. "He looks like he needs to be in a classroom."

"He's a good miner, Doc," Moss said. "He's smart. He watches and listens, does what he's told. Stays away from the roughnecks, most of the time. But he's spent his last day in the mine. He's going to college to be a doctor, just like you."

Doc said, "He better get through high school first."

"I am through high school," I said. "Finished early. I'm mining for a while to earn money to go to school. Going to be a doctor, like Moss says. It takes a lot of money."

"Well, that's a fine aspiration, but you aren't going to be mining for a couple of weeks. You stay off this leg, LC, or you're going to have blood poisoning and whatever you do, you'll be doing it with one leg. You understand that?"

I dropped my head. "Yes, sir."

"You got a way to get him home, Moss? Better yet, you got a way to keep him there?"

"If you can let him rest here a spell, I'll get Stub's truck and take him out to the country to stay with Maw. She won't be happy with either of us. She's still upset with me for helping LC get on at the mine, and for the first time in his life, she's angry with him for wanting to come here to work."

"I've got an idea," Doc said, "Let him stay here with me and my wife. Emma needs somebody to fuss over. Maybe she'll let me breathe if she's got somebody else to baby. I can teach him about doctoring, too, before he goes off to school. Help him compete with some of those boys who come from a line of doctors. Might even be able to get the company to pay him a little salary, you know, as my assistant."

"We don't need charity," Moss said. "I got some money from Aunt Minnie." He looked at me and said, "Five hundred dollars. You can have it all for college."

"That won't pay for four years of college and medical school, too," I said. "Besides, I want to pay my own way. You've always given us everything you make." I looked at Doc Timer and said, "Can I really stay here and learn about doctoring?"

"You bet your boots, you can."

"Say I do this. What kind of rent would you need?"

"Oh, you'll earn your keep. And God knows Emma will love having you here. She drives me crazy. I'm not complaining, you understand. She's been like that ever since—ever since we lost our little boy to pneumonia." He paused and ran his hand through his thinning hair. "She'll mother you to death, I need to warn you, but you'll love her, and she'll feed you well."

"I can't let you feed him and take care of him for free, Doc," Moss said.

"I need help in the clinic, have ever since I lost Sadie to Jim Johnson, lucky son of a gun. It'll be kind of like an apprenticeship, at least when his leg heals. He can study some medical books while he has to be off it. What do you say?"

Moss looked at me. "You're old enough to work in the mine, you're old enough to decide this for yourself."

"I'd like it a lot."

"Then it's settled," Doc said. "Go on to work, Moss. LC'll be fine, won't you, boy?"

Moss said he'd bring me what I'd need after he got off in the evening. Then he went back to the dark mine. I had such a lump in my throat I couldn't even thank him for taking care of me. But at the same time I was thrilled I could take care of myself and have the chance of working in medicine. I hoped that someday Moss would be as proud of me as I was of him.

Moss

I had been worried about LC not having a real home in Outcropping ever since Aunt Minnie'd died. While our house was being repaired, we'd moved into The House where Paw had stayed, and we continued to stay there. Neither of us wanted to go back to Engineer's Row to the house where Aunt Minnie had been killed. I didn't want to be beholden, but LC staying at the Timers solved that problem, at least for a while. And it wasn't really my decision anyway. So when the men were able to go back to work, LC wasn't among them, and I breathed easier.

The ground was still unstable, especially under the river. I'd recently put Dicey's boy Henry on as a driller's assistant. He'd been roustabouting for a while. Drilling was a place to make good money in time, and I wanted to give him a chance. I sure didn't do it for Isaac, but for Dicey and, of course, for Henry. He was a good boy, a steady worker. He just had no backbone. No wonder after having to walk on egg shells when Isaac came home drunk and mean for all those years.

I put him on with a driller named Robin Hood who was something of a legend in the mine. You couldn't keep but like him for the very things that drove you crazy. True to his name, he robbed from the rich and gave to the poor, at least that's the way he saw it. He stole hammers, drills, flashlights, carbide lights, dynamite, anything he could get out of the mine, and he distributed them among the people of Lowtown. I prayed I'd never catch him at it.

Sometimes it was hard to decide if Hood was a blessing or a curse. He ignored safety precautions, but he knew more than I did about so many things, and he never got himself or anyone else hurt.

When I went to check on him the first day Henry worked with him, they weren't where I'd sent them. I asked Stub where they were, and he said he thought they were still down under the river.

"Damn," I said. "I told him to clear out of there. Too much popping going on."

"Aw, he's all right," Stub said. He'll leave if it gets too bad. They's still good ore up that way yet."

"I know, but it's not safe, and he's got Henry with him."

As I approached the drift heading, I could hear the ground popping, even above the sound of the drills. I yelled at them, and neither of them could hear me. As I got closer, Henry saw me. He stopped drilling and patted Hood on the shoulder.

"Chief's here," he yelled into Hood's ear

"Shit," said Hood, shutting off his drill.

"What do you think you're doing?" I said. "Can't you hear that popping?"

Henry looked up at the rock above him and nodded.

"Don't go on the warpath, Chief," Hood said. "We hear it. Aint nothing to get yore dander up over. Looky here, look at this ore." He pointed to the yellow vein running through the rock. "Yeller gold. And you wonder why we don't leave."

"Forget the zinc. Listen to that," I said, pointing to the rock above us. "I told you to get out of here."

"We're moving, aint we, Henry? Just as soon as we finish."

Henry looked up again at the rumbling rock and nodded slowly as Hood added, "Don't you think I know when it's time to clear out? Been drilling since before yore mammy met yore pappy. And I aint about to let nothing happen to this here boy."

"I'm not, either. I want you both out. Now. Get your drills and go. If I have to come back, you're both off without pay for a week. You got that?"

"Okay, okay, we're packing up," Hood said, "but we're leaving a hell of a lot of good zinc."

Henry was so proud to be working with Hood, I knew he wouldn't leave as long as Hood didn't, so I added, "I'll be back to see if you're gone."

"We'll be gone. Right, Henry?"

Henry nodded, but wouldn't look me in the eye.

221

I said, "Henry, you want to stay on as a driller?"

"Yes, sir, Chief."

"Then, Leave, now."

"Keep yore britches on," Hood said, "I told you we're leaving. He's coming with me."

"Okay," I said and started down the drift. If Hood wasn't the first man to get killed under me, I'd be real lucky. I just hoped it wasn't Henry. I turned around to go back, thinking maybe I should've waited to make sure they left, even though they said they would. I couldn't believe my ears as I heard the sound of drills start up.

"Son of a bitch," I said, running towards them.

Instantly the popping overhead turned into one large crack as though the earth were being torn apart. All I could see was a huge cloud of dust. I'd been taught to run, to get away from falling ground, but I couldn't budge. My eyes stung as I squinted to see what was happening. A mountain of rock had replaced the openings where Hood and Henry had been drilling, and large boulders lay near where I stood. My heart pounded like the earth overhead. I ran towards the pile of rock, yelling their names, stumbling, falling and clawing, ignoring debris raining down on me as I climbed toward the exact spot where I knew they'd been— and still were.

"Hood," I yelled. "Answer me, goddamn you. Say something."

I began throwing rocks I could pick up. At last I dropped to my knees and looked down at my shaking hands covered with my blood and rock dust.

"Oh, God, Paw," I said, "I didn't want nobody ever to die working for me."

Then I heard my name being called. I looked up and saw Lightning climbing towards me. "Mr. Moss," he yelled, "get off these rocks. Ground's still popping. It's going to fall again. You get off."

"Lightning," I said, "Thank God. Help me. Hood and Henry's under here."

"God in heaven," he said, shaking his head. "No way we can help them. We got to get out of here ourselves or we be joining them."

The earth thundered and shot down more rock. Blood trickled over my brow and into my eyes. Lightning scrambled faster over the rocks toward me.

"Help me get them, Lightning," I said. "God, help me get them."

Lightning moved through the bullets of rock that were still firing from above. When he got to me, he put his hands on my shoulders and shook me.

"Listen here, boy," he said. "Aint nothing we can do for them. If you don't get out of here, you going to be buried with them. And me with you, 'cause I aint leaving without you."

The earth shook again and belched rock from above us. We both threw our arms around our heads and huddled like babies. When the rumbling subsided, we raised our heads slowly, and we saw more rock piled only feet from us. I looked at Lightning. He was gray as ash and streaked with blood.

"We both going to die if we don't get away from here. You know that."

I nodded, and we climbed down, helping each other as the earth continued to crack above us.

As we rode the cage up to the surface, I sat in the floor with my head in my hands. Lightning sat beside me. The only thing I could feel thankful for was that LC wasn't in the mine that day. But that would not be consolation for Dicey. The only light in her life was snuffed out, and I hadn't been able to do a damn thing about it.

Doc

LC never went back to the mine after the rat bit him. I saw to that. You can't save the world, but once in a great while you get a chance to help someone, and I decided this was one of those times. Of course, as most things we do for someone else, I had a bit of a selfish reason. The boy was smart, knew a lot about animals, therefore people. He'd become a real help around the clinic, and Em had someone to dote on. But even more than that, the boy cared for the folks that came to the clinic. I wasn't going to live forever, not that I wouldn't have liked to, but I was getting old. It wasn't easy getting a doctor to come to the mining towns, and I saw LC as someone who would make a great physician for the folks in Outcropping. He understood them. He was one of them.

Em and I talked it over. We'd never had a chance to send our own child to medical school. His untimely death ended that dream. But after we got over the shock, we toyed with the idea of setting up a scholarship for a child from the town. We just never got around to it. I guess we couldn't accept the fact that it'd never be our child. But when LC came to live with us, we both decided it'd be good if we could send him.

I made a proposal to him, to pay his way through college and medical school if he'd agree to come back to Outcropping after he finished school for at least five years as a doctor. We had a hard time convincing him that we weren't doing it for charity. I had to convince him he'd earned a scholarship that we were going to give to someone, if not to him. And it was also a way for Outcropping to get a good doctor when I got too old to practice. Once he'd agreed, we had the more difficult task of convincing Moss. Moss was smart, and he knew how to survive. But sometimes he didn't know when to let other people find their own way to survive. Thought he had to take care of the world.

Naturally he said, "Sending LC to school's my job. He's my brother. I've saved some money and, like I said before, I've got a little from Aunt Minnie."

I told him to try to forget LC was his brother and to think about it as though he was just a deserving student who'd earned a scholarship. "You've earned your way," I said, "and he's earned his."

It was Emma who got through to him. She said, "We've come to love LC like he was ours. The hardest thing about sending him to college for us isn't the money, it's letting him go, giving him a chance to spread his wings. But, don't you see? He wants to be independent, just like you. We all have to let go. Let him find life for himself. For once, you worry about yourself and your own life. We love you both, don't you know that? Someday you'll have children of you own who will need your help. Save your money for them. Let us do something that will last longer than ourselves."

Moss nodded and said, "I'm not going to say more about it."

"Thank God," I said, "because he's been accepted at the university for next semester."

Moss

I knew Abe wouldn't stay gone forever. Sooner or later he'd come back to see his family. Whenever I took Stub's truck to go to Maw's, I'd drive out to where they lived in what wasn't much more than a shack off the main road. I never drove down the lane to the house. Figured if Abe was there, I'd see an old car or truck.

For months, I never saw a sign of him. But one day as I came close to the road, a rickety truck came from the opposite direction and turned down the rutted lane. My heart pounded. I slowed down and watched the truck pull up near the house. I went on past, then turned back around and parked on the far side of the road where I could see down the lane. The truck was black and rusted, looked like Abe's—the one he was in when he threw the dynamite into Aunt Minnie's flower garden and killed her.

I gripped the steering wheel till my knuckles turned white. I took some deep breaths, then got out of the truck and reached behind the seat for Stub's tool box, got the revolver we'd kept in it ever since the strike, and loaded it. I held it with both hands and rested it against my chest. I'd waited for this day too long. This'd be the time to get him. He didn't expect me. Even if folks suspected it was me that shot him, nobody'd blame me. I wouldn't get arrested.

While I was trying to decide whether to sneak down the lane, hide in the undergrowth and shoot him when he came out of the house or just wait for him to drive back to the road, he came outside, followed by three or four children. They grabbed boxes and pokes from his truck and carried them in the house. I felt like I'd been kicked in the gut. Leaning against the truck, I lowered the gun and held it in one hand, dangling by my side. I slowly opened the door and got back in, laid the gun on the seat beside me and leaned my head against the steering wheel. Don't know how long I sat there like that before his truck rattled back up the lane. Suddenly he stopped in a lurch and slid in the dirt and gravel. After a moment, he inched on up, leaned forward and squinted to see inside my truck. Our eyes locked, and his mouth dropped. We sat staring at one another. Then he sped out, flipping up rock and dirt behind him, and tore off in the direction he'd come. I drove away slowly towards our farm, my heart pounding and my hands shaking on the wheel.

Hope

I couldn't believe it when Stub said we were going to a dance at the community center. He never cared nothing about going before. I asked him why he wanted to go, and he said I needed to get out, get to know folks better. We didn't either one know how to dance, and he really wasn't able to since his bout with pneumonia. He was back to work, but his cough was still bad, and he didn't have the energy he had before. I didn't want him to go back to the mine, but he said, what else would we do? I said we could use the money he had for me that Paw had saved. He said I'd need that soon enough, and I knew what he meant. Besides, he said Moss needed him while the men got used to him as foreman. I didn't think Moss needed anybody, but I didn't say nothing.

When we got to the center, Stub introduced me to a man at the door named Red Smith. I'd met him before, but didn't really know him. Stub said he was the spotter for the night, said they always had a spotter to make sure none of the men brought in liquor or caused any problems.

We hung around for a while near the door, standing out like two awkward teen-agers. A few of the men come up to us and started talking to Stub, and I stood there staring at the large room with chairs lined along the wall. A few tables at a corner in the back were covered with food and drinks. A handful of men in middle of the back wall played banjos and guitars, and one man sang. Finally I went on in and sat down. Avery Hought came over and asked me to dance.

I shook my head. "I don't dance."

He said he'd teach me, but when he looked over and saw Stub staring at us, he went on his way and pulled another girl onto the dance floor. I decided to tell Stub we needed to leave when he finished talking to his friends. I watched the dancers and swayed in my seat to "When the Moon Comes Over the Mountain." Then folks started whispering and pointing toward the door. I looked and saw Red trying to keep a man from coming in. I inched toward

228

the commotion, along with other people.

Someone said, "It's Rocky again."

The man staggered around, punching the air and yelling for Red to get out of his way.

Red grabbed his arm. "Come on, Rocky. You need to go home and sleep this off."

Rocky yanked his arm out of Red's grip. "Sleep off what? Let go me, you over-grown ox." He tried to push Red, but he fell down.

Red helped him up and said, "Let's go. You're too drunk to be around the women and children."

About that time Moss came up. He said, "What's going on, Red?"

"Well, if it aint the bossman." Rocky leaned back so far he nearly fell off the porch. He pointed a finger toward Moss and said, "This aint none of your business, Chief. We aint in the mine."

Moss looked at the group of people who gathered around the door. His eyes caught mine, and he shook his head.

"I'm trying to get him to leave," Red said. "He's drunk as a skunk."

"I'm not drunk." Rocky slurred his words. "Reckon I'll go inside if'n I damn well want to. It's a free country."

"Have a smoke and cool off. Then go home," Moss said to Rocky. "You're not coming in." He turned to Red. "See he goes home."

"Whoa," Rocky said, "You taking orders from the company man, Red? He aint the boss of us here. Not enough he kicked me outta the mine today. You know he costed me a day's pay for dry drilling?"

"We don't allow drinking in the center, Rocky," Red said. "It's got nothing to do with Moss or the mine. Come on now and quit making a fool of yourself."

Rocky pulled his arm from Red's grip, shoved him, and pointed to Moss. "If'n he wants me to leave, he can try to make me."

229

Red's face darkened. "If you're wanting to pick a fight with someone, Rocky, I'm your man. You got no call to bring Chief into this. Let's go down to the parking lot and settle this." He grabbed Rocky's arm, twisted it behind him and pushed him down the steps.

"I got no quarrel with you, Red." Rocky struggled to wriggle out of Red's grip. "It's Chief I want."

A lady beside me said, "Oh, lord, somebody's going to get hurt."

I felt sick at the pit of my stomach, and wished we had already gone home. I stood on my tiptoes and looked around for Stub. He was heading over to see what was happening. I pushed between people to get a better look at Moss, as Stub worked his way to me. I was afraid he'd try to help Moss, and I said, "Red's got Rocky now. It'll be okay." But Stub pushed past me and headed toward Moss.

When he got down the steps, he told Moss to let Red handle it, but Moss said, "He needs help."

"Then I'll set him straight," Stub said.

"No, stay back," Moss said. "Keep folks from coming out and getting in the way. I'll help Red. Rocky's mad at me for sending him home today."

Stub came back up on the porch, and I went out to him. He said, "Don't worry. No big deal. Moss can handle it."

Red and Rocky squared off, and some men who'd been on the porch smoking circled them. A few were encouraging Rocky. Most were telling him to go home.

As Moss pushed through them, I heard Rocky say, "Back off, Red, or I'll cut your damn guts out."

Red jumped back, and the men scattered as Rocky made jabs at the air with a knife. The blade flashed in the lamplight. "Come on, Chief. Make me go home."

"You're crazy, Rocky," Moss said. "Put that down. You're apt to fall on it and cut yourself."

The men laughed, but Rocky cupped his free hand and motioned at Moss. "Why don't you take it from me?"

Red pulled out a knife of his own and opened it. "Get back, Chief. I'll take him."

"No," Moss said. "He's just an old drunk. We can take care of this some other way."

I stepped out on the porch, and Stub followed me, telling me it'd be okay.

Rocky bared his teeth and growled. "Who you calling old? Come on, company man. You don't seem so big now."

Moss took a handkerchief out of his pocket and tied it around his right hand. My heart stopped beating.

He moved in a little toward Rocky, saying, "Now, Rocky. Put down the knife. You don't want to hurt nobody."

"The hell I don't. I'm about to cut your goddamn throat."

My whole body jerked as Rocky lunged at Moss who stepped aside. As he did so, he put out his foot and tripped him. Rocky dropped the knife as he fell, and Moss leaned over and picked it up. He put one knee on Rocky's back. Then he folded the blade, but touched it to the back of Rocky's neck and said, "You aint going to cut nobody tonight. Next time you come at me with a knife, you better kill me, because if you don't, I'll cut you in so many pieces, they'll never find you. I'll feed you to the fish in the Holston."

Rocky's face was gray, and he didn't say another word as Moss pulled him up. He staggered away, bent over. Moss pitched the folded knife to Red.

"Want me to give this back to him?" Red said.

"Hell, no."

Stub said to me, "See, I told you Moss would handle it."

As Red and Moss came toward the porch, Red said, "Would you really do that, what you said?"

Moss attempted a laugh. He looked up at me and said, "That'd be way too much trouble. Figure if I scare him enough I won't have to live my life wondering when he might come after me."

"Well, I reckon he'll keep away from you," Red said.

They both leaned against the posts on the porch with Stub. Red lit up a cigarette and offered one to Moss and Stub. People began to go back to the dance floor. I plopped in a chair near the door, fanning myself with a handkerchief I'd pulled from the pocket in my dress. I wondered if there was always that much excitement at the dances. Folks were already dancing to "I Want to Be Happy" as though nothing had happened. About the time I decided to go out and ask Stub if we could go home, Moss came back in. As he passed near me, he looked into my eyes. I looked down, hoping no one had noticed my flushed cheeks.

Moss

All in one day I sent Rocky McNish home for dry drilling, was attacked by him with a knife, danced with Hope, and stood face to face with Mr. Rogers in his front yard.

Ever since I'd been made foreman, I'd had a real hard time getting the miners, especially the old ones, to use water when they drilled. The union had made the company get wet drills, but the men still fought turning the water on. The water caused the drills to gum up some, and the men liked being able to keep mining and not have to stop to clean their bits. I understood that, but breathing the fine dust full of slivers of rock caused silicosis. Nothing sent a message like time off without pay. I hated to do that, but I'd given Rocky plenty of warnings. Guess I just caught him on the wrong day.

I'd promised Stub to come to the community center that Friday night even though I was really too tired. When I got there, Rocky was giving the spotter a hard time. I went over to see if I could help, and Rocky lit into me. We wound up outside in a fight.

Afterwards I talked with Red and Stub for a while on the porch. When I went in the center, Stub sat down on a step with Red, said he needed fresh air. As soon as I got inside I saw Hope sitting near the door. Her eyes caught mine, then she looked down.

I went over and said, "I'm thirsty. You had any punch?" She shook her head, and I said, "I'll go get us some."

When I came back, I sat down beside her. We watched the dancers sway as the band played "All Alone."

"You and Stub never come to the dances," I said. "What made you come tonight?'

"I don't know. Stub wanted to come. Told me to put on my prettiest dress, and here we are."

"You look nice."

She blushed and looked away.

"Having fun?"

She looked back at me and grinned. "Not really."

"Well, we need to do something about that. Want to dance?"

She shook her head. "I saw what happened."

"Sorry about that. Not a good way to start the night. There's not usually so much excitement. Come on," I said. "Dancing will make you feel better."

She said, "I . . . I really don't know how."

"Then it's high time you learn."

"No, really, I can't," she said, but I pulled her toward the floor.

The band struck up "Let Me Call You Sweetheart," and I said, "Just relax and follow me. It's easy to learn on the slow ones."

I leaned over her at first, telling her what steps to make and counting one, two, three. I was no great dancer myself. Gradually Hope fell into step with the music. When the song ended, she backed off the dance floor.

I turned to go get another cup of punch and saw Stub watching me from across the room, but the look on his face wasn't angry. Sad, maybe. I felt the strain of too long a day and too strange an evening. I nodded to Stub, gulped down the punch in one swallow and left.

I walked quickly through the parking lot and headed toward the dorm. The music of "It Isn't Fair" faded and blended with the sounds of insects. I found myself thinking about Madeline. Through the years I thought of her less and less, but that night my feet took me down the road towards Nobb Hill.

When I came to the house, I stood staring at it, thinking of the day she had led me into the big, white kitchen. I relived the dinner with the fancy dishes and silver, the day I ran up the porch steps and found her sick, and the ugly confrontation with Mr. Rogers at the front door. At first I hated him for not allowing Madeline and me to stay together. But in time it had become less a hatred for him and more of a disgust for an order that was as hard as rock to break. Mr. Rogers was just a part of the system that couldn't change. I wondered what dynamite it'd take to bust it up.

I was startled when a tall, thin figure appeared from behind the once-white scroll on the front porch, now covered with ivy. Mr. Rogers' hair had grayed completely, and he no longer stood straight. I nodded, afraid of what he'd do or say.

He nodded in return and said my name, as though he were used to seeing me walk through Nobb Hill in the evenings.

"Sorry I interrupted you," I stammered. "It's a beautiful night, and it's very nice up here."

He didn't respond, and I turned to go. Suddenly he said, "You were right." His voice sounded as though it was coming from a long way away. I turned back around, and he again said, "You were right."

I didn't know what to say. I wasn't even sure what he was talking about. He could've been talking about my actions the day of the flood, for all I knew.

He put his hand on the screen door as though to go inside, but he turned to face me again and said, "You'll be glad to know you won't have to see me any more. I'm leaving Outcropping. Retiring. Bought a little house in Knoxville. Nowhere particular to go. No reason any more to go back to North Carolina."

I couldn't say I was sorry he was leaving Outcropping.

"It should give you pleasure," he said, "to know that when I forced Madeline to give you up, she gave me up. She gave up everything here. She wouldn't come home. When I went to her home, she was cold and distant. So I quit going. My grandson hardly knows me."

Grandson. *My son.* I fought the need to grab him and force more out of him. I took a deep breath and said, "Where is he?"

His head jerked, and he reached out a shaky hand as though to grab an invisible rope. I almost felt sorry for him.

"There's been enough hurt over all this," he said. "The boy thinks he's Clyde Richards' son, the doctor Madeline married. It should be of some comfort to you to know that the person hurt most by all this has been me. You both have moved on with your lives. I've been living in a vacuum. I've come to see that you're not a bad person. You've done well with the company. I could've helped you do better. I'm sorry. But it's over." With that, he turned slowly and walked inside.

I needed a rope to grab, too. My heart was racing and my head was reeling. I didn't feel I'd gone on with my life at all. A part of it had stopped in the summer of 1924. But even the anger had faded over the years, along with hope for Madeline and my child. Working hard had been my salvation. And Aunt Minnie. And Stub and Hope. LC, the girls. My heart began to slow down again. I had much more in my life than he did. And it was time to let go of the past.

The next morning, news spread around Outcropping that Mr. Rogers, the company's chief engineer for the past twenty-eight years, died of a heart attack in his sleep. Folks said it was good he'd died peacefully.

––––––––––––––––

The following November, Lightning ran toward me in the main drift of the mine, yelling, "Moss, come quick! Stub's been blowed off the bench."

"What?"

"Come quick. Aint no time to talk."

As we ran, I said, "Is he dead?"

"If he aint, I'm going back to church."

We ran past Red, and I yelled to him to go get Doc and bring him down. When we got to where Stub lay, his helper George Turner said, "It's my fault."

Fats, an old friend of Stub's, was beside him. He looked up at me and said, "He's still alive, Chief, but he aint good. Waiting on you. Been saying your name. Not 'Chief.' Been saying 'Moss'."

I dropped to my knees. His face was the color of rock, and blood was spreading underneath his head.

"Damn you, you old cuss. You cut them fuses too short again, didn't you?"

He tried to lift a bloody hand covered in rock dust to me. I grabbed it and felt coldness. "Don't damn me now," he said. His chin shook, and I couldn't tell if he was trying to laugh or cry. The only other thing he said was "Hope."

"I'll take care of her and William. I promise. Hang on. Doc's coming."

He tried to say something else, but blood bubbled in his mouth. He stared upward, and his body stiffened. I touched his throat and felt the utter stillness. Only the scurrying of the rats could be heard.

I looked down at my bloody hands. No amount of soap could wash away Stub's blood or Hood's or any other miner who had or would die under my charge. I couldn't stop accidents, not even the stupid ones.

I told Lightning to go get a basket. "If you see Doc," I said, "tell him we don't need him."

George said again, "It's my fault he didn't get down in time, Chief. I lost my footing in the rope ladder."

"No," I said. "Stub cut the fuses too short, right?"

George nodded.

"He always did," I said.

"When I got tangled up, he never said my name or nothing."

"He was afraid he'd make you nervous."

"Hell, I was."

I put my hand on his shoulder and said, "Stub knew the risks. He's the one who took them and made you take them, too."

When Lightning returned with the basket, we arranged Stub's broken body in it. Then he and George and Gadget and me rode up with the basket in the cage surrounded by the rock.

Doc

I arrived shortly after they got Stub to the surface. From what Red had told me, I wasn't surprised Stub was already dead. I found Moss in his office, standing in front of the map.

"Heard the news," I said. "If it's any consolation, he didn't have much longer, anyway."

He nodded and pointed to a spot on the map. "He was right there, Doc." He wiped his finger on his pants and muttered, "Damn dust. He said he didn't want to die from his lungs, so I guess he got his wish."

"He was a good man," I said.

"The best." His voice shook as he added, "He stood by me no matter what."

"That's what friends do."

"You want me to tell Hope?" I said.

He shook his head. "I been standing here getting up my nerve to go tell her."

"I'll drop you off on my way back to the office."

"Thanks, Doc," he said, "but no. I'll walk."

"It's snowing pretty bad. Going to be a cold winter, already snowing this much in November."

"It aint far. The cold air'll do me good."

"Don't envy you what you got to do. Done it too many times myself. Never gets any easier." He walked out with me to my car, and as I started to get in, I said, "Know what you're going to say?"

"No. Any suggestions?"

I shook my head. "Never know what I'm going to say till I say it. And then it never makes much sense."

"There aint no sense in it."

Moss

The sky was gray as I trudged through the snow to Mechanics Row, trying to decide what to say to Hope. I could say he died quickly, hardly suffered at all. But the gory details always circulated. News would get out about Stub's bloody death. Stub, the dynamite expert, the invincible, blown forty feet to strike hard rock, knowing he was falling and not able to do anything about it. I felt real pain in my back, thinking of Stub's broken back and fractured skull. I thought of the pain he must have endured trying to stay alive till I got to him. I wiped away icy tears with the back of my hand.

I stepped up on Hope's porch and knocked, shattering the cold air. She opened the door like always.

"Moss?" she said. "You look frozen." She stepped back for me to enter, and said, "It's not time for you to be off work." Then her face went pale and she said, "It's Stub, isn't it?

I nodded.

She took my wet coat and hat and laid them on the back of a chair while I took off my boots on the newspapers that she had laid at the front door, like she always did when it snowed or rained. Then she slowly turned to face me. I opened my mouth, but nothing came out.

"What is it? What's happened?"

I stepped toward her and took her hands. "He—he got hurt. He didn't make it."

She shook her head. Her lip quivered, and she shut her eyes tightly. We both stood there without saying anything. Her eyes teared up and she wiped them with the tail of her apron. Then she took in a deep breath and said, "Tell me what happened."

"He was cutting in a bench, opening a new stope, you know, up high. He had this new man with him, Cleve's nephew George, and you know how Stub always cut the fuses short to save time. Well, maybe you don't know, but he did. I always warned him. He never gave time for anything unexpected to happen."

239

"What unexpected thing happened?"

"George tripped getting down the ladder, but it's not George's fault. It's my fault. I never could get Stub to quit cutting fuses too short. I've been preaching at him about that for years. Tried to tell him you can't count on nothing going wrong. Things, well, things go wrong. Your name was the last word he said."

Her hands went up to her ears. I thought how much she still looked like a little girl in her worn, plain dress, her curly hair falling down her back. I pulled her close, and she clung to me and cried.

After a few moments I said, "Come sit down. I'll fix us some coffee." I'd been in the kitchen enough to know where things were. I'd even poured coffee, but this time, I only carried two cups into the living room. Neither of us spoke for a while as we sat on the old blue couch sipping the warm liquid.

Then she set her cup down, looked at her hands, and said, "He was good to me—he was good. I know what folks thought when we got married, but we didn't either one know what to do, you know. We all came here from Kentucky when my mother died of lung disease. Me and Paw and Stub. Stub's wife and baby had died the same winter of typhoid. Anyways, they heard about the mines down here in Tennessee. I was just little when we came. Paw said we wouldn't die of black lung here. Reckon he didn't know about silicosis. But he didn't live long enough to worry about that, either. Got his head cut off by a broken cable. He and Stub both made sure I went to school. Paw was really proud." She smiled and wiped her tears. "I taught him to read and write as I learned. We did a lot together, me and Paw. We cooked and cleaned and did laundry. He wasn't like most men who won't do what they think is woman's work. And he never went out drinking at night."

She sat up tall as she could and straightened her apron over her lap. "Then one day he didn't come home from work. Instead, a man from the mine come. I didn't know what to do. There wasn't nothing I could do in Outcropping. We didn't have no close kin left back in Kentucky, and I couldn't stay in the house without Paw. The company didn't see me as nothing without Paw. Stub'd been living in the dorm, and he moved in here so I could stay on. He was a lot like Paw, looked like him, smelt like him. Like earth and rock. Anyway, after a while we got married."

She bit her lip and said, "How soon will William and I have to move out?"

"Not right away," I said. "Don't worry about that. You want me to stay here with you till William gets home from school?"

"No. I'll tell him myself."

"I'll stop by on my way home from work. Wish there was something I could do. Let me know if you need me."

"I may, uh, I may need help with the arrangements. I've never done that."

"Sure. Anything special you want?"

"No. I don't care. Whatever you think. What you did for Aunt Minnie was fine, except Stub once said he wanted the service real short. Just keep it short, he said. A couple of hymns and the Psalm that starts out 'I will lift up mine eyes unto the hills.' He said he hoped heaven was like the hills of Kentucky. That's all he said, because I told him to hush talking about such things." She laughed nervously. "I guess maybe I should have listened to him."

"It doesn't matter," I said. "We'll make it short."

It probably wasn't the right time, but I reminded her she'd be getting some insurance money from the company to take care of the funeral. The $1,000 life insurance policy was something the union had pushed for that the company would never have done otherwise.

She nodded and said, "Thanks for coming over here yourself to tell me. You didn't have to do that. You could have sent somebody, but I'm glad you came."

"Stub would've wanted me to." I put on my coat and hat that were still wet and pushed my feet into my cold boots, then turned back around and said, "I'm sorry, Hope. About the fuses. I tried, but I always knew he did it when I wasn't around. I should've done more to stop that."

She managed a weak smile. "He told about scaring you with dynamite the first day you worked with him at least a hundred times. It's one of William's favorite stories."

I laughed for the first time that day. "He was a good one, all right."

When I started to open the door, she put her hand on mine and said, "You can't hold yourself to blame for other's people's decisions. A man does the best he can do."

"My best wasn't good enough."

———————————

When I stopped by to check on Hope and her son on my way home from work that evening, William answered the door. His eyes were red, but he smiled when he saw me. For an instant the boy was myself standing on our porch in 1918, hearing Ray Lindsey say, "No, he aint hurt. Your Paw's dead."

"Hi, Uncle Moss," I heard William say. He stepped back for me to walk in.

I wanted to take him in my arms, but instead I reached out my hand, and William put his small one in it. I searched for the right words but, like Ray Lindsey, could not find them. All I could say was, "I'm sorry, Will. I'm so sorry."

Hope came into the living room. She'd washed her face, changed her dress and put her hair up.

"You okay?" I said.

She nodded. William went over to stand beside her and reached for her hand. She looked down at him and said, "I'm going to let you visit with Uncle Moss while I fix us all a bite of supper." She looked over at me and said. "Eat with us. Folks has already brought food. All I have to do is put out some plates."

William and I stood awkwardly in the living room after she left, looking at one another.

"You all right, Will?" I said.

"Yes, sir. I knew my paw was gonna die soon. He told me so. Told me to take care of Maw. And I will." He looked up at me, trying to blink back tears. "'Cept I don't know what to do. Will you show me what to do? Paw said you would." His lower lip quivered, but he did not cry.

"'Course I will," I said, "but you're doing just fine."

I put my arm on his shoulder, and we walked over to the couch and sat down. I propped one leg upon the other and looked at him. He propped one leg up, also, and looked back at me.

"The funeral's arranged, and you and your maw will have enough money to live on for a while. You can stay here as long as you need. I'll see to it." I was talking to him like he was an adult, but he'd never again be a child in the way he had been before.

"Is Ellie going to sing?" he said.

"You mean at the funeral?"

He nodded. "'Amazing Grace,' like I've heard her sing as she cooks. She sings prettier than anybody I ever heard. I think Paw'd like that, don't you?"

"Yes I do."

"Paw, he never went to church. You think he'll be in heaven when we get there?"

"If he aint, then there isn't any heaven."

Suddenly he leaned over and held out his arms to me like the child he was and cried, and I cried, too.

Hope

After Stub died, Moss continued to drop by most days after work, and I'd fix supper for him and me and William. Sometimes he seemed uneasy, like he didn't belong. I wasn't sure he did, either. Still I couldn't help but look forward to his coming.

Thanksgiving was nearing, but I wasn't feeling very thankful. I knew things would get better. They always do in time, but it'd be hard without Stub. Especially for William. I decided to ask Moss if he'd like to share Thanksgiving dinner with us. William thought it was a great idea.

One evening after we finished eating, he said, "Aren't you going to ask, him, Maw?"

"Ask me what?" Moss said.

"Well," I said, "we were wondering if you'd like to spend Thanksgiving with us, if you don't have other plans."

He coughed and said he'd never missed a Thanksgiving at his maw's, that she'd disown him if he did.

William dropped his head. "Aw shucks."

I told him not to make Moss feel bad for going to be with his maw.

"But his maw's got all kinds of people out there," he said. "We just got us."

"We're lucky to have each other, honey," I said, feeling my throat tighten. "We'll have us a good time. Why if I had a family nearby, nothing could keep me away. We'll do something special and start our own tradition, you and me." I looked at Moss. "We understand."

But then he asked us to go to his maw's with him, unless we'd rather just be with each other. "I know you don't know everybody, and that can be kinda hard, but I thought maybe it'd be good for William to get out, be with other children."

"We can't barge in on your family get-together," I said.

"Please, Maw," William said. "They got pigs and chickens and cows and dogs and cats and horses and everything. Uncle Joe lets us ride the horses. You'll love it. We won't eat that much. They'll never even notice us."

"You can eat all you want," Moss said. "There's always more food there than you've ever seen." He smiled at me. "But, as for going unnoticed, well, I doubt that. I've never taken a girl home for Thanksgiving, so you're forewarned, and Maw's crazy about William. I think he reminds her of LC when he was little. She'd be mighty proud to have you both. And, I'd be real proud to take you with me. LC's in school. Probably won't come home this year. The girls both have families of their own. I'm the one who's left out these days. I'd be thankful if you'd come with me."

"Please, let's go," William said.

"Be good for him," Moss added. "Keep his mind off, well, things. Except for eating, he'll be outside playing all day."

I was pleased he wanted us to go, but I always felt awkward and out of place in a crowd. Neither Paw nor Stub was much for going places where there were lots of folks. But William's smiling face made me feel weak. It was the first time I'd seen him excited about anything since Stub'd died.

I looked at Moss and nodded. "What should we wear?"

"What you always wear. We don't dress up. William'll need play clothes."

"Well, then what should I bring?"

"Nothing. There's always more food than everybody together can eat."

"I won't feel right if I don't bring something."

"Then bake one of your apple pies," I said. "They always have pumpkin, and I don't like pumpkin pie."

"Me neither," William said.

"Well, then, I better take apple pie." *And pray for strength.*

245

Moss

I was so glad Hope and William went to Thanksgiving dinner with me. Each year it was getting harder and harder to get through the day. It was amazing how alone I could feel with the family I'd always fought to keep together. LC's studying to be a doctor had made everything all right for Maw. His studying medicine was more important to her than marriages, new grandbabies, than anything.

As we walked toward the porch of Maw's house, Hope moved slowly, but William ran up the steps and knocked before we even reached the porch.

I could feel Hope holding back as we went up the steps. I took her elbow and said, "Come on. It's okay. They won't bite."

When Maw opened the door, she smiled and said, "Well, what a beautiful sight." She bent over, reached her arms out to William and said, "Give me a hug." Then she looked up at me. "You're looking good, Moss." She said to Hope, "And you're a breath of fresh air. I'm so glad you're here."

Hope dropped her eyes and said, "Thank you for having us."

"We hear so much about you from Moss. But we don't have to visit on the porch. Come on in. I have to warn you, there's a houseful of people here."

Hope slid her arm through mine, and I said, "Come on."

The house was full of smells of turkey, hot breads, pumpkin pie and coffee. Our family had grown with in-laws and grandchildren. Even Ray Lindsey was there. People cluttered around us, and everyone hugged everyone. Even though William knew all them, he slid his hand in mine and held on tightly. Children were running and squealing, and shortly they whisked William off with them. Kathleen passed her new baby girl Mattie around from person to person, and Ellie's toddler Raymond was into everything.

246

Maw ignored all the noise and said to Hope, "I'm so sorry about your husband. My Moss thought the world of him. And William has already become a part of our family. I'd like to keep him."

It was a real mouthful for Maw. Hope said, "Thank you for including us. It's good we didn't have to be alone."

Maw waved her arm around the room and laughed. "It'll be hard to feel alone here with all the commotion."

Not really, I thought. Used to be, they all needed me. Not any more, not even LC. William reminded me of LC. He was small and blond-headed, smart, too, like LC. I'd spent much more time with him than I'd ever spent with my brother. I'd known him almost his whole life, knew him much better than I knew LC when he was a child. I didn't intend to let gaps grow between me and William.

Even after Thanksgiving I was still uncertain what to do about Hope and William. I wanted to see them, but I wasn't sure what was proper. Stub had only been dead a little over a month. I was scared when I was comfortable and even more scared when I was uncomfortable. The Friday before Christmas I was supposed to go for supper, and planned to take them into Knoxville to see the Christmas lights, but when I got there William wasn't home. Hope said he was spending the night with Roger McNeil, one of Cleve's nephews.

She said, "Tomorrow they're going to practice for the Christmas play at the church, so Maude called to see if William could sleep over." She lowered her eyes and said, "I'm sorry he's not here, but I thought it'd be good for him."

"Sure," I said. We ate in silence. As we cleaned the dishes, Hope grinned up at me.

"What?" I said.

"Stub would roll over in his grave if he could see you in that apron. He wouldn't be caught dead in the kitchen except to eat. He'd declare I've ruint you."

We both laughed. I said, "I 'spect he'd washed a dish or two before you all got married. Just wouldn't admit to it."

She quit laughing. "I doubt it. He ate with me and Paw all the time. Then he went back to the dorm, and me and Paw'd clean up. Paw didn't care to do dishes. I think it's nice when you help in the kitchen." She hung her head and blushed.

"Look," I said, "I'd planned to take you and William into Knoxville to see the decorations. Let's go anyway. You and me. What'd you say? Do you good to get out."

She smiled and inspected the dish in her hand. "William would really have enjoyed that, Moss. It was a nice thing to think of. If I'd known, he wouldn't have gone over to Roger's."

"We'll go next week with him, maybe take Roger, too, but let's go tonight, anyway. What'd you say?"

"Do you think we should?"

"Well, who could we ask? We're the adults."

She laughed again, folded her dishrag and said, "What should I wear?"

"What you've got on's perfect."

She looked pretty in her red plaid dress with the white collar and her thick curly hair hanging loose.

She took off her white apron with red poinsettias embroidered on it and said, "But shouldn't I change?"

"No. You look nice. You always do." She reddened again. I said, "We're not going to do nothing special. Drive around, see the lights, maybe walk on Gay Street. See Santa Claus." I winked at her and said, "Santa won't care what you got on."

Her face brightened. "Okay, let's go."

As we put on coats and hats, I said, "Get your gloves and boots. Looks like it could snow."

As we neared Knoxville, we began to see brightly colored lights.

"Oh, Moss, it's so pretty," she said. "I've never seen nothing like it."

"We'll drive out to Kern's Bakery before we stop anywhere," I said, as I headed towards Chapman Highway. "I want you to see it. They always have nice decorations."

"You sound like you're used to all this," she said.

"Not really. But I've come on the train for the last three or four years. Nothing else to do. This year I feel really up-town in my new Ford with a lovely woman in it."

She grinned and looked out the window.

"Look," I said. "There's Gay Street Bridge, and that's the Tennessee River. The Holston back home runs into it."

The moonlight was reflected in the river, as well as the colored Christmas lights that lit up the town.

"Oh, it's so beautiful."

"Maybe sometime this spring you'd like to drive up to the Forks of the River and see where the two rivers meet."

"Oh, yes, that would be wonderful. Oh, look."

We were passing the bakery. The decoration for the year was the nativity scene with life-sized wooden figures of Mary and Joseph and the baby. There was a stable, shepherds, wise men, and camels and sheep, too. A star was overhead, and the entire scene was lit up with big spotlights.

"We'll turn around and come back," I said. We pulled over next to the curb on her side of the car. Other cars had also stopped. Hope put her face up to the window. I watched her long curls, wanting to touch one, as she gazed at the scene.

"It looks so real," she said.

"Yes," I said, realizing what I needed was a real woman who lived in a real world.

When she turned back toward me, she had tears in her eyes.

"What's wrong? I said.

"Oh, nothing. It's just so beautiful. And to think that somebody carved out that scene so everybody can look at it."

"It's supposed to make you feel good, not bad."

"Oh, I do. It's just, well, haven't you ever felt so good that somehow it made you sad, and it all mixed together?"

I nodded. It always seemed to me that pleasure mixed with pain. But somehow it didn't seem so bad when she said it.

I pulled the car back onto Chapman Highway, and said, "Take a last look. We're going back to Gay Street. I think we should park the car and walk."

After we re-crossed the river, I pulled into a parking spot. The air was brisk as we walked down the street crowded with shoppers. Hope walked close to me as though she was afraid she would lose me, and maybe to ward off the cold air. I was glad, for it gave me a good excuse to pull her arm through mine.

The noises of the city and of Christmas rang in the icy air. Trolleys clanged, carolers sang, automobiles tooted, Salvation Army Santa Clauses rang their bells, and coins jingled as people dropped them into the tin cups of beggars who sat huddled against cold buildings. Some had bells, too, which they rang for attention. They were all dirty and ragged and shivering. Some were missing legs, some were blind. The contrast to the happy, hurrying shoppers carrying their packages was disturbing. People seemed to be used to walking around the beggars and pretending not to see them. I wondered what was wrong with the city. We didn't have beggars in Outcropping. I dropped a few coins here and there into extended cups, knowing it wouldn't really make a difference in their lives.

"I've never seen a real beggar before," Hope said. "It's like in the Bible." She hung onto me more tightly than before. "Don't these folks have nobody to take care of them? No family or nothing?"

"I don't know. Never saw a beggar either before coming to Knoxville, and there's more than usual out tonight. Guess it's Christmas. When I was a kid, we had people come by the farm wanting a meal or a place to sleep in the barn for a night once in a while, but they always chopped wood or carried water or

250

something. It wasn't like this. It always makes me feel so helpless—and hopeless."

As we came to Miller's Department Store, I wheeled Hope through the revolving door and tried to forget about the beggars. "Come on," I said, "help me pick out something for William for Christmas. What would he like?"

"You don't have to get him nothing."

"I didn't ask if I had to get him something. I asked what he'd like. I want to get him something special. He's had a rough year."

We looked at toy cars and trucks and trains. Hope kept saying everything cost too much, and I finally decided I'd have to come back without her to get him something. I got her interested in looking at watches for Maw. She'd never had one. Hope's eyes lit up as I had her lay different ones on her arm to look at them, and it occurred to me that I'd never seen a watch on her arm. I decided that'd be another thing I'd return for.

We drank in the smells of chocolate and nuts as we passed the candy section. I bought some chocolates in a bag to take to William, and also a box to give Maw. For many years I'd bought a box for her and for Aunt Minnie at Christmas. It didn't seem right when the lady rang up only one.

"Let's go," I said.

"Are we going home?"

"One more stop," I said, as I guided her through the crowd.

I loved the dime stores. I pulled her into Kress's, where the scents of food from the lunch counter mingled together with popcorn and salted nuts. We worked our way through the mass of people to the counter in the basement and waited to sit on the revolving stools until we saw two together empty. Hope's eyes were as bright as the Christmas lights as she whirled around on her stool seat.

"Whee! I love it," she said.

"What would you love to eat?"

"I don't know. What do you want?"

"How about a warm piece of apple pie and a cup of coffee?"

"Sounds delicious," she said.

After we ate, we pushed our way back through the crowd once again. We stared at all the toys for sale. Neither of us had ever really played with toys. But there was nothing as fine as what I'd seen in Madeline's room she'd had as a child.

Hope was fascinated at the assortment of dolls, and I stood behind her to protect her from being pushed and shoved by the mob of people. She was particularly taken with a doll carriage.

She looked up and said, "I always wanted a doll carriage. I never even had a carriage for William."

At that moment I wanted a child, a child of my own that I could raise. I'd never pictured myself with a little girl since I'd known I had a son, but all of a sudden I wanted a little girl with a doll carriage. It was also the first time in my life I'd thought of having a child with anyone other than Madeline. The urge was real and strong.

I let Hope look as long as she wanted, and I took a lot of bumps from shoppers while I did.

"I know I'm foolish," she said, "but I guess I've never grown up."

"No, I think it's that you were never a child."

She put her small hand on the fancy carriage and then said, "I'm ready to go."

We again merged into the traffic of people, and left the store. As we walked back toward the car, a few snow flurries began to fall.

"It's such a lovely evening," she said as I opened the car door for her. "I hate to see it end. Thank you for bringing me."

"Thank you for letting me bring you," I said.

I took a deep breath as I walked around to the driver's side of the car. As we turned off Gay Street at Regas Restaurant onto Magnolia Avenue and drove back toward Outcropping, we watched the snowflakes fly into the windshield. Hope snuggled into her coat, which pushed her curls up around her collar.

252

"It's too bad William couldn't have seen all this," she said.

"We'll come back. Besides there's always next year."

She looked out the window next to her, and said nothing.

"What's wrong?"

"Nothing. But we won't be here next year, Moss."

I felt sick. I didn't know of any plans she had to leave, but of course she wouldn't stay on and on in Outcropping, unless . . .

"We can't keep on living in the company house," she said.

"I'll see to it that you can stay as long as you like."

"No, it's not right. There's miners that need the house. We have to go."

I gripped the steering wheel hard. "I don't mean to pry, but do you need any money?"

"No. It's kind of you to ask, and I wouldn't never take anything you ask as prying. But I need help deciding where to go and maybe help with moving. I've never lived anywhere but Outcropping, at least that I can remember much about. I got a little money to work with. Stub had some put back, both from him and from my father. I never knew my paw had left me anything. Then Stub made pretty good as a contractor for years, you know. He never spent much. Always told me he didn't buy me things because some day he would be able to give me money when it would be more important. Then, after he had the pneumonia, he showed me where it was. Said I should know where it was when, well, if he, if something happened to him. Remind me to show you where it is, when we get home. Somebody besides me ought to know. Anything can happen. You never know." Her teeth chattered and she sank deeper into her coat.

For a while we rode along saying nothing. Finally I couldn't stand it any more, and I said, "Where?"

"Why, in the bedroom." She reddened again. "I'll show you when we get home."

"No, I mean, where will you go? You, uh, you wouldn't go back to Kentucky, would you?"

253

I couldn't imagine life without her and William, but it was so soon to ask her to marry me. I didn't know what she'd say. But this time, I swore to myself, the woman I loved was not going to get away.

"Why, no. I wouldn't even know how to get to Kentucky," she said. "I have no idea where we should live. That's what's so hard. Maybe I'll buy a little house in Knoxville for us. I love the city. Of course, William would like the country. But I'd have to make a living, and I don't know what I could do in the country. I could work at a shop or something in town. Maybe selling dolls. I'd like that. And, well, you could come see us."

"You think you got enough money to buy a house?"

She nodded. "I don't really know what houses cost," she said, "but I think so. Stub said I did. But, wherever I go, I'll always keep whatever money I got left in the same drawer of the same chest it's in now. That way, if anything ever happens to me, you'll know where it is for William. You would take him, wouldn't you?"

"Nothing's going to happen to you."

"You never know. My maw died when I was little. So, just in case."

I never wanted her to marry me because she had to, and Stub wouldn't have, either. But the fact that she could be independent scared the hell out of me. It'd never occurred to me that maybe she wouldn't want to marry me in time. I didn't want her to move away and maybe meet someone else. Neither of us spoke as we drove the last few miles with snow flying into the windshield. When we pulled up in front of her house, it was late.

"Come on in," she said. "I want to show you where the money is."

"It's late, and maybe I shouldn't know."

"You got to know," she said. "I've got nobody else. You'll need it if you ever have to take care of William."

"Promise you'll always let me know where you go."

"Oh, I will, of course" she said.

We entered the house, and she turned on the light and walked toward the bedroom. I stood still, watching her.

"Come on," she said. "It's in here. In a chest."

She had no idea of the feelings she was arousing in me, and I was afraid to move.

"Well, come on," she said. "It's right here. See?"

I could see her through the open door, standing at an old oak chest of drawers. I walked slowly into the room. She pulled out the top drawer.

"Watch closely," she said.

She put her small hands down on one end and pried loose a board that lay next to the side of the drawer. I would never have known it was a fake side.

"Isn't that something?" she said, smiling. "Stub rigged it up."

She took out an envelope and handed it to me. I looked in. I was afraid to speak, as though unseen ears might hear. I leaned over to her and whispered, "There's all kinds of money in here."

"I know," she said. "Enough to buy a house and live for a while, isn't it?"

"Looks like it to me."

"Stub said a lot of it was money Paw'd put back for me." She bowed her head, and her voice broke when she said, "Stub never spent one penny of it."

"Hope, you ought to be happy. My God, you can do whatever you want. You're free to, to, well, to do whatever you want. You can get away from all this dust."

Without raising her head she said, "But I don't know what I want. I don't know nothing but here. This is where everybody I— love—is." She looked up at me and quickly lowered her head again. After a moment she said, "Are you really free if freedom takes you away from where you want to be?" She pushed the back of her hand against her eyes and attempted a little laugh. "Guess I'm just a little scared. I'll be all right."

I took hold of her curls that flowed down her back, the curls I'd always wanted to touch. She didn't do anything, and I touched her face with my other hand and bent over to kiss her. When I pulled her to me, she made a quiet cry.

We kissed for a moment. Then we stood for a while with our arms around each other and her head buried in my shirt. I think I could have stood like that forever.

When she finally moved, she looked up at me and said, "I'll stay here for a while if they will let me."

I was happier than I had been in years. Not just happy. I was at peace. I had never known such a peace, at least not since I was a little boy, back when Paw lived at home with us. "Marry me, Hope. Now. Tomorrow. Next week. Quick. God, I was so afraid you were going to leave me."

She laughed and cried at the same time. "I was afraid you were going to let me. But shouldn't we wait a little while?"

"I've waited all my life. I'm taking no chances you're going to go away."

"I'm not going to go away," she whispered, "not until they put me in the earth."

Gadget

Moss'd told me he was going to get my boy on as night shift foreman when an opening came up. He's a good boy, smart. He always admired Moss, wanted to be like him. He worked hard to learn all the jobs as had to be done in the mine, and he was anxious to move up. Moss'd put him on drilling under Fats, who'd been drilling for years. Sometimes that's good. Sometimes it's bad. Fats knew his job well, but he was set in his ways, which was older than the union's regulations. Moss was on him all the time about dry drilling, like he had to be on all the old timers. I told Junior when he went to work with him, I said, if Fats sets into dry drilling, you cut his water on anyway. But what happened to Junior didn't have nothing to do with dry drilling anyway, even though Fats had been doing just that when it happened.

Moss said he'd come up on them working, and Fats was hidden in a cloud of dust, which you don't get if you use water. Moss went up to him and tapped him on the shoulder, and he said Fats jumped so he almost dropped his drill.

"Damn you, Chief," he said. "You near scared me to death."

"You know what I'm going to say," Moss said.

"Yeah, yeah, but we're trying to finish up here 'fore we stop for the day. You know that water's a pain in the ass."

Moss told him he didn't care. It saved lives. The old timers know wet drilling keeps them from breathing in them rock slivers and solves the problem of setting off misfired dynamite, but they insist it slows them down. Moss told Fats he was going to give him days off without pay if he come back around and he had his water off. Gave him a lecture about how if he hit dynamite, he'd not only hurt himself, but Junior, too, and him with twins to feed. Moss didn't leave till Fats started drilling again, his water on. He walked over to take a look at the ore they were uncovering when he said Junior dropped his drill, fell back and covered his eyes with his hands, yelling that his eyes was burning. Moss looked to see what had happened, and so did Fats. Moss said he couldn't see nothing that could be causing the burning. It had to be gas. Then his own eyes began to burn and so did Fats'.

Junior kept yelling that he couldn't see, and Moss and Fats got him to the cage, with their own eyes burning and watering. Moss sent for me, and Avery went topside with me. We found them in Mr. Frazier's office. They'd washed out their eyes, and Mr. Frazier was fixing to drive them all to Doc Timer's.

Junior reached his hand for me and said, "Daddy, I can't see."

I never felt so bad in my life.

We all piled in the car, and when we got to Doc's office, he said they had to get Junior to Knoxville, that they all needed to go, but Junior'd took the gas full force. I told Mr. Frasier I could take them all in my car and sent Avery over to my house to get it.

On the way, Junior was moaning and saying he couldn't see and how would he take care of his babies. We tried to assure him everything would be all right. Fats felt awful, saying he was sorry for not using water in his drill.

Moss said, "It not your fault, Fats. Gases hide in pockets in the rocks, waiting to be set free, and sometimes dry or wet, the drills open them up."

"Maybe water would've help filter it," Fats said.

Moss told him Junior had his water on. "Nobody knows what can be done about gases that don't smell or show themselves till you hit them. But I'm going to try to find out."

The doctors cleaned out their eyes and said Moss and Fats would probably be all right, but they don't know about Junior. Fats said he wished it'd been him, he was old and didn't have many years anyway. Junior had his life ahead of him.

Moss felt awful, too. Blamed hisself, even though he told Fats it wasn't nobody's fault. I told him wasn't nothing nobody could've done, that some things is in the hands of the good Lord, and we have to trust he knows more than we do. Moss said when he was young, he'd swore to stop accidents in the mine, that he'd thought they were caused by mistakes people made, and so could be done away with.

Avery said, "You aint God, Moss. You can do a lot, but you can't do everything. You can't even stop all mistakes, let alone things that's got no rhyme nor reason to them. None of us is perfect, not even you."

Moss said he knowed that better'n anybody.

For once, Avery was right. He wasn't trying to be smartelecky. He was just telling it like it is. Pain and suffering will always be around on this old earth. It aint no respecter of persons. The book of Job says that. The doctors say only time will tell about Junior's eyes. And we don't like to wait. We want answers in our time, not God's. Me more'n anybody. Junior's my boy. I'd give anything if I could make him well. Was a time when I thought there couldn't be nothing better in the world than having that car I drove Moss to Doc's in, way back yonder that day at the creek. But now I'd give ever car that's ever been made if Junior could just see.

Moss

The spring after Hope and me got married, we were expecting a baby. She needed some time to rest, and one Sunday afternoon I took William out to the country to visit Maw and the family. It was a perfect day for a drive. Leaves were popping out, and grass was tuning green. New calves nursed from their mothers, and baby colts ran on spindly legs. The woods and fields looked like patchwork quilts of green and yellow and purple.

"Can I take Maw some flowers, Uncle Moss? They don't have no dust on them out here. You reckon it'd make her feel better?"

"I'm sure it would," I said, "but let's wait till we get to Grandmaw's, and you can get Maxine to help you pick some."

I slowed down and pointed to a white horse in a pasture with a colt by her side. "Aint that about the prettiest thing you ever saw?"

He stuck his head out the window. "It sure is. I like to ride Maxine's horse at Aunt Kat's."

"Would you like to have a horse?"

"We can't have a horse in Outcropping. Where would we put it?"

"We could keep one at Grandmaw's, keep it with Maxine's."

He settled back in his seat and said, "Would you really get me a horse?"

"I think a horse would be good for us both. I'll talk to Grandmaw."

When we pulled up at Maw's, Maxine ran out to meet us. Ellie was busy with her baby, and Maw fixed us some lemonade and cookies. William was already off with Maxine, and Maw and me settled in the rockers on the porch. I asked her about keeping an extra horse or two.

"I'll buy feed and anything else they need, and I'll pay Maxine something for tending to it."

"You know you can keep a horse or anything else you want here. You don't need to pay Maxine. She loves to work with the animals, like her Uncle LC. And William needs a horse. He rides like you, always puts me in the mind of you when you was a little boy ever time I see him sitting on a horse." She looked over at me. "You got a good life for yourself."

"I know."

"I thank the good Lord for that," she said. "Was a time when I worried—well, that you spent your life trying so hard to make a life for us that you wouldn't take time to have a life of your own." She reached over and patted my hand, which wasn't like her. "We never talked much, you and me."

"Reckon we didn't have to, Maw."

She nodded and sat leaning forward with her arms on the sides of the rocker, staring across the fields. Then she pulled her shoulders up and settled back into the chair. She crossed her legs and pressed her apron down neatly. She still wore her thick hair pulled back severely from her face, but her black hair was streaked with gray. Her high cheekbones were more pronounced than ever, and the fine lines around her eyes and mouth had deepened.

As she reached down to pick up her glass of lemonade off the porch beside her chair, I noticed her long fingers were more slender than ever, and veins mapped her hands more than I remembered. She was getting old. Like so much else, I hadn't noticed before. She'd always been so strong, so permanent, like the dark mountains beyond the fields. She shifted in her chair, uncomfortable when she saw me looking at her.

"You all right, Maw?" I said.

"Why, yes. Fit as a fiddle." Her smile came easier than I remembered, and it reassured me. She'd never been one to waste smiles any more than she wasted words.

We sat quietly for a while, listening to the noises of spring, hearing the children every once in a while. Then she said, "I don't rightly know how to put what I got to say."

I looked over at her. "You said you were all right."

261

"Oh, I am. Never better. But I've been meaning to talk to you. There never seemed to be a good time. You know, Ellie and Joe's got their own little family, now that Raymond's here, and, well, I think it'd be nice if they had this place to theirselves."

"Where would you go? You want to come live with me and Hope?"

"Oh, no. I want to stay out here in the country. I'll never leave little Mattie."

"Have Ellie and Joe said anything to you?"

"No, no, nothing like that."

"Well, if you want a place to yourself, me and Ray's boys could build you a little house. Or I'm sure the Lindseys will help build Ellie and Joe their own place."

"I don't need a house. I'm just trying to tell you something."

She'd rarely tried to tell me anything since I was thirteen and went to work in Outcropping, except to tell me not to let LC work at the mine.

"What I'm trying to say is that I'm going to be moving out of the old place."

"I thought you said you wouldn't leave the grave plot."

"I'm only moving a few acres away, I'm, I'm going to . . . that is, me and Ray, well, we're going to get married."

I couldn't take it in. She was fifty-three years old!

"I'm going to marry Ray Lindsey," she said again. "He's been alone for a long time now. I been alone over half my life."

She'd never been alone. At least one of my sisters or LC had always lived with her. As if in answer to my thoughts, she said, "Even old folks needs a partner, Moss. You're married now, with a fine little family. Max and Kathleen's got their family, and Ellie and Joe's got Raymond. And, LC, well, he's all set in that fancy college. Going to be a doctor." She paused and smiled. "You all got lives of your own now. You don't need me no more."

She patted the air for me not to say anything. "Ray, his kids is all moved out now, and he's in that big old house by hisself. Fred

and Molly's built them a house on the farm. Ray
between Joe and Fred, and Joe took the acreag
fingered the rim of her glass. "Me and Ray's b⟨
understand what I'm saying, Moss?"

I was having a hard time with it, but I nodded.

"I aint said nothing to the girls yet. Wanted to talk to you
first, but I'll be telling them now, that is, if it's all right by you."

"You don't need my permission," I said. "It's just that, I
never thought, I mean, nothing here ever changes."

"Things always change, son."

"Yes, I guess they do, but we'll always need you, me and LC
and the girls. You know that. I don't want you to do this on
account of anybody else. And I don't want you to go over there
because you think Ray needs somebody to wait on him, either."

"Oh, I don't think of it as going to work for him, Moss. I've
been working for him for years, anyway. That's what I do, you
know. And he needs somebody to provide for, to feel responsible
for, too. He's a good man. He's worked hard all his life. So've I."

I couldn't picture Maw with anybody but Paw, but he'd
been dead for so many years, for more years than she'd lived with
him. Then I thought of Stub, and what he'd told me about Hope,
and I knew Paw wouldn't object to Maw marrying someone else.

"When we get married, that'll give Ellie and Joe this place
to theirselves," she said, "lessen you got any objections to that, of
course. They done a lot of work on it, you know, added rooms and
all. But you've put money into the place before they were married,
and they wouldn't want you to think they're taking it over."

"Lord, I don't care what you all do with the house, Maw.
Mostly what I put into it was work, not money. Do whatever you
want with it. But the land, the land needs to stay in the family."

"It will. Kathleen and Max don't want it. They're thinking
of moving into Knoxville, be nearer to the university." She held her
hands together in her lap and smiled. "Max is working on some big
degree, you know. Then he hopes to teach there, and Kathleen
plans to teach when the kids is both in school. Joe and Fred's

ıming all Ray's land and ours too now, along with Ray, of course. He's still going like he always did, but one of these days, he'll have to let up, and the boys will run it, so it makes sense for Ellie and Joe to have the farm, 'cept for what you want of it. God knows you ought to keep some of the land. We can split it between you and Ellie, let Ellie have what joins Lindseys', if that suits you. That would give you the burial lot, and it'll stay in the family. Joe and his brother can work it all until you retire. Maybe you'd like to come back here then, build you a house, keep a few animals. None of us want to do anything you don't want us to do."

We sat quite for a while, and finally I said, "Let me think on it, Maw. I never thought I'd be able to come back home, and I hate to take land that Joe needs to farm. But maybe I'll keep just a few acres on the far end near the creek. That'd be a pretty place to build a house. I like the idea of retiring out here someday. Being near everybody."

"Wouldn't that be something?" she said.

"It sure would. And, if the graveyard winds up being on Ellie's part, that's okay. She and her children will probably stay on the land longer than any of us."

"This has been a wonderful day," Maw said. Her face reflected none of the strained look I'd seen her with for so many years. A gentle breeze blew across the porch, and she said, "Gonna be a shower, I think. We need us some rain. Keeps everything growing."

———————————

We were at Ray's house for Thanksgiving the day Grace was born. I still couldn't think of it as Maw's house, but I guess it was. The big house was full of people, with all the children and grandchildren that could get there from both sides of the family. William was in heaven with so many children to play with. Even LC came home from the university. He was spending his three or four days with Doc and Aunt Emmy, since they had no one to stay with them, but he'd come to the country to be with the family for the evening meal. We'd invited Doc and Emmy, but they said they'd be overwhelmed with so many people. I didn't blame them. Sometimes I was, too. Hope was heavy and swollen and looked miserable, but she insisted we should join the family for dinner. After we ate, I watched her laugh weakly at stories people told and constantly shift her position on the couch. Finally she said she thought we should go. LC went out and hollered for William, and we all piled in the car and set off for Outcropping.

As we pulled out of the lane, Hope held her belly and said, "I think you better hurry."

"Lord," I said, "why didn't you say something?"

"I wasn't sure, and I didn't want to spoil everyone's day."

"You all right, Maw?" William said.

"Sure, honey. I just think it might be time for the baby."

I bit my lip and pushed harder on the gas pedal. The drive back seemed longer than the time it actually took, as her pains began coming regularly. I was driving so fast, LC finally said that we didn't need a wreck to add to the problem.

When we pulled up to Doc's, he came out to greet us. He took one look at Hope and said, "Get her in here. LC, run tell Emmy we're coming into the guest room with the little mama. Then, wash up."

He helped me get Hope to the bedroom. When LC came in he said, "You brought any babies into the world yet?"

"Only animals."

"Good enough." He told me to help Emmy with William and for us to stay out of the way.

I wanted to help, but he said, "I don't do well with daddies. Besides, LC knows what he's doing."

Hope said, "Do as Doc says, Moss. Stay with William."

As I left the room, Doc said, "Tell Em to heat me some water and some towels."

When William saw me come down the hall, he ran into my arms. "Can I see Maw?"

"Me and you better stay out here," I said. "It's okay. Women have babies every day. I guess they think me and you'd be in the way, huh? They always get the men out of the way, you know."

"But LC's in there."

"That's different. He's going to be a doctor, like Doc."

"I'm going to be a doctor, too," he said.

"I'm warming coffee," Aunt Emmy said. "You boys ready for some supper?"

William groaned, and I said we ate so much at Maw's I didn't think I'd ever eat again and that Doc wanted hot water and towels.

"Maybe after I take care of that I could interest you boys in some stack cake."

Later we both sat at the kitchen table and picked at a piece of cake. William said, "How long does it take to have a baby, Uncle Moss?"

"I reckon there's no set time," I said. "Depends on the mama and the baby."

"My cat had kittens last year, and it didn't take her very long."

"Well, it will probably take your mama a little longer."

Doc had warned us that it might take a good while, as it'd been so long since she'd had a baby, and since she was so little and I was so big. When we first heard Hope scream, William bolted out of his seat and ran for the bedroom. It was all I could do to catch him before he got there.

"Let me go," he said. "I got to see 'bout my maw. Let me go."

He beat his fists into my chest, and finally he buried his face into my shirt and cried. I put my arms around him and took him back into the kitchen.

"It's all right," I said. "She'll be all right. There's some pain now and then. But it's natural."

"What if she dies?"

266

"She's not going to die," I said. "She's just having a baby. Women have babies all the time."

"My paw died, and he was just at work."

"That was different," I said.

He looked up at me with big, round eyes and said in a shaky voice, "Will you send me to a orphanage if she dies?"

"I'll never let you go," I said, "even if something happened to your Maw. And if something happened to me, you'd still have LC and Aunt Kathleen and Aunt Ellie and Grandmaw and even Doc and Aunt Emmy. Only problem you'd have would be keeping them from fighting over who'd get to keep you."

"You mean it?"

"Of course, I mean it. You'll never, never be without family."

He reached up and hugged me and said, "I'm sorry I hit you."

"Yeah," I said, "it's a wonder you didn't kill me. Let's go into the library and listen to the radio."

I shut the library door and turned on the radio, thinking he might not hear any more screams. We listened to Charlie McCarthy until late, and William fell sleep on the sofa. I covered him with an afghan that lay over the back. Then I went into the kitchen where Aunt Emmy was boiling more water.

"What's going on?" I said.

"It's slow. But nothing seems to be wrong," she said as she poured me a cup of coffee.

Then I heard Hope, and jumped up to go check on her.

Emmy put her hand on my arm. "Wait. Let me go see if it's a good time for you to see her."

I followed her to the bedroom, but waited outside the door until she came back to get me. As I entered the room, Hope was gripping the spindles along the headboard. Emmy dampened a cloth in the bowl beside the bed and wiped her forehead.

She said, "Moss's here."

I walked lightly as I could to the bed, afraid I might somehow jar the room. Hope's face and hair were wet. Her lips were swollen, and her eyes were dark. She let go of the spindles and grasped my hands. I reached over and kissed her forehead. She grinned at me, then said, "I'm sorry I'm so much trouble."

"I'm sorry it's so hard," I said.

Suddenly she arched and screamed, and squeezed my hand so hard I wanted to yell.

"Do something," I said to Doc.

"It's about time. Now, go, and let us do the doctoring."

I went back to the library to check on William. He was still asleep, and I sat in a big chair beside the sofa. I let my head rest against the back and shut my eyes, though I couldn't sleep. Shortly I heard the sound of a baby crying. I laughed out loud and ran down the hall. As I barged into the room, LC was cleaning a red, wrinkled baby. Her tiny head was covered with dark hair.

Doc was still working with Hope, and he said, "Hell, man, can't you give us time to finish?" But he looked up and smiled. "Did all right, didn't we, the little mama and us?"

Hope looked as though she were asleep. I went to her and touched her face. She opened her eyes and slowly lifted her arm as though it were weighted. I knelt by the bed and grasped her hand.

LC wrapped the baby in a towel and laid her beside Hope. "Look at my beautiful niece," he said to me.

"She is beautiful."

"Count her fingers and toes," Hope said.

"Ten all together," said LC. "Already counted them. What's her name?"

"My maw's name was Grace." Hope looked up at me. "You think that'd be okay?"

"It's perfect. Could we put it with Aunt Minnie's name? Maybe Minerva Grace? We'll call her Grace."

"That's nice," she said and fell asleep. I was full of most every emotion a man could feel, all at once. I couldn't keep from thinking of Madeline who'd gone through this all alone, at least with no one close to her. I swore Grace would never go through anything like this by herself. I'd be there for her, no matter what.

The pleasant spring of 1940 turned into a hot summer. One morning Mr. Frazier had me come up from the coolness of the mine to the sweltering July humidity and heat.

"I need you to run an errand for me," he said.

When some stuffy company official came in from St. Louis, he usually sent me to get him. The company chauffeur picked up inspectors and anyone else who came, but for some reason, Mr. Frazier'd always get me to meet the big shots.

I asked him who I was meeting.

"Don't think you'll mind playing chauffeur today." He grinned. "This isn't the usual run-of-the-mill mine president. It's a lovely lady."

"What?"

He nodded, pitching me the keys to his Packard. He always had me use his car. Guess he thought my Ford wasn't good enough.

"She's expecting someone at the station at 10:15," he said, "so you better head on out."

"Who am I looking for? How will I know her?"

"She'll probably be the only lady to get off the train. I don't know exactly what she'll look like. Haven't seen her in years, not since she was a very young woman. She used to be tall and thin and blond. For all I know, by now she might be gray and fat. Remember Carl Rogers who used to live across the street from me and Mildred?"

I lost my breath when he said that, but he didn't seem to notice. "His daughter is coming in. She called to see if I could have her picked up when she arrived."

I sat down in the nearest chair. He looked at me. I never sat while he stood unless he told me to.

"It's hot," I said.

"Hotter'n hell." He looked at his watch. "You better get going."

I needed a few more minutes. "What's she coming for? She didn't even come in for her father's funeral."

"I know. Odd. But I understand she was ill at the time. Anyway, it seems her husband passed away recently, and she always wanted to move into her folks' homeplace. Her family was quite wealthy, you know. Lived in a beautiful home on a big farm down by the river. She's kept it all these years. Must be in a pretty serious state of disrepair. Anyway, she says she's gong to fix it up and move into it. The land hasn't been farmed in forever. Carl never would move to the country, but Madeline spent a lot of time there when she was a little girl. The place must hold lots of memories for her. Drove her out there myself a few times."

I sank deeper into the straight chair and leaned my head against the back.

"You all right?" he asked.

"Sure, but this heat is getting to me."

"Well, go on and get out of here. It's bound to be cooler outside. She'll be going to The Inn. She'll stay there until she gets the old place fixed up enough to live in."

My head was pounding. Maybe I was asleep and would wake up to find this wasn't happening. But I tripped over my own feet walking out, which reassured me that I was indeed awake.

"Careful," Mr. Frazier said, "I'd like you to get there in one piece. And don't wreak the car."

As I drove to the station, thoughts flooded my head. Why was this happening now? Why not two or three years sooner? The timing was always off with Madeline. Everything was either too soon or too late. Not that it mattered. She'd take one look at me in these dusty mining clothes and be glad she escaped a life with me. I arrived before the train did, pulled over under a big elm tree and got out of the hot car. I leaned against it and tried to breathe the air deep into my lungs, but only coughed. My mind raced. I pictured Madeline coming up to me coolly, saying, "Did I keep you waiting long, Moss?" I'd say, "Oh, of course not, only sixteen years." I heard the whistle and shook my head to erase the crazy vision.

She stepped down from the train and looked around, her beautiful head turning on her long, thin neck. All I could do was stare. She was still slender, even thinner than I remembered, and her blond hair fell to her shoulders. She looked cool in a white linen suit. I didn't know if she'd recognize me. I hadn't meant to her what she'd meant to me. When her eyes found me, her hand went to her mouth, and she stood still on the platform, like she'd turned into a statue.

My eyes drank her in, but I still couldn't move. Then she was coming towards me, floating like a fairy in a dream. Suddenly she was in my arms. There was the same fragrance, the same fit. I'd always been amazed how her body fit into mine. We were like two parts of a puzzle that merged together. I held her tightly for a moment. She raised her head. Her eyes drew me in, and I realized she expected me to kiss her.

My mind was in a war of feelings. I stepped back and stammered, "Madeline, god, why did you come back here?"

"Didn't you believe I would?"

"Yes, I did. For many years. But not after all this time."

"I came back to The Willows," she said. "I don't really have ties anywhere else. What are you doing here?"

"Same thing as always, working for the company."

"No, I mean, what are you doing here at the station? Mr. Frazier said someone would meet me, and I'm expecting Jim or maybe the chauffeur any minute. They do still have the chauffeur, don't they?"

"Yeah, they do, but Mr. Frazier sent me."

"He sent you? But why?"

"He often sends me to meet folks. Jim's not here any more."

"He's not? Where is he?"

"He was sent out West as a supervisor."

271

"He was?"

"Yes, he was. And he finally married Sadie, or she married him."

"Well, I'll be. I wondered when or if that was ever going to happen."

We stood there a minute, not knowing what else to say. Finally she said, "That still doesn't answer my question. Why you?"

"I guess I was in the right place at the right time—or maybe the wrong place at the wrong time, depending on how you look at it."

She made an attempt at a laugh. "Well, whatever. I'm glad you came. You, uh, you look good."

I pulled out my handkerchief and wiped my forehead. "You do, too. But, then, you always did. I better go get your things." It took me two trips to get all her luggage loaded into the car. It was a good thing I had the Packard.

As I opened the door for her, I said, "Mr. Frazier says you'll be staying at The Inn for a while, till you get the house ready."

"Yes, but I'd like you to take me to the river first." My face must have registered my shock, for she added, "Don't worry. I want to get an idea of what needs to be done to the house. I'd like to move in as soon as possible."

I slammed the door and went around the car to get in. She didn't say anything else, and neither did I until we left Outcropping. When we turned down the river road, I put my arm out the window and looked at the water, trying not to see her, but very aware of her presence.

At last she said, "Is this your car?"

From her tone I knew she didn't think it was. "Mr. Frazier's. I guess he wanted to impress you. Nice, isn't it? I'm sure he thought you were too good for anything, well, normal. He's right, of course. You always were."

She looked at me without smiling, and said, "How did he come to send you, Moss? Does he know about us?"

"Hell, no. Besides, what's to know?" She looked out the window on her side and said nothing. I felt awful. The whole mess was no more her fault than mine. I said, "Sorry. Actually, I took Jim's place. Don't worry. I'm a good driver because of my experience dodging all the rich ladies on Nobb Hill."

She looked over at me. "You like it?"

"Picking up people?"

"No, of course not. Your job. That's quite amazing."

"Can't complain."

"But it's so unusual. I mean, you're very fortunate to have moved up to such a position with the company. They don't usually, well, you should be very proud."

I turned up the lane to the house. "I worked hard for my job, Madeline. It's cost me dearly."

"I, I didn't mean anything."

"What about you? You like yours?" I said.

"My what?"

"Well, you know, your life, whatever it is you do." She was bringing out the worst in me. She sat silent as I took in a deep breath and looked at the old house that we were approaching. It was smothered in bushes and vines and did not seem as big to me as it had when I was young.

When I parked the car and started to get out, she turned towards me and put her hand on my arm. "We need to talk, Moss. We're avoiding what we really need to say."

"I guess you're right. No point putting it off."

"You're angry and I don't blame you."

"Yes. I am. Why didn't you contact me, or at least Annie? She has worried herself to death. If you didn't want to marry me, you didn't have to. But surely you knew we both needed to know if you were all right. We didn't know if you had the baby, if you lost it, if you gave it away." A big lump came up in my throat. "Or even if you were still alive."

"How much do you know?"

"I finally found out you got married. And that you had a son. My son."

She said, 'Yes. His name is Clell. That was my grandfather's name. He looks like you." She looked away and added, "But I couldn't very well name him Moss."

I wanted to grab her shoulders and shake her. When I could get my breath, I said, "There was a lot of things you could have done that you didn't. Where is he?"

"He's staying with friends until I get situated."

I wanted to ask her more about him, but the words wouldn't come. I reached for the handle and said, "I need to get out of the car."

In a quiet, shaky voice she said, "I'm not sure I ever decided to do anything, Moss. Except to know you. Everything was always chosen for me. Until now." I turned towards her and she was looking out the window on her side of the car. She said louder, "Coming back to The Willows is my decision." She looked back at me. "It will be beautiful again."

It didn't seem likely to me. We sat in silence a moment until the heat became oppressive. I opened the car door and got out and wiped the sweat off my brow, then went around and opened her door with a shaking hand. I watched her long, slender legs come out first. I wanted to hate her, to be angry at her. Part of me did hate her, but part of me was drawn to her.

She stood beside the car, pulled her little white jacket down neatly, and looked as cool as the river water. "For the first time in my life I'm free to do what I want to do and live where I want to live. I'm going to fix up this old house and live in it, and I'm going to see cattle and horses once again in the pastures." She nodded her head firmly.

I shut the car door and said, "Nothing's ever the same, Madeline. And nobody's ever free."

"I know it'll never be like it was before, but it will be as good as it gets in this life. This farm will become home again for Clell and me."

"It'll take a lot of work."

"I know that. I'll hire people to work the farm and to keep the house." She paused, like she was thinking of what to say next. "I'll bring Annie out here."

I knew Annie couldn't come, but I didn't say anything. We went up the walk with weeds growing between the bricks without saying a word. When we got to the porch, I saw the doors and windows were boarded up. Madeline went over to the wall of the house, and ran her long, perfect fingers over the bricks.

She turned around and looked at me. "You would realize this dream, too, if you could, wouldn't you, Moss?"

I nodded and dropped my eyes. My legs felt like rubber, and I sat down on a step, thinking that at one time I could've had all this. I could've had Madeline, my son, this home, the river-bottom land. Except for a hardened old man and a hardened old system.

She sat down beside me, took my sweating hand and said, "It's not too late. We can still have it." I shook my head and she moved against me, put her arm on my shoulder and said, "Yes, we can."

I stood up, leaned against one of the pillars and said, "It is too late."

"Moss," she said, "I know I should've defied everybody years ago, but you don't understand."

"No, that's not it," I said. "I understand."

She raised her eyebrows and said, "Then what?"

"I'm married."

"Married?"

Her face went pale, and suddenly I was angry again. She'd gone off and had her own life. She surely didn't expect me to jump when she was free to come back and start again.

"Married," I said. "What did you think I'd do? Wait around for your husband to die?"

She got up off the step, and stood there pale and quiet. Her fingers formed into fists. Finally she said, "No, of course not."

275

"I shouldn't have said that, Madeline. I'm sorry. This is damn tough, and I didn't have time to think about it. I know life's been rough for you. But I, I waited so long, so many years. I felt sure I had a son, but I didn't get any validation of that until your father told me."

"My father told you?"

"He said the boy never knew I existed. He told me the night before he died. By then it was too late for us, but if it means anything to you, he was sorry."

"Damn him," she said.

"I think he damned himself."

"I hope so."

"He made a mistake, like we did."

She straightened and again tugged at her little jacket. "So, we made a mistake being together?"

"No. That's not what I meant. We didn't handle it right. Then again, maybe there was no good way to handle it. I guess your father didn't know what to do any more than we did."

"But we were kids. He was my *father*."

"Even fathers make mistakes, Madeline."

"But how could he send me off sick and scared like that—and even without Annie? I was caught up in something I couldn't control. No one seemed to know or care." Her words ran together as she paced back and forth on the porch, never tripping over broken brick. "Everyone wanted me to give up my baby. Said I could go back home as though nothing had happened. They kept telling me it would be much better. How could that have been better?"

She stopped pacing and stared down at me, her eyebrows knitted, as though she expected me to say something, but the breath had been knocked out of me.

"They couldn't make me do that," she said. "Or, maybe they could've. I don't know. But I wasn't about to go back to my father. Then, there was Mark, the doctor they took me to. He was so good to me when everyone else was so awful. He was much older, had never been married, and he very much wanted children. He offered me a way to keep the baby, and I took it. It was—convenient. I got someone who was kind and gentle, who made no demands on me, and who was able to take care of me and Clell, and he got a wife of some standing, if somewhat tarnished. I'll give him credit, he didn't seem to care. Of course, everything got covered over. My husband had died of a tragic accident, and I'd come to relatives in North Carolina to get away from all the memories."

"He must've been a good man."

"He wasn't you."

"Why didn't you write me and tell me where you were? I would've come and got you. I could've taken care of you."

"No, you couldn't. I couldn't live with you the way we'd have had to live. I would've been a great burden to you, instead of a help."

"Lightning says a man doesn't know he can walk away from his halter, like a mule."

"What?"

"You know, mules just walk out of their harnesses when there's too much for them to carry. They walk away from the load. Horses, they don't do that."

"Oh." She took out a handkerchief from her small white purse and wiped her upper lip. "It's very hot, isn't it?"

"Miserable," I said. "We could've made it, Madeline. Folks do. It wasn't right for you to keep my son from me."

"Maybe. It's clearer now. But at the time, I didn't know how to live without . . . without . . . well, you know, l needed someone to take care of me. I was a spoiled rich kid. But I was sick, too, and alone for the first time in my life, and I was helpless." She flipped her hair back, looked me straight in the eye and said, "But I will not be again."

We stood there for a moment looking at each other. Then she said, "Clell has very broad shoulders, too. And dark hair." She wiped her forehead again. "God, I'm so hot. Can you get us in? It'll be cooler inside."

I looked at the boards. "I'm older now, and not so quick to break the law."

"This place is mine. I give you permission."

"Yes, I guess it is." I pulled the planks off the door.

It was stuffy in the dark hall with the staircase leading up to Madeline's old room.

She placed a hand on the banister and said, "Do you think people can break from their halters, Moss?"

"I don't know. People are bound by so many things. Not just leather straps. I guess mules don't love like people do."

"Do you love her?" she asked.

"Yes, of course, I do. Otherwise I'd never have married her."

She looked away from me and said, "Does she love you?"

"Yes, I believe she does."

"That's, uh, that's good."

I nodded. "It's not the same as, I mean, yes, it's good."

She took a couple of steps up the staircase, and I leaned against the wall. She stopped and turned around. "Are you coming?"

"No. I'll wait here."

"Suit yourself," she said.

I watched her walk up the stairs, watched the movement of her hips and her long, slender legs. The click of her heels sounded like hammer pings in my ears. I ran my fingers through the dust on the wooden banister, making senseless scribbling. Then I gripped it and pretended my feet were set in cement so I wouldn't follow her. I wanted something, someone to blame. Her, her father, even myself. But there was no one person or thing to blame. And by then it wouldn't have done any good, anyway.

After a while she came back down. I was sitting on the stairs, leaning against the banister. She sat down beside me again. He eyes were red. She looked so alone, I wanted to take her in my arms, but I didn't dare touch her. We sat there for several minutes in silence.

When she got up, she said, "I'm ready to go. It doesn't look so bad, does it? The house, I mean. I can move out here pretty soon, even while some of the renovation is going on."

"I think so," I said. "The old house seems solid."

"Did you know we could've had this all along?"

"What do you mean?"

"My mother didn't leave this place to my father. She left it to me. I inherited everything at twenty-one. I was twenty-one that summer. He didn't tell me. I only found out when he died. I hated Father even more after that. Mark wanted me to sell the place. But I knew I'd come back some day. Just think, we could be living here with our son. You could be running the farm."

My head swam. "I'd rather not know that, Madeline," I said. "Not now."

"Moss, we didn't let anything hold us back before. We can have what we had again."

"No. We can't."

"Yes. I mean, there doesn't have to be anything between us, but you can at least run this place. I need someone to manage the farm. I don't really know anything about it. I'll pay you well. I don't need the money it can bring in, but I want to see it producing. I'll build you and your wife a house on the land and deed you a few acres. You can get out of the mine, get your family out of Outcropping and the dust. You know what it did to my mother."

"It sounds great, but I couldn't be that close to you, to my son and pretend—pretend nothing ever happened. You can find someone to run the farm who'll know a lot more'n I do. I only farmed as a boy, and just a few acres at that. I wouldn't know where to begin."

"You can learn. You love the land. I know you do."

"I'll help you find somebody who knows what they're doing, if you want me to. Mr. Frazier can, too. There's some good people working at the company farm. I'm sure one of them would be happy to have a place like this to manage, especially with a promise of a few acres for themselves."

"I don't want someone, Moss. I want you. Your son needs you."

"My son doesn't need me, Madeline. You made sure he didn't a long time ago. That's okay. But I can't move out here. I wouldn't take the chance of hurting him. I've always loved him, ever since I knew he existed, even though I've never seen him. I'm sure he thinks he's your husband's son. It's hard enough to know who you are in this world without having someone tell you you're not who you think you are. Besides, there's other people to think of now."

"You have children?" She said it as though she'd never thought of that possibility.

"A little girl, Grace," I said, "and a stepson. They do need me."

She walked slowly outside, stood for a moment staring at the river. "Look at it, always there, and always gone."

Then she got in the car. I followed, and we rode to The Inn without a word.

Madeline

I tried not to breathe in too deeply as I neared the dump. You'd think they could do something about that stench. Finally I came to a little gray shack where I was told Annie lived with her niece whose husband was a miner. I had to count the houses carefully, according to the directions I'd been given, because there was nothing to distinguish one from another. I'd never been in Shantytown. Father had always told me not to roam up there, that it was dangerous. He was probably wrong about that, too.

I knocked on the door, as I didn't see a knocker or a bell. I was startled when the door was opened by a light-colored youth with straight brown hair, maybe a little younger than Clell. He looked strangely familiar. His thin lips didn't smile. He stared at me, then looked around me at my Cadillac. "You lost, Miss?" he said.

"Well, I, uh, actually I'm not sure. I was told Annie lives here."

He nodded. "Yes'm. She does."

"May I see her, please?"

A woman came to the door, and the boy said, "Mama, this lady wants to see Annie."

"Annie aint able to work for no white folks no more," the woman said.

"I don't need her to work. I just want to see her. May I please come in? I'm Madeline Richards, uh, Madeline Rogers. She used to work for my family."

She said, "I know who you is." From the scowl on her face it was obvious she didn't like me.

"I've seen you, haven't I?" I said.

"Sometimes I used to come to your house with my aunt when we was both girls. I was a few years younger than you, but we played together until your pappy come home one day and found us. He told Annie not to bring me no more. Didn't want you playing with no colored children."

It wasn't my fault Father didn't want her playing with me. What she didn't understand was that he didn't think anyone was good enough for me. Mama wouldn't have cared.

"Later I worked at your house myself," the woman added, "after your pappy run Annie off. But not long. You wouldn't remember that, noway. You was gone then."

I cleared my throat and said, "Could I see Annie, please?"

She stepped aside. "She won't know you."

I walked cautiously into the dark, musty-smelling house. Annie lay on a narrow cot near the stove in the living room. I don't know why they didn't have her in a bedroom. I knelt beside her. She was so thin and little, as though half of her had vanished.

"It's me, Madeline." I picked up her limp hand, raised it to my face and kissed it. "I'm home, Annie. Back at the Willows."

Her hand felt like a flimsy handkerchief in my hand. I looked up at the woman who was watching my every move and said, "What's wrong with her? Why is she not saying anything?"

"Can't. You done come too late. She old. Wore out. Old and tired and, and disappointed."

"Disappointed?"

She looked at me with cold eyes. "Yes'm. She never got over whatever happened on Nobb Hill. You just up and leave. She give most of her life to you folks, and you couldn't even send her word you was all right." She looked me up and down. "You was obviously all right. You think you can waltz in here after sixteen years and 'spect to find everything like before? She kept saying you'd come and get her and she'd have to move. Well, you come too late, that's all they is to it. She don't know you now. Don't know nobody but me and my boy. And most times she don't know us."

"Oh my god," I said, turning back to the cot and fighting back tears. "Annie, I'm so sorry."

"Too late for that, too," the woman muttered, but I ignored her.

"Annie, you were always so strong, I thought you knew I'd be back someday. I always loved you more than anybody in the world."

"I'd hate to see them you didn't love," the woman said.

"You don't understand," I said to her.

Annie's eyes blinked, and I felt a light squeeze.

"Baby," she whispered, "that you?"

"Oh, Annie," I said. "Everything is going to be all right. I'm going to take you home, to The Willows. We'll live on the river. You'll be out of all the dust and smells. I'll get you a doctor, and I'll fix you a big, airy room overlooking the river."

Her hand went limp again, and her eyes went dull.

"Annie?"

Again there was no response. "She needs a doctor," I said. "I must take her with me."

"Dr. Timer sees her right here, You aint taking her nowhere. You aint back home in Outcropping, Miss. You just back. Annie home here with me, and I'm taking care of her. She aint going to die in some fancy house where she was run off from. And she aint going to die in some hospital. She going to die in her own home here, near the dump, here in Shantytown, where she belong. I think you best leave."

When I got to the door, I turned around and said, "If there is anything I can do for her, or for you or your son, please let me know."

"We don't need you or nothing you got," she said.

I cried all the way back to The Willows. I don't know what I was thinking when I came back. Surely not that Moss and Annie would be waiting for me, ready to receive me with open arms. Maybe that I could somehow make it all right again, make it up to everyone. As I drove down the lane where the men were already working to clear the wild growth, I brushed away tears and decided I'd come back for the place, the land, as much as for them. I wanted to share it with them, but if I couldn't, well, I'd still make it home for Clell and me. And I knew Moss'd come around someday. We just might be a little older than I'd hoped.

When Mr. Frazier came back to work after having been off for a few weeks, fighting a case of pneumonia, he sent word that he wanted to see me. Usually he waited till I came topside for the day, but we'd been working on opening a new mine about five miles out of Outcropping, and I figured he needed to talk about that. I had done a lot of the planning and hoped he'd be pleased. I was also hoping he might make me manager of the new mine.

As I entered his office, Mr. Frazier was leaning against his desk, smoking as usual and looking deep in thought. His hair seemed whiter than before, and his shoulders sagged. But when he saw me, he straightened up and reached out his hand to shake mine.

"Good to have you back, sir," I said.

"Damned good to be back," he said, then went into a fit of coughing and struggled to take in deep breaths. He spit into a can he had on his desk. "Sorry. Can't seem to shake this bloody cough." He pointed over to a big table that held maps and notes we'd been using as we made plans for the new mine. "You've done a fine job these last few weeks. It meant a lot to me to know everything was in good hands. This has been a hell of a time for me to have to be off. But everything's going like clockwork. New mine's looking good. They're going to call it Frazier Mine, you know." He smiled, leaned back against the desk again and took a long draw on his cigarette.

"It's a good name, legendary around here. And I'm glad you're satisfied with my work. I'd hate to think the mine wasn't worthy of its name."

"More than satisfied, son. Damned impressed. So's the company. Been on the phone to Kansas City just this morning."

"There are some things I need to ask you about the plans, sir, when you feel like it, that is."

"Right. But I want to talk to you about something else first. We'll get to the mine in a minute. Sit down."

Mr. Frazier walked around his desk and sat in his gray cushioned chair. He crushed out his cigarette in his tin ashtray, put both his arms on the desk in front of him and leaned forward. "I want to talk to you about your position in the company. You know I'm going to retire soon. Got to. It's my damn lungs. Gets us all in the end, if we live long enough, I guess. Anyway, you've taken over and carried on as well these past few weeks as if I had been here. Maybe better." I started to say something, but he coughed and said, "I've told them in Kansas City not to send a new superintendent, just to send me a manager for the new mine and two new foreman."

My heart sank. That meant I'd not be getting the new mine.

"They accepted my recommendation, and you'll be the new superintendent. What do you think of that?"

"Superintendent? You mean manager of both mines?"

He smiled and said, "That's right. Over it all, the whole operation. Each mine and mill will have a manager, but they'll all be under you. Somebody's got to run the show."

"My God, what can I say? I was just hoping to be over the new mine. You've been real good to me. Always have."

"I've been good to the company. Got them the best damn man I could find. Congratulations."

He reached out a shaky hand. I jumped up and grabbed it and pumped it up and down.

"I'm glad you're pleased," he said. "Now this means you're going to have to move to the Hill, you know. We've let that go until now, but we can't have the superintendent living on Engineer's Row. I'll be moving in about six months and you can have my house, but the Neils will be moving soon, and their house will be available shortly. Either place would make you folks a fine home. "

I sat back down. Peter Neil had taken Carl Rogers' place, and he lived in Madeline's old home. I saw the house in waves of visions. The dinner. Madeline's room. The confrontation with Mr. Rogers. I couldn't move into the Neils' home. Too many ghosts from the past.

"I thought you'd be happy about the move." Mr. Frazier said.

"Well, I, it's just that I'm not sure we're ready for it."

"Why not, for goodness sake?"

"Well, you know. I'm not sure how folks would take us moving there—or anywhere on the Hill." I smiled weakly and said, "I'm pretty much a back door man up there, you know." As I said it, it struck me odd that someone from Kansas City should be more at home in Outcropping, anywhere in Outcropping, than I was. I'd lived there twenty-seven years, yet I wouldn't fit in, even if one of the houses offered weren't Madeline's.

"You're good enough to run the show," he said, "you're good enough to live on the Hill. There's not a better man up there."

"Everyone won't see it that way."

"'Course they will. You're too modest."

There was a time, a long time ago, when living on Nobb Hill would've solved a lot of problems for me. But not any more. Hope wouldn't like the idea of moving to the Hill. In fact, that's why we hadn't moved there already. She was close to our neighbors on Engineers' Row, and she would be easily hurt by belittling remarks, and there'd be some. She'd worry about the kids, too. So would I, for that matter.

"I'm honored about the offer," I said. "Can I have a few days to think about it?"

"What's to think about? You'll be in a position to put into action many things you've always believed in. You'll make a lot more money, and you'll have a fine home."

"I need to talk to Hope."

"I can appreciate that. If this is too fast, wait till we leave and move into our house. Give you folks time to get used to the idea. It needs some repairs and updates. We've been putting it off because we knew we'd be leaving. But I'll see that's done. In reality you'll probably have about nine months. But whatever you do, do it. Company needs you for the mine, and we need some fresh blood up there." He grinned at me. "It's much too stuffy."

"Thanks, the extra time will help."

"Good. Now, let's get busy with this new mine." He walked over to the planning table. "I'll not leave Outcropping until we have the new managers. I'll help you all I can."

"You always have, sir. I appreciate that."

But I knew he'd have no idea how to help with the problems we'd run into moving to the Hill. For him, it'd be nothing. I'm sure he thought I'd be thrilled to move up with the big shots. And I'm sure he thought I was just as good as any of them. But not everyone would.

Walking home that evening I wondered if I'd dreamed being in Mr. Frazier's office. If I took the job, I'd sure be the last man to rise up from the ranks to such a position without a college degree. Times were changing. In a few years I'd be in an even more awkward position. There'd be more young men coming up with degrees, with intellectual know-how. I suddenly felt old and tired.

Hope

I was so proud of Moss when he told me about being promoted, but I was scared of what that meant for me and the children. I didn't know how to deal with folks on the Hill. Moss reminded me of Doc and Aunt Emmy, and he said it wouldn't be long before LC would be coming to Outcropping and he'd be living there, too. I said that was different.

"Maybe not," he said. "We don't really know those folks very well. Maybe they're like anybody else when you get to know them."

Of course I couldn't keep him from taking the job. He'd worked hard for many years, and he deserved it. But those folks lived in another world from mine.

In October a big party was planned at Mr. Frazier's home to celebrate Moss's promotion. I dreaded going. My friend Effie, who lives next door and whose husband was Moss's night shift foreman, said she'd ride to Knoxville on the bus with me and we'd get me a new dress to wear and she'd help me fix my hair. Effie's pretty, always reads the fashion part of the paper and picks up fashion magazines. We found a nice blue dress, not too dressy and not too casual. Effie said it'd look good with my hair, which she was going to put up into a twist.

The night of the party, it was cool, but not too cold, and Moss and I decided to walk. The climb to the Nobb Hill was a tough one.

"It's real beautiful up here," I said. "Not so much dust. Seems like nothing bad could ever touch it."

He took my hand and held it in his firm grip. "I guess folks got their share of problems up here, too. And there's plenty of dust."

I looked up at him, and he seemed so serious I didn't say nothing. We walked along, neither of us saying another word until we got to Mr. Frazier's house.

As we went up the walk I said, "It was real nice of Mr. Frazier to give this party for you."

He squeezed my hand as he knocked on the door. Mr. Frazier opened it with one hand and held a cigarette and a glass of wine in the other. "Moss, come on in here. My, my, don't we look lovely, Mrs. McCullen. You're lucky, Moss. What more could a man want besides a good job, a nice home, and a pretty wife? Speaking of, we need to talk to you about that home. But later. Right now go on in and see folks. Everyone is pleased about your promotion."

As we entered the living room, I was relieved to see Doc rise from his seat to meet us. "Congratulations, Moss. Em and I are so proud of you. Guess you can't avoid moving up here with us now. We're happy about that, too."

I didn't say anything.

"We've talked about it some," Moss said.

"Will you be moving in the Neils' place?" He looked at me and said, "It's right next door to Em and me. She'd love it."

Moss muttered something about us not being able to move right away, that we'd probably wait until Mr. Frazier left and take his home, not that we wouldn't love living next door to him and Em. He worked at a laugh and said, "Who knows, maybe by then they'll decide I'm not superintendent material and we won't move at all."

"That's not going to happen," Doc said. "And we only live a couple doors up from here, so we'll still be close."

"That'd be the best thing about the move I can think of," Moss said.

Mr. Frazier joined us about that time, slapped Moss on the back, and said, "Speaking about moves, the company says we need a new house for the superintendent, which will leave the two houses in question for the two mine managers."

Moss took a step back. "You didn't say anything about this before."

"Didn't know myself until near closing time today when I got a call from Kansas City." He looked back at the people in the room and said, "Let's keep this just between us for now, but Mr. Forge himself called. Wanted to ask some questions about the new mine. Then he asked about where you'd live, since we were getting two managers. I said one of the managers might have to live on Engineers' Row. He said he thought the company should build a new place for the superintendent, said we might even have another mine in the near future."

"Well, this is news," Doc said. "Where would the new house be built?"

"Probably in the area in the middle of the drive that was always supposed to have been a park but nobody ever used it." He laughed. "I guess we're not nature people up here, but Moss here's an old farm boy. Be right up his alley. I know you and that boy of yours like to ride horses," he said to Moss. "There'd be plenty of room for you to keep a couple. You'd like that, wouldn't you? I walked around the property today. It's so grown up you can't tell much about it from the road, but it's a fine piece of ground, four or five acres, I'd say. Overlooks the river from the backside. You could have a big back porch. Be real nice."

Before Moss could say anything, several people began entering the conversation, and the news was no longer just between them.

I needed to sit down. I pulled my hand from Moss's and moved farther across the room to a blue velvet chair next to a piano where I could watch Moss and not be asked any questions. I hoped I'd blend right in with the blue of the chair, and nobody'd notice me. But the blue was not the right shade, and I was sure we clashed. Everyone was gathered around Moss. Obviously I was doomed to move onto the Hill. I wished I were at home with the children.

Suddenly all eyes turned from Moss to a woman who entered the room, after pausing at the entrance to ensure she'd captured everyone's attention. She was the most beautiful woman

291

I'd ever seen. Looked like the women in magazines with her smooth, blond hair and a fitted deep-green gown that dipped low at the bust. A single strand of pearls hung around her long neck. Moss was staring at her, as was everyone. The soft material of my dress was sticking to my back, and the collar was choking me. I knew my curls were getting tighter as they became damp. I ran my hand across my forehead and pushed back the loose pieces as the lady floated across the room toward Moss and the people gathered around him.

I was trying to figure out who she was when Mr. Frazier told everyone that she was Madeline Richards, formerly Madeline Rogers. I'd heard about her. All of Outcropping was talking about her and how she'd come back to the area. Most people knew her father, and she was supposedly going to fix up a home she owned just outside Outcropping on the river. Some big place with lots of acres.

Mr. Frazier said, "Moss, you remember Madeline?"

She extended a delicate hand with a pearl bracelet at the wrist and said, "Why, of course he remembers me. He picked me up at the depot when I first came back."

I felt a tightening in the pit of my stomach. Moss glanced quickly over at me and stammered, "Yes, sure. Mr. Frazier sent me. And, of course, I used to deliver groceries up here, if you all recall. I was a regular backdoor visitor."

A few throats were cleared. My mind raced. He hadn't told me about picking her up. Not that he told me everything, but picking up such a beautiful woman at the station had to be unusual, not something he did every day, something he would've normally come home and told. But he didn't. I wondered why she was at Mr. Frazier's home when she no longer had connections with the company.

Mr. Frazier was saying, "I'm so glad you could come, Madeline. We're all happy you're living in the old house again. My wife and I thought this evening would be a good chance for you to renew old acquaintances and to meet the new folks on the Hill.

You can't stay isolated out there all the time. Where's that young man I've been hearing about?"

"Oh, Clell will be along in a second." She waved her long, slim arm toward the door. "He's parking the car."

At that moment a tall, young man strode into the room, perfectly comfortable in the elegant surroundings. I looked at the thick dark hair, the broad shoulders, the high cheekbones, the expressive deep-set blue eyes, and I knew. I knew without a doubt. He was Moss all over. I felt everyone else must have known what I'd just realized. I gripped the chair to keep my hands from shaking. Moss stood still as a fence post. I watched as he shook hands with Clell.

Madeline smiled and said, "Clell, honey, this is Moss McCullen, an old friend."

My head spun. I felt completely alone as I stared into a big, empty stone fireplace. Then a hand was on one of mine, prying my stiff fingers loose from the chair.

"Let's me and you go out on the porch and get some fresh air," Doc Timer said. "I get bored with all the chit-chat. Come on." He was pulling at my hand, and I slowly rose. He put an arm around my waist and took me through some double glass doors onto a large screened-in porch, overlooking the Holston River. I walked to the railing, not feeling a part of anything. I hugged my arms around myself, shivering, and stared at the rock cliffs across the river.

"You're cold," Doc said, taking his jacket off. He put it around my shoulders and said, "Beautiful up here, isnt' it?"

"Moss says there's dirt up here, too."

"Well, sure. There's dirt everywhere, but if you're talking about rock dust, we get some but not as much as most folks. It'll be a healthier place for your children to live."

I looked down at the river and said, "Am I the only one who doesn't know?"

"Know?"

"Don't treat me like a child. I've had two husbands and two children, for God's sake." I knocked tears away with the back of my hand. He handed me his handkerchief. "Am I the only one in the dark?"

"No, no one knows."

"Then, how do you know?"

"I was there. She was very sick, and her father called me. She kept saying his name, but Moss and I have never discussed it."

"Why didn't he tell me?"

"I'm not sure he knows for sure. Her father zipped her away as fast as he could."

"Oh, Moss knows. If he didn't know before he does now. I could tell by the way he looked at him."

"Well, even if he does, what does it matter now? It's over. It was doomed from the start. It's been over since it began."

"It's not over. I can tell by the way they look at each other. Why didn't they get married?"

"It would have been bucking the system. Just couldn't be."

"Then, what are we doing moving up here?"

Doc set his jaw hard and stared for a moment at the river, too. "It's another day. And Moss is in a completely different position."

I looked back through the glass doors at the people surrounding Moss. "Nobody could have drug me away from him," I said. "A team of mules couldn't have drug me away."

"Well, you don't know how she felt back then, but that's neither here nor there. One thing I know. Moss's moved on. He's not one to mull over things he's lost. He goes forward. If he didn't, he'd never have gotten where he has. He loves you and your kids more than anything or anyone in the world. And his love's as solid as rock, nothing will crush it. You do love him, don't you?"

"God forgive me, I think I've always loved him."

"Then don't give up on what you have. You may be little but you're a strong woman. I know. I watched you bring two kids into this world. And you're not as alone as you think on this hill.

You've got Em and me. Mr. Frazier thinks you're great. And there's other good folks. You don't know them, and they don't know you. Give them a chance."

"She's so lovely, like something from a movie."

Doc put his arm around my shoulders and said, "And you are, too. More so than you know. And you're his life. Now, take a deep breath and go in there and help Moss face all these people. He needs you."

I reached up and kissed him on the cheek and said, "Thanks." Then I handed him his jacket, straightened my dress, fought with my straying curls, and walked back through the doors into the room of people. I went to Moss, pushing my way gently between him and Mr. Frazier. Moss raised his eyes in surprise and grabbed my hand.

"Well, here's your beautiful wife," Mr. Frazier said, "Where have you been hiding yourself? I've been looking for you."

"Doc and I have been out on your porch. It's a nice view."

"I want you to meet someone." He nodded to Madeline and the boy. "This is Madeline Richards and her son Clell. Madeline used to live here years ago. You may remember her."

"No, I don't think our paths crossed." I reached out my hand. "Nice to meet you. And you, too, Clell."

"Nice to meet you," Madeline said.

"Have you found things changed much since you left?" I said.

Madeline raised her eyebrows and looked at Moss. "Well, yes. And I hear there's about to be more changes."

Mr. Frazier interrupted and said, "We'll hear more about all that later. Right now, let's retire to the dining room and see about this great meal my wife has ready, shall we?"

Moss leaned over to me and whispered, "I missed you."

"Sorry. I needed some air, but I'm here."

Mrs. Frazier fluttered around, pointing people to their seats at the long dining room table, making sure everyone sat where she had planned. Madeline and Clell were seated across the table from Moss and me, and as ladies in black and white uniforms brought in dinner, Madeline said, "Moss, I hear you'll be moving up here."

"It looks that way."

"As a matter of fact, we were all talking about that before you arrived," Mr. Frazier told her.

Before he could explain, Mrs. Frazier said to Madeline, "Have you heard? The Neil home will be vacated next week. You know, dear, your old house?"

Madeline was raising her water goblet to her mouth, and she stopped in mind-air. She stared at Mrs. Frazier and put it back down slowly. "Our house?"

"Why, yes, your old house. You remember that beautiful entrance? It's a lovely house, isn't it?" She turned to Moss and said, "Of course you'll be moving up here."

"My dear," Mr. Frazier said, "you both missed out on the conversation earlier. Moss and Hope won't be moving into the Neil home. The company's building them a new place. The Neil home is needed for one of the new mine managers, so they're going to build the superintendent a new one."

"Well, that's much better," Madeline said weakly.

Clell said, "Can we see your old house, Mom?"

"I'm sure that can be arranged," Mr. Frazier said.

"It's just a house," Madeline said to Clell. "Nothing special." To Mr. Frazier she said, "Where will the new house be?"

"As I was saying before you and Clell came in, we're thinking about the park area that no one uses."

"I would hate to see those woods destroyed," Moss said.

"We can leave some of the woods. Be nice," he said. "We'll clear enough for a house and a small pasture. Maybe we'll even build a dock. You like to fish?"

"Never took the time, but Cleve takes his nephew and Will. They'd love it. Maybe we could create an entrance so that everyone could use the dock."

Mrs. Frazier coughed and said, "For the people up here, of course. Who's Cleve? He isn't that man who . . ."

"You know, my dear," Mr. Frazier interrupted, "the man who cleans the administration building at the mine. Anyone would be safe around water with him. He's quite the water legend in Outcropping. He could be the unofficial lifeguard."

She stiffened and said, "We don't need lifeguards up here."

"My children do," Moss said.

I put my hands in my lap so no one would see them shake. I could feel Mrs. Frazier looking at me, but she was speaking to Moss, "Well, Mr. McCullen, I guess it's official. You'll be moving up here. You'll want to live around those with whom you work. You simply have to associate with your peers. It's vital for your career."

As she spoke, I felt Moss's hand on my thigh underneath the tablecloth. I looked up at him and he grinned.

Madeline said, "But, Mrs. Frazier, Moss will be working closely with all the men in this town, isn't that right?" Then she looked from Mrs. Frazier to Moss.

Mrs. Frazier's gaze turned slowly from me to Madeline. "Well, yes, of course, my dear," she sputtered, "but you know what I mean. This would be so much nicer for him." She looked back at me. "For them both, of course. And the children will have such good influences. Naturally it'll be an adjustment."

As she continued to talk about the benefits of living at Nobb Hill, I reached for my water glass. If I wasn't mistaken, Madeline had just tried to help me. I looked at her, so lovely, so confident, so graceful. She'd have felt at ease in this neighborhood. It would've been no more than coming home. I became aware of Mrs. Frazier again when I heard my name called, as though from far away.

"Mrs. McCullen. Hope, dear."

"Yes, ma'am. Sorry. I didn't hear you."

Mrs. Frazier stared at me and mashed her mouth together tightly. Then she said, "I was saying, dear, that I was sure you'll want to move where it would be advantageous for your husband in his career, isn't that so?"

I felt like a load of limestone to be milled and refined in an overhead car that needed to be dumped. Life hadn't been easy, but love and care had always been there for me in some form, and I took it as it came. Now I would have to fight for what I had. I couldn't lose Moss, not at least without trying my best to keep him. I looked around at the fancy surroundings, and I knew the struggle might last a long time, maybe always, and it wouldn't just be with Madeline. I was ill equipped.

Mrs. Frazier's shrill voice was rapping at me again. "Isn't that so, dear? Mrs. McCullen?"

I looked at Moss who held a cup of coffee in suspense. He was looking at me as though he were in pain. He lowered the cup and opened his mouth to speak, but I said, "I'll move with Moss wherever he moves. It has nothing to do with his career. I'm his wife."

"Didn't you hear? They're building you a new home."

"Yes, ma'am, I heard."

Moss took a gulp of coffee and winced, as though he'd burned his throat. Madeline looked from him to me to Mrs. Frazier, who sputtered, "Well, perhaps you'd like some help with decorating the new house. You know, it'll be very different from . . . well, it'll be such a big house and all."

"Thank you, Mrs. Frazier, but we'll manage."

"You can always hire a decorator," Madeline said. "That's what I'm going to do at the Willows." She laughed softly. "I'd offer to help, too, but the whole thing of deciding what goes where overwhelms me."

I had no idea of how to go about hiring a decorator, but I said, "We just might do that. Perhaps you could recommend someone."

"Of course. In fact I'm going to Knoxville to interview a couple of people next week. Maybe you'd like to come along and check them out. We could have lunch."

I glanced at Moss who wiped his mouth with his napkin and raised his eyebrows.

"I'd like that very much," I said. "It's kind of you to invite me."

"Not at all. I'll enjoy the company, and I can sure use your ideas."

Mrs. Frazier said, "I'll be glad to go along and help. Monday is the only day I won't be able to go."

As my heart sank at the thought of a day with Mrs. Frazier, Madeline looked at me and winked. "So kind of you to offer, Mrs. Frazier, but Monday is the best day for me to go. Will that work for you, Hope?"

"Why, uh, yes. Monday will be fine."

Moss squeezed my thigh where he knew it'd make me laugh, and I had to cough to keep from squealing. Suddenly I was having fun.

"Well, I'm sure you don't really need a decorator, Madeline," Mrs. Frazier said, "but it would probably be a good idea for Hope." She looked at me and added, "I imagine you'll want to get everything new."

"Well, no, not really. Some of our things have been my father's and Stub's and Aunt Minnie's. I couldn't let them go."

I actually enjoyed the frown on her face as I added, "Losing them would be like losing a part of who we are."

"Yes," Madeline said. "That's exactly my situation. I can't let go of most of the furnishings at the Willows, but much of the upholstery is faded and worn, and the draperies are not worth salvaging. And I want to lighten the place up, somehow make it a blend of the past and the present. I'm at a loss as to where to begin selecting colors and fabrics."

"Well, I've never had a decorator myself," Mrs. Frasier said, "My mother, God rest her soul, was simply a marvelous decorator, absolutely marvelous. Had impeccable taste. Women of her day took pride in decorating. She made certain I learned everything she knew. Yes, I always say . . ."

I tuned out her babbling and tuned into the sensation of Moss's leg pressing against mine. He whispered in my ear, "I'm glad you're here, Hope."

Acknowledgements

I cannot begin to mention all the people who have been influential in the writing of *Deep in the Earth*, but they are all valued and appreciated. Perhaps the most important person to whom I owe a debt of gratitude is my father, Paul Bozeman, who shared his and his friends' and family's experiences on the farms and in the zinc mines of East Tennessee in the early 1900's. He spoke of Depression days, of the World Wars and of mining when virtually the only protection was one's wits. As well as his stories, I loved his voice, his colloquialisms, and his natural metaphors that came from the world around him. I also want to thank countless others who shared their experiences of living in Mascot, a former zinc mining town in East Tennessee. Among these are my friends Zelma and Nettie Cate and Nancy and Angie France.

Without my dear friend and mentor Wilma Dykeman Stokely, I would never have found my writing voice—nor have believed anything I wrote would be publishable. Though she is passed, she will always be a part of my life. Thanks also to Lee Smith who taught me much about writing and living and who, like my father, showed me that everyone and anyone's life deserves a voice. George Ella Lyon's wisdom and insight have also been a continual inspiration, personally and professionally. Gurney Norman had faith in my writing from my earliest stories and has never let me give up. Silas House read and edited some of my earliest writings and made me feel as though I were a "writer." Sandra Ballard supported me when hardly anyone except Wilma knew I was writing. She edited, prodded and begged me to submit manuscripts. She dragged me to writing conferences, lectures and workshops and introduced me to the world of writers. For several years she and Patricia Hudson and I also worked together as a small writing group.

A special thanks also to Cecelia Seale who worked tirelessly editing *and editing and editing* a final version of this book. She also encouraged me, pushed me and inspired me until the novel was completed.

I also want to thank the people at the Jefferson County Historical Archives of Jefferson County, Tennessee, for their assistance with research of information and pictures. And, I must give credit to my husband, Jimmy Hodges, who went with me to zinc mining sites and who investigated leads for information and pictures. My children, Boyd and Amy, read, listened to me read, gave suggestions and expertise on many subjects and encouraged me always to write no matter what else seemed to be begging for my attention. Thanks also to the members of my library writing group who listened to me read and who validated the project.

A final, but certainly no less heartfelt thanks, to the publishers of Sapling Grove Press, Susan and David Underwood, for giving me the opportunity to share the novel with readers everywhere, especially those of my region. I am proud and humbled to give the people of my region voice and to reveal them as a people of integrity, ingenuity, hard work, and compassion.

— Mary Bozeman Hodges.

Mary Bozeman Hodges. Author photograph by Jimmy Hodges.

About the Author

While her works generally are set in her native East Tennessee, Mary Bozeman Hodges lived outside the region much of her adult life. When her husband retired as a federal agent, they returned to her home town of Jefferson City, Tennessee, where she still teaches courses in the English Department at Carson-Newman University after retirement.

Soon after moving back to Appalachia, Hodges took a creative writing class at the University of Tennessee from Wilma Dykeman, who encouraged her to take her writing seriously. Dykeman said of her, "Hodges is a keen observer and an attentive listener in her corner of our human neighborhood. A storyteller in the best Southern Appalachian tradition, at once witty and compassionate, she makes us aware of the daily experiences that bond us to 'neighbors' everywhere."

Hodges has published two collections of short stories, *Tough Customers and Other Stories* (1999, The Jesse Stuart Foundation), and *Plastic Santa and Other Stories* (2003, Iris Press). Her writings have also been included in several journals such as *Appalachian Heritage* and *Journal of Kentucky Studies*, and in anthologies, including *Listen Here: Women Writing in Appalachia*, edited by Dr. Sandra Ballard, editor of *Appalachian Journal*, and free lance writer Patricia Hudson.

In the fall of 2003 Hodges was part of the Appalachian Lecture Series given annually at Maryville College. In spring of 2005, she was inducted into the East Tennessee Writers Hall of Fame.

The author as a young girl, with her big sister,
Paulette, at an East Tennessee zinc mine.

CPSIA information can be obtained
at www.ICGtesting.com
Printed in the USA
LVHW011019240122
709167LV00008B/779

9 780692 182765